A CUTE LITTLE MURDER

Molly Harper

BERKLEY MYSTERY
NEW YORK

BERKLEY MYSTERY
Published by Berkley
An imprint of Penguin Random House LLC
1745 Broadway, New York, NY 10019
penguinrandomhouse.com

Book design by Kristin del Rosario

Library of Congress Cataloging-in-Publication Data

Names: Harper, Molly author
Title: A cute little murder / Molly Harper
Description: First edition | New York: Berkley Mystery, 2026.
Identifiers: LCCN 2025035389 (print) | LCCN 2025035390 (ebook) |
ISBN 9780593817346 trade paperback | ISBN 9780593817353 ebook
Subjects: LCGFT: Fiction | Detective and mystery fiction | Novels
Classification: LCC PS3608.A774 C88 2026 (print) | LCC PS3608.A774 (ebook)
LC record available at https://lccn.loc.gov/2025035389
LC ebook record available at https://lccn.loc.gov/2025035390

First Edition: April 2026

Printed in the United States of America
1st Printing

The authorized representative in the EU for product safety and compliance is Penguin Random House Ireland, Morrison Chambers, 32 Nassau Street, Dublin D02 YH68, Ireland, https://eu-contact.penguin.ie.

Praise for Molly Harper

"Harper writes characters you can't help but fall in love with."

—RT Book Reviews

"Tons of heart, lots of laughs, and of course, kooky locals."

—Harlequin Junkie

"Warm and cozy and full of Southern charm." —Dear Author

"This sweet tale of the city girl finding a home in the country launches Harper's latest series and will go down as easy as honey on a deep-fried Twinkie." —*Library Journal*

"Harper's assemblage of ghostly residents sparkles."

—*Publishers Weekly*

"Molly Harper serves up a smart, hilarious mystery in *A Proposal to Die For*, complete with a remote and luxurious setting and a sexy romance. Pitch-perfect banter and compelling twists will keep readers turning the pages as Harper (gently) pokes fun at the wedding industry without sacrificing charm or heart."

—Tirzah Price, *USA Today* bestselling author of *A Matter of Murder*

"*A Proposal to Die For* is a fun, enticing union of murder, mayhem, and mindfulness. A spa retreat is anything but relaxing when a proposal planner starts to trip over dead bodies . . . and it turns downright anxiety producing when *she* is the one marked for murder. Go ahead, say YES to *A Proposal to Die For*!"

—Juliet Blackwell, *New York Times* bestselling author of *Asylum Hotel*

"Everything I love in a Molly Harper story: quick wit, strong characters, laugh-out-loud moments—with a little murder mixed in. This was a delight from start to finish. I want a dozen more books just like this!"

—Kristen Simmons, Bram Stoker Award nominee and author of *She Waits for You Beyond the Dark*

"A lighthearted murder mystery with plenty of twists to keep you guessing, a heroine to root for, a hunk to drool over, and everything—and I do mean *everything*—you could ever want to know about the cutthroat world of wedding-proposal event planners. While this may be a rom-com, Harper uses her trademark snark to get in a few sly winks at influencer culture, the clueless rich, and the inviolate code that is Southern etiquette. Charming, delicious—and deadly."

—Alma Katsu, Bram Stoker Award–winning author of *Fiend*

"Hooray for this charming and funny mystery from Molly Harper! Buckle up for a love-to-hate-her bridezilla, a winning heroine-slash-amateur-sleuth, and an entertaining and satisfying story. *A Proposal to Die For* is endless fun."

—Kathleen West, author of *Making Friends Can Be Murder*

"*A Proposal to Die For* is a fast-paced, clever mystery that's perfect for a weekend escape. With a lovable cast and twists that keep you guessing, it's an entertaining whodunit that delivers just the right amount of intrigue and fun."

—Melissa Holtz, author of *A Charming Touch of Tarot*

"I'm a longtime fan of Molly Harper's work, and *A Proposal to Die For* doesn't disappoint! Harper's trademark humor and snarky-but-kind characters are there on every page, alongside a satisfying murder mystery plot. Cozy mystery fans will be snickering while reading this page-turner. An absolutely deadly delight!"

—Lish McBride, author of *Most Likely to Murder*

"A witty and engaging story. . . . The characters are quirky and endearing."

—Fresh Fiction

"A charming mystery that ideally blends elements of humor, murder, engagement chaos, and sleuthing."

—San Francisco Book Review

Berkley Titles by Molly Harper

A PROPOSAL TO DIE FOR

A CUTE LITTLE MURDER

For Tirzah,
my public speaking good luck charm
and partner in comedic crime

A CUTE LITTLE MURDER

Prologue

May 14, 2011
Tallen River, Illinois

Lainey Piper liked to think she had a relatively normal high school experience—up until she found herself knee-deep in the thirty-yard line, trying to prove her high school principal was a murderer.

"OK, if we don't find a body here soon, this is just wanton vandalism," Lainey told her partner in crime Harlow Drake, as she tossed a shovelful of dirt onto Tallen River Memorial Field. On any other occasion, this might have been an ideal night for stargazing—cloudless sky, big open field, just enough nip in the air to keep the mosquitoes at bay. The harsh field lights had been turned off in the absence of players or coaches . . . or really anybody but Harlow and Lainey, who were digging up the field by the light of a camping lantern.

"We've already broken into the principal's office," Harlow reminded her, grunting as she stepped on her shovel, spearing it into the dark, dry earth. Being shorter and slighter than Lainey, she had trouble moving as much dirt. There was a metaphor in there somewhere. "Are you really worried about a little unsanctioned gardening? Technically, we're doing chores for the school. The school board should thank us."

"*I* broke into the principal's office," Lainey noted, shuddering at the thought of the evidence she'd found in Mr. Burnham's filing cabinet.

And his desktop computer.

And his locked desk drawer.

The neon-purple thumb drive, onto which she'd copied dozens of files, felt like it was burning a hole in her pocket. The plastic baggie full of thumb drives she'd *taken* from Mr. Burnham's locked drawer were actual stolen property. She wasn't sure how much she should tell the authorities about them. Because she was in possession of just . . . so many stolen files.

"Yeah, because you're taller than me. You can climb in through the window," Harlow scoffed. "It's not a skill issue. And if you didn't want to be in charge of breaking and entering, you should have held on to the secretary's keys—instead of dropping them in the Narc Box like a loser."

"We'd had them for a month," Lainey huffed, tossing aside more dirt. "They were going to fire Mrs. Gates if we didn't return them."

"She kept leaving them in the door of the teachers' lounge where *anyone*—including us—could get them," Harlow grunted, blowing her dark, blunt-cut bangs out of her face. "Maybe Mrs. Gates deserved to be fired. She's the whole reason the school has a security camera trained on the office door now, so really, it's *her* fault you had to climb through the window."

Lainey paused her shoveling and leaned against the well-worn wooden handle for a minute, catching her breath. The tension inside her gut, the knowledge that she was doing the right thing while also aware that she was about to ruin several lives, seemed absent in Harlow.

Sometimes Harlow accused Lainey of having no balls. Lainey preferred to think of it as having perspective. She knew what it was like to have a "high-profile" funeral in your family, to walk into the grocery store and know that conversations stopped because they were about you. Harlow's family scandal had been handled quietly with half-truths that were *just* believable enough for the neighbors to stop asking questions.

"Are you *sure* about this, Harlow?" she asked.

"You're the one who found the letters on Mr. Burnham's computer," Harlow reminded her. "They prove I'm not wrong about GradeGate. And now, I'm going to prove to you I'm not wrong about Ms. Fraser, either."

A sour lump of guilt solidified in her throat. Mr. Burnham had gone to the trouble of writing Lainey a really nice recommendation letter for the University of Michigan just three weeks before she broke into his office. Of course, he'd written a lot of kids nice recommendation letters—factual or not. He'd done that and more to ease the way for *certain* members of their graduating class into some of the best schools in the country. That was sort of the problem.

"I'm just saying that selling recommendation letters to rich kids doesn't mean he killed our guidance counselor," Lainey countered, glancing toward the school building.

"He 'adjusted' some kids' grades, too," Harlow noted. "And the fact that his office *and* his car reeked of Ms. Fraser's awful perfume is a big old neon sign that says something was going on."

Ms. Fraser habitually doused herself in her signature scent, Manifested Visions, an amber-heavy body oil that smelled like crumbled dreams. Harlow seemed to take the perfume's tendency to linger in the air as a personal attack.

Lainey grimaced. It had been a hell of a risk for Harlow to break into Mr. Burnham's precious cherry-red BMW. She'd only managed to get into the Beemer by using some homemade gadget she'd bought off the auto-shop kids. Lainey preferred not to ask questions about it.

"She could be attending that continuing education conference in Milwaukee like Mr. Burnham said," Lainey noted, pushing her shovel into the dirt. She was working through all the possible explanations for herself as much as for Harlow. Lainey knew that something bad must have happened to Ms. Fraser if she hadn't updated her social media with a single Affirmation of the Day all week.

Harlow said, "The conference organizers refused to confirm or deny she showed up. And her front door has a huge pile of newspapers in front of it. If she was planning to leave town, why didn't she stop the deliveries?"

"Who even reads newspapers anym— *Oof,*" Lainey gasped when her shovel hit something distinctly un-dirt-like. "Oh no."

Lainey's hands shook as she crouched down and brushed one last layer of dirt away from gray plastic.

Ms. Fraser definitely wasn't visiting Milwaukee.

Lainey's mouth went sour and watery as the warmth leached from her limbs. She was standing in a *grave.*

"Ten rolls of sod from DIY Depot on Mr. Burnham's credit card," Harlow murmured as Lainey carefully moved her gloved fingertips against the slick plastic. There was definitely a pliant structure underneath the sheeting—forehead, nose, chin.

Swallowing hard against the acid rising in her throat, Lainey was deeply grateful that the plastic wasn't transparent. She didn't want to see what was underneath.

Poor Ms. Fraser.

Ms. Fraser *believed* in the value of education and would never have let Mr. Burnham get away with academic dishonesty no matter how many times he promised to leave his wife—which, according to the emails Lainey had copied from his computer, he had. Repeatedly.

Ms. Fraser would have blown up Mr. Burnham's whole life with the truth. And now she was *gone*, buried under the school football field in some half-assed attempt by Mr. Burnham to hide her body in plain sight.

"Probably should have called the sheriff before we started digging," Lainey said, her hands shaking as she set the shovel aside.

"We tried to tell the sheriff that Ms. Fraser was missing," Harlow reminded her. "He said we were 'entitled little brats' and threatened us with juvenile hall."

"He did do that," Lainey admitted. "I think Mr. Burnham's still in the staff meeting in the library."

"It's Mr. Burnham, Mrs. Gates, and the cafeteria lady running inventory, trying to figure out why we run out of Bosco Sticks every Tuesday," Harlow scoffed. "It's hardly a staff meeting."

"How do you even know that?" Lainey asked.

"I know everything," Harlow told her. "If we're lucky, they'll lock themselves in the Deepfreeze and give us more time."

"I know we have more important things to worry about right now, but we need to talk later about stuff that you don't say out loud," Lainey told her, peering across the field to the parking lot where Mr. Burnham's automotive darling sat cozy in his special spot. The entire student body of Tallen River High School knew not to park within two spaces of it. Of course, if the student body had stopped to ask themselves how a principal could afford a German high-performance luxury sedan, maybe they could have avoided this whole body-finding situation.

Lainey tried to maintain some dignity as she heaved herself out of the grave. It wasn't easy, considering the way her legs were quivering.

Harlow had already climbed out and now tossed Lainey's giant shoulder bag at her. "Call the sheriff and tell him to get here ASAP. I'm going to let the air out of Mr. Burnham's tires."

"What?" Lainey paused while fishing her phone out of her bag. "Why?"

"So he can't drive off!" Harlow cried, jogging away.

"Of all her plans, this is the worst one." Lainey sighed, staring into the latest mess they'd created. Sheriff Arlo Pleasant wasn't really the guy you wanted to count on in a murder clinch. Writing a parking ticket or figuring out which of the neighborhood dogs dug up Mrs. Robbins's tulips? Sure. But a murder investigation? Never.

Even as she gave Dispatcher Peggy her name—yes, it was Lainey calling, *again*—and asked for Sheriff Pleasant to come to the football field as quickly as possible, Lainey wasn't sure that armed people with authority would arrive anytime soon. The girls didn't have the best working relationship with the sheriff. Lainey imagined he'd prefer not to have any relationship with them . . . or that they move to another county and become some other sheriff's problem.

Ending the call, Lainey supposed it would embarrass the sheriff that two teenage girls took it upon themselves to solve the town's first murder in a decade. To be fair, Harlow and Lainey had thought they were only dealing with a grade inflation scheme when they started looking into it. And technically, it *was* Lainey's discovery that escalated the situation. She was the one who realized Mr. Burnham was selling admissions "help" to the richest students in their class. She could have just shut the hell up about it.

"You only have yourself to blame on this one," Lainey muttered to herself, glancing around the ruined grass. What had she even done to the crime scene at this point? There was no giving poor Ms. Fraser dignity before the police arrived. Also, they'd already contaminated *so much* evidence.

Yeah . . . Sheriff Pleasant was going to be pissed.

Their mutual willingness to irritate the people around them was what had originally bonded Harlow and Lainey in the first place. Still, Lainey had absolutely panicked when she realized how far-reaching Mr. Burnham's pay-for-play grade-changing / college recommendation scheme stretched in their wealthy little enclave outside of Chicago. So many people in their graduating class—or their parents—had paid him for outright faked qualifications to get into their dream schools. Lainey had actually *liked* a few of those whom Mr. Burnham had rubber-stamped futures for . . . not that likability should determine accountability. Right?

Harlow suffered no such internal conflict. She'd pushed ahead as she always did. And now, their classmates were going to lose their college admission spots that fall. They were going to lose their scholarships and sports placements.

Sensing the impending disaster, Lainey had tried to get Harlow to drop GradeGate and focus on some easier, lower-stakes mystery to wrap up their *Harlow Drake Investigates* . . . webisodes. She had *begged* Harlow to slow down, think it through, but that had never been Harlow's strong suit.

Then Ms. Fraser had disappeared. There had been a tiny smidge of hope that Harlow might overlook a college admissions scandal, but solving a disappearance—possibly a murder? (Given the giant hole in the football field, that seemed to be the direction in which this case was going.) The obsessive curiosity in Harlow that could not leave a riddle unsolved, the trait that made working with her maddening and rewarding and occasionally life-threatening, just wouldn't let it go.

And honestly, Lainey couldn't let it go, either—Ms. Fraser deserved better than this sad, shallow grave. It just got on Lainey's nerves when Harlow was right.

A shriek echoed across the empty parking lot. Lainey's head snapped toward the noise. Even in the dim, sickly yellow light of the streetlamps, Lainey could see Mr. Burnham's *hideous* sweater—the fluffy pastel Angora kind more suited to children's show hosts than a man built like an industrial refrigerator. Tonight's selection was an awful curdling-egg-yolk yellow that made it easy to spot Mr. Burnham wrestling Harlow away from his rear driver-side tire.

Lainey heard Harlow yell, "Go ahead and call the cops. And then you can explain to them why there's a body on the thirty-yard line!"

"Dammit," Lainey huffed. She bolted across the field, redialing the dispatch number as Mr. Burnham shoved Harlow to the ground. Shouting insults and accusations that Lainey couldn't quite make out, Harlow popped up to her feet, pepper spray in hand. She tried to coat Mr. Burnham's face, but he knocked the little cannister away. He slapped her with that *giant* hand, smacking Harlow's head against the frame of his car. She sagged down bonelessly, a puppet whose strings had been cut.

Lainey wanted to yell, but Mr. Burnham's back was turned to her. He didn't appear to know she was approaching. For the moment, Lainey had the element of surprise. Her legs burned as she ran, praying for Peggy to pick up.

"No, no, no," she whispered as Mr. Burnham grabbed Harlow's thick dark hair. Lainey would never make it to them before Mr. Burnham did something . . . like slam Harlow's head against his car a second time. That couldn't be good.

Also, Dispatcher Peggy appeared to be screening Lainey's calls.

The Tank—her late father's old-school pickup truck—was parked on the closer edge of the parking lot. She'd reach it in ten paces, but Mr. Burnham was already yanking his car's trunk open. The jingling of her keys in her shoulder bag gave Lainey an idea.

A ridiculously dangerous and potentially criminally destructive idea.

Mr. Burnham lifted Harlow's limp body up from the pavement and dropped her into the open trunk with a *fhwump*. Lainey gasped, catching sight of Mr. Burnham's face as he slammed the trunk shut—the desperation, the anger, the wild *annoyance* of having to deal with a murder accusation. He wasn't the kindly administrator she'd dealt with over the years. This man was feral.

Pulling his car door open, Mr. Burnham practically had the

engine revving before he was fully in the driver's seat. Even with a *very* low rear tire, he made pretty good time racing toward the exit.

In the interviews that would follow, Lainey wouldn't remember fishing the keys to the Tank out from the bottom of her giant purse or sliding behind the massive F-150's steering wheel. She wouldn't remember her phone dropping to the floorboard as her truck's engine roared to life. She wouldn't remember aiming directly for Mr. Burnham's driver-side door. All she remembered was the sick roll of her stomach as the Tank lurched forward, an uncaged steel-framed beast heading straight for the zippy little sports car.

The jolt of the collision, the earsplitting howl of metal on metal, would echo through Lainey's head for days.

Hours later, Lainey was perched on the open tailgate of the Tank with her usual post-trauma quilt tucked around her shoulders, mesmerized by the way flashing police lights left beautiful patterns on the shattered auto glass.

That was probably shock kicking in.

Over the past few years serving as Harlow's partner in these wacky investigative hijinks, Lainey found that state-issued foil blankets just didn't do the job. Her grandma's quilt was the one necessity that didn't fit in her seemingly bottomless shoulder bag, in which she carried her entire existence. The "emergency quilt" stayed stashed safely under her passenger seat for occasions just like this.

She pulled the quilt tight around her throat and watched the lights dance. They created a nice distraction from the angry lecture Harlow was receiving from the sheriff. Lainey chose to believe it was the vehicle-to-vehicle damage she'd done to Mr. Burnham's BMW that had the principal furiously smacking his head against the squad car window.

It would have been really helpful if the deputy who'd made the arrest had moved his squad car farther away from Lainey's truck after throwing Mr. Burnham in his back seat. Even if they were muffled by police-grade glass, it kind of hurt to hear so many four-letter insults from the educator who had declared her the Regional Grammar Bee Champion. It was difficult not to take the previously unknown five-letter ones personally. Mr. Burnham seemed to quiet down, though, when she picked up her digital video camera and made a show of framing a shot of his face.

Filming on scene was one of her least favorite parts of creating their popular webisodes. Lainey was just glad she'd been able to talk Harlow into condensing this case into a multi-episode arc on their vlog *after* they'd secured credible evidence of the college admissions scheme rather than live posting it. She was pretty sure that was the only thing that had kept the girls from getting run out of school by an angry mob.

"Has it occurred to you to just stay home on some nights and watch TV?" Deputy Robin Wintrout approached Lainey with a foam coffee cup in hand. He was one of the few first responders who was friendly to Lainey or even acknowledged her presence. While Harlow was loud and snippy, Lainey faded into the background. She was able to move around without being noticed. It was helpful for their cause. Harlow was the face of their little team, but Lainey saw things while other people didn't realize they were being watched.

Unlike his surly colleagues, Robin seemed to see the value in what Lainey and Harlow were trying to accomplish. Or, at least, he didn't outright curse at them while they were filming. When he found them in situations like the football field fiasco, Robin was always the first to ask if Lainey needed her mom, needed an ambulance, needed a left sock. (That one was a long story.) Tallen River hadn't extended much in the way of friendship to Lainey or her mother. She was grateful that Robin turned out to be ninety percent tolerable. The barely visible outline of a wispy blond mustache comprised the remaining, intolerable ten percent. While he was just shy of thirty, the underdeveloped facial hair made him look like an overgrown teenager.

"And miss out on the awesome faces Sheriff Pleasant makes when Harlow gives her 'how I solved it' explanation?" Lainey scoffed. "Oh, look, there's a new one. I'm going to call it 'frustrated disdain with a dash of seething rage.'"

Against the flashing police lights, Lainey could see Pleasant's short frame slumped against his cruiser. He seemed to be pinching the bridge of his nose as Harlow explained how they'd *tried* to tell him Ms. Fraser was missing, but he hadn't listened. Sheriff Pleasant didn't appreciate hearing "I told you so." It was better for Lainey to observe them from multiple car lengths away. In the distance, Lainey could just make out the county's excavating equipment trundling onto the field to dig up the crime scene.

"Three creams, three sugars?" Robin asked, sitting next to her on the tailgate. His gun belt made a scraping *scriiitch* as he hitched his hip over the metal surface. Lanky and lean, Robin had been the first to arrive on scene after she'd Mario-Kart-smashed into the BMW, trapping Mr. Burnham inside until he could be extracted, arrested, and placed in the back of a squad car. He'd helped her pry the trunk open with a crowbar, freeing Harlow, while Lainey word-vomited an explanation. He hadn't even judged her when she'd actually vomited on the blacktop. He'd just patted her back and radioed for more squad cars.

"Thanks," she muttered around a hair elastic clenched between her teeth as she shook her thick coppery hair out of her face. She tied it back with practiced ease.

"You know that's basically hot ice cream, right?" he asked as she sipped her coffee, grateful for the sucrose boost. "It's terrible for you."

"I've taken bigger risks today," she told him dryly. She lifted her long legs to wriggle her toes in sensible, if oversized, running shoes. "Besides, I'm not exactly afraid of stunting my growth."

"So, remind me why you're not over there, helping your equally smart-ass friend explain to the sheriff how you two figured all this out?"

"Well, for one thing, when Sheriff Not-So-Pleasant threatens to throw me in juvie, he means it," Lainey replied. "Harlow has a different level of protection. I don't have a state's-attorney-turned-judge for a dad. It's better for me to stay out of his line of sight."

Lainey didn't add that they were still working on several cases around town, and Harlow didn't want to tip their hand. The sheriff's interference would derail the episodes of *Harlow Drake Investigates* . . . they'd planned to post before they left for college that fall. Harlow wasn't Harlow without her subscriber count.

Robin chuckled. "You mean, Drake doesn't like it when you point out how you contributed to the group project." He had never liked Harlow, but more in a concerned "You should make nicer, calmer friends, Lainey" vein, as opposed to Sheriff Pleasant's irritated vitriol.

"It's better for me to embrace my Fifth Amendment right not to self-incriminate," she replied. "Which is why I would appreciate it if you forgot all the babbling I did when you were helping me pry Harlow out of the trunk."

The deputy snorted into his coffee cup. "So, what set off Harlow's crime antennae this time? Counterfeit prom tickets? The chess team using performance-enhancing drugs?"

Lainey scrubbed her hand over her face. "I'm in the same lunch period as Hoyt Landon. I heard him bragging to his buddies about the recommendation letter Mr. Burnham wrote him for college applications, which wasn't weird. Mr. Burnham is known for writing nice recommendation letters. But Hoyt joked about giving Mr. Burnham a 'German assignment,' which I thought was weird. And not just because of the improbability of a student giving the principal homework, but because Hoyt famously failed Spanish all four years of school, including this one. Anyway, Hoyt read parts of the letter out loud—mocking the hell out of it, by the way, because he's a prince—and Mr. Burnham had called him a 'shining example of citizenship and meaningful student involvement.' *Hoyt Landon*, the same spoiled-ass rich kid who filmed himself while throwing pee-filled balloons at food pantry volunteers last year. It just made me wonder how many of these glowing recommendations Mr. Burnham was giving to people who didn't earn them. And then the school paper published something about Hoyt getting a scholarship for his humanitarian efforts on behalf of the homeless based on one of those classic effusive Burnham recommendations. I put that together with Mr. Burnham's new *German*-made sports car."

She paused and pointed at the famous blue-and-white logo on the mangled remains of Burnham's car. "And things started to make sense . . . on a really terrible level."

"Oh, so *you're* the one who started all this," Robin said.

"Don't remind me." Lainey groaned, even as she smiled a little. That was the danger of working with Harlow: the teensy bit of sensible shame being overwhelmed by the deluge of "Hell yeah, I did that."

For the moment, she was carefully avoiding looking at Mr. Burnham, seated in the back of a squad car. The baleful stares from her (probably former) principal were becoming unnerving. Now that the adrenaline was ebbing and she was beginning to grasp the damage to her dad's old truck, Lainey realized her mom was going to *kill* her.

It had been four years since Matthew Piper had died in what Lainey considered a suspicious car accident. She and her mother still couldn't manage a calm conversation about her dad. The loss had changed both Piper women in incalculable ways *and* established Lainey's hostile dynamic with Sheriff Pleasant. The asshole had the nerve to "offer condolences" at her father's funeral. Lainey had responded that the best way to show that he was sorry was to find out what had really happened to her dad. Lainey still remembered the stunned, offended silence that echoed across the funeral home. It was this ability to establish an archrivalry with a public official that had attracted Harlow's attention.

"Lainey!" Harlow whispered harshly, snapping her out of her fog. Lainey looked up to see Harlow miming winding an old-fashioned hand-cranked camera. Right, Harlow would want footage of the police response, the body being wheeled across the field. She hoped there was enough space on their memory card to handle the kind of video file they would need.

Lainey was so used to this sort of cinema verité, she didn't even have to think about it as she panned across the parking lot. But when the body bag was wheeled past her, she nearly dropped the camera.

Ms. Fraser had been a favorite among the students, but solving her murder was going to set sleepy little Tallen River *on fire*.

Maybe Mom would let Lainey move in with her grandparents this summer.

Robin was staring at her, his expression expectant. "And how did a suspiciously financed sports car lead you to digging up the football field?"

She replied, "I found a receipt in Mr. Burnham's desk."

"You mean, after you broke into his office?" he asked.

"I would argue that the office is public property and I had a right to be there as a concerned citizen," Lainey said, still filming.

"And I don't think that's going to hold up in court," Robin deadpanned.

"Mr. Burnham bought ten sod rolls from DIY Depot last week and marked the purchase as a maintenance expense," Lainey said. "It didn't make any sense. The district pays for a landscaping company to sod the *whole* field, like they just did in the fall. The district wouldn't expect the principal to repatch one tiny area on the fly. But if you wanted to cover up a fresh hole you'd dug in the football field really quickly, that would be the way to do it. I really don't know how he thought that was a long-term solution, but I think he was kind of unraveling."

"And so . . . you dug up a body."

"We did try to tell you, or the department, at least," Lainey said. "The sheriff didn't believe us."

"Maybe you could send me a text next time, before the digging starts," Robin said. From anyone else, this would sound like a pickup line, but the deputy seemed honestly concerned for her. It was an odd and unfamiliar feeling, an adult trying to supervise her.

"Probably a good idea. Fortunately, the Tank fears no midlife crisis car." She patted her truck's solid metal gate with affection.

"And again I ask, why aren't you over there, claiming your share of the credit?"

Staring through the darkened window of the police cruiser to where Mr. Burnham was currently screaming his head off, Lainey mused, "I'm the sidekick. I accept this. I make the funny observations. I occasionally provide snacks. I rein in the worst of Harlow's self-destructive impulses—trust me, I've prevented way worse than this. But if it had been up to me, I would have dropped this whole thing when it got scary. Ms. Fraser never would have been found without Harlow."

"I believe you contribute a little more than you think," Robin told her. "You should be right up there with her."

"Wintrout!" Sheriff Pleasant hollered across the parking lot. "Get your ass over here and explain yourself!"

"Well, right now, the spotlight means getting yelled at, so I think I'm good. Besides, I don't know if you know anything about group projects but getting the credit you deserve isn't how it generally works out." Lainey snickered as Robin slid off the tailgate to try to talk Sheriff Pleasant off his emotional ledge. Harlow was apparently dismissed and was ambling toward the Tank. Lainey was grateful when the cruiser carrying Mr. Burnham finally pulled away, his face pressed against the glass like a compressed, angry goldfish.

"Well, the sheriff says you shouldn't anticipate an accident report listing Mr. Burnham as being at fault, so good luck with the insurance." Harlow chuckled, climbing up on the tailgate alongside her.

She bumped Lainey's shoulder with her own. "Thanks for pulling me out of the trunk."

"I'm buying you *two* cans of pepper spray. I don't care if they don't fit into your tiny impractical purse," Lainey said, bumping Harlow back. They watched a departing cruiser's taillights fade into the darkness. "Unless Burnham pleads out, the trial is going to be an absolute circus. We're talking at least one *Dateline* episode, maybe a *20/20*, meaning a lot of this town's secrets will be exposed like a . . . sucking chest wound. A privileged community, spoiled kids benefitting from a rigged system, wealthy parents behaving badly—"

"Sex scandal," Harlow interjected, pursing her lips. How did she manage to keep a consistent coat of Persistent Plum while stuck inside a principal's trunk? It was one of the greatest mysteries involved in spending time with her partner in true crime.

"Don't stop filming," Harlow reminded her. Lainey rolled her eyes but held up the camera. They would never use the audio from this footage. Harlow preferred voice-over, controlling how much information the viewer got, tantalizing them just enough to tune in for the next episode.

That was one thing Lainey would not miss when she went away to college: the marathon editing sessions, meeting Harlow's exacting standards with video software that she didn't really know how to use herself. Lainey wasn't sure who would be polishing the videos shot at Chawton University, but she doubted that Harlow would give up her growing popularity on social media.

Then again, if this story broke the way Lainey expected it to, Harlow's and Lainey's college careers could be in jeopardy. Admissions offices could decide that any Tallen River High student's recommendation was fruit of the fraudulent tree. They could be stuck in this place. Forever.

For a moment, Harlow's smirk twisted her heart-shaped face into something unpleasant. "I'm betting Mr. Burnham's going to confess to everything. He's too riled up to wait for a lawyer. I could hear him supervillain monologuing about Ms. Fraser's 'betrayal' while I was locked in the trunk. I guess that's how she found out about the grade fixing. Misguided pillow talk."

"Yikes." Lainey shuddered while she pictured fuzzy sweater-vests shed in passion. "Wait. That's weird conversational timing. Why would you bring up a sex scandal right after I mentioned parents? And you have that look on your face. The 'I know something' look."

"Because I always know something. And I'm pretty sure the deputy over there is way more interested in pillow-talking with your mom than fighting crime," Harlow said, ignoring the gagging sound Lainey made. Lainey stared across the lot at Robin. Harlow had to be mistaken. Helen Piper had been alone since Lainey was thirteen years old and hadn't had so much as a valentine from her dry cleaner that whole time. And when had Robin even *met* her . . . Oh, right, all of the times she'd had to pick Lainey up from the station.

Dammit.

Harlow kept talking, completely oblivious to Lainey's turmoil. "Grade fixing. Corruption. Murder. It's a shame that we're not going to be around to cover the trial for the vlog. But we'll be far away at college, where there's less risk of being locked in a trunk. Not zero risk, but less."

Lainey watched, frowning as faint snatches of the sheriff yelling things like "incompetent" and "dumbass" at Robin drifted to them from across the parking lot.

"You're probably going to have to come back and testify against the guy who locked you in his trunk," Lainey reminded her.

Harlow shrugged. "My dad will get them to accept my deposition in place of my testimony. Look, I know you feel guilty about Hoyt and the others, but we did the right thing. We found Melissa Fraser's murderer and we exposed a major scandal in our school system before we even graduated."

"Alyssa."

Harlow scowled at her. "What?"

Lainey said, "Ms. Fraser's first name was Alyssa."

"I know, I know, I'm just a little keyed up from all the adrenaline, you know?" Harlow smiled blithely, flexing her hands. "Don't worry about the trial, OK? If we get dragged back here, we'll get through it together, like we always do. It's not like when our parents were going off to college, where they had to write each other actual paper letters and stuff. We have the internet, email, video calls. When I need you, you'll be *right there* with me."

Lainey tried not to let Harlow see her shudder. What did it say about her that Lainey was so eager to get away from Harlow and their work? In the last few years, Lainey had committed an array of misdemeanors with a disturbingly casual attitude. And while she'd done those things in the course of helping people, finding the truth, Lainey Piper was not the best version of herself when Harlow Drake was investigating.

Fortunately, there was life after high school, and Lainey was going to run out into the world and grab it with both hands.

"Drake, I still have questions!" the sheriff yelled. "I'm not done trying to charge you with something. Maybe your little friend, too!"

"Dad says he has no case," Harlow assured her, tying her dark chestnut hair back into a ponytail, as if she were preparing for a fight. Lainey grumbled into her coffee as Harlow sauntered back toward the sheriff.

"You were just kidding about my mom and Wintrout, right?" she called after Harlow. "Right? Harlow!"

1

Present Day
McGillis Point, Wisconsin

Lainey Piper knew three things to be true. One, she needed to get out more. Two, messages from her credit card reps had recently transitioned from passive-aggressive to downright threatening. Three, grown adults should not have their mommies drop them off for cute little murder getaways.

Lainey should have just risked extended parking in the abandoned lot and left her car to rot in the scrabbly weeds and badly patched blacktop. The McGillis Point Marina was beyond the edge of the proverbial map. Here be dragons, and possibly a meth lab.

"Mom? You really don't need to get out of the car, I can get my own bag," Lainey huffed as she climbed out of Helen's sensible Volvo. Parking for the marina was practically empty. There appeared to be several possibly derelict RVs near the tree line surrounding this little corner of Lake Michigan. If Helen hadn't been willing to drive four hours, Lainey probably would have returned from Bantam Island in two weeks to find her aging Kia rehabbed and occupied by a van-lifer.

"I am not an Uber driver. Pardon me for wanting a look at the strangers who will be sharing an isolated location with my daughter," Helen drawled, her accent dripping with guilt-inducing sarcasm. Her mother was from western Kentucky, something that had always set her apart in Tallen River, and not necessarily in a good way. People had always treated Helen as if she were one step out of the trailer park, while happily making use of her hospitality and natural warmth to benefit the town's tourism bureau.

"You make it sound way tawdrier than it is," Lainey grumbled. She shut the door behind her, blowing her wind-frizzed auburn hair out of her face. She really should have had Sophie drop her off. But her neighbor was under an illustration deadline and had already taken on cat-sitting Lainey's fastidious tabby during her absence. Additional transportation felt like too big of an ask.

The sagging dock barely stood against the ripples of the brown-gray water. Lainey could see people milling around the *Acheron*—four men of varying ages and a slim woman who appeared to be securing several large bags in the boat's hold. The aging day cruiser would take them on this hop-skip-jump from McGillis Rock, around Washington Island, and then another few nautical miles to their destination.

"Let Robin help you with your suitcase," her mom commanded. "Robin, help her with her suitcase."

"Got it!" No-longer-a-deputy Robin Wintrout sprang out of the passenger seat with his usual enthusiasm and practically yanked the hatchback open. Lainey followed him, the strange weight of the inevitable settling on her shoulders.

"We just want you to have a good time, Laines," he told her, giving her his best hopeful smile. It faded quickly as he hefted the battered old black canvas suitcase she'd had for years. "What in the hell did you pack?"

"Same thing I always pack when I'm going somewhere new. Flashlight, pepper spray, digital voice recorder, backup flashlights, first-aid kit, batteries, lock-picking kit, backup pepper spray, protein bars, extra-large bottle of bright purple superfine craft glitter, backup first-aid kit." She paused when he gave her a knowing stare. "I have my reasons!"

"Your adolescence shaped you in ways that other people's did not," he told her.

"I'm just saying that if I'm attacked, can't make the pepper spray work, and don't make it out, you tell the cops to look for the guy covered in purple glitter. That stuff won't come off for *months*," Lainey said.

She glanced down the dock and saw that two figures on the *Acheron* had stilled and were staring at her family. She was grateful that, given the sound of the boat engine warming up, the strangers on the boat probably couldn't hear them.

"I know your mom is being a lot right now, but she worries about you," Robin confided quietly. "No matter how old you are, you're always going to be our little girl."

Lainey snorted, smiling despite herself. "Robin, buddy, we've discussed this. No matter how you mean it, that sounds creepy."

Robin chuckled, throwing up his hands. "I know, I'm just excited to be a dad figure."

Robin was all smiles for Helen as she joined them at the tailgate.

He wrapped his arm around her mother's shoulders. Helen grinned at her daughter, adding, "Well, if you didn't want me marrying Robin, you shouldn't have brought us together so often."

"Yeah, it was your idea for your mom to give me a job working under her!" Robin exclaimed, making Lainey scrunch up her face.

While he hadn't been directly attached to the college admissions scandal, Sheriff Pleasant's reelection bid had failed in the wake of GradeGate. His newly elected replacement had fired every deputy hired by Pleasant, including Robin. Meanwhile, the school district had privately awarded Harlow's and Lainey's diplomas two weeks early and asked them not to come to the graduation ceremony "given the circumstances." The circumstances were that most of their classmates had, as predicted, lost their scholarships or had their admissions withdrawn after the official investigation into Mr. Burnham's actions. Lainey and Harlow didn't have their admissions canceled because the universities seemed to think it would be a bad look to punish the whistleblowers.

"Please don't say 'under her' in reference to my mom." Lainey groaned, making Robin cackle. "The boundary is blurry but it's still there."

She supposed it was worth the indignity of having a stepdad a handful of years older than her to see Helen Piper-Wintrout aglow with happiness. Or at least happiness that had her keeping a skincare routine and a SoulCycle schedule that would be the envy of any internet celebrity.

Tourist traffic to Tallen River had exploded after the GradeGate scandal, which had made it a popular stop for true-crime enthusiasts' road trips. That, of course, increased the demand on

Helen at the tourism bureau, giving her the budgetary space to hire Robin as her assistant. Their Hallmark Channel age-gap romance movie plot had played out very quickly, much to Lainey's personal horror.

"At least she convinced you to shave off the mustache," Lainey said with a sigh.

Robin adopted a more serious tone to say, "Your mom and I think this is going to be really good for you. Meet some new people."

"I know people," she insisted. "I talk to people all of the time."

"Keeping up with former coworkers through group texts doesn't count," Robin told her.

"I also keep up with former coworkers over social media," Lainey objected.

"And make the most of this opportunity," her mother added. "You never know. This could lead to a new job—"

"I have a job!" Lainey objected.

"You work in your pajama pants."

"At my job," Lainey reminded her.

"Honey, you hall monitor the hall monitors," Helen shot back.

Lainey's lips pinched together. Helen had never understood Lainey's job as a freelance forensic accountant. Poring over corporate financial documents, seeking out signs of malfeasance, double-checking other accountants' work—it wasn't quite the career Lainey had dreamed of, but it was a challenge. It kept her out of the spotlight and out of danger. And up until recently, it was a career that kept Lainey and her cat, Locard, in the luxurious accommodations to which they'd become accustomed at the Orchard View Apartments. She was not prepared to admit to her mother that she was on the verge of losing one bedroom and a galley kitchen's worth of decadence. So instead, she stuck with the pajama-pants conversation.

"Why would I wear real pants to work at home?" Lainey asked.

She'd said that a little louder than she'd intended. Lainey realized she could hear her own voice much more clearly than before . . . because the engine noise had died down. And the people on the boat had heard.

Great.

The *Acheron*'s passengers seemed to realize they'd been spotted in their spying and returned to their business—or at least the appearance of it.

"OK, I love you both, but I'm going to go now," she told them.

Helen frowned. "Wait, don't I get to meet your new coworkers?"

"No, you do not," Lainey told her. "Because this is not sleep-away camp. And I am thirty-two years old."

"I know, I know, you sent me all the emergency contact information for the network reps, but I would just feel safer if I had faces to connect to the names," Helen insisted.

"And I would feel like I had a lot more professional standing if my mommy didn't want to introduce herself to said coworkers and regale them with tales about my unreasonable childhood bias against raw tomatoes and my occasional hay fever."

Helen gave her a long-suffering look. "Well, do they *know* about your hay fever?"

"Mom, I know I've given you trouble over the years." Lainey paused to gesture at Robin, as if to include him in the consequences of said trouble. "But I've learned from my mistakes, made better choices, reduced my risks."

"I'll say," Robin muttered, even as Helen said, "But you're rushing right back into Harlow's orbit and I just—"

"You can't tell me to take advantage of a situation while simultaneously fretting over that situation," she said. "Pick a lane."

"She always picks her Laine-y," Robin said, grinning, then added, "See? Dad joke."

Both Piper women groaned as if tortured. Lainey sighed and hugged them both. "OK, I'm going to go before that happens again." Lainey pointed toward her stepfather. "You chose this man."

"Yeah, I did." Helen beamed up at Robin before taking Lainey's face in her hands. She leveled her with the same green-on-brown hazel eyes Lainey saw in the mirror every morning. "Please be careful, baby."

"Believe it or not, I usually am," Lainey replied.

"I do not believe that," Helen told her.

Lainey dragged her suitcase down the dock to where the *Acheron* was idling again. A potbellied deckhand took her bag with embarrassing ease and pointed at the bench seat. The man, his shaggy iron-gray hair sticking out at all angles under a threadbare West Michigan Whitecaps hat, was a fairly typical character around the less glamorous lakeland ports. He carried Lainey's suitcase back to the boat's storage area, carefully tucking it behind several black canvas bags—all embroidered with the True Crime 24/7 logo.

Another man with thick silvery blond hair took her hand and helped her step into the boat without tumbling into the drink. He offered her a conspiratorial grin. "Vern works for the hotel and is a man of few words. I'm Gordy, sound guy extraordinaire."

"Thanks." Lainey fanned her face with her hands as she

plopped down on the bench seat next to a younger guy wearing what could only be called "vacation-business wear"—a white shirt and gray dress slacks that were somehow crisp and detergent-commercial bright despite their surroundings.

He was the type of guy you met at a conference in Vegas, only to end up making a lot of bad decisions involving misspelled tattoos. He had wayward dark hair begging to be tamed by an affectionate hand. Sharp jawline. Dark blue eyes a girl could drown in. She took a minute to very sternly lecture herself about travel safety and impulsive decisions.

She would *not* end up with a misspelled tattoo.

Not today.

Probably.

Lainey wrinkled her nose as Vern loosed the ropes from the dock cleats and tossed them aside. They gave off a waft of mildew and gasoline as he dragged them into place. Vegas Decisions helped Vern and Gordy secure the ropes without being asked. She watched him move, a rangy figure with broad shoulders and a waistline that tapered down to long legs.

Did his unprompted helpfulness mean he was an employee of the hotel? If so . . . why was he wearing such fancy shoes? On a decidedly nonfancy boat? Why wasn't the deckhand yelling at him for not wearing more sensible boat shoes?

Vegas Decisions glanced toward her as if he could sense her watching him. She froze. He stared. She arched her brows in response. He seemed to think better of whatever he was about to say. Probably for the best, for both of them.

Lainey pulled her phone out of her beloved shoulder bag—not the same bag from high school but version 15.0, a durable brown leather specimen that included multiple zipping pockets inside and out, and even more elasticized pockets to store all the things she needed to keep up with life in general. If she was going to see Harlow again, she would need all of its pockets and maybe more.

Vern took his place behind the pilot's wheel while Vegas Decisions sat down next to her. Vern goosed the engine into a dull roar. Lainey wondered if it was big enough to propel the worn vessel around Washington Island, about twelve miles farther into the lake, to their destination.

Lainey leaned back against the fiberglass lip of the gunwale as the *Acheron* lurched away from the dock. Given the clouds of exhaust billowing from the back of the boat, Lainey was starting to get a dreaded three-hour tour vibe. She glanced around at the other occupants of the little vessel.

Gordy's seatmate seemed a little more cheerful—a long-limbed, doe-eyed brunette telling a story about her boyfriend ruining an entire batch of Bellinis during the brunch rush. The brunette's head was pillowed on a backpack as she reclined on the seat, talking loudly enough to be heard over the engine. Gordy occasionally chuckled but mostly just listened to the harrowing tale of lost Bellinis and disgruntled, caviar-less society ladies.

A less audible presence down the bench was the heavyset man about Lainey's age who was gazing at the sky as if it owed him an explanation. His rounded face was red under his thick dark beard. And she imagined he had to be hot under that True Crime 24/7 cargo jacket. People underestimated how warm it could get on Lake Michigan with the sun reflecting off the water, even in September. She wondered what he did for the network.

Was Vegas Decisions with production? He looked like he could cart around a camera if he wanted to, but given the outfit, she was going to guess he was a producer of some sort—not that he wasn't handsome enough to serve as on-air talent. Hell, he ticked off a lot of Lainey's boxes with the eyes, broad shoulders, and damn . . . those were some big hands.

Why was she thinking about this now when she was getting farther and farther from the shore? She turned to see Helen and Robin waving at the departing boat. She waved back but quickly turned away, gripping her shoulder bag to her chest.

For all Lainey's assurances to her mother, the cold weight of doubt was starting to worm its way through her middle. What if this was all fake? What if some Draniac had arranged for Lainey to be abducted in some awful catfishing / human trafficking prank?

It wasn't entirely unusual for the hard-core Drake fans, or Draniacs, to track her down. For all her attempts to obfuscate, Lainey's name was published on multiple internet platforms as Harlow's sidekick. Lainey had found the true-crime community at large to be a safe space full of fun, supportive people committed to finding the truth of most matters or just fascinated by the absurd, macabre riddle of human behavior. But Draniacs tended to be middle-aged guys just a little too interested in a teenage girl broadcasting from her bedroom. It had been one of Mr. Drake's many sensible arguments against their vlog. The fact that Harlow's dad had insisted they keep the vlog "small," exclusive to their own little website instead of hosted on larger platforms like YouTube, was probably what had kept them to a more manageable cult following.

When the True Crime 24/7 staffer first reached out weeks ago, inviting Lainey to be part of *Harlow Drake Investigates . . . The Disappearance of the Blue Rose*, Lainey had ignored their emails, as she always did. She'd turned down multiple invitations to speak at true-crime conventions over the years as Harlow's reputation grew due to a series of True Crime 24/7 specials about infamous historical cases. Lainey hadn't appeared on any of the podcasts or documentary series that made offers. It was financial necessity that had her accepting this one now, but what if this whole thing was a scam? She'd done all she could to vet the network staff that contacted her, but what if someone had managed to fake accounts so they only *looked* like they belonged to the True Crime 24/7 network?

Still . . . maybe it would be worth it. Lainey had been obsessed with the Blue Rose case as a teenager. She'd read the books, watched the documentaries, and, yes, shamefully watched the Lifetime movie at least twenty times. (It was the best one.)

Marguerite Devereaux had been the gold standard of missing persons cases before D. B. Cooper hopped out of that plane. It should have been easy to solve and yet remained a mystery because of a multitude of misdirections and misinformation. It had all the hallmarks of a notorious true-crime case—a missing woman with a hauntingly beautiful portrait, illicit hobbies, relationships with gangsters, even Hollywood connections, or at least attempted Hollywood connections. Lainey wasn't sure how a niche historic hotel in the middle of Lake Michigan played into it. In all her reading, she'd never seen a connection between Marguerite and the Crossings Hotel. Her curiosity was piqued, and sometimes that led her to destructive decisions.

The self-awareness would make being kidnapped in this tiny boat worth it, right?

Breathing deeply through her nose, Lainey rifled through her purse, looking for her wallet, phone, keys, glitter—all there. Teenage Lainey didn't struggle like this, not even when finding bodies and rescuing people from car trunks. Adult Lainey was much more aware of the cost of things—not just the financial but also the grinding strain of disappointment, unprocessed grief, and stress that she never quite learned to manage in a healthy no-one-gets-locked-in-a-car-trunk fashion. Also, she had to pay for her own health insurance, which recently stopped covering her therapy appointments.

Lainey forced herself to take in oxygen. There was no hopping off the boat and swimming back to shore. Her former partner, Harlow Drake, worked for True Crime 24/7, or at least she did as of earlier today. Lainey had specifically checked Harlow's social media that morning for an official Notes app apology or a sad announcement of a "mutual parting of the ways" with the network. No dice. So Lainey was still committed to the Bantam Island project.

Besides, if she were being tricked into thinking that she was working on the network's new *Harlow Drake Investigates . . . History* special, the catfish would have contacted her from a fake Harlow account instead of her producer's assistant's assistant's. And surely, if Lainey were being kidnapped, they would have taken her credit cards and probably the phone in her hand.

She needed to stick this out. She couldn't tell her mom that she'd just lost her biggest client. That was what happened when you had to inform that client that his son was funneling large portions of the company's discretionary funds to offshore gambling sites. Poor Mr. Clary had been so thrilled to bring Bert Jr. into the company right after business school. He'd assured Lainey that he understood she had to tell him the truth about Junior's embezzlement . . . Mrs. Clary, however, was less forgiving. Lainey was pretty sure she recognized the lady's tight, neat signature on the proverbial pink slip accompanying her last payment from Clary Construction Resources, Ltd. It was not the first time she'd been let go for making the holidays awkward for a small family-owned company.

So beyond her fascination with the Blue Rose case, money was a big factor in Lainey's presence on the boat. She was here to chase the sort of money that would keep her creditors at bay and give her time to find new clients for her one-woman operation. The "Associates" bit was what Lainey considered a hopeful bluff. She wanted to eventually take on more accountants, but she'd gotten into unhealthy partnerships before. She just wanted to choose her associates carefully.

Helen had no idea how upside-down Lainey's finances were, and Lainey wasn't about to tell her. Agreeing to meet Harlow on Bantam Island was one stop short of asking her mom if she could move back into her childhood bedroom. The irony of a broke accountant was not lost on Lainey—nor the tragedy of Lainey's financial woes being tied to digging up problems that people would rather stay buried. It was a bit of a lifelong pattern for her. Her therapist—before Lainey had had to stop her *luxuriant* bimonthly sessions—would have been proud of this sort of introspection.

Vern gently sped the *Acheron* into open water. The leggy brunette sat up and tied a floral silk scarf around her hair, protecting it from the wind. It only added to her Audrey Hepburn mystique.

Lainey thought of her mother's cheerful lecture that morning, one of many cheerful lectures during the long drive. This round centered on Lainey "treading water" through life instead of trying to achieve bigger dreams. *"It's just like Freya says, 'See it, believe it, achieve it!'"* Helen had chirped at her.

Was there anything worse than your mom lecturing you because she thought you were lagging behind the goals one should reach at thirty-two? Maybe having your mom's spin instructor's mid-class motivational mantras repeated back to you.

Vern's careful handling of the engine ended as he threw the throttle, jerking the boat forward into the open water. The jolt sent Windburned Bearded Guy sliding a bit in his seat. He shot an annoyed look at Vern. They rode in silence for some time until Gordy shouted to her over the sound of the motor, "Was that your mom back there?"

Lainey nodded, pursing her lips.

"My mom doesn't get my job, either," he told her.

When Lainey frowned in confusion, he pitched his voice several octaves higher to add, "*Why work in television if you're not even in front of the camera?*"

"My mama says I could make way more money doing makeovers for Glamour Shots," the brunette told her, a distinct Southern twang sweetening her vowel sounds.

Now that Lainey looked closer at the other woman's face, she could see the expertly applied false lashes that emphasized her already large dark eyes—that and the four shades of eyeshadow that complemented her golden-brown skin. Lainey could spend hours in front of the mirror and never manage anything so subtly spectacular. She sincerely hoped this lady would be working on her before she stepped in front of a camera.

The pair looked at Lainey expectantly as if they expected a response.

Right, people skills.

"Do Glamour Shots stores still exist?" Lainey asked.

The well-coiffed woman nodded. "Sadly, in some parts of Texas, yes, they do. Even more sadly, my mama's probably right. They spend a lot of money on glittery blush in Texas."

The three of them looked to the deckhand to add his thoughts on vocationally disappointed moms, but he continued to scowl at the clouds overhead. Gordy shrugged it off, leaning forward to shake Lainey's hand.

"Again, I'm Gordy Scott," he said, laying his hand on his chest. "And this is Findlay Reeves, makeup artist to the stars."

"Or what passes for stars on True Crime 24/7," Findlay demurred.

"Elaine Piper," she told them, using her proper full name—the name under which she'd filed her business license to try to escape her limited online notoriety. Their little group paused and turned to the other occupants of the boat, but Vegas Decisions and Windburned Bearded Guy didn't bother introducing themselves. So . . . maybe they didn't all know one another? Huh.

Gordy shrugged off the snub. "And what do *you* do that disappoints your mom?"

"We overheard—at least the 'pants' bit," Findlay added. "And your brother was cute."

"That was my stepdad," she said, waiting for the duo's responses. The slacked jaws did not disappoint.

"Way to go, your mom," Findlay mused.

"Yep. They're very happy, except for my chosen field of being a forensic accountant," she said. "Companies call me in when they notice problems in their books, usually because money they have coming in doesn't match up with what's going out. And it's usually because someone's brother-in-law is paying for a secret apartment for their secretary from a party-planning fund."

Vegas Decisions's dark brows rose at that, but Lainey disregarded him. (But the stepdad thing he ignored? Interesting.)

Findlay stared at her speculatively. "You know, you don't look how I thought you would. We've watched quite a bit of background video on you and all we ever heard was your voice."

Lainey felt like a little bubble of pleasant privacy had popped. She supposed it was silly to hope the network staff wouldn't recognize her. And she was going to have to slide back into "public face mode" earlier than expected if she was going to survive her stay on the island. Lainey's discomfort with the "true-crime wunderkind" label after GradeGate and the ensuing backlash was a big deciding factor in her choice not to engage in the convention circuit, even when she really could have used the money. The Draniacs *thought* they knew her, and what they hadn't gleaned from the webisodes they filled in with their own assumptions. The things they posted in online spaces were disturbing enough—about her diet, her dating life, her choice of sleepwear. So yeah, she didn't want to know what they would say to her face.

Lainey had learned to develop a sort of armor if she was recognized—which had happened less and less over the years. She adopted a pleasant if blank expression, a neutral tone of voice, an understanding that even if she didn't see phones, she was probably being filmed. She found herself disappointed at this pivot in conversation. She had enjoyed this fledgling socialization with Gordy and Findlay. It was the first real, in-person interaction she'd had with nonfamily members in months. Most of her social interactions took place over group texts with former coworkers or with her neighbor, Sophie—the only person Locard trusted enough for cat-sitting. Those were the people who got to see the real, inappropriate-emoji-using, spit-taking-wine-during-a-reality-dating-show Lainey. She didn't want to subject Findlay and Gordy to aloof-and-detached Lainey.

"I think I've got a lip color that's going to change your life," Findlay told her.

Lainey blinked at her. "All right."

Gordy nodded solemnly. "You remember Wilson from *Home Improvement*? You had that level of mystique for me."

"I'm surprised *you* remember Wilson from *Home Improvement*," Lainey told Gordy.

"Reruns," he replied, nodding.

Lainey snorted. Most of the "original" vlog episodes featured Harlow sitting very close to the camera, confessional-style, expounding on her theories about events around Tallen River's latest mystery. Lainey was generally out of focus, shouting observations from her perch on Harlow's beanbag chair. It was not a comfortable position for laptop use, but Harlow's dad had objected to dragging another desk into Harlow's room for a "kid who doesn't even live here."

Darren Drake had never been a fan of their little project, or of Lainey's father . . . or of Lainey. He thought her whole family was more trouble than the social connection was worth. Lainey's father had been a very sweet, very earnest CPA. Matthew Piper was successful because people could count on him to tell them the truth about their financial picture. He was a family man, a person of integrity, the rock upon which Lainey's family was built—until he wasn't.

Even at thirteen, Lainey had refused to believe that the same man who had given her endless lectures around personal responsibility drove drunk, crashing head-on into a family of four. In the months following the funeral, Lainey and Harlow formed, well, not quite a friendship. They didn't sleep over at each other's houses or braid each other's hair, but they had a partnership, a respect for each other's intelligence. They knew what they were capable of, and for teenage girls in the digital age, that was a precious thing.

At first, Harlow posted a few webisodes focusing on her thoughts about the wreck, which Lainey found too painful to talk about on-camera. And while the suspicious death of Matthew Piper had featured heavily in their site's mission statement, their audience was far more interested in the various cases they found around their small town. It was usually small-stakes, small-town stuff, like proving a vegan restaurant used real cheese in its pasta dishes or exposing a sleep-deprived driving tester who slept through evaluations while indiscriminately approving all license applications. Nothing they broadcast was as serious as Ms. Fraser's murder.

And while their work hadn't added to their popularity at school and had definitely attracted the attention of more than a few internet weirdos, it had given Lainey something to *do*—somewhere to channel her anger, her energy, while she waited to get the hell out of Tallen River. But it had come at a cost.

"You don't have a social media presence," Gordy noted.

"Not under my own name," Lainey replied. When their brows rose—in unison, which was a little unnerving—she added, "It wasn't just GradeGate and everything that came after. People tend to shoot the messenger when I give them bad news at work, and the people they fire are usually super unhappy about it. So if I want to use social media, it has to be under a very bland made-up name, with very little in terms of personal info."

Findlay said carefully, "I guess you and Harlow didn't talk much after high school, given that she couldn't give the network your contact info."

Gordy shot her a look, and she shrugged. "I have friends in the network's administrative offices. I give them advice about hair products, they give me nonconfidential info."

"I am not mad, I'm just disappointed this is the first time I'm hearing of it," he told her.

"It's normal for people to lose touch with their high school classmates," Lainey said warily. "It's been more than fifteen years."

"Really?" The pair leaned closer, as if Lainey was going to spill her tea all over the boat's deck. Lainey found herself faintly disappointed in them. Did they really think she'd gotten by for this long by indulging in casual gossip with near strangers? Lainey needed the check at the end of this venture too badly to be so foolish.

Findlay watched her carefully. "But you keep up with her career, huh? Particularly lately?"

Lainey stared back, unmoved. If that was a conversational trap, she would not tumble into it.

"Well, there has been a lot to keep up with," Gordy demurred, glancing at Vegas Decisions. He whispered to Findlay, "Did you see this morning's email from corporate or did your secret gossip pipeline get it to you three days before anyone else?"

"Don't be bitter." Findlay glanced at Lainey, as if vetting her for discretion capacity. Lainey had to work to keep a neutral expression.

Ultimately, Findlay seemed to decide that the risk was worth sharing the gossip. "Are you referring to the email that told us not to talk about Harlow's 'developing situation' outside of the company?"

Lainey sat back on the bench and watched Gordy flush pink, glancing at her. "Well, she doesn't count as outside, right? She's technically a network employee. Freelance. Contract. Sort of."

"Not just talking about her." Findlay shot a significant look at

Vegas Decisions. OK, Vegas Decisions was *not* a network employee then. Interesting.

"So, how close *are* you and Harlow these days?" Gordy asked.

"Yeah, are you text-every-day type besties or comment-on-birthday-posts-only acquaintances?" Findlay added.

"I suppose we're somewhere below birthday comments only," Lainey said carefully, making Gordy blanch and Findlay give her a sympathetic look. Even Vern the boat pilot frowned slightly, making extremely awkward eye contact with Lainey.

Lainey wondered if she'd said too much. Almost instinctively, she clamped her lips together. Vern shook his head and returned his gaze to the horizon.

Harlow Drake had been called many things over the years: "internet darling," "new media powerhouse," "unreliable friend" (but that was mostly from Lainey's mom) . . . and now, Harlow might be considered a "future former network employee."

Harlow had started off her tenure with True Crime 24/7 years before, as a gimmicky side dish to the meatier "current events" style coverage of criminal trials. Harlow translated her teenage-media-celebrity-made-good narrative to launch *Harlow Drake Investigates . . . History,* in which she dissected historical unsolved cold cases and presented the audience with at least three plausible theories. She became a staple of the network, earning herself a new generation of faithful fans. As long as she chose cases in which most of those involved were long dead, Harlow was free to speculate as wildly as she wanted with little in the way of repercussions. Her commentary had been heavily vetted by the network's legal department and everything was fine. Interest in the original vlog was renewed by the old-school Draniacs. Lainey preferred to ignore the unwanted speaking invitations, tighten her social media restrictions, and hope that maybe renewed interest in Harlow could generate fresh information in her own father's case.

And then came the Chicagoland Sausage Slayer Murders.

The network made the fatal error of trusting Harlow to do a podcast interview unsupervised. And when the hosts of *Totally-TrueCrimetastic* had asked Harlow what she was working on next—a reasonable question that any media personality should have been prepared to meet with an informative, innocuous answer—Harlow had rambled freely about tracking a series of unexplained food poisoning deaths in the Chicago area going back to the 1970s. She expounded on her theory that more than forty deaths were linked to a "meat shop on the outskirts of Chicago." She coyly hinted that the owner worked with organized crime families to quietly poison important targets with strategically tainted meat. She said just enough to identify the shop without actually naming it or the owner.

What might have been a sidebar anecdote that slipped into obscurity captured the imagination of the internet. After weeks of Harlow giving follow-up interviews, a comment on a local news station's Facebook page identified Sam Restretto, owner of Restretto's Finest Meats, as the Chicagoland Sausage Slayer.

Which was the *worst* serial killer name ever.

And rather than refute the theory, Harlow had merely shrugged in follow-up interviews and said, "Who knows?"

That was a literal quote, given to an actual national news affiliate, and all it served to do was stoke speculation even more.

The health of Mr. Restretto, who was still running his shop in his late seventies, quickly declined in the maelstrom. People posted fake awful reviews of the shop on platforms like Yelp. The shopwindow was vandalized repeatedly. Kids would walk into the shop and shout rude, leading questions at Mr. Restretto while filming him behind the counter. He found himself the focus of multiple unwanted TikTok campaigns. And when his four sons complained to police, it was shrugged off as "internet stuff."

Sam Restretto died at the counter, surrounded by his distraught children. The public relations backlash was immediate and swift, resulting in tearstained national interviews from the grieving family and huge losses in True Crime 24/7's ratings. It had been a considerable embarrassment for the network, which had just announced a lucrative development deal with Harlow.

Harlow had been set to become the fun, youth-friendly face of the network's cold-case division—appealing to a younger audience without alienating the older viewers. She was slated to head several spin-off series, prime-time interviews, her own podcast, live shows. Hell, probably her own breakfast cereal. But now all of those projects were stalled in development hell.

From what Lainey had read in the news, Harlow had *just* stayed within the lines of her contract by not naming anyone specifically. So the network couldn't break said contract. Or at least, the network's lawyers hadn't figured out how to yet.

Lainey supposed this Bantam Island project was the network's attempt to fulfill Harlow's contract without actually giving her the platform they'd previously promised her. And Lainey was caught in the cross fire, recruited for purely mercenary reasons but also accepting for mercenary reasons. It was an interesting balance.

"Well, does it make you feel better to know that Harlow's not exactly a popular figure among the crew?" Gordy asked, barely audible over the engine and the wind.

Lainey thought about it, and while she didn't answer, she kind of waggled her head back and forth, indicating that it didn't make her *unhappy*. But again, she didn't know these people. She would not endanger her check or its zeros.

"Demanding diva behavior across the board, without the success to back it up yet—I don't think she's had a single beverage served to her without a side of sneeze," Gordy told her. "And that was *before* the Chicagoland Sausage Slayer stuff."

"Such a bad serial killer name," Lainey muttered. She figured that was a safe contribution to the conversation.

"Right?" Findlay cried. "Also, I'm technically not even supposed to be here. Most of our correspondents do their own makeup and hair in the field. It's just how it's done. They work their way up in news, where they learn to do that stuff on their own. Me and my department head are mostly kept around for studio interviews with celebrity types. But Harlow's contract included a demand for on-site makeup and hair for all shoots. As much as I love working with Gordy, I've got to tell you, I lost the coin toss on this one."

Lainey bit her bottom lip and nodded. She supposed that compared to covering current trials or emerging cases, traveling to an island in the literal middle of nowhere to cover the *possibility* of a historic cold case . . . probably wasn't that exciting.

"This does seem like an awfully large crew to pay for just one special," Lainey said.

"It was in her contract," Gordy said, shrugging. "And there's another two people on the ground, doing prep work on the island."

"Oh, so they wanted her *bad*," Lainey replied. She glanced at Vegas Decisions, who still seemed completely detached from their conversation.

"If the hotel's new owners hadn't agreed to feed and house the crew for free, I don't think she would have gotten approval for this," Findlay told her.

"Findlay's too classy to tell you that Harlow will demand at least three hair looks before she finally settles on one. Every damn day of shooting."

"I am not that classy," Findlay scoffed. "She also insists on the same brand of foundation she's used for years, despite the fact that it makes her look all sallow on-camera."

Bearded Guy cleared his throat, staring off into the distance as if he weren't listening to them. And then he jerked his head very deliberately at Vegas Decisions.

Findlay rolled her eyes. "Kenny, down the bench there? He thinks if he clears his throat loud enough, we'll stop spilling our secrets, which is a woeful underestimation of both of us."

Gordy added, "And he won't tell you that the only reason *he* got this assignment is that he was the network's most recent hire and is therefore the low man in the pecking order."

"And he doesn't want to lose the gig, so keep him out of it," Bearded Guy, whose name was apparently Kenny, called to them.

Gordy looked cheerfully undeterred, waggling his eyebrows. Lainey laughed softly, sliding her sunglasses onto her face. She wished she'd thought ahead to bring a scarf, like Findlay. She used this eye camouflage to glance toward Vern, whose expression was impassive . . . if impassive implied he would gladly toss all of his passengers into the water and jet down the coast to Cuba if he thought he could get away with it. It would take work, getting the boat over land, but he looked determined.

This was . . . just not a man who exuded a friendly aura. She wondered why the hotel had assigned him any sort of guest relations. Then again, from what she'd seen online, the century-old Crossings Hotel had seen better days.

Lainey glanced back to the people who seemed determined to

befriend her. Both Findlay and Gordy were staring at her expectantly, as if it were her turn.

"Oh, well, I'm just excited by the novelty of being out of the house," she said, gesturing to her jean-clad legs. "See, I put on real pants and everything."

She thought she was making a clever callback to her embarrassing domestic scene, but both of them looked oddly disappointed. Vegas Decisions's mouth quirked . . . and his eyes flicked down to her lower half.

"Um, so what's your thing that you won't tell me?" she asked Gordy.

His silver-gold brows drew together. "What?"

"Well, you told me the thing Findlay wouldn't tell me, and the thing Kenny wouldn't tell me," she said.

"Leave me out of it," Kenny called from down the bench. Lainey nodded in Kenny's direction and smiled in response, getting a chuckle out of Findlay. She skipped over Vegas Decisions because they seemed to be deliberately shielding him from the conversation.

"So, what's the thing you won't tell me?" Lainey asked Gordy. He stared at her for a moment, as if searching for the best answer. And then he spotted something over Lainey's shoulder and stood, steadying himself on the rust-speckled metal pole supporting the boat's awning.

"Is that it?" Gordy asked, turning toward a shallow split of land emerging in the distance.

Lainey turned to see the Crossings Hotel for the first time and wondered if she'd made a life-altering "secondary location" mistake.

2

Lainey couldn't define the hotel's architecture beyond "dilapidated to the point of pity."

Maybe at one point the Crossings Hotel had been a sexy retreat for the wealthy and well traveled, but now it just looked worn and sad. She wasn't even sure what style of architecture this could be called, except for "fussy." It was neither breezy nor comfortable—all eaves and angles and dusty windows.

From the water, the island itself looked like a mammoth squarish crustacean, waiting to devour unwitting travelers dumb enough to wander close. Unfortunately for Lainey, she was one of those travelers, and she didn't know if she even qualified as "unwitting." The greenery surrounding the hotel seemed overgrown and wild. The forest almost swallowed up the hotel building—but there it was, a narrow, brick, hexagonal tower that stood proudly in the center of two wings that spread diagonally behind it. Lainey could only imagine the hulking steamships that had been required to haul bricks across the lake, but she supposed the wealthy liked to prove they could afford that sort of thing.

The enormous entrance was accented by a porte cochere with similar brick columns. Tall, arched windows seemed to gaze impassively down at the approaching boat from what Lainey supposed were the guest wings.

The overall effect sent a shiver down her spine. "Accommodations at this cute little murder getaway can be yours for the low, low price of being willing to walk into an obvious trap," she muttered to herself in her best radio voice. "Any injury suffered by the guests is their own damn fault. If you have any questions for management . . . well, you probably should have asked those before you got on the boat."

Down the bench, she heard Vegas Decisions snort. She gritted her teeth and shook off this little indulgence in melodrama. The hotel must have been something beautiful once, this isolated spot of luxury built away from the hustle and bustle of Chicago's post–World War I industrial boom. The whole building exuded diminished luxury, a faded prima donna clinging to her ragged elegance. As they moved closer, she could see that the windows got increasingly dirty toward the back of the hotel wings.

Gordy moved to the front of the bench, bracing himself against the gunwale. "Would you look at that."

Since Vern didn't censure Gordy for standing, Lainey rose, too, but almost immediately lost her balance as the small boat hit a wave. She stumbled back and nearly landed in Vegas Decisions's lap. He shot her a surprised look just as she grabbed the awning pole and braced herself, relieved when she didn't face-plant on the deck. This move put her almost shoulder to shoulder with Vern, who looked downright annoyed despite the fact that she hadn't made contact.

"Noticed you're careful about what you share," Vern muttered out of the side of his mouth.

Shocked that he'd actually spoken words, Lainey only stared up at him. He nodded to Gordy and Findlay, who were trying to goad Kenny into standing so he could see the cinematic possibilities of the island.

"Keep that shit up," he told her, and then shifted the boat into a quieter gear. "Now, sit down before you fall."

When she merely continued to stare at him, his graying brows nearly met at the middle of his forehead and he added, "Please."

"OK, but not because you told me to. Just because I am gravity's bitch." Lainey saw the little flash of amusement cross Vegas Decisions's face as she sat down, the quick upward flick of his lips. It felt like something she should lock away for herself.

"Well, the 'please' was for customer service purposes," Vern told her as they idled toward a dilapidated dock. Vern frowned at the sight of another white boat with a pretty official-looking seal laminated onto its side.

As they got closer, she saw that the seal read **WISCONSIN STATE PATROL**.

Well, that didn't seem normal.

A teenage staffer wearing a wrinkled lake-blue collared shirt and cargo shorts caught the landing rope and helped tether the boat. Vern moved away from her, clearly going through a shutdown process before grabbing some boxes from the hold. The small cardboard packages were marked with what looked like an illustration of small engine parts under a logo for a major freezer manufacturer.

What *was* this man's job?

"Hey, Vern, man, you've got to wear the uniform, or at least the name tag," the teenager on the dock called. "You know Mr. Wesley gets all weird when you don't."

Vern hopped off the boat with an ease that Lainey envied, probably born from years of practice. "The place is closing down in two weeks," Vern grumbled. "Not much use in company pride."

Lainey frowned at that. She'd known that the production group was moving in at the invitation of the new owners, who had elaborate plans to renovate the hotel into a private corporate retreat. But to hear the resignation in Vern's voice, it made her feel an unexpected wave of guilt. Was there any chance these employees would be brought back after the hotel's revamp?

Vern strode toward the hotel, only slowing when a pair of state troopers and a woman in a Tyvek jumpsuit rolled a gurney around the side of the hotel's main building. The gurney rattled over the stone pathway, jostling the blue body bag it carried. As they passed, Lainey noted that the badge on the Tyvek jumpsuit read **MEDICAL EXAMINER**.

"What in the hell?" Lainey whispered.

"Yeah," Gordy said, grimacing. "Shelley said one of the guests died during the night. Something about an allergic reaction. He was an older guy. They found him in his bed."

"That's so bleak," Findlay replied with a shudder, watching as the police helped the medical examiner load the body onto the boat.

"People die on vacation all of the time," Gordy said. "How many 'honeymoon killer' episodes have we worked on?"

"Maybe it's time to move you over to the home renovation channel," Findlay told him, scrunching her nose.

The teenage employee seemed eager to change the flow of conversation, clapping his hands together and practically chirping. "Welcome, folks! I'm Tommy. I'll be happy to take care of your bags. Mr. Taggert and Mr. Bagwell are waiting for you inside."

Tommy delivered this line with a sunny smile and plenty of charm. However, Kenny, Gordy, Findlay, and Vegas Decisions simply jumped off the boat, clearly used to handling their own bags. Lainey noted that Vegas Decisions wasn't admonished for lacking a name tag.

Huh.

Also, were they just supposed to pretend there wasn't a police boat parked right next to them receiving a dead body? The answer was apparently yes. The crew worked to disembark while the police quietly pushed off the dock and idled away. Was that standard procedure to protect the deceased's dignity or an attempt not to agitate the hotel guests? Lainey was left to wonder as the boat's engine fired and carried the body toward the horizon.

"Hell of a way to start our week," Findlay observed.

Nodding, Lainey pulled her phone out of her bag and checked for a signal. It would not have surprised Lainey if the signal bar on her screen had read "LOL, no." But instead, it showed two scary dashes. No signal whatsoever.

"Do you need help, ma'am?" Tommy asked her eagerly, even as Lainey died a little inside at the "ma'am" label. She tucked her phone in her bag and handed him her suitcase.

"Thank you, Tommy," she said, wondering if she had enough cash in her knockoff designer bag to constitute a decent tip. She'd been counting on production to cover most of her expenses. That was what was promised in her contract.

"Pretty cool, the TV show coming to the island. Kind of a shame it has to happen right as the hotel is closing," Tommy said as he hauled Lainey's roller suitcase off the boat. She had no idea how he was going to drag it on the cracked brick path up to the hotel, but she figured he had professional expertise. "Most of the guests have cleared out, except for a few diehards who refused to give up their reservations. Old people, you know—stubborn."

Tommy glanced after the rapidly disappearing police boat and flushed red under his summer tan. "Not that we got a lot of young people coming around here."

"I'll try not to take that personally," she told him as she jumped off the boat.

His cheeks flushed even redder. She was going to have to take it easy on the kid. It felt slightly cruel, picking at him when they'd just watched a body being hauled away. She glanced around the hotel's "front lawn"—muted pastel flowers and box hedges that appeared to have been carefully manicured until recently. Had the grounds crew—Vern?—just given up the pretense because of the closure? The other guests were milling around the grounds, pointedly not looking toward the departing coroner's crew, as if that made them not exist.

The hotel's foreboding aura wasn't exactly helping Lainey's nerves.

Lainey studied the building, half expecting to see shadowy figures in the windows or disembodied hands drawing back the mangled curtains. But it was just a sad old building, and it seemed to be mostly empty given the lack of people occupying the beach or the slightly murky pool. Most of the Adirondack-style beach loungers were stacked into two piles. One was clearly the "keep" pile, while the other consisted of those too damaged and splintered to hold on to.

"What sort of guests did you get?" she asked Tommy.

"Well, like I said, mostly older people who used to come here way back when—you know, when the place was super famous. The only younger people or families we got were fooled by the travel website photos, which even I have to admit are pretty good. Or there are the people who think they can find a secret entrance to the Crossings Speakeasy. You know, 'cause it's not like the hotel boarded the entrances up years ago and hid them from *everybody*. The number of people who think I know the secret location and will show it to them for twenty bucks . . ."

"So, you don't take the bribes?" she asked.

"We call them *tips*, please," he said, grinning at her. "And it's not my fault that while I lead them around to the back of the island, near the fishing dock— We have awesome fishing here, by the way, something not everybody knows about. Those are the other kind of guests we get here. Fishermen who can't get reservations at the better, more snobby fishing resorts. But Mr. Wesley hates it. Doesn't think fishing is very fancy, I guess, so he doesn't make it very easy for them. It was his idea, putting the dock all the way at the other end of the island. Anyway, if I happen to get interrupted while taking these tipping guests to some location on the island where an entrance to a secret speakeasy *would* be . . . and I get distracted because one of my coworkers needs me somewhere else, and these guests wander around a beachside hiking path . . . well, that doesn't hurt anybody, does it?"

When she shot him another slightly judgmental look, he added, "It gives them a story to tell!"

"I'm not following you on any hikes," she told him, glancing at the thick trees flanking the hotel. They didn't look like they were meant to be this close to the building, not with the high winds that blew over the lake in winter. It was like they had crept up on the hotel over time.

"Have you worked here long?" she asked.

"Two summers," he said, clearly making an effort to hide how much work it was to roll her bag over the uneven brickwork. "My aunt works in the kitchen as a sous-chef and got me the job. It's not bad. Not super busy and the people are mostly nice. I get to live on-site with my meals covered, so I save a lot for school. I was kind of hoping to stay on after the DBags took over, but I haven't heard anything so far."

"Oh, right," she said. She'd been so focused on the network, the people issuing the checks, she'd forgotten about their hosts. Technically, she supposed DBag Games was her employer, since the company was paying for most of the production costs.

Sigh.

"Are there more boats on the other end of the island?" she asked. "You know, for the fishermen?"

"Nah," he said. "Most of the fishermen cast from the dock. But it's quiet out there. Really peaceful, which is what I think they're looking for anyway."

"Why would a hotel on an *island* only have one boat?" she asked, pointing back toward the underoccupied dock.

"We used to have more," Tommy said. "But profits have been shrinking for years, and the Stanbridges, the owners, well, their grandkids didn't want to throw more money into quote, this money suckhole, unquote. So the boats broke down over the years and management couldn't replace them. The DBag guys? They rode a helicopter out here, landed on the tennis court and everything. And then they kind of freaked out when it took off again. I guess their bosses back at the office wouldn't let them keep it here. I didn't think the guys who owned the company had bosses."

Headquartered in Chicago, DBag Games was the biggest online gaming platform to claw its way into the content-sphere in the last two decades. While the games were aesthetically pleasing and cleverly conceived, the company's secret to success was subscriptions and in-game purchases. Kids weren't happy with having the basic pack. Thanks to very loud, frenetic ads featuring company founders Deke Taggert and Bryce Bagwell, the kids wanted the special perks of the VIP pass ($19.99 a month). The kids wanted their scantily clad lady elf warrior to wear the limited-edition armor ($14.99 each) in every color. They wanted access to the special levels only available to people who paid a million gold coins for entry ($4.99). Parents protested, of course, that the online purchases didn't feel like real money and the kids didn't realize how much they were spending until the parents got their credit card bill at the end of the month.

The company's newest game—into which Taggert and Bagwell had invested an enormous amount of the company's money—was populated almost entirely by scantily clad lady elf warriors whose armor got smaller with each progressive level. In the ensuing parent-sparked backlash, female programmers came forward with documents detailing a toxic work environment in which they were routinely denied promotions in favor of less experienced male coworkers. Female-presenting employees were expected to plan the staff parties, which meant answering party-related texts and calls at all hours and jumping to meet Bryce's whim-based micromanaging. For instance, he insisted that the entire staff would love to eat carrot cake for every birthday. After all, that was *his* favorite. Female programmers were expected to smile and be good sports when major project decisions were made during weekend whitewater rafting trips they weren't invited to. They were denied assignments on the higher-profile "blood and battle" epics and relegated to the less profitable tablet games for younger children.

All in all, DBag Games had had a pretty horrible year so far. Parents' groups protested the half-dressed elves. Women's groups protested the well established corporate misogyny. Everyone protested carrot cake because . . . carrot cake.

And yet DBag Games trundled on—an elephantine machine padded with cash.

According to *Wired* magazine, Taggert and Bagwell had bought Bantam Island to revamp into a corporate retreat to "rebuild trust with their female staff." Lainey wasn't entirely sure how that was supposed to work. Isolating women in a remote location, where they didn't control transportation away from said location, rarely *increased* trust. But sitting in on Harlow's investigation like it was some sort of immersive fan experience got both founders to a secluded location, away from the press . . . and from their board of directors, who were not thrilled with the DBags' decision-making style.

"I appreciate you talking to me, you know, candidly," Lainey told Tommy.

"What do I have to lose?" he said, shrugging. "It's not like they can fire me."

She laughed, but she did note that his posture straightened as they got within sight of the windows. When she gave him a side-eyed glance, he added, "Well, it's not like I *like* getting Mr. Wesley griping at me."

"The manager?"

"He loves this place," Tommy told her. "Like, *loves* it . . . to the point where it's a little uncomfortable. Talks about it like an ex-girlfriend who never blocked him on socials but won't respond to his comments."

She stifled her giggles as they neared the porte cochere, a feature that was a little odd given that there were no cars on the island. Lainey saw two people standing under the shade of the brick portico in front of a tall, carved wooden set of doors. One was a man with dark curly hair, tapping his thumbs frantically against his phone. And the other was . . . someone she hadn't spoken to in more than fifteen years.

"Harlow?"

HARLOW DRAKE INVESTIGATES . . .

Webisode 5, "Introducing . . . LAINEY!"

Posted—November 3, 2007

TRANSCRIPT EXCERPT

HARLOW: Hey, everybody, I appreciate the comments on our first few webisodes. We're still getting things up and running here. And we will start some proper cases soon. Right now, we're just trying to figure out how to explain the weird crimes that happen in this town with no one noticing.

LAINEY [OFF-CAMERA]: What do you mean, "we"? You're one person. Working alone. I told you I don't want to be on your stupid show. I don't want to be the *iCarly* of true crime! I'm only here because you said I could use your Wi-Fi. Do you realize what a freaking luxury a fiber-optic connection is in this town?

HARLOW [SMILING AT THE CAMERA]: That's Lainey. We're in the same grade at school. We've never really hung out, but I was in the library when Mr. Burnham caught her using the school computers to look at autopsy records—

LAINEY: Accident reports. They're public records. I don't see what the big deal is. They closed the case. They barely bothered looking into it.

HARLOW: Lainey's dad died in a wreck a few years ago and her mom doesn't like to talk about it. It's really hush-hush and my dad knows all about it. He's the state's attorney for our county, so he knows everything that happens. But he wouldn't talk to me about it when it happened, so I know *something's* up. And she makes Sheriff Pleasant mad, so she's got to be *sort of* interesting.

LAINEY: Sheriff Pleasant told me and my mom to be grateful that the Carstens hadn't been seriously injured. I don't care what they say, my dad wasn't drunk. He freaked out if my mom drove with me in the car after she took cold medicine. There's no way. Also, how do you have a laptop *and* a desktop?

HARLOW: My dad wants me to have all the tools I need to be successful.

LAINEY: Must be nice. Whoa. This says my dad was under indictment at the time of his death. For *theft* and *embezzlement*? What the hell? My dad would never—

[HARLOW STANDS AND WALKS OUT OF FOCUS TO JOIN LAINEY AT THE BAY WINDOW. SHE TAKES THE LAPTOP AND TAPS ON THE KEYBOARD.]

HARLOW: Yeah, that's an indictment all right. Yikes. Your dad was waiting on his trial date when he died.

LAINEY: Did your dad tell you about this?

HARLOW: He wouldn't. He says I shouldn't worry about adult problems. It's why I spend so much time snooping through his stuff. Besides, a little white-collar thing like this? I doubt it even made the papers, because nobody at school is teasing you about it. It's not that big of a deal.

LAINEY: Why wouldn't my mom tell me?

HARLOW: Same reason Dad says my mom moved to another state "for a vacation" four years ago.

LAINEY: Four years is a pretty long vacation.

HARLOW: That vacation's name is Todd.

LAINEY: Oh . . . Sorry.

HARLOW: Parents think if they don't tell us stuff, it's not real.

LAINEY: OK, if my dad was stealing money from his boss, where did it go? Because I can tell you, he didn't spend it on sports cars or trips to Europe. My mom has sworn to me that my college fund is tiny. The insurance money is probably going to run out in the next couple of years. So where did the money go? What if my dad wrecked the car on purpose? . . . Wait, is that light still flashing? Turn the camera off.

HARLOW [SMILING CONFIDENTLY AT THE CAMERA]: Look for Lainey in future episodes. I'll bring her around. I think this is the beginning of a beautiful friendship.

LAINEY: It's not!

3

Lainey wasn't sure what she expected in her first meeting with Harlow in all this time, but it wasn't for her former partner to push Dolce sunglasses into her carefully highlighted dark hair and say, "Did the network send my vitamin C serum? You did keep it refrigerated, right? It's prescribed by my dermatologist."

Lainey's brows rose. "What?"

Brilliant snappy repartee, Lainey. Nice job.

The man standing beside Harlow glanced up from his phone long enough to look sincerely annoyed. The irritated expression was the most remarkable thing about his appearance—average height, average build, average even features.

And Harlow?

Gone were the boyfriend jeans and Converse of their youth, meant to help Harlow sneak around undetected. Her incredibly impractical heels—putting her at eye level with Lainey for the first time in their lives—had telltale red soles. Also, Lainey recognized this wrap dress from a recent article in *Vogue* titled "Wardrobe Staple Indulgences."

There was something different about the alignment of Harlow's features, as if Lainey was looking at her through a slipped contact lens. The changes weren't noticeable on-camera, but Lainey honestly didn't remember Harlow's cheekbones standing out like that. And her lips looked sort of swollen, as they had after Krissy Ronson socked Harlow in the mouth for posting that Krissy's dad put cameras in the changing room of Ronson's Formalwear Shop—which he had. But Krissy hadn't appreciated the very public dismantling of her comfy life.

Sensing the impending awkwardness, Tommy eased Lainey's suitcase toward the doors and said, "I'll leave this for you at the front desk."

"The network," Mr. Average insisted, looking up from his phone with an arch expression. "They were supposed to send you out here with a little blue nylon bag marked 'Harlow.' I'm assuming you know how to read."

"I'm not from the network," Lainey told him, using the tone she reserved for telemarketers and people who texted in darkened theaters.

Harlow threw her hands up. "Then why the hell are you talking to me?"

"Harlow—it's Lainey."

Don't say "from high school." Have more dignity than that. You cannot just walk away from this interaction. You spent money you didn't have. You borrowed money and you haven't paid it back. Think of the check. There are going to be so many zeros on that check in comparison with all previous checks you've received.

Harlow's face took on all the expression it was capable of.

"Ohmygod, Lainey!" Harlow cried. Suddenly, she opened her arms wide, as if to let Lainey step into them. And for a second, Lainey didn't know what to do.

In watching Harlow's interviews over the years, Lainey had always assumed it was discomfort and stress that caused that manic gleam shining in her blue eyes and added the increasingly strident ring to her laugh—on the rare occasion that Harlow allowed herself to laugh on-camera. But Lainey supposed this *was* Harlow now, and while she was much more aware that Harlow wasn't her friend, the old uncertain energy remained. As she had before, Harlow needed Lainey to make her show funny, more approachable. And now, Lainey needed Harlow for cash. They were not going to come out of this project as renewed friends and social media contacts, and that was probably best for the both of them. Lainey could smile and play along. She could keep the goal in mind and escape this project as unscathed as one could be when serving as Harlow Drake's wacky sidekick.

Lainey hoped she wouldn't be the one locked in the trunk this time.

Think of the zeros.

Lainey stepped forward, letting Harlow sort of awkwardly pat Lainey's arms with her own wrists, but not wrap them around her. It felt like how you might instruct a teenager to hug a dubious older uncle.

Also, had Harlow really not recognized her? Lainey liked to think she'd maintained (mostly) the same shape. Her hair really hadn't been that different in high school—same color, same basic layers. She'd experimented briefly with fringe bangs in her twenties but had learned her lesson on that one. The one area where Lainey hadn't skimped was her skin-care routine . . . because she used the same drugstore brands she'd always used.

That really wasn't something to brag about.

The zeros . . .

Over Harlow's shoulder, Lainey saw Mr. Average's brow wrinkle, as if he were trying to calculate how this relationship worked. Maybe he would share his notes with Lainey if he figured it out. He took a plastic tube out of his pocket, a large lip balm with a little bee on its side. Lainey could swear she detected a hint of eucalyptus in the air. Interesting.

Fully balmed, Mr. Average returned to his phone. It made Lainey wonder how he was getting a signal out here. Was there some lake-based cell tower nearby? Or were they hooked up to the hotel Wi-Fi? Did a hotel this old have Wi-Fi? Lainey's phone hadn't picked up a network. What if lack of cell phone access had made these two snap, and they were just pretending to use their phones? Surely Tommy would have mentioned if two network employees had gone on a screen time deprivation rampage. Right?

Maybe Lainey was spiraling a little bit.

"Have you been here long?" Lainey asked.

"Not really," Harlow said, returning to her phone. "Cameron and Shelley came out a few days ago to lay the groundwork. I mean, I insist on doing all of the research for myself, but they handle the little details and logistics, you know?"

Lainey saw Mr. Average's brow furrow at that. While Harlow had done several of these cold-case specials on location, this was the first one that was so far off the beaten track. Lainey could imagine there was more to "little details"—like how to get lighting equipment, employees, and only partially enthusiastic former collaborators transported all the way out here. Harlow had never been *great* at recognizing the contributions of other people. In the end, Mr. Average was wise enough to say nothing, so Lainey followed suit.

"Of course, everybody's distracted today—so much drama over an old man who died peacefully in his sleep," she huffed.

"I thought it was an allergic reaction," Lainey replied.

"Same difference," Harlow said, waving her hand dismissively. "Anyway, I do appreciate you making time for me in your busy schedule. My dad says you're a bookkeeper now?" When Lainey frowned, Harlow added, "He sees your stepdad at the gym sometimes."

Lainey chose to laugh lightly rather than try to explain how forensic accounting worked. "Something like that."

"So weird that Deputy Wisp-Stache is your stepdad now," Harlow said, tapping on her phone screen. "Ugh, I thought the DBags said their Wi-Fi satellite hotspot thing was state of the art. I can't even download a PDF on this weak-ass signal."

Ah, so there was Wi-Fi available . . . via DBag technology. Should Lainey really entrust her fragile, very outdated smartphone to the DBags' digital influence? The uncomfortable shiver creeping up her neck felt like a no.

"Maybe we should move a little closer to the router," Mr. Average said, glancing at Lainey. Was he trying to get Harlow away from her? Did he think Lainey was some sort of threat? Weird.

Given Harlow's attention to her phone, Lainey supposed this awkward hug and halfhearted small talk was all she would get for her grand reunion with her "partner in crime." There wouldn't be an apology for Harlow ignoring Lainey's earlier emails. There would be no follow-up questions about Lainey's life or "So sorry your existence got run off the rails while I skated off to be celebrated."

Also, were they not going to address the Sausage-Slayer-shaped elephant in the room? They were just going to pretend like Harlow had casually extended the invitation to join this venture spontaneously and out of the goodness of her heart?

Lainey hadn't spoken in so long that Harlow actually looked up from her phone to receive a response.

"It really is. It is very weird that he is my stepdad," Lainey conceded, biting her lip. She made a subtle hand gesture toward Mr. Average. Harlow just stared at her.

Lainey turned to Mr. Average. "Hi, my name is Lainey Piper. Nice to meet you."

Harlow startled, as if she'd just remembered the man existed. She exclaimed, "Oh, Cameron, this is my oldest and dearest friend, Lainey Piper! Lainey, this is my assistant, Cameron Underwood. He organizes my schedule. Keeps me stocked up on everything I need. Screens my emails. Streamlines my interactions with the network. He's basically in charge of my whole life."

"That sounds like a task and a half," Lainey said.

Cameron raised an eyebrow. "I do much more than that."

Lainey frowned. Obviously, that joke hadn't landed.

Harlow had already returned to her phone, making it all the more awkward.

"So, I'm assuming if you're here, the rest of the crew is here?" Cameron said.

"Mmm-hmm," Lainey hummed, even while she asked herself—did she count as crew? The rumor was that she would be expected to appear on-camera this time. Their hosts were practically demanding it.

"So does that mean *someone* on the boat has Harlow's skin-care parcel?" Cameron asked, shaking his head.

Lainey replied, "I would like to say yes, but I didn't see a blue nylon bag on the boat. You might ask Findlay."

Cameron let loose an irritated sigh, locking his phone screen. He told Harlow, "Don't worry. I'll find her somewhere."

He pried open one of the oversized wooden doors, their carved . . . birds? . . . worn blurry by wind and time. Pulling it released a rush of cool, stale air, like the shadowed interior was welcoming them with a clammy embrace.

"Hey, Cameron? Can I have a carrot-ginger juice, when you have a minute? I need the vitamin A. Remember, fresh ginger cut within the last twelve hours. The kitchen tried to pass off dried ginger last time. There's no health benefit to me in that. And make sure that they use the Crystalline Greens NutriScape powder. I left my supply with the kitchen staff."

Cameron's smile was paper-thin as he held the heavy door open. "Of course." He turned to Lainey. "Just to keep things clear from the beginning, I'm Harlow's assistant, not yours."

When Harlow didn't respond to this blatant display of rudeness, Lainey replied, "Wouldn't dream of asking you to trouble yourself on my behalf."

"Good," Cameron told her, releasing the heavy weight of the door. Lainey's nervous energy gave her the reflexes needed to catch it before it smacked her shoulder. Cameron disappeared into the cavernous interior without an apology.

"This place is not the luxury retreat they promised," Harlow muttered as Lainey let the heavy door swing shut behind them. If Harlow was aware of her assistant's rudeness, she didn't say it. "I can't maintain this level of camera readiness if I don't get the full benefits of my juice regimen. The Crystalline Greens powder has been a *life changer.* Antioxidants, vitamins, probiotics . . ."

The conversation was starting to feel like a paid ad. Did Harlow have an endorsement deal with the wellness company or something? Lainey glanced around the entryway for hidden cameras filming this little testimonial.

"Well, I'm sure in its heyday, the hotel was something," Lainey said, examining the feather patterns carved into decorative columns on either side of the darkened foyer. Had the management never heard of LED lights? It was hard to make out the exact shape of the carvings, but Lainey thought she could make out feathers attached to a human torso. Were they angels? That was weirdly evangelical, considering the hotel was supposed to have been quite the party spot once upon a time.

Harlow continued griping. "The socket shorted out when I plugged in my phone. Big sparks. Thank God my phone wasn't on the charger cord yet or it might have fried. And the elevator went out when I was coming down this morning. It's one of those old-fashioned ones with the gates you have to close yourself? I got stuck between floors for almost an hour. I could have *died.*"

"I will avoid the elevators," Lainey said, nodding. "And the sockets."

"Well, the elevator doesn't work anymore, so that's something you don't have to worry about," Harlow told her.

Lainey stared up at the hotel. "This place gives me the creeps, Harlow."

"The school gym gave you the creeps," Harlow noted.

"I stand by that," Lainey replied. "Also, my telling you no was how we survived sophomore year. And junior year. And senior year."

Harlow cackled but then immediately schooled her features into a calmer expression—less likely to leave wrinkles?

"I've missed you." Harlow sighed, bumping Lainey with her shoulder. "Everybody is so serious and they expect *me* to be serious and know everything and how to do *everything* and there's no space for me to just . . . breathe."

It was hard to feel sorry for her, and yet, it was the first glimpse Lainey had of the girl she'd known. Lainey nodded. She could get through this, and she would try not to make life harder for Harlow. After all, complications would endanger the precious, precious zeros.

Maybe stop sounding so much like Gollum, Lainey.

The click-clack of heels drew Lainey's attention to a woman in a rumpled pink linen suit. Shelley McMillan, senior producer, had not looked so frazzled in their handful of preproduction video calls. Today, Shelley's expertly highlighted golden hair hung in limp waves around her red-cheeked face. Her muted pink suit—obviously custom-tailored to her petite figure—looked wilted. And yet, she stared down at her phone, nearly bumping into a nearby column before looking up to spot Lainey and Harlow.

"Oh, good, you're here," Shelley said, finally looking up to shake Lainey's hand. "So nice to see you in person, Lainey. So sorry to be out of sorts today. Everyone's really looking forward to you joining Harlow on this project."

The unspoken "while she still has projects" hung in the air between the three of them. Even Harlow seemed faintly uncomfortable at the resigned tone in Shelley's voice. Someone who hadn't known her as long as Lainey had might have missed the telltale tremor to Harlow's hand as she returned her attention to her phone.

Looking faintly embarrassed, Shelley pulled an inhaler from her pocket and took a puff from it.

"Shelley's from New Mexico. I don't think the chilly Midwest wind agrees with her," Harlow informed Lainey in a tone Lainey suspected was *supposed* to sound sympathetic. But given the way Shelley's mouth tightened, Lainey didn't think it was received that way.

"The air's a little damper here," Lainey conceded in an attempt to be kind.

"We're on a lake," Harlow observed flatly.

"Anything you need, you tell me. I'll do whatever I can to make it happen," Shelley told Lainey, coughing lightly as she pocketed her inhaler and returned to her phone. Lainey supposed that a producer had to accomplish a lot of tasks while working on location with a skeleton crew. Still, eye contact would be nice.

"Oh, Lainey's always been so independent," Harlow said, waving her off. "I'm sure she won't be any bother."

With that, Harlow turned on her heel and walked off. Lainey didn't know whether to laugh or roll her eyes. Shelley was too busy texting to comment, absolutely laser-focused on her screen. Lainey waited several very awkward silent seconds to clear her throat. Shelley's cheeks flushed slightly redder. She took Lainey's arm in a companionable hold while keeping her phone in her free hand. It reminded Lainey of how fancy ladies used to grasp their cigarette holders.

"The DBags—" Shelley stopped herself and said, "Deke and Bryce have asked us to join them in the Gentlemen's Lounge for a little welcome drink."

"I suppose it would just show my poor upbringing if I said that sounds like an on-site strip club?" Lainey asked, following Shelley into the relatively brighter lights of the lobby.

Shelley's face finally relaxed into a semblance of a smile. "An affectation from the hotel's origins. Couldn't have the delicate ladies sitting around and breathing in cigarette smoke and hearing *blue language*. Now no one gets to smoke there because of health codes. But it's a nice little lounge area with a bar."

Lainey finally got a proper look at her surroundings. It was a sanctuary, dedicated to the worship of Prohibition-era opulence. This seemed to be one of the few buildings on Lake Michigan that avoided taking advantage of the waterfront views, but she supposed the high, small windows were an effort to keep in the heat during brutal winters. Large, old-fashioned windows could let in too much wind. Could people even get out here during the winter? The light seemed to filter through those windows with a slightly purple-tinted softness, making Lainey wonder if the glass was leaded.

That couldn't be good in terms of environmental safety.

The lobby's overall effect was of a shadowed cave, with intricately paneled walls made of bubinga wood, a tropical hardwood that reflected a garnet glow. That seemed like a bit of a miracle given the low light and the age of the wood, which Lainey was pretty sure was endangered. The panels alternated between plain and intricately carved relief scenes of—well, Lainey couldn't tell what. The images seemed to involve sweeping . . . clouds? Writhing animals? She thought it would probably make her look like a rube, walking up to the walls to squint at them. Also, Shelley had a pretty firm grip on her arm. Was she afraid Lainey was going to run away?

The oddly intricate yet hard to pin down decorative theme continued through to the enormous check-in desk, more pinkish-red wood, which was overseen by a sweet-faced, gray-haired lady in a crisply ironed lake-blue Crossings uniform shirt.

"This is Lainey Piper, Cassie. She should be on our list," Shelley called in a considerably friendlier tone than she'd used with Harlow. She took a black, branded True Crime 24/7 gift bag from Cassie, the front desk clerk, with a wink. "Please add her to our block of rooms. I'll be back for her key in a few."

Cassie glanced down at some papers on her desk and gave Shelley a warm grin. "She's right here. Thank you, Ms. McMillan."

"Just a little welcome from the network," Shelley said, handing Lainey the gift bag.

As Shelley lead her across the white-and-carnelian tile, Lainey glanced down into the gift bag. It was necessary to avoid looking at the floor with its strange red-and-white wave pattern. It was making her a bit dizzy. Ooh, there were all sorts of network-branded goodies in there—hat, shirt, coffee mug—and a eucalyptus-scented lip balm from Dancing Driftwood Apiary. It looked like the tube that Cameron had been using. Maybe the network gave them to everybody on-site?

Lainey cringed. She tended to stay away from eucalyptus products thanks to her mom's essential oils phase. She would never say anything to Shelley about it, though. That would be rude.

Lainey turned her attention to the dozens of framed black-and-white photos of better times at the Crossings. Girls in flapper dresses pouting at the camera. People awkwardly posed mid-Lindy-Hop. Elegantly dressed cigarette girls hawking their wares to men in dinner jackets.

Wait. Was that Marilyn Monroe? Not an impersonator, but the real Marilyn Monroe?

The archivist didn't display photos taken after shaggy hair and casual clothes took hold in the late sixties. Lainey couldn't help but notice that most of the photos were centered on women in tight-fitting evening wear . . . which was uncomfortable, but she supposed the owners knew what drew the eye of the general public.

The furniture was in less-than-pristine shape. The cream-colored settees and sofas, grouped into little conversational pods, were showing wear at the seams. The foam showed through splits in the grubby off-white material like pus leaking from a wound. Also, there were splashes of an unknown gray-brown substance on the armchair in the corner near the sweeping double staircase. The grand staircase split on either side of an old-fashioned brass birdcage elevator. An inelegant orange **OUT OF ORDER** sign was taped across the elevator gate.

A little extra light might have made the overall effect less "haunted hotel chic." It also might have helped her spot the other people in the room, like the older woman sitting on the couch nearest to the phone booths—an honest-to-God wood-paneled bank of tiny phone booths that Lainey couldn't imagine spending any time in. The little ash-blond-haired lady sat primly on the lumpy couch, reading a novel with a hot-pink cover. It clashed horribly with the light peach cardigan twinset she was wearing, but Lainey admired the way she didn't seem self-conscious about that or the lurid cover illustration of a shirtless hockey player.

The lady glanced up when Lainey walked by, and a flash of disappointment flickered across her softened features. Lainey supposed she was staking out the lobby in hopes of glimpsing Harlow. Lainey felt a little sorry for disappointing her.

Lainey turned her attention to an elegant middle-aged woman wearing a floral-print tea dress who sat near the enormous white marble fireplace. The mantel took up most of the wall over the empty hearth and was shaped like an enormous inverse . . . beehive? (Featuring more difficult-to-distinguish-at-a-distance carvings.) The woman was knitting something fluffy and yellow.

Who came all this way to sit in this weird room to knit?

Lainey supposed these were the last of the hotel's real guests. She had to wonder what would possess people to stay in this creepy place when it was mostly empty . . . without the monetary incentive that attracted Lainey.

OK, maybe she was being a little hypocritical. The mood lighting wasn't helping.

Lainey spotted a sign that indicated the Beatrice Dining Room was on the far end of the lobby, through a closed pair of double doors. And something called the Rosemont Archive and Museum was next to the gift shop. She could only imagine the gift shop—bags of salt, exorcism kits, presharpened wooden stakes . . .

What Lainey didn't spot were security cameras. Anywhere.

They passed a door marked LIBRARY—GENTLEMEN ONLY . . . which, honestly, tracked with the rest of the building. Why would women want to *read*, she thought grumpily. Yeah, Lainey was going to have to hydrate and get some sleep before that sort of thought actually left her mouth.

"I have been assured that the library is open to everyone," Shelley told her. "The hotel only keeps the signage up because of the nostalgia factor."

Lainey hummed and chose not to comment.

The zeros . . .

They took several short turns away from the main lobby. Apparently, the owners had wanted the lounge to be out of sight of the general public while remaining close to the "action."

As Shelley led her toward a door marked GENTLEMEN'S LOUNGE in dull gold Poiret font, Lainey noticed that the tile formed an alternating foursquare pattern around the central decorative tiles, which were pressed with flame-shaped indentations.

Huh.

Lainey touched the brass door handle for the Gentlemen's Lounge. She immediately withdrew her hand at the sticky sensation against her palm.

"Yeah, a lot of the doorknobs are pretty grubby," Shelley said, wrinkling her nose. "I think it's some old-fashioned paste polish or something that never comes off."

Lainey stared at her hand. This didn't feel like cleaning paste. It felt—

"Or it's possible the housekeeping staff was fired, considering that the place is closing," Shelley supposed. "It could be doorknob germs from six months ago."

"Oh, come on! Why would you say that?" Lainey demanded, making Shelley chuckle.

"We're going to have fun," Shelley told her.

Despite herself, Lainey laughed as she wiped her hand on her jeans. "Are we?"

4

When they entered the even darker lounge, the smell of long-stale cigarette smoke practically choked her. The overwhelming scent reminded her of some of the old-school office buildings across Chicago that she'd worked in over the years. She glanced around at the bizarre red velvet wallpaper, flocked with a black lace motif. The paper was spattered with strange smearing patterns, making it appear blurry. Had the nicotine soaked into the velvet over the years, contributing to the stench?

The dark walls plus the overstuffed chairs, cases of camera equipment, and a large projector screen all crowded in, making the room feel even more claustrophobic. The brightest spot in the space was a man in a vibrant lake-water-blue dress shirt and white sweater knotted around his shoulders. The man in question was shuffling through a file folder, looking awfully stressed as he talked with Vegas Decisions. The besweatered file shuffler had intense dark eyes and dramatically feathered, too-dark-to-be-natural hair.

Was it a wig? In terms of style, it was pretty outdated. Surely, if it was a wig, he would buy *fashionable* hair, right?

Gordy and Findlay were already seated, talking quietly with Kenny, who still seemed to be in a sour mood despite the beer in his hand. Harlow had taken her seat in an armchair near the darkened fireplace. It was definitely the cleanest chair in the room.

Lainey noticed that Harlow didn't speak to anyone on the crew. She looked up and acknowledged Shelley's entry with a nod, but that wasn't exactly the deference Lainey would have paid her de facto supervisor for the network.

Looking considerably more relaxed than anyone else in the room were two guys behind the bar, cackling to themselves as they attempted to juggle bottles like flair mixologists. Lainey was pretty sure she spotted a pricy bottle of tequila in the taller guy's hand. One did not simply walk into a bar and manhandle Don Julio 1942.

Lainey's mouth fell open in dismay. She didn't even drink tequila, but honestly—

The disrespect.

Behind them, she noted two boxes labeled with far less impressive whiskey and tequila brands. Considering that the Don Julio appeared to be full with the wax seal intact, she could only imagine the prestige brands were strictly for show while the staff served well liquor at premium prices. It was highly illegal, but she couldn't imagine this place got to its neglected state by slinging the high-end stuff.

Thanks to her internet searches, Lainey recognized the two bartender wannabes as the founders of DBag Games. Deke Taggert, the company's CFO, was pale and slight with an angular, freckled face. His eyes and hair were almost-matching reddish shades of sherry brown. Bryce Bagwell, on the other hand, was dark-haired, a foot and a half taller, and solidly gym-built and fake-tanned. Both were wearing cargo shorts and T-shirts advertising their own games.

So they were *those* guys.

Shelley gestured to the DBags. "Deke and Bryce recently purchased the hotel, and they were gracious enough to let us use it as a location before their renovations. Guys, this is Lainey Piper."

It was like being scented by a pair of velociraptors. Both heads snapped up and then toward her. They moved in unison, practically crawling over the bar to get to her. Lainey resisted the urge to step back. They would never respect her if she retreated now.

"It's you!" Bryce said, surging ahead while Deke hung back, watching. "The other half of Draney!"

"I'm sorry?" Lainey paused mid-protest. She'd heard of Draniacs, but never "Draney."

"'Drake' plus 'Lainey' is 'Draney.' We could have used 'Harlow' plus 'Lainey' equals 'Harley,' but we wanted to avoid confusion in the online fandom forums. We didn't want to conflict with the Harley Quinn content," Deke drawled in an accent that sounded Southern—well, southern New Jersey. "And I'm Deke. Glad to meet you."

"I still don't love the Draney thing," Harlow muttered into her drink.

"They could have used both last names and gone with 'Diper,'" Lainey noted, making Harlow shudder.

Deke threw his head back, laughing, while simultaneously elbowing Bryce. "See? I told you this would get funnier once Lainey got here."

Harlow's frown deepened. She probably didn't appreciate the

notion that she wasn't the most entertaining factor of their little crime-fighting team.

"We never thought we would get to meet you in person. I mean, Harlow we met on the party circuit in New York, but you? You're like a recluse," Bryce said in an earnest tone, like calling someone a hermit was an overture for lifelong friendship.

Lainey told herself she should probably be flattered by this attention. Ostensibly, Bryce was a good-looking guy with bottomless pockets. And she was basically a bankrupt single mom to a cat. If this were a Hallmark movie, the pair would enter a gingerbread house competition together, fall cozily in love, and discover the true meaning of Christmas.

And yet she said . . .

"Hi, nice to meet you." Lainey extended her hand, only to have it nudged aside by Bryce's giant paw.

A brilliant smile split his tanned face. "Oh, I don't shake hands. I'm a hugger."

Several things happened at once. Lainey pictured the total balance of her checking account, which was depressingly low. She estimated how much lower it could get if she stamped on Bryce's instep in response to a hug. As an alternate plan, she planted her left hand on Bryce's shoulder and slipped her right hand, eellike, back around Bryce's wrist until she managed to reestablish a grip on his hand. She maintained eye contact and pasted on a saccharine smile and shook it. They were standing awkwardly close while shaking hands, but still, she'd managed a handshake.

Remember the zeros . . .

Bryce glanced down at her steadying hand on his meaty shoulder as if it were a dead squirrel. In her time dealing with grabby businessmen who also conveniently defined themselves as "huggers," Lainey had discovered that the best way to avoid unwanted contact was to disrupt the embrace before it started. And most people were made sincerely uncomfortable when a stranger's hand was this close to their neck.

"Accidentally" poking the hugger in the eye while making a sweeping hand gesture was also an option. Honestly, Bryce was lucky she wasn't using the pepper spray. Or the glitter.

Over Bryce's shoulder—still braced by her hand—she caught sight of a smirk on Harlow's face. Lainey wondered if Harlow was treated to Bryce's brand of hugging and figured . . . probably not. Guys like Bryce were generally intimidated by Harlow. Lainey was somehow considered more approachable, despite her waking up feeling like a feral cat most mornings.

"I am not a hugger," Lainey said. Behind Harlow, Shelley was setting up a collapsible projection screen. She'd actually put her phone aside on a nearby table to do it. She turned her head to check on the device multiple times, sure, but she'd put it down.

Bryce's brow furrowed as if this were an inconceivable concept. "You're not?"

Lainey pursed her lips and shook her head. "No."

Bryce's lips tilted at the corner. "Are you sure?"

Lainey's chin retreated into her neck. The shrewd look in Bryce's eyes, like he was calculating all the angles of this social interaction, knocked the practiced, pleasant expression from her face. Maybe Bryce wasn't nearly as goofily harmless as he appeared.

Deke gave Lainey an apologetic smile as Bryce stepped away from her. He accepted her offered hand with comparatively little drama. "We're still working with the sensitivity coordinator to unlearn some of the habits that have gotten us into . . . difficulties."

To Lainey's right, Vegas Decisions made a muffled groaning noise into his scotch.

"Do you want a drink?" Bryce asked, gesturing over his shoulder. "We've got a fully stocked bar back there, some stuff I've never even heard of before. Absinthe. Chart-rooze. Crème de cases."

"Cassis," Deke corrected him.

"No, thank you," Lainey told him.

"Maybe later," Bryce said, grinning at her. "Did you hear about the dead guy?"

"I did," Lainey said, frowning. Shelley had finished the projector setup and now scooped her phone up from the table like it was her newborn child.

Bryce seemed to realize right away that his cheerful announcement of a senior citizen's death was inappropriate. He rearranged his features into a semblance of grief. "Very sad. He will be missed."

"We're just so excited to meet you and Harlow. We were hardcore Draniacs from the beginning—you know, old-school fans," Deke told her, obviously trying to maintain his cool. "We were early adopters."

"We found you by accident, when we were in college," Bryce said. "On a countdown blog."

Lainey arched a brow. "Countdown blog?"

That caught even Shelley's attention. She actually looked up from her phone, while Deke shot Bryce a venomous look. Bryce scratched the back of his neck and hesitantly answered, "You know, one of those blogs that kept track of hot teenage celebrities and counted down to when they turned eighteen. Technically, it was Harlow whose birthday it was counting down to, because you never mentioned your birthday on-camera. Otherwise, we totally would have tracked you—"

"Bryce!" Vegas Decisions barked, his expression livid. Bryce clamped his lips shut.

Lainey stared at Bryce, attempting to formulate a response. She'd known those blogs existed but had never thought she or Harlow would show up on one. So much about her adolescence had just taken on a darker, seedier feeling. She supposed there was some comfort in the fact that her face had been barely visible on the vlog.

Shelley, sensing how hard Lainey's silent *yikes* response was kicking in, seized control of the situation, announcing, "Thank you, everyone, for being here, participating in this project. Of course, this wouldn't be possible without our hosts, Deke and Bryce, whom I believe most of you have met already."

Deke and Bryce raised their hands, waving casually, as if they hadn't just admitted to tracking the legal status of underage girls. Lainey noted that Findlay had shrunk back behind Gordy, using him as a sort of human shield between her and their "hosts."

"Milo Wade works for DBag Games. Think of him as a compliance officer, interested in maintaining and promoting the company's image." Shelley nodded to Vegas Decisions, who was still wearing that vacation-business outfit.

Vegas Decisions apparently didn't work for the hotel. He worked for the sketchy guys who were sponsoring this whole exercise. And he looked very tired.

Ohhhh no.

What had Lainey said on the boat that could be construed as destructive to this opportunity? She tried to mentally review all of her boat conversation comments, but she couldn't remember anything in particular except the one thing she'd said about not wearing pants to work. Had Findlay and Gordy known that he worked for DBag Games when they were critiquing Harlow's behavior? She glanced at the pair and they didn't seem particularly concerned . . . but then again, they were long-term network employees who probably had contracts and unions and stuff.

Far too casually, Bryce said, "Milo handles all the boring corporate stuff. He's here to make sure we don't piss off the board."

The dismissive tone in Bryce's voice did not communicate an urgency to stay on the good side of someone who could persuade their bosses to oust Bryce and Deke from their own company. For a reason she could not name, Lainey felt very sorry for Milo and his thankless job.

Nonetheless, Bryce's comment immediately set a stern line across Milo's full mouth. "Yes, like, say, if our founders spontaneously decide to take the company helicopter off-site and try to keep it with them indefinitely—which absolutely pisses off the board."

"We paid for the helicopter, so we say where it goes," Deke said, shrugging. "We can always buy another one and write it off as a corporate expense."

"Just the sort of thing you'd hope your CFO wouldn't say," Milo told Lainey . . . because his eyes landed on her first, maybe? But it was very obvious he was making a comment pointed in Deke's direction.

Lainey didn't respond. She wasn't about to come down on the wrong side of a conversation involving the title "CFO."

Milo was fussing at Deke like an exasperated stepdad. "They sent me out here earlier than planned, bud, because they were *terrified* when they heard the crew was already on their way. They thought that you might film without me being here to supervise you. I had things to do at the office. And *I* didn't get the helicopter."

"Sorry, Milo," Bryce mumbled.

Deke simply stared. "We go way back, Milo. You know I don't apologize."

Milo shook his head and turned his attention to Shelley. "Please don't take it personally if I ask you not to film something because it will reflect poorly on the company—for instance, if their founders are recorded saying something along the lines of 'being able to see both sides' of prank videos involving flammable spray-on party decor and birthday candles."

"We don't know *for sure* that Nikki from graphics is permanently bald because of us," Bryce protested. "Who develops stress-based alopecia as an adult?"

"Nikki from graphics," Milo told him. "After you turned her office party birthday cake into a firebomb. And Deke told a reporter from the *Journal* that he could see both sides of the 'should some pranks be illegal' debate. You, of course, stated that 'all pranks are jokes, so that means they're fine.'"

"That quote was taken out of context," Deke replied dryly.

Milo's nose wrinkled. "Was it, though?"

When Deke didn't reply, Milo added, "That kid in Akron was severely injured because your antics inspired copycats. Multiple copycats at the same birthday party. The headline was 'First Grade Inferno.'"

Lainey shot a glance toward Harlow. She was watching Milo. Honestly, Lainey couldn't blame her. Milo was non-icky, age-appropriate, and traditionally employed. Also, he was gorgeous and clearly understood how grooming tools worked. That was Harlow catnip.

Deke and Bryce seemed to be in conflict with the one guy on the island there to represent their interests, and if Harlow set her cap for that guy . . . Well, Harlow had never been a fan of romantic competition. Her motto in high school had practically been "All's fair in love and mashing your opponent into a fine paste."

"Moving on," Shelley continued, gesturing to the man in the era-inappropriate possible wig. "Gregory Wesley has been the general manager here at the Crossings for the past twenty-nine—"

"Thirty," he interjected. "I prefer to think of myself as the steward of this establishment for thirty glorious years. I started off as a porter and worked my way up. I'm so very pleased to meet all of you and serve as your initiator at the world-famous Crossings Hotel. Words cannot express how much I envy your position. Not only have you ventured into the rarefied air of this beautiful historic landmark, enjoying its many delights for the first time, but you have the honor of being among the last guests to enjoy the Crossings and her copious charms."

Tommy had been right. There was definitely something . . . off in the way Mr. Wesley spoke about the hotel—festering, unrequited longing. It was as if the Crossings was Mr. Wesley's ex-girlfriend and he had made her his emergency contact and refused to change it, even after the Crossings asked him to.

"On that note, we aren't alone," Milo interjected. He shot an annoyed look at Mr. Wesley. "Before our arrival, I was told we could expect total privacy on the island, but now I'm informed that these reservations had to be honored or it might be a violation of some sort of obscure innkeeping law. The remaining guests couldn't be bought out. And trust me, we tried."

"They were determined to have their experience at the Crossings," Mr. Wesley replied, his own mouth quirking into a smug smile. "The lady commands respect, even as her time comes to a close."

Yeah, Mr. Wesley had some questionable attachments to the hotel. Lainey was deeply regretting her refusal of that drink.

"We figured it was a better look to just let them stay on, as opposed to booting a couple of seniors from their vacation," Milo added. "That's the kind of thing that shows up on indignant social media feeds."

"You'll officially meet your fellow guests at dinner tonight, which will be served in the Beatrice Room at six sharp, preceded by a cocktail hour," Mr. Wesley told them. He clasped his long-fingered hands together. "Now, a few ground rules. You will notice, of course, the hints of Dante throughout the hotel. The architect, Dennis Rosemont, was an enthusiast of Signore Alighieri's masterpiece, the *Divine Comedy.* Rosemont and the original owner, Michael Hinchcliffe, wanted guests to think of the Crossings as the place where the Devil took his due, a waypoint between the workaday world and the escape to the fantastical. At the Crossings, guests must decide whether to choose a sunlit path or give in to their darker desires. Rosemont was sure to make both available on the grounds. Tennis courts, a sun-room, multiple gardens, and the occasional spot where one might imbibe a cocktail. Most of the fixtures are original to the construction in 1914. For the protection of the tiles, the artwork, the woodwork, and the other surfaces, we ask you to refrain from food or drink outside of the lounge or dining spaces."

Lainey grimaced and thought of the mysterious splashes on the lobby furniture. Was Mr. Wesley refusing to replace the furniture because he was clinging to it out of nostalgia?

"You know we're going to tear half of that stuff out, right?"

Deke asked, even as Mr. Wesley visibly blanched. "Crew arrives in two weeks for the demo."

Lainey thought of the strange, sinister charm of the lobby and found herself very upset by the idea of overhauling it. Were they going to turn the Crossings into one of those start-up havens with swinging egg chairs and foosball tables? Yes, those places tended to have amazing snacks, but she just didn't think a boba tea bar would fit into the lobby.

"The board says we have to go forward with the project, whether you're done shooting or not," Bryce said, his face scrunched apologetically. "Otherwise, the board pulls funding for the project. They're not super hyped about it in the first place, even though we think it's going to be a big step forward in building relationships with our chick employees—"

"Lady," Deke interjected.

"Lady employees," Bryce said. "We're gonna look *so* committed to trying to make our lady employees happy, so, you know, they'll stop filing complaints about us."

Milo sighed and pinched the bridge of his nose. He seemed to do that a lot.

"The Hinchcliffe family dedicated their lives to this hotel. Some of the previous owners are buried here on the island."

"Because the hotel's already healthy creep factor needed a boost?" Lainey asked aloud, drawing an offended gasp from Mr. Wesley.

Bryce's face twisted in discomfort, while Deke told Milo, "Check to see how fast we can dig them up and get them out of here."

His tone was so casual, as if he were ordering a pizza. But Milo simply frowned and began tapping his phone screen.

"I intend to keep the hotel to the same standards instilled by the Hinchcliffe family on the day it opened. Until the last guests check out, this is a hotel, and until it ceases being a hotel, it is still under my protection," Mr. Wesley informed Deke, his voice growing thin and almost trembly. "Every square foot of the hotel is devoted to enjoyment, but of course, those facilities have aged over time, as all landmark buildings do. We have taken care to mark any facilities in need of love and attention, so if you see a sign that asks you not to enter, please obey the sign. I must ask you not to explore the halls of the hotel on your own."

If she were still an obnoxious teen detective, Lainey might have seen that sort of vaguely sinister statement as a challenge to seek out whatever Mr. Wesley was hiding in the halls of the Crossings. She would have snuck out of her room with her handy lock-picking kit and sought out the speakeasy entrance herself. But she was not that girl anymore.

Adult Lainey was more self-aware and considerate . . . and she paid for her own health insurance, which meant she was uniquely aware of how much crawl-space-related injuries would cost. Lainey found herself comforted by the presence of Mr. Wesley *and* Milo. Maybe Harlow and the DBags' baser impulses could be tempered if they had sensible adults around.

"So, we're supervised, no matter where we go on the island?" Lainey asked.

"Ideally, yes," Milo said. "It's one of the points on which Mr. Wesley and I firmly agree."

"And I've told you, close supervision is going to make filming difficult," Shelley noted.

"My job is to protect the hotel," Mr. Wesley told her. "You'll have to find a way to film that allows for that."

"I'm just here to protect DBag Games from liability," Milo said. "And that includes whatever your families might file against us if some part of the roof falls on you. So yes, consider me your full-time babysitter."

"I'm sure we can find a way to compromise to create the best footage possible." Harlow stood and tossed her hair back in a strange swooping motion Lainey had never seen her use before. She offered the group a brilliant smile. "And thank you for that segue, Mr. Wesley. It brings us to why we're all here. The disappearance of Marguerite Devereaux, the Blue Rose of the Crossings."

Harlow opened her PowerPoint presentation with a flourish. A black-and-white photo of a flapper girl bloomed into view, her short, scalloped dress tin-typed blue.

Apparently, Harlow had not lost her flair for drama.

5

Lainey sat on the smoke-stained banquette, accepting the bottle of water Findlay handed her. Lainey kept her smile measured, still guarded, but not aloof.

"We expect this to be a very important meeting," Gordy told her. "Shelley put away her phone and everything."

"Shelley *never* puts her phone down," Findlay added.

"I have noticed some device separation anxiety." Lainey held up the water bottle. "Not to look a water-bearing gift horse in the mouth, but don't you want to sip the free booze?"

"Four years sober," Gordy replied. "And Findlay abstains out of solidarity."

"It works out better for me anyway. I get shoppy when I drink," Findlay said. "On one particularly martini-heavy weekend, I bought five pairs of shoes. And I didn't realize what happened until the Ferragamo shipping boxes showed up."

"She was a footwear after-school special," Gordy whispered,

shaking his head. "The returns involved much weeping, but we got her through it."

"I aspire to this level of friendship," Lainey told them. She sipped her water and tried to ignore the shiver of discomfort from being around this many people at once. Moving to Ann Arbor for school had been a much-needed change, giving her the chance to start over without all the small-town baggage hanging around her neck. She'd found that she was actually pretty good at reading people, finding stuff to talk about, and when she wasn't invading their privacy and accusing them of felonies, people responded pretty well to her. And yes, maybe it was a little manipulative to use people skills she'd picked up while working with Harlow, but she wasn't pretending to be someone else. She was still herself—observant, sarcastic, full of random trivia. She wasn't exactly the life of the party, but she wasn't a recluse.

Lainey had returned home for Thanksgiving during freshman year, ready to regale her mom with stories of her safe, relatively well-adjusted life on campus. But before she could even reach her house, she had a cherry cola Mega-Glug tossed at her at a gas station on the county line. And then she'd walked into the house unannounced to find her mother in a naked yoga position with Robin on their couch.

Lainey hadn't been able to stomach the smell of cherry cola since.

Meanwhile, Harlow's part in GradeGate had been forgiven since it had led to her TV appearances, her book deals, and her True Crime 24/7 show taking off. She'd made good, so Lainey supposed the ends justified the means in the eyes of Tallen River.

All those methods of communication Harlow assured Lainey would keep them together? Harlow didn't use any of them. They'd drifted apart, as Lainey had expected. So Lainey settled into a quiet life that suited her. She made friends. She honed her financial investigation skills. She stayed away from her hometown, the Draniacs, and sugary frozen drinks.

Sipping her water, Lainey stared at the opening slide of Harlow's PowerPoint with the Blue Rose moniker. The best-known photo of Marguerite featured her wearing that blue beaded dress, holding a rose that some photo "expert" had colorized to match. Badly.

"This is a case I've been obsessed with since high school," Harlow said. "So you might call this a passion project."

Lainey tried to remember a single time Harlow had mentioned the Marguerite Devereaux case in their years of hanging out. She couldn't remember one, but if anyone was going to solve the Blue Rose case, it was Harlow. Lainey was honestly happy to be along for the ride.

The first slide showed a more intimate studio portrait of a stunningly beautiful woman with finger-waved dark hair framing her elegant oval face. Her brows were thinned to conform to Prohibition-era beauty trends, but her mouth was the definition of bee-stung, defying the highly defined Clara Bow lip. She had painted it a deep and unrelenting color that stood out against the pale luminosity of her complexion. The photo was black-and-white, but Lainey could practically *feel* the boldness of that color. The woman stared directly and defiantly into the camera, not lowering her carefully curled lashes in a typical-to-the-period pout.

Lainey knew most of the story Harlow was telling them. From the time she was thirteen, Marguerite—who was born Margaret Ploppe—told her family and friends in Ishpeming, Michigan, that she was destined for silver-screen stardom. She just had to make it to California and meet the right people. She had faith in her own face and her talent. And that sounded easy enough, but Marguerite didn't want to ride a bus to Hollywoodland. She wanted to arrive in style—with train cases of the latest fashions and a hairdresser on call—so she would have the means to attract attention from the "right people."

"The best way to attract the right attention, in Marguerite's opinion, was the support of a wealthy benefactor," Harlow said. "She moved to Chicago in 1925 at age eighteen, tried to establish herself with a couple of mid-level bagmen with some vague connection to Al Capone's organization. But they didn't have either the funds or the enthusiasm to put her up in the style to which she wanted to become accustomed. She went to all the best speakeasies, where the sons of America's richest families were delaying their adulthood with booze and broads. She roomed with a sultry Southern juke-joint songstress named Gladys McComber, who was dating a married Chicago police detective at the time."

"Shouldn't we be filming this?" Lainey whispered to Gordy out of the side of her mouth while Harlow spun her tale. Harlow had gotten better over the years, Lainey noted. Less personal interjections of opinion. Fewer tangents.

"Oh, no," Gordy assured her quietly as Harlow continued speaking. "The lighting in here is terrible. Suitable for film noir, maybe, but Harlow has a whole 'flattering illumination' clause in her contract. Poor Kenny has his hands full with that. *And* Findlay hasn't worked her magic. So we'll shoot this whole presentation again in a much more attractive setting after we get the lighting rig set up."

"How did Harlow get them to sign this contract?" Lainey asked.

"She was a hot commodity at the time," Gordy said. "She had quite the buzz going. The teen sleuth made good, all grown up. She had earned some public goodwill with that missing girl she helped locate in Kansas. The network had high hopes."

Lainey hummed. The "girl" in Kansas was actually a seventy-two-year-old woman who had disappeared from a city park as an infant. Harlow did a special on the case in which she reunited the woman with her family after using a forensic genealogist and commercial DNA testing sites to search for her. The story was splashed all over mainstream and digital media, hailing Harlow as a heroine. It was a brief moment of hope in which Lainey thought maybe Harlow had gotten more noble as a person. But then the Chicagoland Sausage Slayer comments happened and Lainey was back at Opinion Square One.

Harlow continued. "We know that in May 1927, Marguerite told Gladys that she'd met a swell guy named Timmy who was going to take her to a swanky hotel 'off the coast.' It was supposed to be a real classy gin mill. Marguerite said she hoped Timmy would be nice enough to set her up in an apartment in California."

Lainey could practically see Harlow editing and rewriting this speech inside her own head. She was using the "narrator voice" she used for TV, smooth and deliberate and very limited in her use of contractions. Lainey wondered if the network had sent her to elocution lessons or something.

"Gladys loaned Marguerite a couple of her nicer stage outfits and a few travel essentials, and off she went. When Marguerite didn't return to their apartment when she was supposed to, Gladys gave her a couple of days. Travel was different then, delays happened, trains derailed. There was no checking in over text. But when the rent was due and Marguerite still wasn't home, Gladys got mad enough to talk to her cop boyfriend about it. The problem was, Gladys was an unreliable narrator. She was a known drinker, back in a time when that was considered a character flaw. Gladys was a mouthy type, Southern and known to tell long rambling stories after a couple of cocktails. She was very annoyed with Marguerite for leaving her high and dry with the rent, plus the lost clothes. The cop boyfriend didn't listen, so she told a reporter, known to be one of her steady drinking pals, that her roommate had disappeared after visiting a fancy hotel.

"In her haze, she seemed to think the hotel was off the coast of Florida. But she couldn't remember which one Marguerite had mentioned. She named three different hotels in three different states, including Florida. And none of them had heard of Marguerite when contacted, which hurt Gladys's credibility even more. Charles Lindbergh's plane landed in France on May 21, and the usual newspaper headlines that might have screamed over a missing beauty and a rich man's son— Well, that didn't match the public's taste for Lucky Lindy."

From what Lainey had read, when Gladys finally did remember the name of the hotel, it was months later. The local police did a halfhearted courtesy search of the Crossings as a favor to the Chicago PD. Obviously, they didn't find anything, so they moved on. They figured Marguerite ran off somewhere with a boyfriend and disappeared the way people could before the internet existed.

"So, why do you think that Marguerite was here as opposed to the other locations Gladys named?" Lainey asked, then clamped her lips shut, remembering how much Harlow hated being interrupted.

To her surprise, Harlow beamed at her. "Exactly like that, Lainey, yes! Set me up to answer questions so I can explain to the audience that, up until recently, there was no photographic evidence that Marguerite set foot on the island."

Harlow had switched back to her narrator voice with an ease that was sort of disturbing. "But in 2015, a woman named Erin Nefflin was going through a box of her grandparents' old albums for a reunion and noticed *this*."

Harlow tapped her laptop to change the screen and displayed a very carefully posed, slightly blurred black-and-white photo of a couple standing close together, the lady's head tilted tentatively toward her partner's, as if she wasn't sure how to smile. In the background, a woman in a light-colored dress was caught glancing toward the camera. A thick, sparkling rope of gems dangled around her neck. Something about it was familiar, but Harlow disrupted Lainey's train of thought.

"Erin had heard of Marguerite's case on a Macabre Mysteries of Chicago ghost tour while on vacation with her family. Marguerite's ghost is supposedly wandering a cemetery in her old neighborhood, searching for her own grave. But the brochure included a head shot of Marguerite, which Erin remembered. And she recognized the logo of the Crossings on the band shell in the background," Harlow said, pointing to the curlicued "C" on the screen. "Her grandfather was a frequent guest of the Crossings, back when the family had considerably more money."

"According to our records, he vacationed here no less than ten times," Mr. Wesley announced proudly.

"You have records going back that far?" Lainey asked.

"In our archive," he replied, his tone going colder.

"Guests used this place as an escape from the heat and smells of the city," Harlow said, the annoyed expression returning to her face. "There was no air-conditioning in most homes and there was no EPA to limit emissions, so it was considered healthful to leave any city for long periods of time. The longer you could leave, the better off you would be. And I believe that on one of his trips here, Eugene Nefflin captured a photo of Marguerite on the lawn during a garden dance."

"Our summer garden dances are the highlight of the season," Mr. Wesley interjected, eliciting an annoyed sigh from Harlow. "A chance for our guests to take advantage of the Crossings' full lake views and gentle breezes, lightly scented with our famous lilac trees—"

"When was the last time you held one of those dances?" Harlow asked, and before Mr. Wesley could answer, she added, "Where more than three people attended?"

Mr. Wesley frowned. Lainey supposed that hit a nerve.

"Right." Harlow turned her back on Mr. Wesley to tap on her laptop and progress to the next slide, zoomed in on Eugene Nefflin's hazy photo to show a close-up of a woman in a slinky, sleeveless dress. Lainey imagined it as light blue. The waistline was dropped and the hem was covered in scalloped patterns of slightly darker beads. The woman was twisted at the waist, looking back at the camera over her shoulder, her smile sort of tilted and sly. The fact that her face could compete with the jewels around her neck was proof of her defiant beauty.

Harlow tapped again and showed a side-by-side comparison of Marguerite's known photo and the garden party guest. They were the same woman.

"And Erin just . . . emailed you?" Lainey asked.

"She contacted our Facebook page a few months ago, after she saw the *Kansas City Connections* episode," Cameron said. It had been so long since Cameron had spoken, Lainey had sort of forgotten he was there. "And then Harlow's . . . schedule opened up."

Harlow ignored Cameron's suspicious pause, which he followed by swiping on more lip balm. Harlow continued, "We heard about DBag Games purchasing the hotel. We made contact with Deke and Bryce here—"

"We 'replied all' *so* fast," Bryce said.

"We told the network that we would pay anything you wanted," Deke added. "Our only condition was that we got to watch."

Milo sighed and pinched his nose at the double entendre. Harlow ignored it and finished with, "And here we are."

Harlow said, "According to the hotel's records, *Timothy* Dandridge, of the Dandridge Razor Blade fortune, checked in to the hotel on May 17, 1927. He wrote 'and guest' on the register, which was typical when you were trying to hide an illicit girlfriend's name. Or boyfriend's name, for that matter."

Harlow tapped her laptop to summon a slide featuring a stocky young man in a dark, sharply cut suit. The collar was starched, white and high, and the creases nearly cut into the round weight of his cheeks. His face was cherubic and almost boyish despite the fact that he had to be . . . twenty-seven? Twenty-eight? His mouth was full and almost pouty, which was sort of off-putting when combined with the narrow-set eyes so light blue they seemed almost white in the photo. He was smirking, as if he knew something the photographer didn't, a joke that was about to be played, and only to his own amusement.

In short, his was a face that was highly punchable.

Harlow continued. "Timmy Dandridge was known as a bit of a ne'er-do-well, second son in a family in which his older brother had already taken over the family business to great praise. There wasn't much for Timmy to do except run around to various gambling establishments, houses of ill repute, gin joints, and speakeasies, like the one that was reported to be here at the Crossings."

"I can neither confirm nor deny that," Mr. Wesley said loudly.

"Come on, man, we *bought* the building," Deke huffed, annoyed. "You can't just not tell us where stuff is."

"*If* a speakeasy existed on the property, an outside entrance was probably boarded up when the property was renovated in the late 1960s," Mr. Wesley sniffed. "Any other entrances are unknown, even to me."

"There was an outside entrance to the speakeasy?" Milo asked, sounding intrigued despite his protests.

"For performers and staff who arrived by boat," Mr. Wesley said. "Until it closed in spring 1928 . . . if it ever existed."

"Anybody else feeling like they're being gaslit really, really ineffectively?" Findlay asked Gordy quietly.

"Did they give a reason for closing it up?" Lainey asked. When Mr. Wesley hesitated, she added, "If it ever existed."

"Why?" Harlow turned to her, a gleam in her eye.

"Because 1928 would have been the height of Prohibition. The stock market hadn't crashed yet. People who had the means were living large. Kind of weird that the hotel would close down something that was probably bringing in a lot of guests. Hell, it doesn't make sense *now.* The whole Gatsby thing is really trendy."

Harlow's lips twitched. "Exactly. In the 1960s, the owner married a devout Catholic girl from a timber family in Oregon. Sarah Murphy-Hinchcliffe wanted to align with the squeaky-clean Camelot vibe. So she pretended the hotel's rum-running days never happened, boarded everything up, and fired anybody who had been with the hotel long enough to remember the speakeasy. Mr. Wesley claims the speakeasy location has been lost to time."

"It *has* been lost to time," Mr. Wesley insisted. "And I don't see any reason we need to dredge up the hotel's unsavory past. It was forgotten after Mrs. Murphy-Hinchcliffe sold the hotel to the Stanbridge family in the 1970s. And that's for the best."

"Mr. Wesley will not be helping us with production," Shelley deadpanned.

Mr. Wesley looked vaguely offended. "I will be caring and providing for your party while you are guests here. I simply won't be providing you with information that could damage the hotel's reputation."

"Will you prevent *us* from finding information that could damage the hotel's reputation?" Harlow asked pointedly. "Because it seems like you have your own problems . . . what with guests dropping dead in their beds and all."

Even from across the room, Lainey could see the tension in Mr. Wesley's face as he tried to maintain his customer service expression. "The new owners' contract dictates that I can't interfere."

Deke and Bryce both frowned at the implication that Mr. Wesley wasn't one hundred percent on board with their every whim. Harlow navigated back to the party photo, which showed Marguerite wearing the fancy necklace. She pointed to a stocky man even farther in the background who bore a striking resemblance to Timmy Dandridge. "It was supposed to be *the* speakeasy—luxurious, secluded, the kind of place where the filthy rich rubbed elbows with mobsters and everyday joes alike. From what I've read, Timmy Dandridge would have *loved* a place like that. And he would have brought a woman like Marguerite. He had a taste for women who would probably have upset his mother, which is something we don't have time to explore in our episode."

Lainey squinted at the ill-defined image of the necklace. She'd never seen photos of Marguerite wearing anything like it in her research. Even at paste prices, a girl in Marguerite's socioeconomic bracket couldn't have afforded a fake. Was Timmy Dandridge the sort of guy who would have gotten naughty enjoyment out of draping his practically penniless arm candy in real jewels? Probably. Something about it was . . . familiar, but not something she remembered from her own experience. She remembered the shape from a picture.

"According to the hotel register, Timmy Dandridge checked out of the hotel the following Friday, leaving a generous tip. No fuss, no muss," Harlow said. "He supposedly left on a sailboat with some friends who were staying at the hotel at the same time, but no one could remember who. No mention was made of Marguerite leaving with him. Private boat was a pretty common method of getting back to the mainland. After that, Timmy Dandridge was never seen again. His family sent Pinkerton detectives to investigate, but they found no trace of him. They followed his route back to Chicago and searched all his known hangouts. They even contacted his old school friends, who he was known to travel with—nothing. His belongings did show up at a pawn shop in Eau Claire, Wisconsin, about a year after he disappeared. The seller pawned the suitcase and pocket watch and chain, all personalized in some way with Timmy's full name. The police made note of it when they raided the shop for suspected gambling in the back and reported it to the Pinkertons."

"Whose name was on the pawn slips?" Lainey asked. "Maybe

we can figure out if it was a Crossings staff member if the archive includes employment records."

Mr. Wesley drew in an offended gasp. "From the beginning, the staff of the Crossings Hotel has been the very essence of honesty and—"

Harlow cleared her throat, interrupting him. "The name was Seymore Keyster."

Deke and Bryce snickered to themselves. Milo gaped at Harlow. "So that joke was around even then?"

"Worth noting that 'keister' was also a Prohibition-era slang term for 'suitcase,'" Lainey said.

When Milo, Harlow, and the crew turned to stare at her, she cleared her throat. "My mom really likes old movies."

Deke and Bryce positively beamed at her. Meanwhile, Shelley was furiously scribbling notes.

"Lainey did a whole research project on the problematic behaviors in *The Great Gatsby* our junior year," Harlow added, sounding both amused and vaguely irritated by the disruption. "Because she knew it was the teacher's favorite book."

"Mrs. Lafferty was not happy with me," Lainey said, shaking her head. "Had to give me an A minus, though. I had *so many* footnotes."

"And what did Mrs. Lafferty do to deserve this provocation?" Milo asked, smirking at her.

"We had conflicting opinions on Shirley Jackson," Lainey said primly. When Findlay laughed, Lainey added, "She said that *We Have Always Lived in the Castle* was overrated!"

Several people in the room chuckled at her overwrought testiness. Harlow resumed her narration while Lainey stared at the necklace around Marguerite's neck. Gems like that always had a story. The Hope Diamond. The Koh-i-Noor. Hell, there were theories about Daisy's pearls being cursed in *The Great Gatsby*. That had been one of the footnotes that had upset Mrs. Lafferty so much . . .

Dandridge.

Jewels.

Curse.

Lainey blinked as several connections gelled in her head in a dizzying rush.

"Is Marguerite wearing the Star of Sikkim?" Lainey blurted out. Loudly.

Loudly enough that time seemed to stop and everybody turned around to stare at her.

"I do that sometimes," she muttered, making Milo snort.

"I think so!" Harlow exclaimed. "I hope you're prepared to do that again later, Lainey. Your acting skills were never great. Maybe practice in the mirror."

"What's the Star of Sikkim?" Gordy asked. He turned to Shelley. "Did you know about this?"

Shelley, whose expression was one of someone who was thoroughly confused, said very pointedly, "Jewelry with names was not discussed in any of our meetings."

"Isn't Sikkim one of those countries that doesn't exist anymore?" Deke asked.

Bryce nodded. "Yeah, like Morocco?"

"Sikkim still exists. It's a state in northeast India," Harlow told him.

Lainey added, "Also, Morocco still exists. It's important to me that you know that."

"I knew that," Bryce grumbled, looking slightly pouty even as Deke elbowed him in the ribs.

Harlow pulled up a new slide showing a sketch of a multitiered choker centered around a very large pear-shaped diamond. The multifaceted briolette shape dangled free from the diamond throat band from which several long looping threads of diamonds dripped over the wearer's collarbone. Back when Lainey was a nerdy kid who devoured library books about such things, she learned the supposedly cursed diamond was at least twenty carats. The smaller diamonds together totaled more than fifty carats. And despite its eye-watering value, it was also linked to a number of kidnappings, murders, and ironic accidental deaths.

"In today's market, even without considering the whole legendary jewels thing, the Star would be worth about thirty million dollars," Harlow said. "It was part of the crown jewels of a small southeast Asian nation and migrated across distances, like most significant jewels have done throughout history. And then the Dandridge family 'located it' around 1924."

"I thought the Star of Sikkim was lost in some shipwreck?" Milo asked. "Isn't that the story?"

"It went down with a yacht called *The Lucky Edge*, which makes sense if it was owned by a razor-blade-making family. *The Lucky Edge* sank in a tsunami created by an earthquake off the coast of Newfoundland," Lainey said. "It's said the owner's daughter-in-law thought it was appropriate to wear a legendary necklace to a boat party off the coast of Canada . . . in November 1929 . . . less than a month after the stock market crash that brought on the Great Depression . . . which doesn't sound suspicious at all. The daughter-in-law went down with the ship. Her body was never found. The policy on the necklace saved the family fortune but bankrupted the British insurance company that covered it."

"If Dandridge let Marguerite wear the necklace while she was hanging on his arm, maybe someone killed them for it while they were here?" Harlow suggested. "Even if someone didn't recognize the Star as a famous diamond, they would have seen it as valuable. Or maybe Marguerite stole it, running off to live a life of expat luxury in Europe or something. Timmy disappeared because he knew his family would never forgive him for the loss? Maybe the story has a happy ending."

"You don't believe that," Lainey observed. "You've never been a fairy-tale kind of girl."

"No, I think it's far more likely that Timmy Dandridge killed her in some stupid accident involving a croquet mallet and a crossbow. But that's not a theory people will want to hear," Harlow shot back, rolling her eyes.

For a moment, the energy of their former partnership was there, crackling between them. A familiar feeling stirred in Lainey's gut, the initial thrum of excitement, a puzzle waiting to be unlocked, questions to be unraveled. It was the same craving some people felt for the level of a video game they couldn't beat. It was what had kept her coming back to Harlow over and over again.

Secrets left an itch on both their brains that they couldn't leave unscratched. It was what had made them so effective and yet so deeply toxic for each other. They encouraged each other to push and make exceptions, and while Lainey tried to put the brakes on, she was far too easily swayed toward that chase. Even now, when she knew there was a very high probability that running down this trail would blow up in her face, she would follow Harlow. Because at the end of it, they would find answers and the compulsive brain itch would be eased.

Note to self: Stop making sleuthing curiosity sound like an incurable disease.

Lainey had to admit, it had felt good to kick the cobwebs out of said brain, even if her only conversational contribution so far had been random trivia and snark. During their vlog days, she'd thought of herself as the voice of the viewers, saying what they were probably thinking as they watched. But that had felt so much smaller than Harlow's job, and she'd barely made an appearance beyond her voice. Now? She still hadn't figured out how she felt about her face having a national platform. And Harlow? Well, Harlow wasn't to be trusted. Lainey knew that now.

"Wait, so, under your theory—the Dandridge family kept it quiet? And the Pinkertons?" Lainey asked. "Why?"

"Because Timmy was an embarrassment to the family? Because the family didn't want to put a target on his back as he ran around God knows where, unprotected?" Harlow said, grinning back at her. "I looked up the old Pinkerton files on Timmy's disappearance. They tried to keep things discreetly nondescript, only saying that the family was concerned that Timmy took off with *a* necklace before he left for one of his 'jaunts.' That's why they were looking for Timmy so frantically. Oh, sure, they would have been happy to find Timmy, even though he had always been a 'concern' for the family, but they really, *really* wanted the necklace back. As for the Pinkertons, are you aware that bribes are a thing that exist?"

"Oh, trust me, we are," Bryce told her. Deke shook his head and Bryce quieted down. Milo looked like he was warding off a cardiac event with happy thoughts.

"So, the family kept quiet about it, searched for Timmy, and then . . . faked the necklace going down in a shipwreck to save their asses after the stock market crash?" Lainey murmured. "*The Lucky Edge* was never found. People have been searching off the coast of Canada for that necklace for *years*."

"I know," Harlow squealed. "It just adds one more awesome element to the story, right? Missing treasure!"

"The necklace is supposed to be cursed," Lainey reminded her. "Of course, the curse story seemed to get way more common after the shipwreck."

"What if it's still here? What if we found it?" Harlow asked, waggling her eyebrows.

"I'm just going to remind you of the lesson of Geraldo and Al Capone's secret safe," Lainey told Harlow.

Harlow waved her off as if she wasn't concerned with real-time national humiliation. "Back to Timmy's suitcase. My best guess is that a staff member of whatever hotel Timmy ended up at stole his belongings and pawned them when they realized he wasn't coming back for it. It could have been an employee of the Crossings or any other hotel in the Midwest. It's possible they were trying to mislead the authorities about where he stayed." Harlow nodded. "No trace of Timmy was found after the pawn shop. Marguerite's disappearance never really got the attention it deserved, in my opinion. But it has everything a good story needs—rich spoiled people, beautiful women, possible mob connections, the glamour of the Gatsby era, *and* possibly cursed jewels."

In her library hauntings, Lainey had read speculations that Marguerite saw too much while spending time with her mobster ex-boyfriends. Or that one of those connected boyfriends got violently jealous. Or that she ran into a 1920s serial killer. Did any of these theories still apply if Marguerite died here at the Crossings? Could one of those sketchy boyfriends have caught up to her here?

Poor Marguerite. She was just trying to make the best of the shitty circumstances that life had dealt her. She hadn't stood a chance against people with money and the power to cover their tracks. Lainey had seen enough in life not to believe in happy endings, but she wanted to believe in that for Marguerite—an easy life in Paris, funded by diamond money from the indecently rich. And stupid.

Harlow announced, "We're here to look for proof of what happened to Marguerite while she was on the island and explain why she never made known contact with anyone after that. I have plenty of off-island pre-interviews from historians to fill in the gaps. We're here for action shots. I hope that at the end, we'll have a fantastic two hours of television in which we can say *something* definitive about the fate of Marguerite Devereaux. And maybe, *just maybe*, recover cursed jewelry, or at least prove that it didn't go down in a shipwreck in 1929."

At the end of this declaration, Harlow clicked back to the photo of Marguerite. She beamed at the room in general, as if she expected applause. The closest she got was contented sighs from Deke and Bryce, who were hunched over the bar, their chins propped on their hands. They looked like two very large children being told a very upsetting bedtime story. Nope, Bryce was standing up now, clapping those big meaty hands together, wolf-whistling.

"That was *awesome*," Bryce told her. "It was just like watching one of your old webisodes."

"The interaction with Lainey, the surprises, the twists," Deke said, grinning. "But it's even better, because we get to watch it play out in person. It's like *Harlow Drake Investigates . . . The Live Show*."

Something about the purr in Deke's voice made Lainey deeply uncomfortable. She was acutely aware of the *one* boat that could get her out of this place, and even more aware of the fact that she didn't know how to drive it.

Right. This was another danger of spending time with Harlow—the exposure to unseemly elements and the risk to life and/or limb.

Remember the zeros.

Harlow preened a bit and winked at Deke and Bryce. She turned to Shelley. "I think I'll just let Lainey be the one to deliver that Seymore Keyster line."

"Sure," Lainey said, staring at the photo comparison of Marguerite. "The lack of poise will be more believable from me."

HARLOW DRAKE INVESTIGATES . . .

Webisode 16, "Raine of Road Terror"

Draft Episode—Not Posted—February 3, 2008

TRANSCRIPT EXCERPT

HARLOW: So . . . that is where we are on Mr. Raine. I do feel bad that he had to work multiple part-time jobs, but sleeping his way through driving evaluations and rubber-stamping approval for kids' licenses—when they have no business driving—because he didn't want to admit he slept through the tests . . . has led to the worst cohort of drivers in Tallen River history. Click on this link to view a summary of accident reports involving drivers between the ages of sixteen and nineteen in Tallen County in the last five years. You'll notice a sharp increase three years ago, when Mr. Raine was hired as the county's driving assessor.

[LAINEY ENTERS THE ROOM.]

LAINEY: I thought you weren't recording today.

HARLOW: Why wouldn't I? You got me the info I needed from the sheriff's department. It proves we're not just being judgy about Mr. Raine's performance. He's not doing his job.

LAINEY: Yeah, but I wasn't supposed to be looking into Mr. Raine and his very loose definition of what counts as parallel parking. Look, the whole reason I got involved was to look into my dad's accident. And that's going nowhere. Because I keep getting distracted by your little side projects.

HARLOW: You always say that, and yet you always end up getting pulled into those little side projects. Because you love the chase as much as I do. You're no better than me.

LAINEY: I never said I was better than you. I'm just a little more cautious about putting people's business out on the internet. You know they say that stuff is forever.

HARLOW: Right, which is why we need to let people in our town know about a guy who runs one of the biggest clothing boutiques in town installing secret cameras in the dressing rooms.

LAINEY: What?

HARLOW: Two girls at school swear they spotted lenses when they were trying on prom dresses.

LAINEY: OK. So . . . videotaping our underage classmates. That's concerning. Also, gross. And super illegal.

[LAINEY GROANS.]

HARLOW: Look, either quit or don't. But stop jerking me around.

LAINEY: Well, you know I'm not going to quit when you tell me something like that.

HARLOW: Yes, I do.

LAINEY: My mom is getting really tired of picking me up from the sheriff's station.

HARLOW: Well, until our sheriff comes to accept our looser definition of trespassing laws, she's just going to have to make it part of her routine . . .

LAINEY: Because I'm the one who's breaking into buildings all over town.

HARLOW: I can't help it that you're better at lock-picking than me.

6

Lainey tugged at the sleeves of her dark blue dress as she picked her way carefully down the sweeping staircase. Apparently, Mr. Wesley insisted on formal dress for dinner, like something out of a BBC drama. Lainey tried not to think about the fact that on those shows, someone was usually murdered before dessert.

While the dress fit her well, pulling her waistline in the right places and making her legs look a mile long, she'd packed it because it was the sort of classic cut that stayed stylish for years. It was a "no statement" type of garment, appropriate to wear to a wedding and a funeral on the same day. It would be a complicated day, but the Illinois side of the family had been known to maximize the rare occasions when they all got together.

It felt weird to have left her shoulder bag in her room in favor of this tiny handbag, big enough for her phone and a lip gloss and not much else. She felt exposed and rudderless without her giant bag. What if there was an emergency? The only thing that made her feel somewhat settled was leaving it inside her suitcase, secured with a TSA lock. Like a normal person.

Yeah, that probably wasn't normal.

The setting sun didn't exactly give the lobby a warmer and more welcoming feel. Cassie had abandoned the check-in desk, so Lainey was the only soul wandering around the vast, empty space. The mile-deep shadows only added to the inscrutability of the decor. Her heels clacked ominously on the tile as she drew nearer to the fireplace, which went unused despite the relatively chilly state of the room. She passed the **OUT OF ORDER** elevator sign, which had a new context now that she knew about the DBags' plans for the hotel. She doubted they would repair the elevator when they were probably going to just rip it out and put a water-slide or something in its place.

As Lainey walked closer, she realized that the panels on the walls didn't depict writhing animals and clouds; they depicted writhing *souls*. The panels showed twisted bare tree limbs and lustful demon hands clawing at sinners and hands reaching through the icy mud of the circle of gluttony. Just a lot of hands doing things they weren't supposed to.

The floor's red-and-white pattern wasn't waves. It was flames. The mantel wasn't a beehive. It looked very much like Botticelli's *Map of Hell*. Each circle of hell had its own layer depicting the punishments heaped on sinners for their various transgressions. It had creeped Lainey out years ago when it graced the cover of the paperback she'd read in college. And it creeped her out now as a twenty-foot-tall marble rendition of suffering that swept up to the ceiling.

Lainey took a step back from the massive sculpture, suddenly very concerned about the wall's ability to anchor it. It felt like the architect was giving the Crossings' revelers a fair warning of the stakes of their indulgence. Or maybe he'd been trying to titillate them with vague threats of blood rivers and Minotaur mishandling.

She shook off the sensation that the marble figures were watching her as she walked away. The gift shop was closed, no wooden stakes or holy water bottles visible through the darkened glass door. But the Rosemont Archive . . . the lights were burning low under a series of green-glass banker's lampshades, casting a peridot radiance over enclosed wooden display cases. She stepped through the door, the stale, slightly warmer air welcoming her. Her hand, however, was very sticky from some substance smeared on the doorknob. What was with this place and sticky doorknobs?

Lainey sniffed at her hand, expecting lemon polish. Instead, it smelled old and sort of woodsy.

She stood in the middle of the room, turning in circles. It was a tiny museum to the greatness of the Crossings—glass-encased photos of the construction, preserved blueprints covered in Rosemont's scribblings. Clothes left behind by previous guests. More framed photos of former guests, one of which looked familiar. (Holy hell, Marilyn Monroe *had* stayed here.) In a display entitled *Common Household Items from the Crossings at Its Zenith*, there were several tins of household cleaners and beauty treatments and . . . poison. Just straight-up poison. There was a bottle of mercury chloride to treat "social diseases." A tin of something called carbolic acid. What the hell was "Liquid Nova Radium Water"? That couldn't possibly be good for you. A caustic soda for cleaning was labeled **Dirt's Doom**. There was a particularly nasty-looking tin of household pesticide—the label featured a legs-up dead fly centered on a chrysanthemum. It read **Your Best Pest Powder**.

The case needed a good editor, someone to make space. The only gap was at the rear of the dark blue velvet display cloth. Whatever had rested there left a palm-sized hexagonal mark in the material. *Hmm.*

Maybe the container had corroded or something? Started leaking?

Also, why did so many commercially available products in the 1920s seem designed to kill people?

Lainey turned away and studied the fashions on display from "notable guests over the years," which centered on a collection of rather fabulous hats. Maybe this was just a collection of lost-and-found-type items guests had left behind. The jewelry had to be costume. No one would forget a real emerald the size of an apricot. Timmy Dandridge notwithstanding, rich people weren't *that* careless, right?

She glanced down at the front of the case. Yeah, there was no way they would display real jewels with locks this simple or this old. Lainey could pick these with five minutes and a nail file. In fact, she had a whole lock-picking kit upstairs in her shoulder bag . . .

She snatched her own hands back and tucked them behind her. She felt like she was sliding down a slippery slope toward those destructive Harlow-adjacent activities. She wondered if Harlow had intentionally brought Lainey in on a case that featured her areas of interest. Harlow had always made fun of the nonfiction Lainey read about Bigfoot and cursed gems and the Bermuda Triangle. She had to know that Lainey would recognize the Star of Sikkim, leading to on-camera exclamations.

Lainey sighed. She didn't mind the machinations. She just didn't want to be treated like she was too dumb to recognize them.

"Lainey?"

She glanced up to see Milo standing in the doorway. He was a striking image framed in that light, wearing a full suit, dark blue and devastatingly tailored. Lainey's knees actually wobbled a bit. But that could have been because she was wearing heels for the first time in a while.

"What are you doing in here?" he asked, frowning at her. She supposed that a random person he didn't know or trust standing next to a case full of poisons couldn't feel comfortable to Mr. Corporate Compliance.

"I'm just, you know, casing the joint," she said, tugging at her sleeves.

"Smart," he said, nodding, while a little dimple appeared in his left cheek.

The universe is a cruel and unfair place.

"I hear the black-market value of old feathered fascinators is indecent," he said. "I mean, that's your whole retirement score, right there."

She grinned at him, pleased that he knew a fascinator from a full hat—not the kind of detail a lot of men would notice. "I was actually aiming for the fishing reels from the 1950s."

"OK, those might actually be worth some money to collectors," he told her.

"Really?"

"No clue," he said, opening the door and none too subtly indicating *Get the hell out of this space full of expensive, irreplaceable things.*

"Huh," she said, shaking her head. "Well, clearly my life of crime is going to be pretty short."

"But highly entertaining," he replied, ushering her gently but firmly through the door. "I have to admit, I was surprised that you agreed to do this project with Harlow. I kind of thought you would grow up to be the smart one. I thought you would have a nice, calm normal life away from all the true-crime murder and mayhem."

"To be fair, we really only handled the one murder case, and that was sort of an accident," she told him. "And as for the murder stuff, that's not why people like true crime."

"I'm just saying, there are a lot of women out there devouring the murder podcasts to a degree that makes the people around them uncomfortable. They don't seem to understand their search history never really gets cleared from the corporate servers. I've seen things that cannot be unseen." He paused and shuddered. "I won't pretend the subject isn't interesting. But the obsession people have with the news, the documentaries, the TV series *based* on the documentaries—I don't know. It feels a bit ghoulish."

Milo's stupid, handsome face could not atone for the flash of annoyance she felt toward him. It was not the first time she'd heard this response. The whole "bloodthirsty woman who loves true crime" narrative was part of the reason she stayed off most social media, the culture-at-large's inclination to demean something just because it drew female interest—like romance novels or fundamental human rights.

"You do realize you're participating in one of those programs, right?" she asked.

"I realize now I am undermining my own righteous indignation," he muttered, making her snort.

"True-crime stories warn people of what to look for in others," she said. "And people want to know that even when they don't see the red flags, the criminal is going to do something stupid and get caught. They want to know that justice exists. And maybe they just want to assure themselves that they could kick the taillight out of a car, find help, and survive."

"Oh." He stopped and looked at her as if he were seeing her for the first time, a human being in uncomfortable shoes instead of just a potential threat to his bosses and stock options.

His expression became thoughtful, and Lainey felt a twinge of guilt for lecturing him. And so she fell to her go-to defense: humor. "But also, we enjoy marveling at the assholery of men who try to get away with shoving their wives off a cliff on a camping trip and blaming it on Sasquatch."

"Yeah, even I watched the Movieflix special on that one," he said, shaking his head. "How did he think that was going to work? He had his plan written out in his Notes app."

"It was a flawed plan from the start," she said, shaking her head. "Sasquatches have a reputation for being the peace-loving vegetarians of the cryptid world."

He stared at her. "I can't tell if you're kidding or not."

"And that is half of my mystique."

Milo snorted but didn't deny it.

"So, I have to ask, how did you even meet these guys?" she questioned, her voice echoing through the cavernous corridor. It felt like they were sneaking around an abandoned school building after dark, a scheme at which Lainey had some practice . . . never this dressed up, though, and never with someone who looked like Milo. "You seem so . . . I don't want to use the word 'non-DBag-gy' but . . ."

"I was their suitemate in college," he said. "You share a communal bathroom with a man, it bonds you for life."

She laughed. "So you go from roomies to basically being in charge of protecting the DBags from themselves?"

"I would not phrase it that way," he said, although he was nodding. "Even if it is the correct way to phrase it. Just please, let me know if you feel vaguely uncomfortable or unsafe during filming—so I can work ahead of the situation and nobody gets hurt. Or harassed."

She nodded . . . because she also wanted to avoid being hurt or harassed.

"As a corporate officer of DBag Games, I probably shouldn't tell you this, but if you marry either one of my bosses, you'll be set for life. In terms of their personal lives, they do not think ahead. Neither one of them will ask for a prenup."

Lainey felt her entire face convulse in an expression of horror so acute, it made laughter explode out of Milo. It was vaguely humiliating, and yet worth it, to see that honest joy light up his face—even if that joy was at her expense.

"That was wrong," she grumbled, even as her lips twitched into a smile.

"And yet, I feel no regret," he said. "It was a little bit of a test, just to see if I could trust you around Deke and Bryce. Or vice versa, I guess."

"Honestly, they're safe from me," she muttered. While she prided herself on seeing Harlow's machinations coming, Milo had caught Lainey off guard with the prenup comment.

"Well, thank you for humoring me. Please don't make me give you the 'don't stray away from the group' talk. You seem like an intelligent person. I should not have to explain why you shouldn't be Scooby-Doo-ing your way through a hotel that has only partially passed safety inspections over the last few years," he said, leveling her with a look far more suited to a contentious boardroom than a conversation with a near acquaintance.

She stepped just a little closer, because, well, he started it. "You don't. Just like I don't have to explain to you how *not* introducing yourself on the boat came across as a little unscrupulous, if not downright manipulative."

The corners of his mouth lifted, even as challenge sparked in his oceanic eyes. "How can it have been manipulative if I didn't say anything?"

"It's like a lie of omission. You never said you work for DBag," she countered. "You just sat there, eavesdropping to see what we would say about the company if we didn't know we were being heard."

"It wasn't just eavesdropping. It was *really, really advanced* eavesdropping," he insisted, his smirk deepening. "Because you knew I was there and you talked anyway."

She frowned, stepping back. He was right. And she reminded herself to keep her armor up around Milo. He might seem less offensive than his bosses, but that didn't make him harmless.

"Am I going to have to explain basic conversational etiquette to you?" she asked. "Besides, we didn't say anything terrible. I don't make it a habit to engage in gossip with people who manage video equipment for a living."

His smile was smirk-free now, even as he said, "Your new friends said some pretty unflattering things about Harlow."

"Trust me, they could have said worse," she replied, turning down the hall toward the gilded doors of the Beatrice Dining Room.

He followed. "Trust *me*, I know. She didn't make the same horrified face you did when I mentioned the unlikely prenups. My question for you, to settle my mind, is . . . how did you get here, Lainey Piper?"

"We just talked about arriving on the same boat . . ." she said, making a vague gesture toward the dock.

"No," he huffed, mildly annoyed, prompting a hum of satisfaction to warm her belly. "You'll forgive me for saying so, but how does someone who presents as a reasonable, responsible adult get caught up in this circus? Again?"

She stopped and stared at him, considering. She'd never appreciated being *told* that she would excuse someone before they said something rude. It was presumptuous. But she was also aware that he probably knew her background and there was no point in lying. "I got recruited to a pretty big accounting firm in Chicago after college. They sent me all over the place to work with difficult clients in person, to root out their secrets and the problems even they didn't want to admit to—even when it might make more sense to handle everything by email."

"Because you picked up on more clues when you were staring them in the face?" he asked.

"Because I showed no fear of corporate bullies and the attached bullshit," she retorted. "Once you've had to ram your high school principal's car on purpose to keep him from escaping murder charges, some random associate vice president throwing a stapler at you because he's unhappy with his quarterly statements doesn't really seem so scary."

"Someone threw a stapler at you?"

She shrugged. "Just once, and I ducked out of the way. The whole murder-y principal thing gave me incredible reflexes. Anyway, I was doing well at the whole forensic accounting thing. My mom and stepdad got married a few years ago, but before then, I was making enough to help my mom out with bills. My dad's insurance money ran out a long time ago. And it's possible I led her to believe that I was making more than I was. And then the house, which we'd worked so hard to make sure we could keep after Dad died, needed a new roof. And then the foundation had a crack. There was a plumbing issue and then a mold problem. The house is a money pit, but it's a money pit that I grew up in. I couldn't let her just sell it off, even if it is a little weird that she lives in it with my stepdad now. Every time there was a repair needed, I told her I could take care of it. Mom and Robin work at the town's tourism bureau, which isn't exactly a lucrative gig. It probably wasn't the healthiest way to handle it, but I didn't want to tell her that I couldn't help her after she basically raised me alone. And I didn't make things easy on her. I got into a cycle where I spent a lot of money just trying to keep her afloat. And then there was the money I spent on trying to find out what happened to my dad—independent autopsy reports, private investigators, legal bills."

"The accident that probably wasn't an accident," he said, nodding. When she arched a brow, he added, "I lived with your superfans."

"I feel bad that I didn't talk about *who* my dad was on the webisodes," she confessed. "I was just so caught up in everything else. He was funny. He could quote entire episodes of *The Simpsons*. He was vicious at trivia. I mean, he was kicked out of a bar league once because he heckled the other teams. It was really the only thing that he was kind of a jerk about—except for not letting me win at board games. My mom was always telling him that he was scarring me psychologically, but he thought that people learned more from losses than victories. And he was right. When I finally beat him at chess, my victory dance was epic. There was so much mockery."

"But you never found out what happened to him?"

Lainey shook her head. “The police weren’t exactly helpful. The autopsy report showed a *lot* of alcohol in his system. We didn’t know who he was meeting with or where. They searched our house and his office but couldn’t find anything on his phone or laptop that wasn’t related to his own business. And there were some issues with chain of custody of the evidence—as in, the state police lost it.”

“And there was no way that he just . . . had an accident?”

She shook her head. “I think he found something in his work that he wasn’t supposed to know. And I think that whoever that information affected found a way to make him go away, and then they found a way to make evidence of what happened to him go away. One of the frustrating things about the true-crime genre is that sometimes cases are unsolvable. And thanks to a lot of therapy, I’ve figured out how to live with that.”

Lainey had limited regrets. She was rewarded in other ways for walking away from her father’s case. Her relationship with her mother became so much easier when she stopped bringing it up around Helen and Robin. She was able to focus on other things in her life. Her work became easier. The persistent pain on the right side of her neck went away . . . sort of.

“Did you lose the fancy accountant job because you were too distracted by your dad’s case?” Milo asked.

“No, because it was more important for the firms to hold on to their clients than to hold on to me. The client might begrudgingly pay the firm when I find some huge error in their financial system—caused by theft or incompetence—but sometimes they also wanted the ‘rude girl’ who found all this information punished, even if I delivered it in the gentlest way possible. I was fired several times, not as gently.”

"I have been part of several 'shoot the messenger' firings, I'm ashamed to say," he mused. "Deke has a tendency to blame the marketing department for a lot of stuff."

"Yep," she said. "Eventually, I opened my own one-woman operation. I really like the work. I like math. But it also turned out that people are much more likely to fire a one-person firm because there's no one for me to hide behind. I'm the problem. And I mentioned Mom needing help and the irresponsible investigative habits. It's all congealed into a perfect financial storm. The bills are piling up. So here I am, trying to pay them off."

Milo was quiet for a moment. She asked, "Are you horrified by my fiscal irresponsibility?"

"No, I already knew most of it," he said. "But I wanted to see what you would tell me yourself."

"Again, I would like to ask if I need to review basic conversational etiquette with you," she said.

He put a hand on her arm. They were almost at the door now. Lainey had a feeling their time alone was coming to an end, and she found herself lamenting it. "What you are to those executives—who didn't really want to know about their financial disasters—I am to Deke and Bryce. I root out the problems *before* they happen. I see around corners. It doesn't always make me the most popular guy in the room, but I think you would understand my position. It's not personal."

There was an apology in those dark blue eyes, even if he wasn't saying the words. Lainey stepped back, eyeing him speculatively as they walked into the dining room. But she'd had enough mind games and unspoken words with Harlow. "Look, I like you, or at least, I want to like you," she told him. "But I know where your interests lie. And they do not align with mine."

He held his thumb and forefinger a tiny bit apart. "They align with yours a little."

"You would toss me into a well if you thought it would keep the DBags from giving a bad interview."

"Don't be silly," he scoffed. "We don't even know if they have wells on this island."

7

The Beatrice Room must have been glorious once. Lainey wondered if the architect had lost control of the project at this point in the design, because there was actual *light* in this room. Floor-to-ceiling windows displayed the previously missing lake views, energy efficiency be damned. The orange-and-purple-watercolor sky drew the eye away from long-faded Art Deco designs that danced across the high ceilings—more hellish visions, more punishments in the circle of gluttony. The never-ending storms of sleet and snow, centered on a drooling Cerberus, were a real mood killer, considering the setting.

At one point, the floor had been an exquisite parquet design made of repeating cherrywood sunbursts. But some genius had decided to put down a godawful pea-green carpet that did not remotely match the gold patterns painted on the white plaster walls. At least the carpet-happy idiot had known not to mess with the large dance floor at the lakeside end of the room. That would have been criminal.

Small round tables for three or four seats dominated the space, with the exception of a few long captain's tables. Maybe for VIP parties? Most of the TV crew was hovering near the bar, where Vern was wearing an honest-to-God vest and bow tie and pouring the contents of a shaker into a glass for Harlow. He didn't look particularly cheerful about it. Then again, he didn't seem to be someone made for happiness.

There were strangers in their midst, the two ladies Lainey had seen in the lobby earlier and an older man wearing a slightly shabby gray suit. They didn't appear to be mixing in with the production crew; they were sticking close to the windows or lingering alone at tables. It was strange to Lainey that these holdout guests had stubbornly clung to their reservations to keep family vacation plans. They were determined to stay in this place. Alone.

Why?

"So, fair warning—Mr. Wesley is insisting on assigned seating at dinner," Milo murmured out of the side of his mouth. "To 'make for stimulating conversation.'"

Lainey cringed. "Like on cruise ships?"

"Mr. Wesley calligraphed the fancy little place cards himself," Milo told her, prompting a tired sigh from her.

She *would not* scrub her hand across her face. She was wearing mascara for the first time in weeks. "Well, it couldn't be more awkward than sitting next to Harlow."

"Reuniting doesn't feel so good?" he asked, glancing across the room to where Harlow stood, chatting with Deke.

Lainey pursed her lips. She had not meant to say that. Lainey stared at Milo's handsome face, wondering if she could or should trust him. Then again, it was Milo's job to protect his bosses from fallout related to the shoot. He should probably know what he was up against. "I don't think she knows what to say to me. And I guess the same is true on my side. We haven't spoken in years. And sometimes, I have trouble connecting to people, places, and things. Nouns, I guess."

"You two seemed to work well together on the show," Milo noted.

"Yes, we *worked* well together. Past tense," she reminded him. "Also, I still don't know how I feel about you watching the webisodes."

"The guys are not kidding when they say they were obsessed with you," he told her, quiet enough so that no one at the tables or bar heard them. "If you didn't post new episodes, they would just watch old ones on repeat. Sometimes I would walk into their room at night and it would just be the two of them, in the dark, watching you two."

"Oh, I wish I could go back in time to when I didn't know that." She made a face that was no doubt more dramatic than her reaction to the prenup information. "I guess it's better that Harlow was the face of the team."

"No, they considered you all the more mysterious and alluring because they never saw you."

"Oh, come on!" she exclaimed, shuddering. He guffawed as he walked away. *Jerk. Beautiful, fascinating jerk.*

"Miss Piper?" Mr. Wesley, who seemed incapable of *not* wearing Crossings blue, was waiting for her to move past the threshold of the room. He was displaying his loyalty through a smartly knotted blue tie. OK, if he really loved the hotel that much, how could Mr. Wesley let the carpet thing happen? Lainey felt offended on the Crossings' behalf.

"You've been assigned to table six with your fellow guests Mrs.

Maynard and Mr. Spiros, lovely people. I'm sure you'll find all sorts of things to talk about," he told her. "Chef Andre's special tonight is a local whitefish, poached in a delicate lemon caper sauce. And you should really try one of Vern's brandy old-fashioneds. He makes the best in Wisconsin."

"And he makes a hell of a bee's knees."

Lainey turned to find Harlow standing behind her, wearing designer jeans and a blouse that cost more than most of Lainey's appliances. She sipped an opaque yellow drink from a rounded martini glass, then made a little "ah" sound of satisfaction. Shelley was standing nearby, her phone posed at that "fancy lady cigarette holder" angle again.

"Shelley, please offer the network my thanks for the thoughtful gift bag," Lainey said. "The lip balm is a brand I've never seen before."

Never mind that Lainey didn't like eucalyptus. Shelley had tried, and that counted.

Shelley smiled and opened her mouth to reply but Harlow interjected, "Oh, sweetie, Shelley didn't touch those bags. She probably had some intern or Cameron put them together. And for the love of God, don't send the network a thank-you note. I don't care where your mom was raised."

"Duly noted," Lainey replied curtly. Harlow had never thought much of her mother's "country-ass" manners, probably because her mother saw through Harlow's fake parent-friendly charm.

Shelley shot Lainey a sympathetic look and quickly crossed the room to Findlay and Gordy. To their credit, her crewmates welcomed her warmly to their little table.

It appeared that there was a clear dividing line in the group: those who felt inclined to follow the dress code and those who didn't. Deke and Bryce were wearing what seemed to be their uniform of T-shirts and cargo shorts. They were clean, unripped T-shirts advertising their own games, but still, T-shirts. Harlow had opted for dressy jeans and a pale green linen blouse. Shelley was wearing a much crisper lavender pantsuit while Kenny, Findlay, and Gordy had at least put on the sort of outfits that would be acceptable at an office holiday party. The same went for the outsider hotel guests. So . . . the people not worried about losing their jobs were comfortable, which was probably a metaphor for life in general.

Wait, shouldn't Harlow be worried about her job?

Meanwhile, Harlow gave Lainey's outfit the once-over. "Oh, Lainey, did you take that whole dress code thing seriously?"

"Yes, because I was asked to," Lainey replied. "Politely."

"Well, I've never been much of a rule follower," Harlow sniffed.

"Trust me. I remember," Lainey shot back.

Harlow grinned cheekily as she sashayed to her own seat at one of the longer VIP tables near the windows. Deke was already sitting there, playing on a handheld game console. Lainey was grateful to be spared his company for the evening but figured that was not the sort of luck that would hold out.

Harlow called over her shoulder, "Just ask Jerry for anything you want."

As Lainey neared the bar, she picked up on the look of irritation on *Vern's* face.

"You are clearly not Jerry. Sorry about that," Lainey told him. "I spent most of my high school years correcting Harlow's incorrect name guesses."

"That's OK. I've been putting half measures of booze in her drinks this whole time." Vern shrugged, making Lainey laugh.

"What can I get you? I'm not the regular bartender. 'Fraid I can't make you a cosmo without looking it up."

She lifted her chin. "How do you know I won't ask for bourbon?"

Vern gave her a hard stare with his rheumy brown eyes. "You're not angry enough for bourbon."

"Well, you're clearly not reading the room," she muttered, making him snort. She lifted the slightly sticky cocktail menu from the marble bar. Several drinks featured gin. The bee's knees. The gimlet. The gin rickey.

"I've never heard of a bee's knees," Lainey told Vern.

"Wesley's attempt to be 'era appropriate.'" Vern uttered the last bit in a mocking airy imitation of Mr. Wesley. "Gin was pretty popular with the Prohibition types. Easiest to make at home."

Lainey shuddered at the idea of making gin in the bathtub considering the cleaning products available at the time. And also, poison.

She felt a faint pang of envy toward Findlay and Gordy, who were clearly enjoying a cozy chat with the casual closeness that came naturally to longtime friends. Shelley wasn't a factor in the conversation. She was still nose-deep in her phone, tapping out what Lainey assumed was a text message. At one point, she picked up Findlay's soda with her free hand, her eyes still focused on her screen, and took a deep drink before she glanced up and registered the bemused looks on her coworkers' faces. Her cheeks flushed prettily as Findlay giggled. Gordy gently patted Shelley's shoulder while she offered apologies that Lainey couldn't hear over Deke loudly listing his favorite *Harlow Drake Investigates* . . . episodes. Lainey couldn't help but notice that Deke described the webisodes based on which outfit Harlow was wearing, as opposed to the subject of the investigation.

Ew.

"I'll get the makeup lady another Diet Coke," Vern muttered.

Lainey chuckled, wondering what Shelley was texting about that would keep her from detecting the difference between a soda and a gin. Had the network already decided Harlow's employment status?

"Another bee's knees, Jerry!" the possibly-ex-correspondent in question called from across the room. Vern rolled his eyes and reached for the shaker, to which he added gin and a honey-colored syrup from a squeeze bottle.

Vern huffed, "She's the only one here ordering the bee's knees. Pain in the ass drink. I have to make this syrup from scratch so the honey doesn't congeal at the bottom of the shaker."

"I will leave the bee's knees to Harlow," she promised, nodding at the gently curved glass he'd set aside for the cocktail. "Are the glasses bee's-knees-specific?"

"It's a coupe glass," he said, somehow managing to shake the cocktail vigorously without dropping the container or spilling anything—something that Lainey knew she'd never be able to accomplish. "Another Wesley thing. They loved 'em, back in the Prohibition days. And Wesley gave us a big speech about how the round shape lets the guests smell the aroma of something or other. But honestly, I'm pretty sure it was cheaper to buy a whole bunch of these than to buy different types of glasses."

"Sensible," Lainey observed.

"Well, I'm not one to try to twirl the booze bottles around like those two idiots," he said, nodding toward Deke and Bryce. "Aw, hell, here comes one of 'em."

She turned to see Bryce walking toward her, wavering a little bit in his neon-yellow designer sneakers.

"Thank you, Mr. Wesley, for the dress code!" Bryce crowed,

taking Lainey's hand and raising it, attempting to make her give a little spin. When she stayed stubbornly stationary, he frowned. "Oh, come on, give us a little twirl so we can all see how you're wearing that dress."

Are there enough zeros in the world to tolerate this?

Milo cleared his throat from across the room.

The corners of Bryce's mouth pulled back into a grimace. "Sexual harassment?"

Milo nodded. "Pretty much the textbook definition."

Bryce dropped her hand and seemed sincere when he said, "Sorry."

Lainey shrugged. "I'm not going to say it's OK because it's not. But what you have done is also not unforgivable. Which I realize is a double negative, but it applies as long as you keep it at this line."

Bryce chuckled, and his breath smelled like cotton candy vape juice. "*You're* a double negative."

She shook her head. "What does that even mean?"

Bryce grinned and jerked his broad shoulders. "Not sure. But what kind of vodka do you like? We brought all kinds of fun fruity girl flavors—blueberry caramel and habanero lemonade and marshmallow licorice."

Lainey was pretty sure she would rather lick the nicotine-infused wallpaper in the Gentlemen's Lounge than drink marshmallow licorice vodka.

"And there's a lot of cool weird liquors that were already here, and fancy stuff we can't even find sometimes. They have Don Julio 1942. Did you *see* the 1942?" Bryce asked, his eyes aglow.

"Not much of a tequila drinker," she told him. "Lost a couple of fights with it in college. You know that really cheap brand with the little plastic cowboy boot on the cap?"

Bryce shuddered. "We don't talk about the cowboy boot."

She found herself laughing, despite knowing it was a bad idea. Lainey supposed this was the seductive nature of dealing with people like Deke and Bryce. They weren't *always* terrible. They could have their moments when they could be charming and cheerfully take correction. And it was easy to lower your defenses only to get stomped all over when you least expected it. Worse, they had money and influence *and* power. They could dismantle Lainey's life with just a few social media posts. She had to force her feet to stay in place, even though she didn't enjoy standing this close to Bryce. She *would not* lose ground.

Deke called Bryce over to watch some video clip on his phone, and Lainey practically sagged against the bar in relief. Vern slid the finished cocktail across the marble. The drink was the color of weak early spring sunlight and smelled of sickly sweet denial. Lainey reached over the bar for the honey syrup bottle and sniffed it.

Vern frowned at her, deep furrows digging into his jowly cheeks. "Um, I don't think I'm supposed to let you do that."

"Do you care enough to stop me?" she asked him.

He thought about it for a moment. "Not really."

Lainey sniffed the bottle again. All of the natural mellow subtlety of honey was boiled down into something heavier. The cloying scent settled unpleasantly at the back of her throat. She wrinkled her nose and set the bottle aside.

"I'll take that to Harlow. Thanks, Vern." Cameron had appeared at Lainey's side without her even registering his approach.

He stood beside Lainey, pretending to sip from his martini so no one would hear him say, "I will not be running or fetching for you. Not even if I am getting something for Harlow."

"Understood. Because you've already told me that," she said. He nodded curtly and didn't say more.

Lainey watched him walk away with Harlow's drink. She didn't know if Cameron wanted to work for Harlow or just slowly take on her personality. After ordering her own (unflavored) vodka martini, Lainey found her attention drawn to the older lady standing at her side. She was a real looker. Her carefully dyed blond hair was cut into a smart pageboy. And she was wearing even more pearls this time, at her ears and both wrists. She ordered a gin rickey and smiled at Lainey.

"I think we're at the same table for dinner," she said sweetly, reaching out to hug Lainey. Lainey found that she didn't mind the hug from this lady, which enveloped her in the scent of Elizabeth Taylor's White Diamonds. Her grandmother had *loved* that perfume and received a bottle every Christmas. This woman seemed a little young for it; she was probably around the same age as Lainey's mom. Maybe she had a favorite grandmother she wanted to remember?

"Are you one of the TV people?" she demanded, but before Lainey could answer, she was off to the races. "I'm Lucinda Maynard. 'Cinda' to my friends. My daddy always hated it because I was named for his mama and he didn't like the idea of shortening it. He thought Lucinda made me sound like a movie star. And that man was awful fond of his mama. But we spent so much time with my mamaw and it was *so* confusing having two Lucys."

Lainey wondered if maybe it was the elder Lucy who was an Elizabeth Taylor fan.

"People would call out, 'Hey, Lucy,' and we would both just pop our heads up and say, 'Whatcha need?'" Mrs. Maynard continued, not even slowing for breath. "And then everybody would laugh, but we hardly ever got anything done because we were always trying to figure out who they were talking to, and then the family tried to fix it by calling me 'Little Lucy' and her 'Big Lucy.' But Mamaw wasn't at all fond of that, lemme tell you. We thought about calling her 'Lucinda' and me 'Lucy,' because Lucinda was such a nice grown-up name. But she'd been 'Lucy' since Adam was a boy and said it just didn't feel right to her. So finally, we settled on her being Mamaw and I got to be plain old Lucy. But then *my* mama didn't like how close 'mamaw' sounded to 'mama.' And that started off a whole new argument. And by the time I hit my rebellious teen phase, I thought 'Cinda' sounded awfully sophisticated, so my mamaw and my mama spent all those years feudin' over nothing."

Lainey blinked at her. She seemed to say it all in one breath. Hell, she didn't seem to need to breathe at all. Where did all those words come from?

Vern seemed to be making her drink extra fast just to make the source of the talking go far away from him. He pushed the highball glass across the bar to Mrs. Maynard with a customer service smile. She accepted it and asked, "Now, what's your name, hon?"

"Lain—" She hadn't even finished the syllable before Mrs. Maynard's baby-blue eyes went wide with excitement and the words came tumbling out again, "Oh, Elaine Piper, yes, Mr. Wesley told me all about you! I can't tell you how happy I am to see some new faces here this week. It was getting so boring with such a small crowd—nothing like it used to be. Why, my daddy used to sneak up here all the way from Mobile to meet up with his old college friends back in the forties. Used to drive my mama crazy the way he'd tell everybody he was going fishing, but he'd always come home smelling like three kinds of hell with poker chips in his pocket." Mrs. Maynard paused and winked at her. "'Course, he always told me what he was up to, because we were always close like that. After he passed, I started coming up here every year, on the weekend of his birthday. And I'm glad I got one last chance, now that I know they're shutting down. The game people tried to buy my reservation back, but I said no sir, I want a last chance to drink these awful rickeys, enjoy my daddy's favorite perch omelet for breakfast, and sleep in these sad-as-sin rooms one last time. For Daddy's sake."

Lainey could only stare. So. Many. Words.

Also, perch omelets sounded disgusting.

When she recovered the power of speech, Lainey finally asked, "If you don't like the rickeys, why do you drink them?"

"Tradition. They were Daddy's favorite. Honestly, I would much rather have a bottle of pop and be done with it," Mrs. Maynard insisted, taking her glass and tucking her hand in Lainey's arm. Lainey allowed herself to be pulled along to stroll down the length of the rectangular bar. "So, you're here with the TV people? Do you work for them?"

"Sort of," Lainey said. "It's . . . freelance work."

"Well, isn't that interesting? Now, how's your room?" Mrs. Maynard asked. "I'm always in the east wing, toward the back. And I swear, the closer to the back you are, the dingier the room. They used to be so bright and pretty. Cleaner, you know? But I think the hotel staff just stopped caring a while ago. It just hurts my heart. Daddy would have hated it."

Lainey sipped her drink. She had to agree. The theme of the Crossings seemed to stop at the lobby. The guest room hallways were furnished with threadbare brown-green carpet and these weird little half-chandelier lighting fixtures that seemed to attract cobwebs like something out of *Tales from the Crypt*.

Her own accommodation was, in the barest of terms, a room. It had a ceiling and a narrow barely queen bed and a door that locked. There was even a worn blue love seat, for some reason facing away from the window's sweeping lake view, which was the best thing about the room. She supposed the charm of staying on a small island was that all rooms had a water view.

The love seat *and* the room had definitely seen better days. The environs smelled like old air-conditioning—a sort of corn-chips-and-musty-socks odor. But the sheets seemed clean and the bathroom tile only looked a little bit like the shower set in *Psycho*.

At this point, she felt lucky she didn't have to share a bathroom with everybody on her end of the hallway. But, smells aside, it was clean. There were no bugs. She hadn't detected any hidden cameras . . . yet. And yes, she would continue looking after dinner.

Mrs. Maynard stopped near the bar's opposite end and gently squeezed Lainey's arm. "Oh! CeeCee, honey, this is Elaine Piper. She's my dinner partner for the evening. She's with the TV people."

It was the knitter from the lobby. Tall and willowy, the lady was encased in a long, red, silk crepe dress. There was no cheerful drugstore-brand perfume in the air around her, just the subtle notes of a warm, floral scent. Expensive. The woman had only bothered with minimal makeup. Her dark hair was shot with silver and tied back in an elegant chignon. Everything about her spoke of old, quiet money—the kind that snuck up on you with better lawyers.

What was *she* doing here?

"It's Cecelia," the woman told Mrs. Maynard, her voice laced with very deliberate patience, like she was trying *so hard* to remain polite. Maybe she'd made the correction a few times already? Cecelia turned a slightly warmer expression on Lainey. "Cecelia Rowland, nice to meet you."

Harlow crept behind Mrs. Maynard as she attempted to get another cocktail from Vern. Mrs. Rowland reached toward the charcuterie plate displayed on the bar top just past Mrs. Maynard and Lainey and moved it toward herself, out of Harlow's reach. Weird, and maybe a little rude. The plate contained several elegantly arranged cheeses and fancy crackers, interspersed with little piles of pistachios dusted with different seasonings.

Nope, that was just plain weird.

Harlow had claimed to be allergic to pistachios since tenth grade. She'd never had any strong preference for or against pistachios. She'd definitely *never* had any sort of allergic reaction to them. Harlow claimed that telling waitstaff she had an allergy kept them honest and tested whether they paid attention to her order—sort of like that rock band who'd demanded their candy get sorted by color. Lainey thought this was the sort of thing that made people take allergies less seriously and made life harder for people who had them, but Harlow insisted Lainey was overthinking it.

Had Harlow been peddling the fake allergy story since she'd arrived on the island? Or did Mrs. Rowland just want the pistachios for herself? Harlow slunk away with her drink without Mrs. Maynard detecting her.

"I'm Lainey. What brings you to the Crossings?" Lainey asked Mrs. Rowland.

"A birthday trip," Mrs. Rowland said, plucking at the neckline of her gown. The wedding set on her finger centered around a diamond solitaire of at least three carats. *Dang.* "My daughter and I used to come here every year for her birthday, and when we found out the Crossings was closing, we knew we had to make one last visit. Unfortunately, she was called into work this weekend, so here I am. Alone. With you people."

Lainey didn't love the implications of "you people," but at the moment, Deke and Bryce appeared to be trying to spin plates on their fingertips like basketballs, so she supposed she couldn't begrudge Mrs. Rowland her irritations. The lady also seemed to have a problem with Cameron applying lip balm at a nearby table and Findlay checking her eye makeup in a compact, given the way she was frowning at them.

Right, no at-table grooming in front of Mrs. Rowland.

"Oh, are you going to sit with the crew people?" she asked, nodding to table 9, where Cameron, Gordy, and Findlay were seated.

"Apparently," Cecelia said. Lainey noticed that she wasn't holding a drink. Was it a choice or the result of servers being overwhelmed by the DBags' demands? "It should be a pleasant break from Mr. Spiros and his tall tales of fishing adventure."

She nodded toward an older man in an ill-fitting but expensive suit. His white-on-silver hair was brushed back in a pompadour that had probably been quite stylish in his day. It struck Lainey, the age divide between the DBags' group and the "regular" guests. When was the last time someone under fifty booked a room here for vacation?

Deke and Bryce were loud and boisterous . . . and definitely skirting the boundaries of what Mr. Wesley's dress code deemed "dining room appropriate." Lainey noticed several of the non-TV-crew crowd giving Bryce annoyed looks—apparently based on Bryce's horse laugh. Even Shelley looked up from her phone when Bryce wandered near the crew table to offer them champagne from one of the less expensive bottles. She immediately went back to her phone, but she had looked up for two whole seconds. Lainey hoped the difference in decorum didn't cause tension between the crew and the guests. The odds in a fight would be . . . sad, just sad.

Also, she really didn't love that she was technically aligned with something called a "DBag group."

"Oh . . . great," Lainey said, making the other ladies laugh. She tried to recover some sort of composure. "But you'll like Gordy and Findlay. They're really nice. Funny."

She paused and tried to think of a way to say "they have all the good gossip" but came up with, "They're very informative."

Cecelia chuckled. "Thank you. Good luck with the fish."

With that, the woman sauntered away on heels as red-soled as Harlow's.

"Did she mean with the main course or the tales of fishing prowess?" Lainey asked Mrs. Maynard.

"Oh, he's harmless—Mr. Spy-ross? Spee-ros?" Mrs. Maynard said, sipping her rickey as they walked to a little table at the center of the room with a large 6 printed on its place card and took their seats. "You know, you'd think I'd be used to these Eye-talian names, spending all this time up here, but I never can get the hang of them. And don't ever ask if they're in the mob or know anybody in the mob. That gets their drawers all up in a bunch. No sense of humor about it at all."

Lainey looked across the room at Milo to see if he'd heard any of that. Given the width of his eyes, she was going to guess yes. Mrs. Maynard's voice carried. Yeah, this was going to be a long dinner.

"I'm pretty sure it's a Greek name," Lainey said quietly.

"Well, it's all Greek to me, honey," Mrs. Maynard said, laughing a little louder than Lainey was comfortable with. She glanced toward Findlay and Gordy, who seemed to be receiving a chilly reception from Mrs. Rowland. At least "CeeCee" was consistent.

"You know, she thinks I don't notice that she ignores me," Mrs. Maynard whispered. "And that's OK, I don't have to be everybody's cup of tea. She's still better than sitting with—"

She stopped herself and seemed to pale a little bit. "Oh, that's terrible. I shouldn't speak ill of the dead when he hasn't even been gone for a whole day."

"Did you know the . . . deceased? I don't even know his name. That's sort of embarrassing," Lainey admitted.

"Mr. Hornsby," Mrs. Maynard told her. "Poor man. He was an anxious type, you know? Kept talking about late-life-onset allergies. Didn't trust any of the food coming out of the kitchen. He went over the menu and ingredient lists with Chef Andre every night."

Mrs. Maynard paused long enough to nod to a large, somewhat sweaty, and ruddy-cheeked man in dingy chef's linens. Chef Andre appeared to be having an animated discussion with Mr. Wesley while gesturing to Harlow.

Mrs. Maynard said, "And even after all that, some nights he would just go upstairs and eat his protein bars for supper."

"Why bother coming all the way out here to eat protein bars alone in your room?"

"He said it was a 'bucket list' thing," Mrs. Maynard said. "He's always wanted to stay here, and when he heard the hotel was closing, he figured this was his last chance, poor man. I mean, he had to be in his late seventies. How much longer was he going to wait on that bucket list?"

"Oh, man, that adds a new sad angle to the story." Lainey sighed.

"Doesn't it just?" Mrs. Maynard tsked.

Mr. Spiros joined them, a beer bottle in hand. Lainey glanced at Mr. Wesley, who seemed to be unhappy about the lack of formal glassware.

"So, more people, eh?" Mr. Spiros said, tapping his bottle on the table. He had a bit of a Chicago accent, and it was like hearing a piece of home. Lainey automatically relaxed around him.

"I'm Pete Spiros," he said, patting his hand on his chest. He nodded at their tablemate. "Cinda, I've already met. Who are you? Are you with those video game people?"

"Do you not like video games, Mr. Spiros?" Lainey asked, smiling.

"Doesn't seem like a way for a grown man to make a living," Mr. Spiros muttered. "Then again, none of those guys look like grown men. Soft, sissy hands, all of them."

Lainey's brows shot up. As much as she would like to dismantle Mr. Spiros's toxic notions on masculinity, she just didn't have the emotional bandwidth to spend her evening that way.

"I'm Lainey Piper. Nice to meet you, and no, technically, I don't work for the video game company," she said. "Is this your first time at the Crossings?"

Mr. Spiros grinned, showing a mouthful of carefully capped white teeth. "My daughters gave me this vacation as a Father's Day present last year. They heard the fishing out here was supposed to be fantastic, which makes sense when you figure how far away we are from the big-boat channels. I kept putting it off and putting it off. The hotel people emailed me to say they're closing. They told me they'd let me cancel, get the cash value, but I didn't want my girls to be cheated. This place sold me a fishing weekend. They're gonna give me a fishing weekend."

"And you'd rather fish here than, say . . . Florida?" she asked.

Lainey realized there were no menus on the table and Tommy and Cassie were carrying trays of plated salads over to them. Did that mean there was only one meal option for dinner?

Well, that explained the number of questions Lainey had to answer about dietary restrictions. She tried not to let her disappointment show. Just because she wasn't allergic to fish didn't mean she *enjoyed* it.

"I get seasick," he confessed sheepishly. "And airsick. Traveling anywhere big is kind of rough and my girls figured this was the closest option. You got no idea how much shi—" He paused, glanced at Mrs. Maynard, who was giving him an arch look. He corrected himself, "—guff my buddies give me about it. A man living on one of the biggest lakes in the world can't go out in a boat. They had to knock me out with Dramamine for the ride out here, but now I can fish from the pavilion out back just fine."

Lainey wondered if his girls secretly disliked their dad to put him on the *Acheron* to get him here, but she didn't ask questions.

She was distracted by Harlow announcing very loudly to Chef Andre, "I left very specific instructions with the kitchen. I won't be taking the salad course or the main. I left the recipe for my Crystalline Greens NutriScape juice with the kitchen staff."

Chef Andre looked very tired as he replied in a smooth French accent, "Madame, I assure you that I can prepare an entrée to whatever specifications you prefer to meet your health needs."

Harlow responded as if he hadn't spoken. "You can't use dried ginger. It has to be fresh ginger cut within the last twelve hours. The cannister should be on the counter. If it's not there, someone needs to find it immediately."

Chef Andre took this instructive rant with grace, giving Harlow a sweet customer service smile. It did not reach his large, watery blue eyes. "Of course. I'll see to it right away."

"Well, that was rude," Mr. Spiros muttered as Chef Andre retreated back to the kitchen. Lainey nodded, keeping her lips firmly pressed together. While she agreed, she wasn't about to jeopardize the zeros by adding her opinions. "What the heck is a Crystalline Greens Nutri-whatever?"

"Not a clue," Lainey told him.

Apparently, Tommy's delivery of a delicately dressed spinach salad was the signal that Mrs. Maynard had held off long enough. She practically burst out, "So, how exactly are you helping the TV crew? It's so exciting, knowing that Harlow Drake, the TV star, is here solving a real-life mystery!"

"Never been much of a TV watcher," Mr. Spiros commented, his mouth full of greens. "I got the sports package at home, but that's only for the Cubbies."

"Well, I watch *all* of her specials," Mrs. Maynard said. "She really seems to understand the details that people need about the past, you know?"

"She always enjoyed history," Lainey conceded. "It was one of her best subjects."

"Did you know her in school?" Mr. Spiros asked, frowning.

There was a commotion at the crew table behind Mr. Spiros, a shriek. He stood and whirled around, watching as Shelley scrambled to mop up the champagne Bryce had spilled on her *and her precious phone.* At the VIP table, Harlow had thrown her head back laughing, assuring Bryce that it was no big deal. Of course, it wasn't *Harlow's* phone doused in lesser champagne.

Mr. Spiros frowned and sat, his expression . . . confused? His hand was shaking as he reached for his beer. She'd seen that sort of response before, when they sat in restaurants when Robin couldn't get a seat with his back to the walls. It always made him edgy, not knowing what could be walking up behind him.

"Were you ever a police officer, Mr. Spiros?" Lainey asked as Shelley passed, popping her phone out of its sleek black True Crime 24/7 branded case and wiping it with a cloth napkin.

Mr. Spiros burst out laughing. "What? No, electrical supplies. Owned a whole store before the big-box chains moved into my neighborhood. Retired a couple of years ago."

"I guess the business gave you quick reflexes," Lainey mused.

"Is that why Harlow brought you to assist her, because you notice the little things?" Mrs. Maynard asked.

Noticing the little things. Better people skills . . . sort of. Being the target of misplaced nostalgia from two possibly predatory tech goons.

Lainey just nodded and tucked a bit of salad into her mouth. The salad dressing was of indeterminate origin . . . and she thought maybe it had gone sour. Were Deke and Bryce really going to be able to eat like this? Or were they going to summon a helicopter delivery full of Thai food? Frankly, Lainey was kind of rooting for the helicopter. There had to be some plus-side to tangential connections to gazillionaires—like airborne emergency takeout.

"So do you know what she's looking into?" Mr. Spiros asked.

"I signed a bunch of paperwork that says I'm not allowed to talk about it just yet," Lainey said.

"Oooh, exciting," Mrs. Maynard said. "Well, don't mind if I try to ferret some of your secrets out of you."

Lainey chuckled. She'd decided she was going to like Cinda Maynard. She was at least open about her agenda.

She glanced across the dining room at Milo, who was still dealing with the spill-related uproar at his table. Lainey waggled her eyebrows at him and couldn't help but feel this was karma for the prenup test.

HARLOW DRAKE INVESTIGATES . . .

Webisode 9, "Lainey Overshares"

Draft Episode—Not Posted—December 12, 2007

TRANSCRIPT EXCERPT

LAINEY: I still don't like talking about my dad like this. People don't need to know how I feel about him dying.

HARLOW: If you want access to information from my dad's files, we talk about it in front of the camera.

LAINEY: I'm pretty sure admitting to going through the state's attorney's files is a crime you don't want to record yourself admitting to. You're going to want to delete this.

HARLOW: Not my fault he uses the same password for everything.

LAINEY: You're *definitely* going to want to delete this.

HARLOW: So I guess you don't want to know that my dad kept notes on your dad's accident.

LAINEY: What?

HARLOW: They did a forensic review of your dad's computer. They found evidence that some files had been deleted, most having to do with the community center.

LAINEY: My dad volunteered there, something about their finance committee chair quitting. They needed help. Mom didn't like it. She said some of the business guys who ran it were sketchy. You know, construction. Waste management. I'm not going to say anything else on-camera.

HARLOW: Your dad was tracking big donations coming through the community center from various "civic groups" that had very flimsy paperwork. The center would make expenditures in the same amounts, for new playground equipment, repairs to the roof, with no actual receipts and no actual improvements. Your dad started asking questions, and three weeks later, he had his accident.

LAINEY: He wouldn't tell my mom what was going on, but he was super stressed out. Break-ins at his office. His internet was suddenly really unreliable. There were problems with his brakes. And then he told Mom he was meeting a potential client for dinner one town over, which was kind of unusual in itself because he didn't like to meet clients outside of the office. He wasn't home by midnight that night, even more unusual, because he was someone who was usually in bed by nine thirty. The next morning, the state troopers came to the door. It was like all the air had been sucked out of the house.

HARLOW: I felt the same way when my mom died.

LAINEY: Your mom moved to the Florida Keys.

HARLOW: She's a forty-six-year-old woman who's painting flowers on seashells because a Reiki instructor named Todd told her that was her path. I'll call it what I want.

LAINEY: I get that that hurts, but it's not the same thing. Your mom sucks, but there's a chance in ten years she'll age out of her seashell phase and you'll be able to talk to her again. My dad is *dead*. I keep expecting someone to tell me it's not true. That it was a misunderstanding, a joke. At the funeral, I thought I would walk up to the casket and some other man who looked a lot *like* my dad would be in there. But the day of the funeral, there he was, in his sensible stripy blue tie.

HARLOW: Well, I didn't find anything about which civic groups your dad was tracking. Or what he thought the money was for, but I'll keep you updated. Just like I'll keep you lovely viewers updated! Click the link to subscribe!

LAINEY: You should delete this now.

HARLOW: Probably.

8

Lainey openly defied the door declaring that the library was for "Gentlemen Only." Even though the rule wasn't enforced, she took great delight in spending a good twenty minutes contemplating one of the well-stocked room's shelves. The odd combination of titles followed neither the Dewey decimal system nor alphabetical order, which was weirdly frustrating.

"Hey, Shelley sent me looking for you," Kenny called from the library's entrance. He was drinking coffee from a Crossings Hotel mug. The caffeine seemed to have him in a friendly mood. "She wants to do a background interview about you and Harlow. We're setting up in the Gentlemen's Lounge."

"Because Harlow wants me filmed in the unflattering noir lighting?" she asked. Kenny nodded. "Is she up yet?"

"Oh, no," Kenny huffed. "We don't bother her before ten. Besides, she shoots her 'talking heads' in the nice, controlled studio environment back in New York."

That made sense, Lainey supposed. Harlow wouldn't want to

spend any more time in that nicotine-soaked room than necessary. It might mess with her complexion, which was probably under considerable stress already, given the hours Harlow was keeping. She'd still been holding court with the DBags in the lobby when Lainey had drifted quietly upstairs long after midnight, pleading travel fatigue. It had been awkward, with Deke and Bryce staring her down, opening another bottle of marshmallow-licorice-flavored vodka. They clearly expected more face time in exchange for their cash.

Even now, Lainey shuddered. What exactly was the expectation there? What were Deke and Bryce anticipating . . . in terms of personal contact? They hadn't made any demands exactly, but they seemed to think they *knew* Lainey and Harlow, that they were old friends separated by the cruel vagaries of time and geography. Knowing that master keys existed, she had slid her dresser in front of her door, fire codes be damned. And then she'd checked every light socket and lampshade for hidden cameras.

Lainey could go home. She knew that. She could ask Vern to put her back on the *Acheron*, and he would grumble as he piloted her all the way back to the mainland. Milo would probably commend her common sense. She didn't appreciate being in this isolated location, ordered for two DBags' entertainment. She wanted to move with integrity through the world. Unfortunately, that required having a place to leave her stuff and a cell phone that worked. She supposed she should be grateful this gig didn't involve dancing on tables.

Standing in front of a bookshelf, Lainey pulled at a bright green leather-bound book titled *A History of the Order of Carthusians.* She frowned when it didn't budge. "Did you know the Carthusian monks are responsible for making Chartreuse liqueur? A bunch of them spent years mixing together herbs and flowers and tree bark and stuff in the French Alps because they thought the ingredients would make an elixir that helped you live longer. Instead, they got liquor that tastes minty and vegetable-y at the same time."

"No, I didn't know that," Kenny told her. "Because no one knows that. I'm not even sure what 'Chartreuse' is, other than a color my mom likes for blouses. And it's not particularly flattering on her."

"Well, the liquor helped make the color popular." She snickered, staring up at the library shelves. The other stacks were floor to ceiling, but this one, topped by a bas-relief statue of the archangel Gabriel, was only about eight feet tall.

"Miss Piper."

She turned to find Mr. Wesley standing at the library door, and despite the fact that he was back in his signature Crossings blue, he did not look happy. Fortunately, even Lainey had trouble taking someone seriously when they were dressed like a villain in a 1980s comedy who was probably centered on dismantling a beloved summer camp.

"OK, I know I'm not supposed to be in here this early, but in my defense, the library wasn't locked," she said.

"Yes, but the computer at the front desk was," he noted, handing her the article she'd printed from the Madisonian Institute's website entitled "History's Most Haunted Gems." Another article detailing Marguerite's disappearance from Gladys McComber's home. "The printer is located in my office."

"I did not know that," she said. "Also, the desktop's password was 'password.'"

Mr. Wesley frowned at her. Lainey pressed her lips together to keep herself from adding criticisms of Mr. Wesley's approach to cybersecurity. This was a familiar feeling. Mr. Burnham had frequently given her put-upon looks. Of course, Mr. Burnham had locked Harlow in the trunk of his car . . .

Lainey had decided to seek out the internet articles the previous night while she was lying in bed, praying that she hadn't missed any cameras hidden in the light sockets. She thought she'd practiced restraint staying in bed and waiting until morning to print the articles. She could have crept through the darkened hotel in the middle of the night to get to the front desk computer and research her suspicions.

Her tombstone was going to read *Lainey Piper. Curiosity got her* and *the cat.*

She sighed. She was doing it again. Less than twenty-four hours back in Harlow's orbit and she was stomping over boundaries. And Lainey's mom couldn't even blame Harlow for this. Harlow hadn't asked Lainey to do any of it.

She was mulling these things over in her head while Mr. Wesley was staring at her—probably expecting an apology, like a reasonable adult person.

"I'm sorry. That was an overstep. I would have looked it up on my phone but I haven't had a signal since I got here," she said. "I'm kind of enjoying the break from emails and texts, to be honest, but I did need information. I'm assuming the hotel's guest Wi-Fi has been shut off?"

Mr. Wesley said, "Yes, the former owners decided it wasn't worth the expense to keep the handful of guests happy. And the landline service was canceled before you arrived. The owners have returned the phone units to the provider, as per the hotel's contract."

She stared at him. "We don't have any way to contact the mainland?"

"It was not a decision that I would have made, but it has been made clear to me that I am not in charge. I've been assured by the new owners that should we suffer an emergency, they'll 'figure it out.' I assume that means they will use their portable hotspot to contact the authorities." The manager's frown only deepened as he paused to consider his words. He handed her the much-lamented papers. "In the future, would you mind asking before accessing sensitive hotel resources?"

Lainey nodded. "That is reasonable, yes."

Mr. Wesley looked less thrilled with the solution, and Lainey had to admit that she didn't love the idea of connecting her phone to anything involving the DBags' tech. It would feel like giving her phone a digital STI.

"Thank you, Mr. Wesley. Please feel free to leave me to think about what I've done. You should see to the guests. I'm sure Mrs. Maynard is just dying to enjoy a perch omelet this morning. She said they were a particular favorite of her father's. She makes it a point to eat them every time she's here."

Mr. Wesley stared at her blankly as if he didn't know what she was talking about. That was odd. Of course, it was possible that he was also disgusted by the idea of fish and eggs this early in the day. He gave Lainey one last put-upon look and quit the room like an Austenian matriarch.

"Maybe make her a rickey?" Lainey called after him.

"You're a weird girl," Kenny told her.

"You're not the first person to say so." She pulled at the Carthusian history again and then lifted it a few inches. Her breath quickened as metal creaked behind the shelf, which jolted. The Carthusian history couldn't be moved any farther, but when she pushed it back in slightly at this new height, she felt a tension behind the book that quickly gave a little. The metal, which she assumed to be gears, clanked even louder.

Even though every cell in her body *insisted* that she push the book in farther, complete the circuit of motion, she turned to Kenny and said, "You're probably going to want to wake Harlow up, but tell Shelley to do it without Mr. Wesley noticing."

"Why?" Kenny asked. "Also, how?"

Lainey grinned at him, making Kenny shudder. "Oh, something about that smile scares me so much . . . To be clear, I am not your sidekick. I will not be split off from the group. I will not investigate strange noises by myself. I will not follow you down dark hallways."

When the comment on dark hallways made Lainey dial back the grin to a discomfited smile, he added, "Oh, dammit, there's a dark hallway, isn't there?"

"It's going to be a *really cool* dark hallway," she told him.

"You have no way of knowing that," he groaned, making her chuckle.

It was fascinating, watching the crew quickly and quietly create a set out of nothing. They were like a perfectly timed watch, parts moving around one another in unison, accomplishing a goal without bumping into one another. Shelley kept it professional and cool, occasionally looking up from her phone while Kenny and Gordy tossed nonbreakable filming tools back and forth with practiced ease, all while Findlay transformed Lainey into a "natural beauty" . . . with about fifteen different products.

On Findlay, it worked. Lainey wasn't sure *she* would be able to pull it off.

"Harlow asked that you not be assigned a lapel mic," Gordy told her, wielding a long metal pole tipped with a fuzzy black microphone. "So just try to keep my position with the boom mic in mind if you're going to be talking a lot."

"Why would Harlow specifically request that?" Lainey asked Findlay.

"It would be a shame if your audio was so bad that your video was unusable, limiting your input into the final product," Findlay murmured so only Lainey could hear.

"We can always rerecord it later, as a last resort," Shelley said.

"Meaning Harlow can rerecord it," Findlay added quietly.

Lainey nodded. "Kind of keeps me where she's comfortable with me."

Findlay patted her arm gently, winking at her. "Forewarned is forearmed."

While Lainey should have probably been annoyed by this, she knew her participation didn't determine how much she was paid. So, she kept the main goal in mind and let Findlay apply a sweep of powder down her nose.

Milo appeared at Lainey's left, looking downright scrumptious in a white dress shirt and tailored gray slacks. Milo looking this good under these circumstances was just unfair.

To his credit, if he registered that she looked different with a fully made-up face, he didn't mention it. He handed her a cup of black coffee. "I didn't know how you liked it."

Lainey stared at the cup. She didn't want to confess to her usual coffee milkshake concoctions, a concern which was rendered moot when Findlay immediately took it out of her hands.

Findlay gave Milo a pointed look. "She likes it in a form that doesn't smear her lipstick," she said, turning to Lainey and adding,

"Which I told you would change your life. And obviously, I was right."

"You got me there." Lainey chuckled, glancing in the pop-up mirror Findlay had set out for her mobile makeup station. The pinkish-coral color with its gold undertones was something Lainey never would have chosen for herself, but it really did bring out the "roses in her cheeks," as Lainey's mom would say.

"Thank you anyway," Lainey told Milo. "Am I already in violation of company policy?"

"No, but the guys are on their way," he said. "And I figured you'd need to be caffeinated for that."

"You're a nice man," she told Milo. "Like, eighty percent of the time."

"Is that the sort of thing that people judge by percentages?" he asked.

"Keep arguing with me and I'll make it seventy," she retorted.

Down the hall, she could hear shouts from Deke and Bryce. It sounded like they were arguing with Mr. Wesley about ripping out the archive's displays to put in a climbing wall. While Bryce insisted that "chicks love that sort of thing," Mr. Wesley was incensed at the "shocking lack of respect for the history."

So . . . that was going to keep them all occupied for a while.

"I'm judging you by the company you keep," Lainey told Milo. His cheeks flushed an adorable crimson. Unfortunately for Lainey, Harlow chose that moment to storm into the room, a large brush roller in her bangs. Her juice—a cloudy pumpkin color, which was weird considering it had "Crystalline Greens" right there in the name—sloshed onto the well-worn imitation Aubusson carpet as she slammed the glass down on an end table.

With Cameron at her heels, Harlow began, "Why are we setting up in the library when the call sheet clearly—"

But Shelley shushed her, pulling her aside and quietly explaining the shooting schedule shift.

"That judgment cuts both ways," Milo told Lainey.

"Touché," Lainey murmured as Findlay lightly dusted Lainey's forehead with powder.

Harlow suddenly turned away from Shelley, moved swiftly across the hardwood floor toward them, and demanded, "What are you doing?"

"Just touching her up," Findlay replied. "Don't want her to be shiny on-camera."

"I wasn't talking to *you*," Harlow huffed at Findlay, turning to Lainey. "I don't know what you think you're trying to do. But I'm telling you now, you don't tell the crew where to film. You're not a producer. You're not even on-camera talent. I could add you as a voice in postproduction and no one would notice."

"There's no reason to talk to her like that," Milo protested.

Lainey felt the blood drain from her face. All of the noise in the room seemed to stop as the people around her paused to watch how Lainey handled this confrontation.

Also, it was interesting that while Milo let the DBags behave any way they wanted, he'd just stepped in front of a Harlow-shaped bullet for Lainey.

Harlow seemed to realize she was being watched, and not in a way that benefitted her.

"Archive, now." She strode out of the library, clearly expecting Lainey to follow.

"If you fight her, don't let her touch your hair," Findlay whispered after her. Lainey huffed out a laugh.

They walked far enough away from the library door to avoid being heard before Harlow whirled around to face her. "Look, I know that came across as bitchy, but I can't have you sucking up all the crew's time and attention. It's *Harlow Drake Investigates*, not *Lainey Piper Is Too Nice and Worries Too Much About What Everybody Thinks of Her*."

Lainey rolled her eyes. "I really thought you'd have developed some more insightful insults since high school."

"Well, if you'd developed some other irritating qualities since high school, I would come up with some new insults," Harlow shot back. "I'll bet you don't even go back home to visit, do you? Too scared to face people?"

"You know, we should probably focus on the shitty way you're treating your coworkers, but sure—let's go back to the beginning. No, I don't go home to visit much because the first few visits home after graduation, people threw drinks at me. Because we prevented their friends and loved ones from being able to attend college. When I was lucky, they were *cold* drinks."

"So you got a little soda thrown at you. Big deal." Harlow shook her head. "You're being dramatic."

"You're being obtuse because it suits you," Lainey retorted. "You never seemed to get that, yeah, we uncovered something important, but there were consequences. There are *always* consequences, Harlow."

"Look, I'm sorry I dropped you as a friend. I'm sorry I outgrew you," Harlow told her.

"I don't care that you dropped me. It helped me stop making some of the shitty choices I made when we worked together."

"Oh, so you're going to blame me for that, too? I forced you to do those things?" Harlow demanded.

"No. I did those things because I *loved* doing them, or at least the results I got from them, which was sort of the problem. But unlike you, I saw the ripples of our actions and how those ripples ruined lives. Firsthand. People don't forget stuff like that in a town that small. You weren't there. You don't know what it was like, the looks that people gave me. Somehow it's OK for you, because you at least went out and made something of yourself, but it's like I did it for no reason. Which is worse."

"People always have hard-luck stories when their college plans don't turn out the way they want," Harlow scoffed. "Danny Conforth wrecked his knee our junior year and lost his football scholarship. Julie Hill got kicked out of State for setting all the test rabbits free from the lab building. My roommate died sophomore year, and you don't hear me complaining that the whole 'free straight A's' urban legend turned out to be a lie."

Lainey shuddered at the cold tone Harlow used when complaining about the rumored perk denied to her. Lainey remembered seeing multiple social media posts around the time that Bella Faris died in a horrific crash on icy roads driving home for winter break that year. Harlow had tried to argue that this tragedy meant she was entitled to an automatic 4.0 and a single room for the rest of the year. Harlow had a new roommate by mid-January. According to scuttlebutt Helen had picked up at the grocery store, Harlow had attempted to file a suit against the school before her dad convinced her it would destroy her public image.

"Those weren't situations that *we* created, unless you have something to tell me about your poor roommate," Lainey shot back.

"We didn't create the GradeGate situation!" Harlow cried. She stopped herself and lowered her voice. "Mr. Burnham did. We just made sure people found out about it. You want me to cry for the people whose lives we 'ruined'? Well, boo-hoo, if they didn't want their future wrecked, they shouldn't have tried to buy their way into college."

"Some of the kids caught up in GradeGate had gotten *real* recommendations from Mr. Burnham that they deserved. Some of them didn't know their parents were paying off Mr. Burnham. They just thought they got lucky with the grades and the recommendations."

"They did get lucky. And they should have known that nothing comes for free," Harlow insisted. "If it were up to you, we never would have done anything. You would have given up the minute you were accused of the weed cookie thing and gone back to being boring, moody set dressing. You wanted to drop GradeGate before we even got started. If it were up to you, Ms. Fraser would still be buried under the football field and Mr. Burnham would be funneling rich kids into the Ivy League."

Lainey gritted her jaw to the point that her teeth squeaked. Harlow was right.

"You could have used GradeGate as a springboard like I did, but instead you chose to worry about what a bunch of small-town nobodies thought of you," Harlow said. "If you keep this up, you're going to waste this opportunity, too. I'm handing it to you, gift-wrapped, because I care about you. And you're *wasting* it. Now, suck it up, know your place on the marquee, and stop trying to coproduce."

Lainey forced herself to breathe. No matter what she told herself, she could not financially afford to simply walk away from this island. Also, if she smacked Harlow over the head with one of the hotel's heavy brass lamps, she would be booted off this island *and* go to jail.

People did not change. Harlow was who she had always been. She did not care about Lainey. She needed to know she was the best, the smartest, the most likely to be chosen, the top billed—but she also wouldn't turn down the chance to be handed the answers to the test. Lainey had to choose to be better, and she had to stop bitching about it. She would go all in on this project. She would engage. And she would make Harlow remember who usually found the answers first.

She took a breath and squared her shoulders.

"Ultimately, you're right. I could leave the island right now and no one would notice," Lainey told her as Gordy appeared and moved to wrap a body pack microphone setup around Harlow's waist. Lainey expected some objection, but Harlow simply lifted her shirt slightly to accommodate Gordy's maneuvering without even looking at him. "We'll go tell the DBags that you *don't want* to find the secret passage to the speakeasy and you can go back to strictly adhering to the call sheet."

Harlow's eyes narrowed as if Lainey were trying to trick her. Gordy smoothed her shirt down over the mic pack and silently stepped away. Lainey grinned at Harlow and followed Gordy into the library.

Close on Lainey's heels, Harlow huffed, "You did not. You did *not* find it on your first damn day."

"I found *something*," Lainey told her. "If it's not the passage to the speakeasy, it's definitely more interesting than me talking about our high school antics in the Gentlemen's Lounge."

"Other people have been looking for the speakeasy for the past sixty years," Harlow shot back.

"And 'other people' didn't find where the lacrosse team hid our rival school's mascot head . . . in exchange for keypad access to the sheriff's department's evidence lockup," Lainey replied.

Shelley shook her head as they rejoined the crew. "Why did you need access to an evidence lockup?"

"The coach was a first-year teacher. He wasn't happy that our lacrosse team stole the head and hid it somewhere in the school. But he didn't have the clout to confront them or their parents. Or make them tell him where they hid it," Harlow explained. "What he did have was a cousin who ran the sheriff's department's evidence lockup and who used the same passcode for everything."

"I thought maybe there was evidence from my dad's accident that might be helpful," Lainey said. "I was wrong. We got caught."

"My dad got us out of it with community service," Harlow added. "He convinced the judge it was youthful hijinks."

"And thus the sheriff's chronic frustration with us was born," Lainey said with a sigh.

"Never did figure out how you managed to crawl under the auditorium stage to get the mascot head back," Harlow mused.

"Yoga and determination," Lainey replied, making Harlow laugh. It was a tentative step back to their equilibrium, but they'd made it. And all was right with the world. At least for this project. At least for now.

"You get all of that?" Shelley asked Kenny, who gave her a thumbs-up. "We'll cut everything before the lacrosse story. The audience doesn't need to see you bickering."

When Harlow turned to Shelley, the producer added, "The only reason we didn't open it before you came along is that we were afraid there would be cool cobwebs draped across the opening or something. We didn't want to waste the visual opportunity."

"Also, there could be booby-traps," Gordy suggested, grunting when Findlay kicked his leg on her way past him. Harlow stared at him, calculating, even as Findlay removed the roller from her bangs and fluffed her hair out. Harlow barely had time to look annoyed before Findlay brushed finishing powder over her already made-up face.

"Just trust me, Harlow," Lainey said. "But you're going to want to change into some practical shoes. Do you have some?"

"I brought them!" Cameron said, holding up a pair of designer running shoes.

"When did you get those?" Harlow asked him, frowning.

"I'm always prepared," Cameron replied, though he was looking at Shelley. "Always."

Lainey arched her brows. Was *Cameron* trying to translate his position as Harlow's assistant into a production credit? Did he think Shelley gave them away like candy?

When Gordy and Kenny gave Shelley another thumbs-up, she turned to Lainey with an expectant smile.

"Mr. Wesley?" Lainey asked.

"I told him there was a leak in the ceiling in my room," Gordy told her. "Water damage galore."

"That was mean," Lainey replied.

"Do you *want* him coming in here, finding us fiddling around in areas Shelley promised we would leave . . . un-fiddled?" Gordy asked pointedly.

"I do not." Lainey shook her head. "Wait, if Mr. Wesley is searching out water damage in Gordy's room, where are the DBags?"

As if on a sitcom cue, Deke and Bryce came tumbling through the open door like a pair of gamboling puppies.

"No fair!" Bryce yelled. "You're shooting without us?"

"Yeah, what's going on?" Deke demanded. "We're supposed to be able to watch *everything.* You can't just leave us out!"

The petulant edge to his voice set Lainey's teeth on edge. The charms of being live entertainment were starting to wear thin.

"We were just setting up," Kenny assured him. "All the boring, time-waster stuff."

"Oh, I guess that's OK," Bryce conceded.

Deke seemed less convinced and required several minutes of small talk from Harlow *and* Lainey before he was appeased enough for filming to start. They both perched on the library sofas in a way that probably would have made Mr. Wesley swallow his tongue. They watched, rapt, as Lainey pointed to the bookshelf that contained the history of the Carthusian monks. "Go over there and pull on that green book."

"Are you sure this is it?" Harlow asked as Lainey lurked behind Kenny, out of frame. Shelley tried to motion her forward, but Lainey shook her head. This was the position that would cause the least friction with Harlow, and it would make sense to anyone who had seen their webisodes.

Lainey threw up her hands. "I think so. And if it's not, at least we're not broadcasting live."

"Because Milo took our phones," Deke grumbled.

"I knew neither one of you could resist live streaming, which violates our contract with the network," Milo shot back. Deke shrugged.

"Well, you were right not to do this without me," Harlow said primly, straightening her shirt. "I would have been furious. So just for narrative's sake, Lainey, why am I doing this? Cameron, take notes. I'll dub over this shot in postproduction."

"Always am," Cameron told her, dropping his lip balm into his pocket. Was the lip balm application an involuntary nervous impulse?

Lainey pointed to the bright green book on the shelf and said, "The Carthusian monks created Chartreuse. You know, that green liquor in the bottle that Bryce mentioned?"

"*That's* how you say it?" Bryce whispered. Harlow shushed him even while she smiled at him.

"Chartreuse is . . . an acquired taste, but it was popular in the 1920s," Lainey continued. "Probably because it was bright green and that was a novelty. Also, people were trying to cover up the taste of alcohol in their home brews, which may or may not have been poisonous at the time, depending on who made it and how."

Harlow smirked and whispered to Shelley, "She loves doing this. Let her have her moment for now."

"The owners built the speakeasy in this heaven-and-hell-inspired hotel during Prohibition. And there's this whole history of the monks who make a popular Prohibition-era booze right next to a copy of John Milton's *Paradise Lost*—the placement of which flies in the face of the Dewey decimal system. If you were a free-living jazz junkie who had just lost access to your favorite substance, it probably did feel like you lost paradise," Lainey said. "I thought there might be a connection . . . And when I tried to pull the green book from the shelves, I couldn't."

Milo frowned. "What do you mean you couldn't?"

"I was met with resistance, and not just 'a book wedged between two other books' resistance. That book is connected to something behind the shelf. If I wanted to hide an interior entrance to a speakeasy, I would probably choose the quietest, most boring location in my hotel," Lainey said. "If we closed those doors behind us, no one—particularly the cranky manager who is not a fan of anyone here—would see us open this door."

Deke and Bryce scrambled to close the solid wooden doors that were carved with more angels' wings. They remained at the back of the room guarding the entrance while practically wriggling with excitement. Harlow took hold of the Carthusian history and looked back at Kenny, who nodded.

"Wait," Milo said, stepping forward to stand next to Lainey. "What if it *is* booby-trapped?"

"Why would they leave booby-traps in a hotel?" Harlow asked.

"To keep people out of the forbidden speakeasy?" Milo guessed.

"Stop interfering, Milo!" Deke hissed.

Bryce actually booed. "We'll cover all your medical expenses, Harlow."

"Very comforting," Harlow muttered. Lainey watched, rapt, as Harlow pulled the book. She seemed to meet the same resistance as Lainey. She pulled the book up and then pushed it back in slightly, following the motions that Lainey was miming for her out of Kenny's camera range. A metallic clang rang out behind the bookshelf, and the whole wall unit swung forward with a loud creak.

"Oh, shit!" Deke cried. To her credit, Harlow didn't respond. She simply pulled the shelves away from the wall. Lainey gave the camera a wide berth, viewing what stood behind the bookshelf from across the room. It was, indeed, a very cool long, dark hallway.

Lainey's body was in chaos. She couldn't believe it had actually worked. She'd *thought* she was right when she'd felt the tension behind that book. Still, a hunch was one thing. The reality of finding a hidden hallway behind a bookshelf was another.

"Anybody bring a flashlight?" Harlow asked. Lainey reached into her shoulder bag, which she was carrying around the hotel for moments just like this. She claimed her favorite flashlight (the largest one in her collection—purple with an emergency window breaker in the handle) for herself and tossed another one of her Maglites to Harlow, who gave her a fond look. "Thank you."

"Get in the shot, Lainey," Shelley whispered. Lainey shook her head slightly. Harlow took a few steps into the dark corridor and flipped a heavy switch that brought dingy submarine lights to life. Rows of them seemed to go on forever into the darkness.

"So . . . a secret passageway . . . full of unknown circumstances," Lainey said.

"I know!" Harlow squealed and disappeared into the hallway.

"I *knew* you were going to end up luring me somewhere dark and unsafe," Kenny grumbled, even as Gordy shushed him.

"It's *partially* lit. And it doesn't have a 'Do Not Enter' sign that Mr. Wesley said would mark damaged areas," Lainey said.

"Because he probably doesn't know it exists. Maybe we wait on an engineer or some construction types to inspect this before just hurling ourselves into the unknown?" Milo said, barely suppressing the anxiety in his voice.

Bryce scoffed, charging ahead of Lainey and almost tripping over the lower lip of the passageway entrance. Deke patted Milo's shoulder. "You thought we would find a secret door in a building *we* own and *not* go in?"

"The board is going to kill me," Milo said.

"Don't worry." Lainey winked at him. "I'll protect you."

"Do you have an extra flashlight?" he mumbled.

She reached into her shoulder bag and handed him her medium Maglite, shiny and bright pink with little rhinestones around the base. "Of course I do."

"Of course you do," he said, leveling her with a bemused look as he clicked on the decidedly ladylike flashlight. "Someone should probably stay in the library, just in case the door swings shut and we get locked in."

"I volunteer as non-tribute!" Findlay said. "My claustrophobia is a living thing."

Gordy nodded. "We got stuck in a crowded subway car during a rolling blackout. I thought she was going to fight a guy who kept making sardine jokes."

"And I could have taken him, too," Findlay insisted.

Gordy gave her a loose side-hug before he hoisted his boom mic into position. "Of course you could have, sweetheart."

9

Stepping across the threshold into the dimly lit hallway felt important, like setting foot on the moon.

It was possible that Lainey was a little too excited about this.

Cameron and Kenny stuck close to Harlow—Cameron following so closely that Shelley had to yank him out of Kenny's shot. But of all the people in the group, Lainey chose to stick close to Milo. She told herself that it was because he was most likely to make sensible, corporate-influenced decisions, but also . . . he smelled nice. And in this dry and dusty environment, the scent of amber and linen was comforting. The submarine lights were the typical practical bulbs protected by thick rippling glass. But they were surrounded by black metalwork flames.

"Whoever decorated this place was a drama queen," Lainey observed.

"They did love a theme," Milo agreed. "So you managed to find a secret passageway in a haunted hotel. Did you do research ahead of time or . . . ?"

"Are you accusing me of cheating?" she said. "At detective work?"

"You're not a detective," he told her.

"Well, what else am I supposed to call this very useful set of skills at which it is impossible to cheat?" she asked.

"I don't know," he conceded.

"Just admit that even if I didn't open the door myself, that was the most awesome thing you've ever seen," she teased him. "And a little hot."

She bit her lip. The looming partial darkness of the corridor was giving her way too much confidence. Milo paused, turning to her, making Lainey inhale sharply through her nose. His face was unreadable in the shadows, but she could feel his minty breath on her face. He moved close until she was backed against the wall. Her shoulder bumped against the cold concrete. The contact sent a shiver down her spine.

"Not just a little—" he began just as they heard Harlow cry out. Milo startled, grabbing Lainey's arms. The warmth of his hands radiated through her sleeves, giving her thoughts a focal point. Had they found Marguerite's remains in the passageway? Was it weird that Lainey was a little disappointed the adventure was over so soon?

It probably didn't make her a *great* person.

"What is this?" Harlow gasped.

Milo seemed to realize how hard he was gripping Lainey's arms and released her. Lainey moved forward through the group to find Harlow standing at a side wall, in front of a riveted metal door with a spinning wheel in the middle.

"Is this a submarine door?" she asked.

"Not exactly conducive to a party atmosphere," Gordy muttered, adjusting his grip on the boom mic.

"We didn't really go that far," Harlow mused, shining her flashlight toward the library. "If there was a swinging jazz club this close to the rest of the hotel, wouldn't the normie guests have heard it?"

"Old walls. Stone and plaster muffle more than you think," Deke suggested. "And with a property this size? No one would be able to tell for sure where the noise was coming from."

When the rest of the group turned to him, he shrugged. "I remodeled an old estate in Ibiza into a vacation home. The VIP room is amazing and undetectable."

"You have a VIP room in a house?" Kenny asked. "Your own private house?"

"Why not?" Deke asked, genuinely confused.

Kenny just shook his head.

"Well, we opened one forbidden door, might as well open another one and find the architect's idea of paradise," Lainey said, trying to steer the conversation back on track. "Or Narnia."

Harlow grinned at her. It took both of them, but once they put enough pressure on the wheel, it spun easily enough, cranking open the T-handle ground rods on the door until it swung open.

"You ready?" Lainey asked, looking to Shelley and Kenny. Shelley made a *Get on with it* gesture.

Harlow pulled the door open and found . . . a wooden wall. It looked like the back of a shelving unit or dresser that covered the entire opening. That felt like a really weird place to put furniture. Lainey looked down at the metal rails at the bottom of the wooden unit. It looked like it was designed to glide aside on casters. Lainey and Harlow nudged it, pushing it open like a sliding glass door. A puff of dust swirled toward their faces as they broke dozens of cobwebs between the dresser and the frame.

Lainey shone her flashlight into the darkened room and saw gray metal bunk beds. Harlow stepped inside, carefully navigating stacks of old towels and canned goods on the floor. She made it across the large room and flipped a light switch on the wall. The crew was left blinking as the overhead fluorescent lights hummed to life.

This was not a glamorous speakeasy of bygone days. This was a hoarder basement.

With bunk beds.

"Suddenly feeling really sorry for Geraldo," Lainey muttered. Cameron glared at her, but Lainey shrugged him off. She stood by the reference.

Harlow laughed, but it was a mirthless sound of disbelief. "What is this?"

Unlike the rest of the hotel, this room was strictly utilitarian, slick greenish-white plaster walls and dulled chrome surfaces. Metal shelves were crowded with old trunks and suitcases. Multiple rows of bunk beds, their tick mattresses and bedding rolled up neatly at the foot of each. Much older canned goods were neatly stacked in the corner, as if someone meant to take them to the dump at some point but kept forgetting.

"Is that . . . fruit cocktail?" Lainey asked. Harlow inspected the pile and handed her the can.

"Expired in 1996," Harlow noted.

Lainey reached up and swiped at the dust covering the metal plaque on the wall. It was ocher yellow with a gray fan symbol. It read **FALLOUT SHELTER**.

"Why would the hotel need a bomb shelter?" Deke asked.

"The Cuban Missile Crisis scared everybody," Milo said. "A lot of people had shelters then."

"Kind of cool, though," Bryce mused. "Like a secret hideaway. But, you know, hiding from bombs."

Deke sounded so disappointed that Lainey actually felt sorry for him. "This can't be it, though. They wouldn't build a bomb shelter in an old speakeasy, right?"

"Maybe they added it in the 1960s, not knowing where the passageway ended?" Harlow suggested. "The submarine door could be like an emergency exit. Mr. Wesley did say that the Kennedy-oriented wife had no interest in the hotel's seedier past."

"It kind of looks like they've been using it as a lost-and-found-slash-storage space," Lainey said, nodding at the Christmas decorations and discarded suitcases stacked in the far corner of the room. The luggage ranged from old steamer trunks to Samsonite roller bags. A stamp on one of the metal trunks caught her eye: **FROGMOUTH, ALABAMA–THE MOUTH OF THE SOUTH**. Next to it someone had scratched *GM* near the carved wooden handle. It looked like a scar. Lainey shuddered.

There was another heavy metal hatch door on the far wall of the shelter. When Lainey tried it, this second hatch opened much easier than the first, as if someone had used the door more recently. The beige-painted corridor shone harshly under fluorescent lights and smelled like grilled onions. Maybe this hallway connected to the kitchen behind the library? Taking a few steps into the beige space, Lainey could hear raised voices and the clang of pots and pans.

"Don't talk to me like that!" a man's voice bellowed down the hall. "You asked me to be your head chef. I didn't want this job. I wanted to work at a damn country club and retire!"

"Dammit, Andy, you explain to me how you, the cook, aren't responsible for someone dying from an allergic reaction," a voice she recognized as Mr. Wesley's yelled.

"We don't know that he died from an allergic reaction!" the other man shot back. Apparently, the hotel's fancy French chef was named "Andy." Lainey noted the distinct lack of Gallic accent. "Old people die in their sleep. It happens!"

"You didn't see him!" Mr. Wesley hissed. "There wasn't an inch of that man that wasn't covered in a rash. His hands looked like those puffy cartoon gloves."

"Look, you know I keep a safe kitchen. I take this shit seriously. As soon as I heard there was a tree-nut allergy listed in the guest notes, I used all the right protocols. I eliminated nuts from the menu—no almonds on the green beans, no pecans on the waffles. I marked Mr. Hornsby's preassigned table number and made sure that all dishes cooked for that table were made with nut-free utensils and pans. I just now started setting out bar snacks because I figured the threat has passed—"

"What is it?" Harlow asked behind her, prompting Lainey to withdraw and close the door.

"Service corridor," Lainey said, keeping her tone neutral. She wasn't sure of how to process what she'd just heard, much less how to explain it to Harlow. "We're near the kitchen. Given the number of cobwebs on the back of the sliding dresser, I don't think the staff has been in the secret hallway in a while. Maybe they forgot it was behind the shelter?"

She latched the door as quietly as she could. It wouldn't do for Mr. Wesley to know they were snooping around in the staff-only areas of the hotel. But it was good to know they could get out of the secret hallway if they wanted. They weren't trapped.

But . . . if Mr. Hornsby was so careful about what he ate, what had he been exposed to that gave him an allergic reaction? Food labels had so many warnings about processing in facilities with trigger ingredients. Maybe his protein bars hadn't been safe after all?

She turned to find Deke and Bryce staging a lightsaber battle with spare fluorescent light tubes. By some miracle, they hadn't broken one yet.

"Kenny, please stop filming," Milo said firmly but politely. Then he turned to Deke and Bryce and barked, "Guys. Eye injuries, both of you, 2018. Doing the exact same thing."

The DBags froze and swept the fluorescent bulbs behind their backs. Bryce's slipped out of his hands and flew across the room into the far wall. The ensuing crash had Milo sighing and closing his eyes.

"Are you praying?" Lainey asked him. He nodded. She added, "For patience?"

"Yes." He sighed again.

"Sorry, Milo," Deke and Bryce chorused, sounding like two scolded schoolboys.

Lainey gazed at them in wonder. She did not understand the DBags. Had they forgotten that *they* signed *Milo's* checks? She eyed Milo carefully. Who was this man, and what sort of strange power did he wield over these indecently rich tech bros?

"Well, this has been a little disappointing," Harlow huffed as they moved out of the shelter into the dark corridor.

"It's still amazing content," Cameron assured her. "Think of the jump-scare value of turning on the lights and finding . . ."

"Ancient fruit cocktail?" Lainey suggested.

Cameron glared again, but the filthy looks were starting to lose their impact.

"Cameron, get behind Kenny and stop talking," Shelley snapped at him.

After the "palate cleanser" of the bomb shelter's onion-infused air, it was remarkable how dry and cold the dim corridor smelled—like old cement dust. It was the common smell of Midwestern basements, so far under the permafrost that the space didn't have a chance to mildew. Without the comforting traces of Milo's no-doubt-expensive cologne, the change left her a little dizzy.

"I don't think this has been disappointing. I am *enthralled*," Deke assured Harlow. She gave him a close-lipped smile, communicating no warmth. Then she winced as Kenny turned on the camera's brighter "action spotlight." She glared at the cameraman, which wasn't a great way to guarantee Kenny would only get her good side.

Kenny's chin retreated into his neck as he turned off the spotlight.

"The flashlights give it more of a cinema verité feeling," Lainey assured him, turning her beam on Harlow. Kenny grumbled wordlessly to himself.

Deke said, "I am having a *great time*."

"This is like a game but better," Bryce insisted. He grinned, waving his hand at the darkened hallway. "The graphics are amazing."

Lainey snickered. Despite the turmoil, this was the most fun she'd had in years.

"We might actually have something worth airing here," Shelley mused to Kenny. "I should let the network know."

"What does that mean?" Harlow froze in her tracks, looking for a moment like Bigfoot in profile against the backdrop of Milo's flashlight. "The network didn't think we would have something worth airing?"

In Lainey's experience, there was always a moment when someone knew they were caught—the realization that they made a mistake flickered across their facial muscles. Their eyes reflected a mental review of what they'd just said and how it hurt their cause. One could practically see the gears turning inside their head as they tried to figure out how to pivot. Shelley's choice was to wave Harlow's concern off as if it were pesky mosquitoes. "Don't be silly. Of course we did. We have complete faith in you."

It was said too swiftly, too casually to be believed.

Harlow, being Harlow, would not be deterred. She stepped forward, toward Shelley, in a way that made the woman step back and smack into the wall. "I'm not being silly. It's not just that you said we might 'actually' have something worth airing. It's the way you said it. Was the network not *planning* to air the special?"

To her credit, Shelley maintained eye contact as she replied, "After . . . everything, the executive board thought that maybe a return to web-based content might be the best place for you. It's your wheelhouse. It's where people are comfortable seeing you."

Lainey could see Harlow's eyes narrow, even in the low light. "They were going to webisode me?"

"That's not important now. Even if you don't find Marguerite or even the speakeasy, you found *something*, Harlow," Shelley assured her. "Secret passageways hidden behind a bookshelf? That's some Nancy Drew stuff. And it's *amazing*. And it's going to make for great TV."

Harlow stared at Shelley for a long moment while Deke and Bryce eased the sliding dresser in front of the secret shelter hatch door. There was no reason to let Mr. Wesley know they'd been there.

A heavy sense of inevitability settled into Lainey's belly. She'd seen that look on Harlow's face before, right after the incident involving Krissy Ronson's punch. Krissy had blamed Harlow for her father's arrest—which was technically correct, because Harlow was the one who told the police about the cameras in Mr. Ronson's shop changing rooms. Shortly after the nose punch, Mr. Burnham received a mysterious anonymous tip that Krissy had definitely-not-prescribed-to-her pills stashed in her locker. The family's legal budget was doubly taxed defending Krissy from a possession charge.

"So do we head back to the library or keep going?" Lainey asked in an attempt to distract Harlow.

Harlow's head whipped toward her. A familiar warmth bloomed in those blue eyes, and she laughed. "Oh, please, I have never once in my life just gone back to the library."

Lainey chuckled and slipped her arm through Harlow's. "True."

Shelley and Lainey shared a significant look. Lainey was taking one for the team and wanted Shelley to recognize it. Lainey and Harlow drifted apart as the group pressed forward slowly into the darkness, down inclines and around corners. They seemed to walk for longer than should have been possible on an island. There was only so much real estate.

Harlow naturally pulled ahead, sure the next turn would open up onto the entrance to the speakeasy. Lainey felt like a hapless character in one of those found-footage horror movies, wandering around catacombs *not* expecting to find flesh-hungry zombies lurking. Kenny was so close behind her, filming over Lainey's shoulder, capturing every moment as Harlow bravely breached the unknown.

It was surprising how little debris there was. No random bits of paper or garbage. Lainey trailed her own Maglite up and down the floor.

Had no one come down this hallway since they'd closed the speakeasy? What if there was no speakeasy? What if this whole thing was a wild-goose chase and they'd been Geraldo'd? They could cobble something out of footage of Harlow searching through the bomb shelter, right? There had to be something in those old lost-and-found suitcases. Some of them looked really old.

The hallway seemed darker here, which made sense considering there were no submarine lamps. Harlow stopped in her tracks, and it was all Lainey could do not to run into her back. She peered over Harlow's shoulder to see a bunch of garbage stacked against the wall. It was an oddly shaped construction of pallets, discarded mops and brooms, tarps, and cans of substances that were probably also dangerously poisonous.

It looked like a set piece from a very seedy scene in *Cats*.

"No, come on," Harlow huffed. "This can't be it. Not after all that buildup. What was the point of a big winding hallway if it just ends in a pile of garbage?"

She looked toward Kenny and Shelley and made a cutting motion toward her throat. Gordy shot a commiserating look at Lainey. She stepped toward the garbage pile and studied the cans of paint and pesticides. (Yep, also poison.) The tarps were propped up against the wall, pinned by two-by-four boards. It all looked so intentionally staged, artfully random. Lainey nudged a can of paint thinner with her fingertip.

The debris appeared to be glued down.

"Yeah, a pile of garbage in a hallway where there has been absolutely *no other litter.* Not weird at all," Lainey said, giving Harlow a pointed look. She nodded at a mop handle that looked darker and smoother than the others, even under the soft patina of dust, as if the oil of hundreds of hands had polished it over the course of years. "With that mop handle sticking out of the pile at that very convenient angle, unlike all of the other mops and brooms."

Harlow stared at Lainey as if she were spouting nonsense . . . which Lainey supposed was fair.

"It's just asking to be pulled down like a lever," Lainey added. Frustration bloomed on Harlow's face, and there was a sharp satisfaction for Lainey, knowing how much Shelley was going to edit the footage to make Harlow look good.

Harlow turned to the crew and barked, "Kenny."

Kenny turned his camera on while Lainey shone her flashlight on Harlow. She illuminated Harlow as she tore down the tarps, which had been strategically nailed to the plaster to make it look like they were just naturally draped.

Harlow pulled on the mop handle. The floor beneath them lurched, making them all yelp. Milo grabbed Lainey's arm, holding her upright as she wobbled on her feet. She swept her flashlight over the floor and saw that they were standing on a circular platform, which rotated counterclockwise. It took the crew with it as the garbage-pile wall turned. When it stopped moving, the crew was standing in front of a large metal door surrounded by sculpted black metal flames.

This was the end of the road to hell. Lainey was still searching for the good intentions.

"Huh," Lainey said. "Didn't expect that."

"You told me to pull the lever," Harlow reminded her.

"Yeah, but I thought the garbage pile would split and reveal a door or something," Lainey said, waving her hands. "I wasn't expecting a rotating wall reveal. I can see now the potential danger of that. I'm sorry."

"I am all tingly inside," Bryce whispered into the darkness. When the others stopped talking, he seemed to realize he had said something out of pocket and added, "What?"

10

Tingles aside, Gordy was the first among them to question the safety of trapping themselves between a door and a secret garbage wall. Lainey thought this spoke well of his survival instincts.

"Are we stuck in here?" Gordy asked. "Or is this a 'the only way through is forward' thing?"

Harlow pulled the mop handle again, which rotated them back into the hallway. They could walk back to the library unobstructed . . . other than the darkness. Lainey pulled the handle, taking them back to the flame door. Gordy sagged in relief, smiling at Lainey when she reached over and patted his back.

"I'm going to need you to stop doing that," Shelley wheezed. "Getting a little motion sick here."

"But now we know we can get out," Lainey noted.

Shelley grumbled as Harlow stepped forward to examine the door. Lainey shone her flashlight at the little sliding panel, set at eye level so revelers could give the bouncer a password to prove they were cool enough to enter the speakeasy.

"Maybe we should 'speak friend and enter'?" Lainey asked.

"You never stopped with the nerd references, did you?" Harlow muttered.

Harlow had never been a *Lord of the Rings* fan.

"No, I did not," Lainey retorted. "Do you think they locked the secret speakeasy when they closed it down?"

She turned the handle and found that no, whoever had closed down the speakeasy had *not* in fact locked the door on their way out.

"I guess they figured the decoy garbage and secret passage were enough security," Lainey mused.

The group filed through the open door. Harlow patted the wall until she found a mechanism that looked remarkably like the switch for an electric chair—*bleak*—and flipped it, bathing the huge space in low, flickering light. It was sort of amazing that the dangling schoolhouse lights still worked, but it wasn't like the bulbs had burned in all that time, Lainey supposed.

In the back of the cavernous room, one of the lights sputtered and burst. It sent shards of glass and sparks hurtling to the floor. So there was that.

The room was cave-like but somehow cozy. An elegantly simple maple stairway led down into a room crowded with red-draped tables. The paneling, not nearly as expensive or pinkish as the lobby, offset walls that were a combination of dark red brick and natural granite bedrock. The Dante themes were minimal here: flames carved into the base of the bar, the sconces. Lainey wondered if the lack of underworldly decor was evidence that the architect had little to do with the speakeasy's construction.

Moldering red curtains hung at the end of the room, marking a stage where Lainey could envision jazz singers wailing over the tunes of a big band. But the main feature of the room was the bar, which ran the entire length of the space. It was backed by shelves that held dozens of bottles wrapped in browning linen and stacked on trays. It was as if the staff had shut the door and pretended this place never existed.

Were they really standing in a room that had been abandoned for almost a hundred years?

The DBags were overjoyed, whooping and high-fiving as if they'd just beaten the final boss standing between them and dominion over their newly purchased building. Shelley was more subdued, whispering to Kenny, suggesting shots, making notes. Did she ever do one task at a time?

"We're gonna look around, right?" Deke asked. "We can't just turn back after finding a legendary secret speakeasy!"

"It's a *lair*," Bryce whispered reverently.

"You can look around, *very* carefully," Milo told them. "And for the love of God, do not drink anything in those bottles. Who knows what's in them."

"We weren't gonna—"

Milo interrupted Bryce's protest with a sharp look. Bryce pinched his lips together.

"The booze itself could be valuable," Deke suggested. "Maybe selling a rare bottle of vino could offset the cost of construction."

"Any wine that you find down here would probably taste like vinegar," Milo told them.

"Stick with Harlow and Lainey," Shelley whispered to Kenny.

The next few minutes were kids-in-the-possibly-haunted-candy-store chaos. The supposedly responsible adults were suddenly transformed into children scampering around, exclaiming over every old poster and bottle.

In the noise and scramble, Lainey noticed that Cameron was nowhere to be seen. Where had he disappeared to?

"Do you think we can keep this as, like, our own secret clubhouse for when we use this place?" Bryce asked Deke. "I mean, the girl employees can't have everything, right?"

"Sure," Deke told him. "We can get this place wired right, set up monitors over there on the far wall. Keep the bar, but like clean it up. Put some couches over there when we want to watch hockey."

"That sounds almost wholesome," Lainey told Milo.

He shook his head and whispered, "Wait for it."

"Put a couple of poles in on the stage," Deke continued.

"There it is," Milo said, nodding. Lainey cackled and he gave her an amused grin in return.

Shelley motioned for Lainey to join Harlow, whom Kenny was filming as she rummaged behind the bar. Bryce was following close behind, repeatedly picking up and dropping antique bar tools.

"What's this?" Bryce asked, attempting to stick his hand through a rounded opening in the bar top, but it wasn't quite big enough for his rather sizable fist.

"It's a drop box," Harlow said. "You see them in gangster movies sometimes. Bars use them to keep their cash safe instead of having an unlocked stash in a rowdy bar. With modern ones, the cash drops right into a safe with a timer on it."

Harlow leaned down and pried open the sliding latch on the cabinet under the bar. Kenny dutifully moved into position to film it. Lainey drifted away from the shot, even as Shelley made frustrated hand gestures indicating Lainey should move back into frame.

"Maybe that Star diamond is there!" Deke exclaimed, running

around the bar to watch Harlow pop the door open. Lainey peered over the bar to see Harlow come up with a stack of very old leather-bound books marked **Crossings Hotel—Manager's Diary**.

"Ugh, it's just books," Bryce huffed. He caught himself and glanced at the camera. "Um, not that I don't enjoy books. But they're just not secret hidden treasure . . . Oh, look, a roulette table!"

"Very graceful exit," Lainey teased him. He shushed her, but he was grinning as he bounded over to admire the gambling equipment.

"I think these are like the captain's log, but for a hotel," Harlow said. "They go from 1920 to 1929."

"So they kept track of everything that happened in the hotel while the speakeasy was open, and then they tossed the books behind the bar, boarded the place up, and ran?" Lainey asked her. Harlow shrugged as she carefully turned the brittle yellow pages of the 1927 edition. "Anything interesting?"

"I don't recognize this language," Harlow said, sliding the book across the scarred oak bar toward Lainey. Kenny took a step back to reframe the shot. Lainey scanned the pages, which seemed to be written in fully punctuated paragraphs of the Latin alphabet, but not in a language Lainey recognized. She turned the book over in her hand. It was just a simple brown leather journal with lined pages. The dates were carefully penciled in English, but the journal entries had no discernible structure. Consonants and vowels all jumbled up into a word stew.

"Why would the dates be handwritten in English, but not the journal entries?" Harlow asked.

"The entries could be written in code," Lainey suggested.

"Do you think Mr. Wesley has the other diaries in his office?"

Harlow asked. "Could be interesting to ask him why these were stored down here but not the others."

"I think I'll leave that to you," Lainey said. "I think he likes you better than me."

"Because I've never insulted his greatest love." Harlow snorted.

"I never insulted the hotel," Lainey insisted. "I simply pointed out its inherent creepiness."

"I'll leave figuring all this out to you," Harlow told her.

"Ah, yes," Lainey muttered, carefully sliding the 1927, 1928, and 1929 books into her shoulder bag. "The homework."

"It likes you better than me," Harlow told her, making Lainey roll her eyes.

"Classic Harlow." Deke sighed, watching them with rapt attention. And then suddenly, his attention was redirected to Bryce, who had managed to get the roulette wheel spinning. "Hey, man, you can't play roulette without me!"

"And as soon as they might learn something . . . *poof*," Lainey murmured as Harlow turned to examine the framed posters on the walls. Kenny was filming Harlow examining the posters. That left Lainey free to explore.

She sat at the nearest poker table, carefully arranging her weight in a rickety wooden chair. Furniture was made for much smaller people a hundred years ago. Many of the tables in the speakeasy were dedicated to cards or craps or roulette. The designers seemed to have operated by the Las Vegas hotel principle that if you're going to sit, you're going to lose some cash.

The cards themselves were beautiful—thick, yellowed vellum printed with almost baroque versions of angels and demons as face cards.

Maybe the gambling was the point of the Crossings speakeasy?

Maybe illegal alcohol hadn't been illicit enough for this wild and privileged crowd? Lainey ran her hands over the ancient green felt. The staff hadn't even bothered to collect the cards from the table before closing this place down. What had made them so panicked that they just threw the door closed and ran? Had they planned to return at some point? Or were they too scared? Maybe Marguerite's disappearance had far more impact on the Crossings than anyone there wanted to admit.

"Ow!" Lainey yelped and withdrew her hand from a stinging sensation on the tabletop. Milo was immediately at her side. He took her hand in his, turning it over and checking it for wounds. Thankfully, there was no blood. Lainey wasn't prepared to deal with the era-appropriate tetanus.

"You OK?" Milo asked.

"It's fine," she assured him. "I just don't know what I touched—What the hell?"

Upon closer inspection, Lainey found tiny metallic bits on the felt, twinkling under the low light. It was like a hidden minefield of tiny, finger-poking gold pieces.

Lainey stood to get a better look at the table. Her foot scraped over some sort of gravel on the floor, but it made a grating metallic shriek between the wood planks and the sole of her sneaker. She panned her flashlight beam under the table and over more little bits of gold, twisted and bent. Someone had dismantled a piece of jewelry in a hurry. She crawled under the table, prompting Milo to ask, "Um, did you lose something?"

"Don't worry," she told him. "I will not hold DBag Games responsible if the table collapses on me."

"I'm not worried about that," he told her. When she looked up at him, he added, "I'm not *only* worried about that."

Lainey vaguely heard Shelley say, "Move over to the table. Focus on Lainey."

Milo crawled under the table with her. "So, what are we doing?"

She grinned up at him. Lainey had some reservations, but she liked Milo. He was prickly and practical but seemed earnest. However, she'd only known him for a day, and she'd been burned before. Then again, she was always suspicious of any man she dated. If she wasn't suspecting them of cannibalism or trying to steal her identity, she fretted about the regular horrible things women worried about when dating.

"I think I found something . . . don't know what," she said, bending closer to the floor so she could examine the gaps in the old wood grain. She was fully aware that her ass was sticking out from under the table, and given the proximity to the DBags and their pole plans, she was deeply uncomfortable. The camera crew was a secondary concern.

"Is this what your whole life is like?" Milo asked, moving his own flashlight beam around the floor. Lainey caught his wrist and pointed the beam back where she wanted it.

"Decidedly not," she told him. She opened her shoulder bag, unzipped a pocket, and pulled out a pair of long, pointed tweezers.

"You just carry those around?" he asked, shaking his head.

"No. Most of the time, I am at home with my cat in pajama pants, doing math," she told him. "Tweezer-less. Which is just as sexy as it sounds."

Beyond the table, Kenny's legs moved into view. He crouched, his lens focused on Lainey. For a second, she considered handing her tweezers over to Harlow, to let her be the one to find what she was rooting around in the floorboards to extract. But in that moment, she stared at the camera and made a choice.

In the name of sidekicks everywhere, fuck it.

When the tweezers finally closed around the object she was seeking, she carefully pulled it out into the open. The tiny jewel flashed brilliantly under Milo's flashlight, which he promptly dropped.

"Holy shit!" he cried, fumbling for the pink metal cylinder, nearly knocking Lainey on the temple.

She looked at him and tilted her head at a *What the hell?* angle.

"Oh, come on, like you wouldn't yell if our positions were reversed," he insisted.

Milo's exclamation brought Deke and Bryce running. Because she didn't want to be trapped under a table with them, Lainey very carefully crawled out, holding her hand under the tweezers because she was afraid of dropping the jewel and losing it among the dust bunnies. She carefully set the gem on the table's felt top.

While it wasn't a sizable stone, it still sparkled, all these years later. Lainey thought of the photo of Marguerite Devereaux in her pretty blue dress and the ropes of jewels around her neck. Even after the bomb shelter and secret doors, something about this shiny little rock made it all real. She was standing in the same room where Marguerite probably spent her last days before . . . dying? Running off with millions of dollars in diamonds and living the high life in Europe? Lainey still wasn't sure what had happened there. She was rooting for a cozy international retirement.

Had Timmy Dandridge dismantled the necklace at the card table to pay off gambling debts? Somehow that seemed like the real crime, a stupid, selfish boy destroying a work of art to cater to his own vices. Poor Marguerite. It had been about a year since Lainey had been on one of those aforementioned dates, but at least she'd never been trapped in an illegal subterranean gambling den with a rich, obnoxious asshole.

Then again, she was trapped in an illegal subterranean gambling den with *two* rich, obnoxious DBags. So what did she know?

Lainey supposed that was unfair. Deke and Bryce weren't the worst people she'd ever met. They were just cheerfully oblivious in a way that drove the responsible people around them mad with frustration.

"What did you find?"

Harlow stared down at the gemstone in Lainey's hand. Lainey watched the Five Stages of Harlow Drake flash over her face. Surprise, pleasure, annoyance, calculation, adaptation.

"Are we sure it's not just a rhinestone?" Harlow asked, picking it up and inspecting it under a flashlight.

Lainey waved helplessly at it. "No idea. I'm not an appraiser."

"A diamond will scratch glass, right?" Deke said. "Use it to scratch the mirror over there."

"A lot of things will scratch a mirror if you press hard enough," Harlow pointed out. "The only way to know for sure is to take it to a jeweler. They have all sorts of tests they can run to verify it."

"Yeah, unless you have a black light or something," Lainey suggested.

"Why a black light?" Deke asked.

"Real diamonds flare blue under a black light," Lainey said. "Or at least some of them do. Fake ones won't do that."

"I have a black light," Bryce said. "Back in my room."

"Do I want to know . . ." Milo began before shaking his head. "Never mind, I think it's better you don't tell me."

Lainey pulled a tiny plastic baggie from her shoulder bag and handed it to Harlow.

"What *don't* you have in there?" Milo asked.

Lainey shrugged as Harlow dropped the stone into the baggie.

"A jeweler's loupe? A thermal conductivity tester? Anyway, if you put the stone under a black light and it flashes blue, you probably have a real diamond. If it doesn't, just send it to a jeweler you trust."

"Do you think the Star of Sikkim could be down here somewhere? How cool would that be?" Deke asked her, his eyes wide, seemingly eager for Lainey to assure him that, of course, it was possible. And he would definitely be the one to find the long-lost diamond.

It was sort of sweet, seeing the more reserved of their financial overlords so excited over lost treasure and secret hiding places. It gave Lainey some confidence that she hadn't made a huge life-derailing mistake, traveling to the Crossings Hotel.

"OK, so we're going to film the whole thing over again, with Harlow under the table, finding the diamond," Shelley said. "Lainey, can we use your tweezers?"

Maybe just a minor life-derailing mistake, then.

"Sure," Lainey said, handing them over. Harlow crawled under the table.

"Wait, it doesn't make sense that I'm just carrying tweezers around with me in my pocket," Harlow said. "Lainey, can I borrow your bag?"

Lainey responded by taking a step back and clutching her shoulder bag to her middle like a much-beloved child. Her entire life was in this bag—ID, phone, charging cords, snacks, multiple tools. She couldn't just hand Harlow her whole life. Her bag was her identity, the source of her strength, and as sad and weird as that was—it was genuine, and it was her own.

"Wouldn't that cause continuity problems considering I've been carrying it around this whole time?" Lainey asked. Harlow's eyes narrowed at her. It wasn't the first time Lainey had told her no, but it was the first time she'd done it in front of the crew. It was odd how the presence of others could change a dynamic.

"Not really, since you've been hiding off-camera for most of the shoot," Shelley noted archly. To her credit, it was the first time Lainey had detected irritation in Shelley—well, irritation with Lainey, at least.

"Or you could simplify things and just find the stone out in the open," Lainey suggested. "It would probably be easier on Kenny's back if he didn't have to shoot under the table."

Behind Harlow's and Shelley's backs, Kenny mouthed, "Thank you."

"Well, that's less fun," Harlow said, pouting.

"Hey, Harlow!" Bryce yelled with all the enthusiasm of a toddler on Christmas morning. He was standing near the drop box, waving her over. "I think we found another one!"

Like a flash, Harlow was out from under the table and behind the bar. Kenny and Shelley followed closely. Lainey slowly turned in the opposite direction, still clutching her bag to her chest.

Lainey moved closer to the stage, just to give herself some space. The band's music stands were still in place, though one of the piano's legs had collapsed at some point. The decayed curtains hung loose over the stage, fluttering in the breeze.

Lainey paused, studying the way the moldering material moved.

Why would there be a breeze in a secret basement?

11

Lainey clicked on her flashlight and moved the curtain aside to find more music stands, some very dirty-looking fans made out of feathers, and a framed poster for a magician called the Mesmerizing Mephisto.

His act seemed to revolve around making chickens disappear. Yikes.

"Lainey?" She shushed Milo as she panned her light across the recesses behind the curtain.

"What are you doing?" he asked.

"Have you ever noticed how often you ask me some variation of that?"

"Yes, believe me, I have," he retorted.

"If there was a band or showgirls performing here, there had to be a dressing room, right? And there would have to be a special entrance for the entertainers that probably led directly to that dressing room," Lainey supposed. "Maybe the hotel management hadn't wanted the entertainment to use the same entrance as the guests. That seems on par with the decade in general."

Lainey moved farther into the space and could now make out an opening partially blocked by the Mephisto poster. Another curtain, rotting, split, and barely hanging on its rings, covered a set of stairs leading upward.

Before Lainey could climb the stairs, Milo reached out to stop her.

"Wait, we should tell—" His hand missed what he probably thought was her wrist in the dark, and he slid his hand across her hip.

Lainey glanced up at his face, seeing that he was staring down at his fingers. And for some reason, she decided to shine the flashlight at his hand, which he quickly snatched away. "I can't help but notice that you're awfully touchy for the guy who's supposed to be protecting his bosses from liability."

"I'm sorry," he told her. "It's dark."

"I'm not sorry," she told him. "Unless you try to shove me into a walk-in freezer, in which case, all bets are off."

"That's an interesting and very specific barometer," he replied as they walked carefully up the dark stairway.

"Well, when you figure out that the lunch lady skimmed thousands of dollars off of the cafeteria's burger budget, then used highly suspicious, lower-grade meat of a dubious origin—and fed it to schoolchildren—all so she could buy her son a pontoon boat, you tend to end up in a few freezers."

He stopped mid-step. She could feel his horrified stare, even in the darkness of the corridor.

"I tried to give Lunch Lady Sybil the benefit of the doubt. Bit me in the ass. After about an hour in the freezer, I decided not to do that anymore," she told him.

"Were you supervised at all as a minor?"

"Nope, not really," she said, and sighed. "In my mom's defense, your parents let you end up in the den of DBags as an undergrad."

He harrumphed as they rounded several corners and passed a door marked **DRESSING ROOM**. If she'd had more time, Lainey would have loved to snoop through the vanity stations of Prohibition-era performers and their makeup—probably poisonous. She pressed on. Because she couldn't wait to see what sort of weird magic trick the owners had designed to hide the speakeasy's staff entrance. Unless Mr. Wesley hadn't been lying when he said it was boarded up.

Hmmm.

Well, if it was bricked over, she could go back and explore the poisonous makeup.

Suddenly, Milo asked, "What's your cat's name?"

"Locard," she said. "After Locard's principle of forensics. It states that no matter what, contact leaves a trace. When someone commits a crime, they will leave evidence behind. Fingerprints or pollen or hair—*something* will connect them to the scene. And they also take something with them, like fibers or—"

"I know what Locard's principle is." He paused and cleared his throat before he added, "Because I saw it on *Jeopardy!* once."

She stopped what she was doing and stared up at him. He added, "My grandpa liked it. I stayed with him a lot after school when my mom was at work."

"Well, Locard is a *Who Wants to Be a Millionaire?* kind of guy," she told him.

Milo gasped in mock indignation, making her laugh. He rubbed a hand over the back of his neck, grimacing before admitting, "My cats prefer reruns of *Press Your Luck.* It's probably the bright flashing lights."

"How many cats do you have?"

He closed his eyes. "Four."

"Four!" she cried.

"It just happened," he exclaimed. "You would think a high-rise apartment building would be free of interfering elderly neighbor ladies, but Mildred next door decided I was lonely and needed one, and that was Frankie. Then she decided that Frankie needed a brother, so that was Sammy. And then Mildred got sick and needed to move in with her kids in Miami, but her daughter is allergic, so I ended up with Frankie and Sammy's parents, Copa and Cabana."

Lainey stared at him, and she thought he could feel it, even in the dark. He added, "Mildred was a showgirl in Atlantic City before she retired, very comfortably, I might add."

"That is so many cats," she told him.

"I have two Roombas to keep up with the shedding," he confessed sheepishly.

She paused, watching his silhouette as he moved up the dark staircase. She knew that it was dangerous to fall in like with an employee of DBag Games . . . but he was a cat person, so he couldn't be all bad.

"You seemed sort of freaked out back there," he said. "When they asked for your bag."

"I'm more freaked out by the small cat sanctuary in your apartment."

"They're my little pride of cats. They're a very calming energy at the end of the day, after I've been dealing with . . ."

When he paused, she suggested, "A snappy Chihuahua and a giant destructive Labrador disguised as people?"

He nodded. "Stop trying to change the subject. You seemed agitated back there. What's wrong?"

"Just trying to cling to the things that keep me, well, me."

"Harlow is . . . an unsettling presence," he admitted. "She kind of scares me."

"Me, too," she said.

"The flow of favors rarely runs in your direction," he observed. "Even when you were kids, you always seemed to be doing things for her, but other than the weed cookie incident—"

"I thought Harlow deleted that episode," Lainey muttered.

"She makes a couple of comments in other episodes about 'saving your ass from the weed cookie consequences' without context, which is very frustrating," he said. "I looked up incidents at your school. When a marijuana-impaired teacher runs out into traffic in front of the school and gets hit by a minivan full of kindergartners, there will be news coverage."

"The cops were ready to charge me with dosing Mrs. Halliday with weed cookies," she said carefully. "I would have been expelled, lost any chance of going to college. Sheriff Pleasant was actively seeking out a reason to send me to juvie. I think he had a vision board or something. My own mom started wondering if I did it, which hurt. Harlow was the one who gave Pleasant proof that it was another teacher's kid who did it. She obtained a printout of the passkey swipes from the school security system. She showed Mr. Burnham it was impossible for Mr. Cappick to have swiped in while he was teaching US history. His son Junior stole the passkey. Junior was excused from Mrs. Bunson's chem class after saying he had to go to the nurse's office, and he left the cookies in the lounge."

Lainey cleared her throat. Better to sanitize the story to avoid unpacking her and Harlow's messy history in front of a stranger, Lainey mused.

"Why would Junior want to give valuable drugs to his teachers?" he said.

She forced a deep breath through her nose. "To embarrass his dad. Cappick Senior had locked Junior's phone in his desk drawer because he threw a party while Senior was out of town," she said. "And to be fair, Junior was right. As soon as the school board found out it was Senior's lax approach to passkey security that led to Mrs. Halliday getting hit by a van, he was fired. They didn't care that she recovered. Then Junior was expelled."

"OK, but why did you get blamed for it?" he said. "Cafeteria ladies aside, I don't see you being a real troublemaker at school."

"Someone left the Post-it note version of a tip about me with the principal," she told him. Even in the dim light, she could see the outline of his frown. "Anyway, Harlow and I didn't share clothes or eyeliner. We didn't stay up late texting about our crushes. None of the adolescent girl friendship benchmarks were met. But we were loyal to each other until . . . we weren't. I'm assuming that given that you knew to google the weed cookie incident, you also occasionally watched the show?"

"Not in a creepy way. It was always Deke and Bryce's thing. But some weekends, when you had new webisodes, we used to play a drinking game, Spot Lainey. Anytime your face showed up on-camera, we had to take a drink. It meant . . . not a lot of drinking, but it was fun. Deke thought it was cute, how shy you were."

"Oh, *Deke* thought I was cute," she huffed as they climbed the stairs. "Deke did."

He rolled his eyes, even as he grinned. "I thought you were cute."

"Milo Wade is affected by my charms," she said, grinning at him.

"You know, my name's not even Milo."

She stopped short. "I'm sorry, what?"

He chuckled, sliding his arm lightly around her waist to encourage her to keep walking. When her feet began moving again, he took his hand away. "It's Mike. And then Bryce gave me the nickname 'Mike Myers.' And then 'Myers.' And then 'Miles.' And then 'Milo.' I don't think they even remember my real name. When the company was incorporated, they ordered me five thousand super fancy linen-paper business cards with 'Milo' on them."

"OK, so should I call you 'Mike'?"

"Honestly, I've been called 'Milo' for so long, I'm not sure I would recognize 'Mike' unless my mom yelled it from across a room," he said. "And it keeps the business stuff from getting too personal, you know?"

"Sure," she said. "Like a layer of detachment."

"Exactly."

They reached the top of the stairs. The landing centered around a black metal spiral staircase that led upward into . . . a large stone box? They tested the staircase to make sure it wouldn't collapse under them. It was surprisingly sturdy and didn't even wobble as they climbed into the large, open, rectangular box. There was a wide ledge they could climb onto, four feet under a flat stone lid. Lainey shoved at the lid, grunting, until it gave a little and slid aside. Milo helped her push it far enough that they could see the lid was on casters to make it easier to move.

Above them, Lainey could see an ornately carved stone ceiling that featured more angels than hellish creatures. Weirdly enough, the carved faces of singing angels were far creepier; their open mouths made them look like they were screaming.

Interesting.

Lainey and Milo popped their heads out of the stone box like a couple of suspicious meerkats.

Unlike the rest of the hotel, this little room was surprisingly funereal. There was a raised crypt on the other side of the small room marked **HINCHCLIFFE**. Tiny square panes of blue stained glass let in minimal light to display a wall of small urns opposite a wrought-iron black gate. Through the opening, they could hear the crash of churning waves. Lainey assumed they were near the water. The urns were labeled with tiny brass plaques naming various Hinchcliffes, without dates—which was sort of weird, considering they were in a mausoleum. There seemed to be a lot of Hinchcliffes with generic names like John and Margaret.

She turned to Milo and grinned. "Cute is meaningless. I was freaking adorable. And sneaky. And kind of manipulative. But fun. I made my own fun."

"I could tell," he said, helping her stand. They were careful not to tumble back down the spiral staircase into the abyss. He climbed over the lip of the sarcophagus easily, despite the dressy pants. "And you forgot 'smart.' You were terrifyingly smart."

"You're terrified of intelligent women?" she asked as he put his hands on her waist to help her step onto the floor without stumbling. She might have felt it was condescending . . . but he'd seen the webisodes. Her clumsiness was well-documented. His fingers flexed around her hips.

"Who can find secret passageways and get people arrested for murder? *Yes.*"

She laughed, gesturing around the room. "I suppose the mausoleum setting isn't helping."

"Not really." He shook his head. "So this is the staff entrance to the speakeasy—hidden in a fake mausoleum."

"We *hope* it's fake." Lainey nodded toward the crypt. "But you have to admit, it would keep the average hotel guest from poking around—out of sheer creepiness or, you know, common 'I don't want to be a grave robber' decency. Also, the architect made it extra creepy with all the angels."

"Should we head back?" he asked, nodding to the open crypt. "Shelley might freak out when she realizes we're missing."

"Shelley has her hands full with Harlow and the DBags," she reminded him. "Also, we'd probably get back to the hotel faster over land."

"I left the guys unsupervised. I was just so caught up in the fun of it all," he groaned. Lainey had the feeling that, cat companions aside, Milo didn't have a lot of fun in his life. "Rookie move. The last time this happened, I came back to a snow-cone machine that ran on tequila and three paternity suits from cart girls at the onsite mini-golf course."

She wanted to tell him she was sorry for distracting him. But she wasn't. Crawling through the butt-end of a fake mausoleum was the most fun she'd had in years. She inspected the mechanism on the inside of the gate, which locked on both sides. Why didn't anyone question why a repository for the dead locked from the inside? Shouldn't control of the gate be managed by the living people on the outside? Or maybe people asked questions and the hotel management's answer was "zombies"? It would probably be more accepted than *We don't want you to discover our illicit booze tunnel.*

Milo slid the crypt lid back into place, and Lainey inspected the heavy iron gate.

"What?"

"Some people get a little weirded out when I do this stuff in front of them," she said.

"What stuff? As long as it doesn't involve shooting milk out of your eye, I'll be fine," he said. When she stared at him, he added, "I have my own lunchroom trauma!"

She laughed as she pulled her lock-picking kit out of her shoulder bag. It only took a few twists and tweaks to get the gate lock turning. She grinned at him triumphantly as it swung open. He stared at her for a moment and then pressed his mouth to hers.

His lips were surprisingly soft and tasted of coffee and peppermint gum. It had been so long since she'd had a proper kiss, the kind that made her want to drag her hand through a man's hair and climb him like playground equipment. And while her entire body warmed at the slip of his tongue against her lower lip . . . they were in a crypt, even if it might be a fake, set-piece crypt. His hand slipped over her shoulder and down her arm—strictly PG areas reminding Lainey that Milo was supposed to be keeping corporate liability in mind. She pulled back to find Milo staring at her like she was some miraculous thing.

She could get used to that.

"You are one of the weirdest, most interesting girls I've ever met," he told her. His breath feathered over her mouth as she stared up at him.

Aw, man, I just kissed a guy in a crypt. I am *weird.*

And because her brain was an asshole that never shut up, she said, "This isn't some low-key attempt to swipe the DBags' internet-obsession target out from under them?"

Her heart sank when he pulled back from her. "Why would you ask me that?"

"People have sent me some really weird emails over the years," she told him. "Detailing my hypothetical relationships, how they would destroy my working dynamic with Harlow, how they would date one or both of us without either of us knowing. Kind of makes you suspicious of relationships. And people. And opening your email."

Milo bit his lip. "Oh, OK, I hadn't considered that."

"You seem really nice," she told him. "And I enjoyed kissing you."

"I *seem* nice?" he asked, using her wounded tone from earlier.

"All indications are you are a kind and thoughtful person," she told him, her tone serious.

"Likewise," he said as they walked out into the afternoon, shielding their eyes from the suddenly harsh sunlight.

How long had it been since she'd seen grass or the unfiltered sky? Lainey had gotten so used to the Crossings becoming her whole world so quickly, it was frightening. This was what happened when she started to chase a problem: She forgot the outside world existed. And it was her own fault as much as anything. She didn't know whether she'd missed Harlow, but she'd missed *this*—feeling capable, feeling smart, being the first one to figure something out. Being unpredictable. Responsible adult life had made her so . . . boring. She supposed that was part of growing up, and yes, it had made her mother a lot less anxious, but had she lost herself in the process? Made herself quieter? Smaller?

Then again, she did receive fewer threatening and/or creepy emails now. Not a total absence of threatening and/or creepy emails, just . . . fewer.

"You know, you could probably turn this experience into a book deal or speaking tour or something," Milo said.

"No thanks," she said. "I mentioned the weird emails, right?"

He laughed. She took a moment to admire how it lit up his whole face. This was the most relaxed Lainey had seen him, well, ever in their short time together, and she was glad she was the one to put that smile on his face. She leaned forward and pressed her mouth to his. "If you turn out to be a murderer, I'm going to be profoundly annoyed with you."

"Same."

Lainey shut the gate quietly, without locking it behind her. It seemed smart to have a quick unlocked escape route from the hotel. She dropped her lock-picking kit into her shoulder bag. Milo tried to peer inside it. "OK, what else do you have in there? More flashlights? A stun gun? A tiny forensics lab? Because it's starting to feel like a crime-fighting Mary Poppins bag."

She opened it so he could get a good look. He gasped. "I have so many questions. Most of them are about the glitter."

"I have informed my family that if I'm about to get taken down, I am dousing my attacker in glitter," she said.

"Smart," he said, nodding. "They wouldn't be able to wash it off for months."

"Exactly!" she cried, making him laugh. He put his arm around her waist as they walked toward the hotel.

The mausoleum was placed almost out of sight of the Crossings, probably on the farthest point of the island, close to the fishing pavilion and the accompanying dock. She couldn't imagine what the speakeasy performers must have thought, arriving on this island in the dead of night, sneaking into a very fake, very dignified mausoleum surrounded by Doric columns and, yep, more angels.

"See, there are some bright spots to Bantam Island," he said. "Look at that sky. Look at the waves. It's like a painting—and I won't say an artist, because I'm sure you will judge me based on the first one I can name."

She shrugged because he wasn't necessarily wrong about that. He asked, "Where else are you going to get a view like that?"

She shook her head. "I'm just waiting for the kraken's tentacles to reach up and sweep me into the water."

"You are just a bundle of cheerfulness, aren't you?" he asked, grinning.

"I learned at a very early age that when you expect the worst, you're prepared," she told him. "Hence, the shoulder bag of doom."

She looked around at the little graveyard arranged about the mausoleum. If the scattered headstones were also fake . . . the hotel management had gone to a lot of trouble. There were at least two dozen small squarish stones, most with names and dates crudely chiseled into their surfaces. Most of them had a death date listed between 1918 and 1930.

"I think this is an actual cemetery," she whispered.

"Yep," he said, nodding as he surveyed their surroundings. "Still, it's kind of nice out here. Peaceful. Which I guess is the point."

"What are you two doing out here?"

They didn't shriek. They did jump and grab at each other like a lifeline as Vern, boat pilot and quietest man on earth, walked into view. Apparently, the far side of the island was also where the hotel hid the maintenance shed.

"Vern, what the fuck?" Lainey growled. "That is *not* cool!"

"That producer lady is running around the hotel trying to find you two," Vern told them, smirking. "If you're gonna sneak around, you should probably find a more romantic location than the graveyard."

"Wait, we're not—"

Vern interrupted her. "Honey, you wouldn't be the first couple I found out here."

"Ew."

"I'll text Shelley." Milo sighed, pulling out his phone.

"Vern, is it normal for old hotels like this to have graveyards attached?" Lainey asked as Milo searched for a signal.

"You ever hear that most cruise ships have a morgue on board?" Vern asked. "Well, so do we. Got a little jail cell, too—a brig—'cause I guess some of the guests used to get pretty rowdy."

"Guests have died—" Lainey asked, then stopped midsentence. "Of course guests have died here, the hotel has been open for a hundred years. Sorry, that was a dumb question."

"At least you answered it yourself," Vern replied. "Saved me the trouble. People tend to put off traveling until they're old, when they don't feel like they have any rainy days left to save for. And sometimes that means dying at their destination. Most guests have next of kin to contact. But back in the hotel's heyday, if they couldn't find you or your family, or your family decided it was too much trouble to have you shipped home—they would bury you right here. Hasn't happened in a while. I think the big boom for the cemetery came around the Spanish flu. Some folks tried to use this place like a fancy quarantine zone, I guess. But they forgot the fact that they had to get food from somewhere and the supplies would mean contact with other people. Most of the occupants of the plots are hotel employees whose families couldn't afford to ship them back home."

Lainey pointed to a smaller headstone with a little bone shape carved into it next to the words FIDO, BELOVED COMPANION—1919. It was one of several pet headstones, including REX—1926, DOTTIE—1924, and one that simply read PEGGY.

Vern shrugged. "Some people like to travel with their pets."

Lainey shuddered. "That's so creepy. And they put it next to a maintenance shed?"

"It was the most out-of-the-way spot on the island. And the fishermen don't seem to mind because of the same thing that brought you two out here: privacy."

"We didn't—"

She stopped short when Milo put his hand on her arm. He held up his phone. "No use in defending ourselves. Also, my text went through. Shelley is happy we got out of the 'death trap' but made it clear that you should probably steer clear of Harlow at dinner."

She stared at his phone. "How far does that hotspot range go?"

Milo shrugged. "The guys sprang for the good gear."

"Well, I'll let you two get back to it," Vern said.

"I would resent the implication that I did naked things in a graveyard, but there were worse rumors in high school," she muttered.

They followed a well-trodden path through a thick pine forest that somehow blocked out the sight of the hotel. They trudged through trees that blocked even more light. Sometimes people forgot how wild the friendly Midwest could be. Sometimes, driving down the highway in autumn, Lainey would study the skeletal fingers of birch springing out of the ground and marvel at how the first European settlers had barged into these woods and believed they could tame them.

About twenty feet off the path, she spotted the dull gleam of metal among the trees. That was weird. Though it was a large and relatively worn-down property, she'd yet to see litter on the grounds of the Crossings.

"What are you doing?" Milo asked as she followed that silver glimmer into the shadows like a particularly gullible moth.

"Being a good citizen," she said, her feet snapping limbs as she walked carefully through the brush. She bent to pick up a small metal cylinder nestled in some creeping green vines. It looked like a combination of bottle and gas can with crimped edges and a wide round mouth. The lid was missing—so was the label, for that matter. Someone had meticulously peeled it off until all that was left was matte tin. She picked up the bottle and sniffed at the opening.

Nothing.

It just smelled sort of woodsy and musty, which, given the rustic surroundings, made sense. Was this a container from the museum display? Recalling that weirdly shaped gap in the case, Lainey turned the bottle over in her hands. It looked too modern and undamaged to be almost a century old, and it was round as opposed to hexagonal. And—final thought—why the hell would anyone peel clean a historical container and throw it out here? Why would anyone peel clean a *contemporary* container and throw it out here?

Both valid questions.

"Are you done admiring the garbage?" Milo called.

She shrugged and carried the bottle back with her.

"Your scout leader would be so proud of you, giving a hoot and not polluting," Milo told her as they continued down the path.

"Doubtful," Lainey snorted. "Troop Leader Marsha's last words to me were, 'You're an awfully mouthy little girl.'"

Milo frowned. "Last words?"

"Before she got arrested for betting our cookie money on the ponies," Lainey said.

He stared at her. "I still don't know when you're kidding."

"And yet you are intrigued, aren't you?" she retorted, dousing the comment with what was probably a little too much sauce. The shoulder wiggle and dramatic chin tilt didn't help.

Milo merely swallowed heavily and nodded.

His hand skimmed along her wrist, keeping her from toppling over when her foot slipped on loose gravel. The hand stayed wrapped around her arm as they passed what used to be a croquet lawn. The rusted wickets had almost disappeared into banks of weeds. Stone benches that flanked the lawn had broken and collapsed into heaps. It was like the trees were reaching out to reclaim the island's "play areas." When they walked by a highly decorative metal trash can—formed out of wrought-iron flames, because of course it was—she tossed the bottle.

"So, I've spent a lot of time over the last two days trying to figure out one thing," she said.

"Whether an egg-sized diamond is lying under the floorboards of the dining room?" he asked. "And how do we find it and then immediately fence it? And then buy a really big boat?"

"No, I mean, yes, those are all pertinent questions. But I will never buy a boat. I don't care how much money we can get from fencing an ill-gotten, possibly cursed, egg-sized diamond. Boats are always a bad purchase. Frankly, I'm a little disappointed in hypothetical you for considering it," she said, making him snicker. "Regardless of marine vehicle choices, that makes *two* things I was trying to figure out. The first thing was why you took on the thankless task of babysitting Deke and Bryce and being the least 'fun' guy in the room. How exactly did that happen? You know you don't have to stay friends with people just because you shared a bathroom in college, right?"

"I know I'm not painting a very nice picture of them in college," he admitted. "Or now, really. But they were different back when they were riding Red Bull highs in their dorm room, programming for days straight. They were decent friends to have then. Funny and shy and kind of goofy. I mean, they were self-centered, like all teenagers can be, but more aware of their surroundings and the stuff that came out of their mouths. And really smart. I don't think that comes across, now that they have money protecting them from things like planning and common sense. But they were doing stuff independently that would have gotten them jobs at Google or Apple the minute they graduated."

Lainey nodded, thinking of the same obliviousness she'd noted in Harlow. "OK, but that doesn't explain how it's, what, ten years later and you're still taking care of them."

"Sixteen years," he said. "And I stopped trying to explain it a long time ago. It just happened so slowly. We graduated, stayed Facebook friends. They kept in touch about their plans to launch some games and I thought, sure, everybody in their computer science classes wanted to invent the next *Candy Crush*. I was almost through law school and I was all they could afford in terms of legal representation—which basically meant I helped read over their early contracts and leases to make sure they weren't getting totally screwed over.

"I saved them from a couple of contractual traps they wouldn't have seen coming," he said. "They started making money. They helped me pay off my last year of law school and my student loans as a thank-you."

"And you felt obligated," she said, an uncomfortably familiar feeling churning in her middle.

"I kept meaning to get another job, find a firm that would have me. But they kept asking me about this project and that project, throwing money at me to make it worth my time. They paid me in stock in the company when it was still like a dollar a share. Which didn't seem like much then, but now it's basically my retirement plan. I've paid off my parents' house. I've paid for both of my brothers' college tuition. Every time I get close to quitting, they do something that reminds me of the lovable goofs they used to be. When my father was diagnosed with cancer, Deke chartered a plane to fly Dad for a consult with the best doctor in the country for his condition. They made sure he had everything he needed, made sure I could take off the time I needed to help my parents. It's stuff like that that keeps me around. And I can't complain. Without them, I would probably be working for a bank somewhere, getting cursed out for turning down loans."

"But you would be called by the correct first name," she noted.

"I never should have told you that," he said. "What about you?"

"I mean, 'Lainey' is a pretty normal nickname for 'Elaine.' My mom started calling me that when I was a baby," she said, giggling when he huffed and rolled his eyes.

"No, I mean, what do you think you would be doing if you'd never met Harlow?" he asked.

She gestured at the woods around them. "Two roads diverge and all that. I either would have gone down a weird Batman spiral where I spent my whole life trying to chase down the people who hurt my dad or I would be a regular accountant, no forensics involved. Maybe a spouse, two kids, and a dog."

"Those are two very different paths," he said.

"I really like my job. The challenge of it. And yeah, it's more telling people what they don't want to hear, but . . . I don't have a justification after that."

"You know, we could use someone like you in our finance department," he said.

She considered it for a moment. Working for a goliath tech company would be dependable, steady income, and she could probably wrangle a ridiculously high, possibly undeserved salary from her biggest fans . . . but she would also face the possibility of Deke and Bryce dropping by her office for daily doses of Lainey, making her dance like an organ grinder's monkey. And if she didn't dance well enough, they could take it away anytime they wanted. Then she'd be right back in this financial abyss. Better to keep her autonomy and a shred of dignity. So she shook her head. "No thanks."

"I don't blame you," he told her. "I keep telling myself, it's not *my* money, it's Deke's and Bryce's money, so it hasn't changed me. But just being near that kind of 'freedom' makes you sort of emotionally lazy. The kind of money they're dealing with brings out your negative traits and makes them so much more dramatic. But I like to think I am making a difference in how they do things. Most of the time, I'm able to slow down the worst of their impulses."

"Really?"

"Oh, yeah, the campaign for the last *Dragon Lord* game could have been way more offensive," he assured her. "So, while I am not the most popular guy in the room with Deke and Bryce or any of their yes-men, the board loves me."

"Could the DBags be fired if the board gets tired of their antics?" she asked.

"Possibly. The board enjoys the clout—and the money—that their stupid ads bring in, but they're only willing to put up with so much. As it is, Deke's and Bryce's creative control over the company has been limited. If their public image continues its descent, they're going to lose control over financial decisions, like buying properties like this. And they'd probably be replaced by an equally annoying but less misogynistic cartoon spokesdog or something. They would hate it, even if it saves their own company. I'm not even saying it would be a bad idea if it happens. I've set up their contracts to make sure they're in good shape if they're forced out of authority. They would have some chance of continuing with the company in a capacity that would make them *mostly* happy."

Milo was talking like someone who was planning to leave. Lainey wondered if offers had been made by any of those board members who loved Milo so much. She understood the impulse to protect someone from themselves, but she'd also found out how dangerous and cyclical that could be. The longer Milo spent keeping Deke and Bryce from feeling the full impact of their choices, the longer he would be stuck keeping Deke and Bryce from feeling that impact. But she also knew Milo had to get through that separation process on his own.

"Do you think this project is going to help their reputation?" she asked.

"The hotel renovation? Definitely not," he scoffed. "Even if it does improve employee morale to be invited out here, the renovation is going to be ridiculously expensive and it's going to come across as extremely insensitive. But bringing justice for a century-old murder case . . . that could help."

"Would you ever leave?"

"I could," he said. "I think I could escape with my reputation intact, even if my entire work experience amounts to defending my clients' right to make game characters with inappropriate pun-based names. But it would feel weird working anywhere else."

They'd walked a little farther along the trail when she asked, "So the cartoon spokesdog . . . Would he be named DBag the Dog?"

"Probably," he said. "Particularly if you mention it to the guys."

"I should probably trademark it now," Lainey mused.

He sighed. "I am caught between abject dread and really wanting to see you convince the guys to use that trademark so they'll pay for it."

"I could do it," she told him. "They have very poor decision-making skills when it comes to me and Harlow."

He muttered, "Trust me, I'm aware."

HARLOW DRAKE INVESTIGATES . . .

Webisode 25, "Lainey Needs a Favor"

Draft Episode—Not Posted—April 22, 2008

TRANSCRIPT EXCERPT

HARLOW: You come to me, on the eve of Spirit Week, to ask me for a favor.

LAINEY: I do not know why you are doing a bad *Godfather* voice right now. I am in *trouble*, Harlow.

HARLOW: It's not that big of a deal.

LAINEY: They think I poisoned a teacher.

HARLOW: They think you laced some cookies with weed, not exactly the same thing. Also, how stupid does a teacher have to be to eat cookies left in the teachers' lounge with no note?

LAINEY: There was a note. It said "Help yourself." Mrs. Halliday did. She ate three of them, freaked out, pelted her freshman class with dodgeballs because she thought they were whispering about her, and then ran out a side door and into traffic. Because that's what happens when someone who has never tried weed suddenly has three doses in them. She got hit by a passing minivan. She has *serious* injuries. The sheriff is looking to charge whoever did it with attempted murder.

HARLOW: And somehow, someone thinks *you* did this?

LAINEY: Mr. Burnham said I was named on a note somebody dropped in the Comments and Concerns Box.

HARLOW: The Narc Box.

LAINEY: Of course it's a freaking Narc Box. It's an anonymous comment box where you snitch on your classmates. What I don't understand is why Mr. Burnham is even listening to this crap.

HARLOW: Yeah, the only time you ever got into trouble was for unauthorized use of the library computers.

LAINEY: Also, I'm a frakking sophomore! People don't sell drugs to underclassmen. Too much risk involved!

HARLOW: Also, because that would be the most polite drug deal to go down ever. *Excuse me, good sir, I would like to purchase some of your delightful marijuana, please.*

LAINEY: That is not funny, even if it is pretty much true. How people treat service workers shows who they are, and that includes drug dealers—you know what, just, never mind! My point is that no one at school would sell me drugs after I started hanging out with you. People think you're worse than the Narc Box.

HARLOW: You know you love me.

LAINEY: I admire the way your brain works. What annoys me is the chaos that brain brings into my life. I was questioned by the cops, in one of the *real* interrogation rooms. Not the usual "pull us into the office and lecture us in private" thing they normally do.

HARLOW: They don't have any proof it was you, Lainey.

LAINEY: Are you *new*? People don't give a s**t about proof in this town!

HARLOW: Easy, I'm going to have to bleep that out.

LAINEY: Oh my God, are you recording me right now?

HARLOW: Of course I am. For one thing, our viewers are going to be furious on your behalf, which will drive up clicks. And if anyone local is watching, they might contact us with valuable info.

LAINEY: Locals aren't going to care about me. They care about quick fixes and keeping the gossip mill going. That's how I ended up in the Narc Box in the first place.

HARLOW: Look, I'm going to help you find the cookie culprit. We'll turn them in and clear your name.

LAINEY: This is a real-world problem, Harlow. I do not appreciate the alliteration. My mom had to retain a lawyer. She didn't trust your dad, which I think says a lot about how they feel about the show.

HARLOW: Which just means that we'll have to work that much harder. Come on, Laines, we can fix this.

LAINEY: F**k.

HARLOW: Bleep button.

LAINEY: Shut it.

12

Lainey was delayed to dinner by her phone, which she supposed would be a self-involved excuse. She was distracted by having a signal after she obtained the hotspot password from Milo. She didn't trust Deke or Bryce, but she trusted Milo. She supposed that was progress.

The sheer volume of texts and emails she had waiting for her after just two days of signal absence was proof that modern life was a digital hellscape. Also, her creditors were getting very tired of waiting for her payments.

Lainey distracted herself by texting her neighbor to ask after Locard and using her phone's internet browser to search various letter combinations from the manager's diaries to confirm that they weren't a language she just didn't recognize. After a couple of searches, recommendations started popping up on how to recognize the signs of a stroke, which seemed ominous. So she searched for codes and ciphers and the various rules for setting them up. And while that was fascinating, something about their little crypt adventure was nagging at her brain—besides the fact that she'd kissed a man in a pet cemetery despite the horror genre's many warnings on PDA at burial sites.

Could there really be that many people named "Dorothy" and "James" in the Hinchcliffe family, or had the plaques in the crypt been entirely made up? And the headstones? How many of those were for show? She was midway through a search of popular nicknames in the 1920s when the dreaded **Cannot connect to the internet** message popped up. She checked her Wi-Fi signal. Apparently, the DBags' internet powerhouse had been knocked offline.

Utterly without informational input, Lainey dressed far less formally for this dinner, donning a simple black sheath and flats, because she did not want to be pulled into another secret passageway wearing dinner heels. She considered that maybe she could be overthinking it, but that afternoon she'd emerged from a fake sarcophagus like she was climbing out of a hatchback. So . . .

The mood lighting in the lobby was even spookier than usual, thanks to the towering storm clouds outside. Weather seemed to roll in faster on a lake. The gathering clouds blocked out the sunset, throwing deeper shadows across the beehive-shaped hell sculpture. She hadn't thought that thing could look any creepier, but the Crossings' architecture continued to defy expectations.

The mood in the Beatrice Room was as unsettled as the storm outside the floor-to-ceiling windows. On one end of the room, Deke and Bryce were jubilantly trying to open a bottle of champagne with a sword while Kenny filmed. Milo stood to one side, visibly restraining himself from wrenching the blade away from them, even as Deke yelled, "Come on, man, we found not one but *two* secret Scooby-Doo entrances in one day! The diamonds flashed blue under the black light! We're on a treasure hunt and we're *winning*! We've got to celebrate!"

Findlay and Gordy were already seated at their table, chatting quietly. They smiled and waved to Lainey as she walked in, but stayed in their seats. Mrs. Maynard and Mr. Spiros appeared to be having a very intimate discussion by the bar. Interesting. Maybe this wasn't the first time they'd met? Lainey couldn't imagine Mr. Spiros involved in a torrid affair with . . . anyone.

Mr. Wesley and Harlow appeared to be arguing close to the bar, with Shelley trying to mediate. Cameron was hovering nearby, maybe eavesdropping? Lainey couldn't help but wonder where he'd been while the others had been exploring the speakeasy, but figured that, given her own wanderings, she probably shouldn't bring it up.

She approached just in time to hear Mr. Wesley say, "I will not confirm that the Crossings managers willingly broke the law. I don't care if the Volstead Act was repealed—"

Harlow looked annoyed, if stunning, in her ultramarine-blue bodycon dress and sky-high heels that Lainey wouldn't have been able to negotiate a flat surface in, much less stairs. It was a definite departure from last night's dinner outfit, but Harlow knew she'd be filmed tonight as part of the celebration. Nothing was an accident with Harlow. "Oh, save it, Mr. Wesley. Why bother with writing the diaries in code if the managers were perfectly happy for the public to know what was happening in the hotel?" Harlow asked. "Why not skip the diaries altogether?"

"I'm not acknowledging that the managers might have dissembled, but even if they couldn't be open in their actions while taking care of the guests during Prohibition, standards had to be maintained," Mr. Wesley insisted. "The diaries weren't merely an exercise in ego. How else were the staff to recall the guests' favorite liqueurs, their favorite table games and dealers, their waking hours? The managers had to find a way to provide the best possible service without implicating themselves. I would imagine that when Prohibition ended, they—with great reluctance, I'm sure—enclosed the diaries in the speakeasy. Now that alcohol and merriment could be enjoyed out in the open, there was no need to acknowledge those dark days."

"And the rest of the diaries are written in noncoded text?" Shelley asked.

Mr. Wesley nodded reluctantly.

"I don't suppose you have the key for decoding the ones we have?" Harlow muttered.

"Honestly, no," he said. "And I don't see why we should delve into those ledgers in the first place. There's no sense in digging up the past."

Lainey wondered if Mr. Wesley was aware that the three volumes she took, the "homework" she'd been assigned in the speakeasy, were currently in her room, hidden in her dresser among her jeans. Given the look on his face, she thought maybe she should find a better hiding spot. She scratched idly at an itch on her right palm, close to the web between her thumb and forefinger.

"That's the whole reason we're here!" Harlow shouted, making Mr. Wesley wince. While the DBags didn't flinch at the raised voice, Mrs. Maynard and Mr. Spiros glared at her from across the room. Lainey supposed shouting wasn't the preferred aperitif for most people. "It's not like you're protecting some pristine reputation for the hotel. You just had a guest die in his bed!"

Shelley laid a gentling hand on Harlow's arm. "I understand

that you don't feel the need to cooperate with us, Mr. Wesley, but I do expect that you wouldn't stand directly in the way of production."

"There's nothing in those diaries that applies to your program," Mr. Wesley insisted. "Most entries include minutiae, guest populations, significant check-ins and checkouts, the most popular dishes from the restaurant. It was meant to help predict patterns in guest behavior before we had computers that would do that sort of thing for us. And of course, notable guests are recorded, notable incidents. It's a history of the hotel. And it's precious. I did attempt to negotiate to take them with me when I leave the island, but your Mr. Wade refused me."

"And you didn't think to share this with us?" Harlow asked.

"I told you I wouldn't help your group gather any evidence that would damage the Crossings' reputation," Mr. Wesley replied. "Those ledgers are property of the hotel, and you have no right to them. If anything, I should place them in the archive so they might rest with the other Crossings artifacts."

"Mr. Taggert and Mr. Bagwell own the hotel and its contents, and therefore they also own the ledgers," Shelley reminded him.

Harlow rolled her eyes and waved to the DBags' table. In a voice that sounded remarkably like a pampered princess asking for Daddy's car keys, she called, "Hey, Deke, Bryce—can we have all the manager's diaries from Mr. Wesley's office?"

"Sure, Harlow!" Bryce called back. "Take whatever you need."

Harlow turned a smirk to Mr. Wesley. "We can take whatever we need."

Mr. Wesley's entire mouth seemed to clench. Lainey braced herself for the hotel manager to finally snap, but he seemed to snatch control of his facial features from the ether and arranged his face into a pleasant, customer service expression. "Of course. I'll deliver them to your room."

"Oh, don't do that," Harlow told him. And for a moment, Lainey worried that Harlow would tell him to deliver the ledgers to *her* room. "I don't have the space to trip over them. I'll just come to your office tomorrow morning and look them over."

"Of course," Mr. Wesley practically seethed. "Please, make yourself comfortable in my office."

He turned on his heel and walked through the swinging doors to the kitchen. Lainey watched the rigid set of his shoulders and felt sorry for Mr. Wesley. She knew it wouldn't make him feel better to know that this wasn't personal. Harlow treated most people as if they were useful office equipment.

"Lainey." Shelley waved her over to the bar, setting aside her gimlet but not her phone. Never the phone. "Come have a drink. We need to talk a little bit before dinner. I'm sitting with you and Harlow tonight."

Harlow's bee's knees sat untouched on the bar. Bryce motioned her over for a glass of champagne, which Harlow happily took. Vern nodded to the abandoned cocktail.

"You can take that one, if that's what you're after," he told her, absent-mindedly polishing a glass. He stared past her toward Mrs. Rowland. The lady was resplendent in a peach-colored dress with long, floaty sleeves. Cecelia Rowland knew how to dress. Lainey couldn't blame Vern for looking.

Mrs. Rowland approached the bar, nodding at Deke and Bryce, who were attempting a sword-versus-baguette fight near their table. She murmured, "Further proof that God protects idiots from themselves."

Lainey chuckled but covered it with a cough, earning a wink from Mrs. Rowland, who glanced down at the spare bee's knees, sniffed in disdain, and said, "Gin rickey, please, Vern."

"Actually, I think I'll try a rickey, so make it two, please," Lainey said, making him shrug and turn to his bar tools.

Lainey looked to Shelley, who was tapping out a text message on her phone. The producer reached for her drink with her free hand and accidentally picked up the saltshaker. She lifted it halfway to her face before she realized the difference. She returned it to the bar top, shooting an embarrassed look at Lainey as she picked up her glass.

"Is this about my wandering off? Because I didn't mean to worry you. I was thinking of it like location scouting," Lainey said.

Shelley glanced across the room at Harlow, who was giggling into her champagne glass. Lainey hoped the drink didn't include broken bottle bits. Poor Milo seemed to be wincing with every glass the DBags poured. Cameron had, of course, followed her, and was hovering nearby.

Shelley absent-mindedly sipped her drink. Her eyes flicked toward her phone screen several times. Lainey could practically *feel* the woman's urge to return to it. Instead, she looked at Lainey and said, "I'm not particularly upset about it, and we'll film the crypt discovery with Harlow later. *But* it would have been better to get both of your real reactions to finding it, together. I can't help but notice that you're not really working *with* Harlow. You're kind of off doing your own thing and then you bring Harlow what you've found. It's not really communicating any trust between you to the audience. Do you think you could work on that?"

Lainey opened her mouth to placate Shelley, but she realized that it would be a stretch to give that assurance. Lainey didn't trust Harlow enough to be completely candid with her about the information she'd already found at the hotel.

And after the fast and loose way Harlow played with facts, she didn't trust Harlow to do Marguerite Devereaux's story justice, either. Lainey wondered exactly when she'd decided that was her problem or job. She just didn't want to see Marguerite made into some lurid piece of Harlow's personal lore.

"Look, Harlow's future at the network is nonexistent at this point, but if she can pull this off, turn the tide of public opinion . . . it will be legendary," Shelley told her. "And I want to be a part of that. After watching you two interact today, I would understand if you don't want to help her, but would you help *me*?"

Lainey lifted her chin. She liked Shelley. But she didn't want to see Shelley's wagon hitched to Harlow's, so there was only so far Lainey was willing to go to help this effort.

"I will do my best to be more cooperative," Lainey said carefully. She noticed a weird watermark on the bar, white and crusty, with squarish angles. And yet all of the glasses in the room, from the rickeys to the gimlets, were round.

Maybe it was from one of the gin bottles.

Vern set the rickeys in front of Lainey and Mrs. Rowland. He stared at the abandoned bee's knees on the bar, frowning. Lainey had worked in enough restaurants during her college years to know a "dying" cocktail when she saw it.

"I'll take it to Harlow's table," she told Vern.

"You're a good egg," Vern replied and moved away to tend to Mrs. Maynard. Mrs. Rowland winked at Lainey and left to join Gordy and Findlay at their table.

Lainey took a sip of her rickey, citrusy and bubbly with the expected after-bite of gin. It wasn't terrible. She supposed she could see how Mrs. Maynard drank them steadily every time she visited the Crossings.

"Ladies and gentlemen, if you'd please take your seats," Mr. Wesley announced. "You'll notice the table assignments have changed to keep your conversations effervescent and fresh, so please look for your name on the place cards."

Lainey frowned. Had she and Milo missed Mr. Wesley's dinner announcement the night before?

"Please make sure my Crystalline Greens juice is served with the salad course. Remember, fresh ginger, not dried," Harlow called to Tommy, who frowned and ducked into the kitchen. Shelley headed toward their table, her posture tense as she checked the place cards, and took her seat.

Given the expression on Tommy's face, Lainey thought the staff had forgotten Harlow's special drink powder existed. Lainey wondered how the juice regimen figured into the number of cocktails Harlow was consuming with dinner, but she knew better than to ask that aloud.

Lainey carried the bee's knees glass, careful not to spill a drop, and set it next to Harlow's place card, close to Shelley's free hand. Shelley was tapping that hand on the table—precariously close to her own gimlet—while scrolling on her phone. She glanced at the fourth seat at their table and grimaced.

"Mr. Wesley might be trying to punish us for all the stress we're causing him," Shelley said. "It's that loud Southern lady—Mrs. Maynard."

Damn. Lainey was hoping the old-school cruise-style seating

gods had assigned Milo to her table. No such luck. She supposed that Milo needed to stay close to the DBags to prevent champagne-related injuries.

"Oh, she's nice enough," Lainey assured her. "She just talks. A lot. All in one breath."

Shelley's phone chirped, prompting her to look down at it. "Sorry, I need to answer this."

"That grumpy fisherman got stuck at the boys' table and doesn't seem very happy about it," Harlow commented as she took her seat. She still had a bit of champagne left in the bottom of her flute. She frowned at the bee's knees by her plate, as if she wanted someone to explain it. "So, what are you two talking about?"

"I was just telling Lainey that I think she needs to spend a little more time with you on-camera, stop lurking so much in the background," Shelley said, already half-checked-out of the interaction. Her thumb flicked over the screen as she opened a text. From her angle, Lainey couldn't make out the words, but she saw enough to recognize all-caps ranting.

"What? Why?" Harlow scoffed, draining the last of her champagne. "Lainey doesn't like being in front of the camera."

"That's really never been our thing," Lainey added. She reached for her own glass and noticed the beginnings of a bumpy red rash on her right palm, close to the webbing between her thumb and forefinger. What the hell? What could she have touched to leave that—

Lainey groaned quietly, not that Shelley or Harlow would notice. Poison ivy. She had been so curious about the stupid bottle in the woods that she hadn't noticed she'd picked it up out of what was probably a patch of poison ivy.

"I just think it's going to flow a lot more naturally if you're not shouting questions at her from behind Kenny," Shelley said, still focused on her phone. Lainey couldn't blame her. She would also like to not be a part of this conversation.

"I told Shelley that *has* always been our thing," Harlow shot back. Shelley wasn't looking at her, and Harlow was starting to glare. Divided attention had always been one of her pet peeves.

"I just think we need to be a little more intentional as we set up shots," Shelley said absently. "Lainey is a resource, and you're not using her. I really think we've got something here. The content we have is really good, and I don't think we should waste the opportunity, Harlow."

"So you went into this project thinking it wouldn't be any good?" Harlow asked.

Shelley finally looked up as she reached for her drink with her free hand. "That's not what I said."

"You were going to shove me off to webisodes," Harlow said quietly, through her teeth. Her expression could have been interpreted as a smile from across the room. Way, way . . . way across the room. "Nobody watches this network's webisodes."

"We have a very faithful online following. We expected healthy numbers," Shelley said, her fingers closing around the bee's knees from Harlow's place. She drank deeply from it and didn't seem to register that it was the wrong cocktail. Lainey figured that was Harlow's fight. A sidekick could only be expected to manage so much.

Meanwhile, Lainey continued to discreetly scratch at her hand. If she didn't get ahold of some antihistamines soon, her hands would swell to the size of Mickey Mouse gloves.

Mr. Wesley had said that Mr. Hornsby's hands were swollen when he died.

Dammit.

What if Mr. Hornsby hadn't been exposed to his allergen through food? Allergic reactions could be topical, right? What if he had touched something covered in nut . . . stuff? There had to be a better way to phrase that. What could Mr. Hornsby touch that would make his hands swell up and a rash spread all over his body?

"It's a step backward," Harlow seethed. "I don't go backward. Lainey, say something."

Lainey snapped out of her hand-related reverie and found the focus to ask, "I still get paid?"

"We will fulfill our contract with you," Shelley said, clearing her throat and taking a longer swallow of Harlow's drink. She glanced down at the drink and seemed to finally register that it wasn't her own. "Sorry, I was distracted. Vern, can we get another drink for Harlow, please?"

"I think Harlow would rather have more of this champagne!" Bryce crowed, waving the bottle around in his usual boisterous, careless manner. Poor Tommy had to duck out of the way before he was clobbered while carrying a tray of salads.

Harlow frowned at the emptied glass before turning her glare on Lainey. "Is that really all you're worried about?"

"Yes, Harlow, cleaning up the mess my choices left me in is kind of a priority to me," Lainey shot back.

"What is that supposed to mean?" Harlow demanded.

"I think you know what I mean," Lainey told her, holding Harlow's angry blue-eyed gaze. Beside them, Shelley cleared her throat even louder. It felt like a hint that they needed to lower their voices.

The corner of Harlow's mouth twitched as she said, "I don't know anything about your life."

"Well, look at all the lovely young ladies at this table!" a Southern voice twanged behind them.

"Hi, Mrs. Maynard," Lainey said, putting on a more pleasant expression. It wasn't Mrs. Maynard's fault she was walking into the world's most awkward conversational snake pit.

"Oh, honey, I told you to call me Cinda," she said as Tommy pulled out her chair. "Now, Miss Drake, I have all kinds of questions for you. I hope you don't mind an old woman's curiosity."

Harlow frowned. "Actually, we were just having a business-related conversation, if you wouldn't mind sitting somewhere— *Ow!*"

Harlow shot Lainey a vicious look as she leaned forward to rub at her shin where Lainey had kicked her. Lainey withdrew her foot, bumping the table. It toppled Harlow's empty flute and would have taken out the bee's knees if Mrs. Maynard hadn't steadied the glass.

"Oops, careful there," she said cheerfully. Her hand hovered protectively over the glass as she put it back near Harlow's place setting. Lainey stared at the thin remains of the opaque yellow cocktail. It looked . . . darker than Lainey remembered it. Maybe Vern had added more honey syrup tonight? Did honey syrup go bad?

Mrs. Maynard began, "Now, Miss Drake, when you're researching an episode—"

"Oops!" A crash behind them had Harlow standing and turning toward the window. Apparently, Deke and Bryce had failed in their efforts to open a second bottle of champagne and had sent the intact bottle flying into the window. It had bounced off a pane of glass intended to withstand a Wisconsin winter and shattered on the floor—spraying Cameron all over with champagne. Deke and Bryce seemed to find it highly amusing. Milo did not.

Cameron didn't, either, stalking out of the room saying, "I'm going to go change."

Laughing, Harlow got up to dutifully check "poor Bryce" over for glass wounds—which felt like she was laying it on a little thick.

When Lainey's attention returned to the table, she saw that the bee's knees glass was toppled to its side. Shelley was rubbing at her throat. Mrs. Maynard was staring at the producer, her brow furrowed.

"Stress can be a trigger. Sometimes that happens when dealing with the talent," Shelley said, pulling her inhaler from her handbag. She laughed awkwardly, but it changed into a cough. Her embarrassed expression was replaced with confusion. She rubbed at her throat, clearing it loudly. The clearing became a deeper raspy cough.

"You all right?" Lainey asked, frowning as Shelley's face flushed red with the force of her hacking. There was a strange smell on her breath, like a cheap candle, sweet and burned black.

Shelley nodded, puffing on her inhaler.

"Vern, can we get a glass of water, please?" Lainey called.

Shelley stood suddenly, bumping their table and fully toppling their cocktail glasses. She stumbled toward the dining room door, fumbling her phone and then her purse as she pressed the inhaler to her face. She was lurching like a zombie, dropping the inhaler as she careened through the door and into the hallway.

"Milo!" Lainey yelled, following Shelley's progress down the hall toward the Rosemont Archive. Where was Shelley going? Lainey stopped to pick up the inhaler. She reached Shelley just as she was bending at the waist to cough. It was a loud grating sound that echoed against the high ceilings. She stood, back bowed, as she clawed at her throat, screaming before dropping to the floor in front of the archive.

Lainey tried to hold the inhaler to Shelley's mouth, but Shelley knocked it aside with a contorted hand. Milo came running, but Mrs. Rowland reached them first. The others simply hovered in the hallway, watching this horror play out.

"I'm a nurse," Mrs. Rowland reminded them. "Is there a first-aid kit?"

Vern nodded and disappeared into the dining room. Lainey pushed to her feet, eager to get out of Mrs. Rowland's way. Mr. Wesley stood in the doorway of the kitchen, his face twisted in abject dread.

Chef Andre was standing behind him, his face red and haggard. He was already protesting, "There was nothing wrong with the food!"

"Not now, Andy!" Mr. Wesley barked.

"Call an ambulance," Lainey yelled to Deke and Bryce, who were standing there, phones in hands. Were those fuckers about to *film* this? Kenny wasn't even filming this.

Lainey didn't have her shoulder bag with her. She didn't have any of the things that might have helped in this situation. Why had she chosen to carry this ridiculous tiny purse to dinner?

Meanwhile, Milo was tapping frantically on his phone. "It's not going through."

"The Wi-Fi's out," Deke yelled, running toward the Gentlemen's Lounge. "I'll go reset the router."

"Where's he going?" Mrs. Maynard asked.

"The company set up a Wi-Fi hotspot in the Gentlemen's Lounge," Lainey told her. "It's how their phones are running."

Mrs. Maynard frowned. "The *what* lounge?"

Shelley was still spasming on the floor, groaning piteously. The fear in her wide brown eyes was feral, an animal caught in a trap knowing that she would die. Mrs. Rowland calmly checked Shelley's vitals and asked her questions, which Shelley couldn't respond to. She attempted to fold Shelley's hand in hers, but Shelley was thrashing so hard, it was difficult to hold on. Lainey felt a flush of guilt at her relief when Shelley's eyes clenched shut.

How long would it take for paramedics to get here, even if they could get a call through? Could the DBags summon a company helicopter? Every time Milo tapped his phone's dial pad, the call refused to go through. Lainey could hear the beeps across the hall. She remembered her phone's internet connection had gone down before dinner . . .

Oh no.

Mrs. Maynard clutched at Lainey's arm, pulling her farther away as pinkish foam bubbled from Shelley's lips. She was turning blue, a pale shade that seemed to creep across her face like she was drowning.

"Come over here with me, hon. You look like you're gonna pass out," Mrs. Maynard said in an accent that sounded . . . wrong. Flat, nasal—not at all the mellifluous Southern tones she'd been throwing at Lainey for the last two days.

Shelley's teeth ground in pain even as the pinkish foam dribbled from the sides of her mouth. She arched off of the floor in her agony. Lainey swore she heard something snap.

From the dining room, Lainey could hear Findlay and Gordy scrambling around, yelling for towels, a first-aid kit. Anything. Harlow stood in the center of the hallway, wooden, staring down at Shelley with an inscrutable expression.

"Mr. Wesley, is there an emergency radio or something?" Lainey asked him. He nodded hesitantly and ran toward his office.

Even with Mrs. Maynard clinging to her arm, Lainey watched Harlow and her strange lack of expression. Harlow had been so angry with Shelley earlier. Could she have done something to Shelley's inhaler or maybe her own drink? Harlow had "joked" a couple of times about dropping Visine into teachers' coffees. Those jokes had stopped entirely after the weed cookie incident.

Or had Mr. Wesley managed to put something in the drink, to punish Harlow for her willful disrespect of the Crossings and its management?

Then again, Vern was the one mixing the drinks, and he'd made it clear he wasn't a fan of Harlow's.

"What's going on?" Cameron came jogging into the hallway from the stairs, his shirt fresh and champagne-free. His head whipped toward the archive door. "Oh, shit, Shelley!"

Deke bolted into the hallway, his face pale and clammy looking. "Somebody smashed the Wi-Fi hotspot with a hammer."

"What?" Milo yelled. "Who would do that?"

"I don't know, man. They left the fucking hammer right there next to the router," Deke yelled.

"Where the hell have you been all night?" Bryce demanded of Cameron. "What, we get a little booze on your shirt and you smash our Wi-Fi hookup?"

Cameron looked honestly affronted. "What? I wouldn't do that."

Kenny asked, "Is there a backup?"

"Why would we have a backup?" Bryce asked. "We bought the best satellite hotspot system on the market . . ."

Lainey's ears felt like they were filling with roaring ocean waves as she stooped to pick up the inhaler and sniffed it. It smelled exactly as she expected—like clean plastic, maybe a little antiseptic. There was no trace of the strange acrid almond smell on Shelley's breath.

She carried the inhaler toward the dining room. Passing the brochure stand on her way, Lainey picked up a guest's guide to the archive. She walked by an immobile Harlow and Milo, who was still dialing desperately on his phone. As she reentered the Beatrice Room, Vern ran by her with a small red first-aid kit and a portable automatic external defibrillator. Lainey supposed they had plenty of use for an AED with elderly guests in the middle of a lake.

Lainey stopped and used a napkin to pick up Shelley's abandoned phone, which was locked. She wasn't sure what was on it, but she was certain the police would be interested. She crossed to the table and used another napkin to pick up the tipped over bee's knees glass. A milky-gold sludge was drying at the bottom of the bowl, forming a sort of crust over the stem. Lainey sniffed it and picked up on that weird bad-candle smell again.

Bitter almonds. Grimacing and pulling the glass away from her face, Lainey moved to the bar and set the glass aside. She rounded the counter, hoping maybe there was a plastic baggie she could save the glass in for the police. She would worry about the fact that her fingerprints were definitely on it at another time.

The weird watermark on the bar caught her eye. Curious, she leaned toward it and sniffed tentatively. Bitter almonds.

Lainey's hands were pretty full, so she set her potential evidence down. She opened the guide to the archive, which included a handy number-coded diagram of every item displayed therein, from the fancy hats to the case full of household cleaners that could definitely do you harm. The hexagonal shape right next to the Your Best Pest Powder in the household case was marked **Rat-B-Gone, Household Vermin Solution**. The void on the blue velvet display had been the same shape.

Breathing heavily, Lainey squinted at the watermark and tried to match its muddled square angles to the hexagonal gap. Didn't companies use arsenic and cyanide in rat poisons during the 1920s? It would have been helpful to go inside the archive to look at the case herself, but it seemed wrong to disturb Shelley to open the door.

Had someone broken into the case and laced the cocktail with cyanide? That would explain the almond smell. Lainey only knew the description because of various documentaries and Agatha Christie readings. It felt like such an arcane and brutal way to poison someone with all of the sneakier modern methods available. Antifreeze. Fentanyl. Why kill someone in such an obvious way? Did they mean to send a message?

Lainey found plastic baggies nearby and sealed the glass, the inhaler, and the phone inside. She searched for something similar to the drop box they'd seen in the speakeasy, but all she found was a locking wooden cabinet. She kneeled, cursing the tiny clutch purse that wouldn't accommodate her lockpicks, but then she spotted a neon-green magnetic Hide-A-Key sticking out ever so slightly from under the body of the bar's mini-fridge.

She slid the old brass key out of the plastic box and unlocked the cabinet. There were two small jars inside marked **Tips**—which were empty. She pushed them farther into the cabinet, secured the bagged items inside, and locked it shut. The key went into her stupid miniature purse, and no one else needed to know about it. She stood, smoothing her dress.

"What are you doing?" Harlow demanded from the doorway.

"Trying to help, which is more than you're doing." Lainey stared at her former friend, walking past her and into the hallway. Mr. Wesley was absolutely ashen, leaning against the wall. Mrs. Rowland was surrounded by the contents of the first-aid kit, as if she was searching for something. Shelley lay eerily still on the tile floor.

Lainey heard Bryce say, "So someone smashed the Wi-Fi hotspot, meaning we have no cell phone signal. Someone smashed the emergency radio. And the landlines are apparently disabled."

"Is the hotspot really damaged, or are you afraid of calling the cops and being charged with criminally negligent manslaughter?" Lainey asked.

"What are you talking about?" Deke demanded, advancing on her. "Why do you have to be such a bitch right now?"

Lainey cocked her head, staring into his wide, panicked eyes. It was interesting how quickly the adoring-fan energy faded when the DBags were in peril.

"Easy," Milo said, but it didn't sound like he was placating Deke. It sounded like a warning.

"Everybody calm down. A phone wouldn't help anyway," Mrs. Rowland told them. "I'm sorry, she's gone."

13

Findlay and Gordy were distraught.

It was one thing to not be particularly close to a coworker. It was another to see that coworker experience death throes right in front of you.

And Shelley was definitely dead. She'd been poisoned. Mrs. Rowland said that was almost certain.

While Shelley had suffered from asthma, neither that nor a seizure disorder would have produced the foam from her mouth that smelled of bitter almonds or the blue tinge to her skin. But according to Mrs. Rowland, asthma could have made her more susceptible to cyanide poisoning since it attacked the lungs and heart.

Suddenly, the hotel loomed larger and seemed claustrophobically small all at the same time. They were utterly without communication with the outside world. The hotspot unit had indeed been smashed with a hammer. So had the emergency radio in Mr. Wesley's office, which had been locked, but his doorknob had also been smashed. It wasn't surprising that no one had heard this happening considering the sprawling size of the building. Still, it was even more unnerving when Mr. Wesley, having located an old phone in the hotel equivalent of a junk drawer, tried to plug it into a jack, just to see if they could get some emergency-only signal. Milo and Kenny went outside to find that the landline leading into the hotel had been cut—because of course there was one old-school line in a barely covered transom leading into the hotel's maintenance shed. Someone had apparently cut the line while they were gathering for dinner.

They were well and truly fucked.

Bryce and Deke were convinced that Cameron was the one who'd smashed the hotspot and the emergency radio when he'd left the dining room. But Lainey thought his reactions were genuine. The DBags accused Cameron of dismantling their equipment *and* poisoning Shelley. They demanded Mr. Wesley lock Cameron in the brig, but Milo talked them out of incarcerating Cameron because, well, they had no proof. And Mr. Wesley really didn't seem to be in the position to be anyone's jailer.

Between the incursion on the peace of the Crossings and the communications failure, Mr. Wesley was insensible with shock.

As a group, they decided to leave Shelley's body covered in a hotel sheet near the archive entrance. It didn't feel right, but Milo had insisted that they shouldn't move or tamper with the body before the police arrived.

The CB radio on the *Acheron* only reached a few miles—not enough range for any nearby island. And because of the weather, Vern didn't feel safe taking the boat out into the dark while it was storming. Their hope was that he could leave in the morning if the weather calmed. Lainey thought he was very brave to offer—even if there was some debate as to whether anyone was willing to ride with him because, as far as any of them knew, Vern could be the poisoner.

It seemed a little odd that whoever had poisoned Shelley hadn't sabotaged the boat, but maybe they simply hadn't had time?

Lainey chose not to share with the group what she'd seen in the cocktail glass until she could get Milo alone to talk it over. She wanted to air her concerns with the other member of Team Reasonable. But because nothing from dinner had been served besides cocktails, Harlow ran with the theory that the drink had been toxic.

"Weren't you the one mixing the drinks?" Harlow asked Vern. "I'm not about to trap myself on a tiny boat in the middle of the lake with a murderer. Unlike some people, I have survival instincts."

"Who was that 'unlike some people' directed to?" Lainey asked.

"If you are the poisoner, the worst that could happen is we get stuck on the island with dead Shelley and a pantry full of canned food until the network realizes we're missing and sends someone out to check on us," Harlow said, ignoring the way Findlay and Gordy gasped with indignation at her use of "dead Shelley."

"So you're saying one of us killed Shelley?" Gordy demanded, his eyes red-rimmed from crying.

"I don't think we should do a full Hercule Poirot accusation," Lainey said. "But unless someone snuck onto the island to tamper with the bar supplies, it's pretty likely that one of us poisoned Shelley. This was clearly not an accident. It was a deliberate effort."

"Who would want to kill Shelley?" Harlow asked.

"I don't think they were trying to kill Shelley," Lainey replied. "I think they were shooting for you and missed."

"Don't be ridiculous. Who would want to hurt me?" Harlow scoffed.

A very awkward pause followed. No one seemed to want to make eye contact, not even the DBags.

"People with ears?" Findlay suggested finally.

"Solid burn," Gordy noted.

"Mr. Wesley, how did you decide which guests sat at which table?" Lainey asked. "Why was Harlow suddenly moved away from the VIP tables to sit with us?"

"Normally, we would use a random assignment, but in this case, Ms. McMillan requested it," Mr. Wesley insisted. "She said she had business to discuss with you both."

Lainey frowned. So that was a dead end.

"What about that pushy chef?" Harlow demanded. "Where did he disappear to? Where are the other two—Bellboy and Check-In Lady—*the hotel people*?" Harlow stepped slightly in front of Lainey.

"Tommy and Cassie?" Lainey suggested.

"They're in the kitchen trying to figure out if anything else in there has been tampered with," Milo added. He was a warm, steady presence at Lainey's side, and she found herself grateful for him.

"How do we know *they* didn't poison Shelley?" Harlow asked.

"Now, wait a minute," Vern snarled. "Cassie and Tommy would never do anything like— You don't just get to accuse people of murder because you think they're less important than you!"

Lainey noted that Vern hadn't said that Chef Andre would never do something like that. Interesting. Lainey stepped between the fuming bartender and Harlow, even if Harlow did deserve to be reminded that random felony accusations were . . . bad. "We don't know that *anybody* is innocent. It sucks, but that's where we are. Everybody is a suspect."

An uneasy silence settled over the group until Bryce broke it with, "This is *awesome*."

"We're living out our own real-life murder mystery," Deke said, grinning broadly. He was apparently over his bad mood. "So cool."

"You two do realize someone *actually* died, right?" Findlay asked them. "This isn't a game. There are no respawns."

"Why aren't we filming this?" Harlow barked at Kenny.

"Harlow, no," Lainey told her firmly. "This is not the time."

Harlow shot her a look that was equal parts surprise and disdain. Lainey stared back, unwavering. This was not a happy coincidence for Harlow, not something to be turned into an opportunity. It would be ghoulish to film the crew's reactions to their coworker *dying* in front of them. Shelley's body wasn't even cold.

"Fine, we'll pick up in the morning," Harlow huffed.

Lainey took a deep breath and added, "Speaking of the morning, I don't think any of us are going to trust food prepared by someone else. We probably need to figure out how we're going to arrange cooking our own meals using industrial-sized canned foods. We only eat from unopened cans in the pantry. We all prepare our own foods, by ourselves in the kitchen."

"I don't know if that's such a good idea." Deke chuckled. "I don't cook. Can't even boil water."

"You would literally rather risk being poisoned than cook your own food?" Lainey asked.

Deke shrugged. "It's better than the fire alarm going off all of the time."

"Can you just do it for us?" Bryce asked. "We trust you, and you're probably better at it anyway."

"The internet is right about everything." Lainey sighed, pinching the bridge of her nose.

The "meeting" sort of collapsed after that, with everyone reluctantly splitting off to their own rooms.

Vern was sleeping on the boat to prevent their saboteur from messing with it.

Saboteur. Such a pretty word for the person who was systematically closing them off from the outside world. Despite the group's agreement that they should all retire to their rooms and try not to get murdered, Lainey tossed and turned, unable to sleep. She snuck downstairs with silent steps that would have made Locard proud.

She crept over to the Gentlemen's Lounge door, wondering if Milo had thought to lock it. The satellite hotspot might be smashed, but it didn't seem like a good idea to leave it unsecured. She jiggled the handle and found that yes, it was locked. And it was still very grubby. Her left hand—because the right one was covered in calamine lotion and a bandage courtesy of her first-aid kit—was now smeared with the same oily, sticky substance.

Ew.

She sniffed at it. It smelled familiar and faintly woodsy. Nutty, even.

Shelley had mentioned that a lot of the doorknobs in the hotel were grubby with some sort of old-fashioned polish paste. What if that was what caused Mr. Hornsby's hand to react? There could be nut-based ingredients in cleaning products, right? She couldn't think of any right off the top of her head, but half the cleaning products in the hotel archive contained poisons. Why not nut products?

Oh, Mr. Wesley was going to be so mad at her if she accused his precious hotel of having fatal doorknobs *and* poisonous cocktails.

"One problem at a time," Lainey said, sighing. "To the kitchen full of thankless tasks."

The general creepiness of the darkened lobby didn't concern Lainey nearly as much as knowing that she had to pass by Shelley's body to get to the dining room. Lainey Piper did not believe in zombies or ghosts, not really. She didn't think the universe would throw supernatural elements at her on top of poisoned guests, fake crypt secret passageways, and DBags. That would just be cruel.

By the time she reached the kitchen, terror and adrenaline had her wide-awake. She perched on the kitchen counter and tried to figure out the stupid manager's diary. It was similar to when she was supposed to have been studying in high school yet found herself absorbed in a one-hundred-thousand-plus-word *Supernatural* fanfic. (Destiel was endgame, and Lainey would happily fist-fight any detractors.)

It was either a genius move—hiding out next to all the knives in the hotel—or it was going to get Lainey killed. She wasn't sure which.

It was well past midnight. She thought 1927 was the best year to start with since that was the year Marguerite had disappeared. It helped to distract her from the big fucking mess she'd found herself in at the Crossings Hotel.

Lainey turned the diary over and over in her hands. It was just a simple brown leather journal with lined pages crowded with code. It would have been so helpful if the former Crossings manager, one Aloysius Crowder, had left a decoding hint. But all he'd left Lainey was his name in careful cursive, inscribed on the front leaf of the journal under the Crossings logo.

She spread the books on the counter and stared at them, biting at her bottom lip. Each diary was inscribed the same way, with the hotel's name, the manager's name, and the year. The "C" in "Crossings" was underlined twice with pencil on each of the diaries' title pages. The "L" in "Aloysius" was underlined twice in the 1927 diary. The "Y" in "Aloysius" was underlined twice in the 1928 diary. And the "U" was underlined twice in 1929.

Based on what she'd seen about codes before the internet had been hammered to death, Lainey thought maybe the diaries were written in a simple substitution cipher, shifting the alphabet's letters a certain number of spaces depending on the difference between the "key letter" and its substitution.

"C" was underlined in all three diaries. Maybe "L" was substituted for "C" in the 1927 diary? And "Y" was substituted for "C" in the 1928 diary, and "U" for "C" in 1929? Each year had its own unique code, centered around substitutions for the letter "C." It would have worked until Crowder ran out of letters in his name.

If "C" was translated to "L" . . . She took out her notebook and translated the rest of the alphabet in this new order. "A" was "J," "B" was "K," and so on. It was nice, giving herself a problem to solve. It made her feel productive, even if she was barely clinging to calm.

The manager had written *years'* worth of business in these codes. It seemed like an exhausting amount of devotion to the hotel, but she got the impression that Mr. Wesley wasn't alone in his inappropriate feelings for the Crossings. What was the name for the -philia where people fell in love with buildings? Was that part of the hiring process?

Lainey turned to the pages for mid-May 1927. She'd translated the first few sentences after Marguerite and Dandridge's arrival date. She was so busy being pleased with her own cleverness that she barely heard the footsteps in the dining room. She froze.

Someone was coming.

Fortunately, the swinging door to the kitchen had no window, so whoever was in the dining room wouldn't see the lights disappear as Lainey flipped the switch. She silently slipped her bag strap around her neck and slid off the counter, grabbing one of the larger kitchen knives from the rack.

She clutched her pepper spray in her other hand, wondering which she would use if it came down to it. She didn't think the glitter would be useful until both those options failed. She'd always kind of wondered what she would do in a truly threatening "me or them" situation, but recalling Shelley's agonized expression, she decided yes, if she was confronted by a murderer, she would mess that murderer up.

A slim form in pink plaid pajama pants and a black tank top padded slowly into view, heading toward the pantry.

Noooo! She didn't want to mess Findlay up. She liked Findlay. And the woman was wearing gold undereye patches on a face shiny-clean of makeup. (Still stunning.)

Murderers didn't care about undereye brightening—right?

Lainey inched backward, crab walking behind a freestanding stainless-steel prep counter. It was perfectly positioned between the giant industrial stove and the counter to give Lainey some cover as she prayed that this wasn't some sort of feint so Findlay's accomplice could sneak up behind her. Also, she had the most inappropriate urge to laugh, like somehow she couldn't be attacked if she was laughing at the ridiculousness of lurking behind the counter like a goblin.

But to her relief, the makeup artist didn't skulk around looking for a weapon among the various clipboards hanging from hooks on the inside of the pantry door. Findlay appeared to be mulling over her choice of oversized fruit cans. Over Findlay's shoulder, Lainey spotted several industrial-sized cannisters of olive oil. They were metal with crimped edges, like the metal bottle from the poison ivy patch. Lainey thought of the old woodsy smell that had clung to the bottle. What if the weird bottle had contained a nut oil like walnut or . . . pistachio?

Lainey was distracted by the metallic rattle of Findlay opening a drawer. She seemed to be searching for a can opener. From a distance, Lainey could see a hardcover romantasy novel under Findlay's arm. Something about dragons and lusty princes with wings, if the cover was any indication. Lainey could not have envied her night more.

Lainey adjusted her hunched position. Being unused to wielding an enormous butcher knife while crouching, she smacked the edge of it against the metal cabinet with an ear-punishing *scriiitch.*

Findlay whirled around, wielding the manual can opener like a dagger. "Who's there?"

For a long silent moment, Lainey considered not answering. It was embarrassing to be caught hiding in the kitchen like a weirdo. Also, it seemed inconsiderate to be lurking in the dark when there was a murderer around. Lainey could just crawl across the floor to the dining room and bolt past the dead body to her room, right?

No, that seemed worse.

"It's me," Lainey said, standing up and waving awkwardly. Unfortunately, she chose the knife hand to do the waving. "I'm sorry, I didn't mean to lurk. With a knife. I realize now, this could be perceived as threatening."

She set the knife on the counter with a clank. But she didn't want to drop it entirely . . . because survival. At least she had the pepper spray—and the glitter as a last resort.

Findlay practically collapsed against the counter as Lainey switched on the lights. "Lainey, what are you doing in here?"

"I couldn't sleep," Lainey said. "Or more like my body refused to sleep, in self-defense."

Findlay sighed, nodding. "I hear every noise and I hate everything."

"Welcome to Insomnia-Town," Lainey said, gesturing to the kitchen. "Population: two."

"Hungry?" Findlay asked, holding up her can of peaches.

"Can we just promise *not* to murder each other and share a friendly can of fruit for the next hour or so?" Lainey asked.

"I'll do my best," Findlay promised, climbing onto the counter and holding out a fork for Lainey. "Do you want some peaches or did you already enjoy a delicious Crystalline Greens juice?"

"No thank you to the green juice." Lainey laughed, scowling at the pearlescent white plastic cannister containing Harlow's favorite supplement. She pulled the cannister toward her and opened it, surprised to find that the powder was white, not green. Again, "green" was *right there* in the name. "I'm kind of surprised Harlow would leave it in here unguarded."

"You don't think she'll still want to use it, do you?" Findlay scoffed. "Her drink was poisoned."

"Harlow's sort of impervious to hints," Lainey said as Findlay cranked the peach can open. "Look, I know this is scary, but we're going to be OK."

"You don't know that," Findlay replied.

Lainey deadpanned, "Nope, but I figured screaming and running around and yelling 'We're all gonna die' would just freak you out more."

"You have a good point."

"Is Gordy OK?" Lainey asked as Findlay peeled off the under-eye patches and massaged the serum they left behind into her skin.

Findlay told her, "He sleeps like a rock, always has—even in the middle of a chaos storm. Something about growing up in Brooklyn and sirens. But I can't get that image of Shelley out of my head. The way her mouth stretched back."

Findlay shuddered, like she was sinking into the memory. Lainey decided to distract her with a question. "So Shelley did something a little weird at dinner. Other than . . . you know, dying—"

Findlay's dark eyes focused on Lainey's face. She guessed, "She took your salad fork? Your drink?"

"No, she took Harlow's drink," Lainey replied. "She was just so focused on her phone and arguing with Harlow that she didn't notice the mix-up."

"Yeah, that makes sense." Findlay sighed. "Shelley lived for her phone. She didn't mean to be rude. She just loved her job and wanted to focus on that more than anything else, even if it was a deep, emotional conversation. I don't think she ever looked at her meal from start to finish. It was just part of working with her. I saw her pick up a burning candle once, thinking it was her drink."

"Ouch," Lainey said, wincing.

"She escaped with her eyebrows intact," Findlay assured her.

Lainey stared into the can of peaches as if she could divine answers from it. Vern probably hadn't known about Shelley's absent-minded phone tendencies unless he'd seen her demonstrating them on previous nights. Could someone have poisoned the drink while Harlow left it on the bar or the table, hoping Shelley would drink it by mistake?

What if Lainey was too stuck on the idea of Harlow as the target? Could Cameron have targeted Shelley to get a job? Shelley had been snappish with him on a few occasions since Lainey's arrival. In fact, Cameron was the *only* person Shelley had been snappish with. She'd only been a little stern with Harlow. Could the motives have combined into an urge to take Shelley out? Cameron had conveniently disappeared right when Shelley suffered the effects. Maybe he'd dropped something into the drink and made himself scarce? Wait, he couldn't have predicted Deke and Bryce spraying him with champagne.

Well, maybe he could have. They *were* DBags.

Lainey wiped at the peach juice that had left her hand all sticky. She was not enjoying the sensation of her bandage being tacky.

Hmm.

What if the grubby doorknobs weren't some misdirected use of nut-based cleaning products? Maybe someone who knew about Harlow's self-proclaimed nut allergy had painted the doorknobs in pistachio oil to get at Harlow, but Mr. Hornsby—with his genuine nut allergy—was exposed instead?

"Poor Mr. Hornsby," Lainey breathed.

"Major conversational lane shift." Findlay frowned at her. "Who?"

"The man who died right before we got here," Lainey said. "If he was exposed repeatedly over the course of the week, unknowingly touching doorknobs contaminated with his allergen as he moved through the hotel, his immune system never got a break. He was probably tired of feeling terrible, took some medication, and just never woke up."

Findlay grimaced and agreed, "Poor Mr. Hornsby."

"Does Harlow still tell everybody that she's allergic to pistachios?"

Findlay shook her head. "Not that I'm aware of. She was militant about her juice schedule, but that's the only time her food preferences were mentioned to me. But she also didn't like talking to me unless it was contouring related."

Lainey tried to review all of Harlow's entourage who had arrived at the hotel before Lainey and who she might have told about the fake allergy. Findlay and Gordy seemed trustworthy. Shelley, Cameron . . . Shelley wasn't really a suspect anymore. And Cameron? He seemed to have a vested interest in Harlow living and having a successful career.

Had Harlow lied to the hotel staff about the pistachio thing?

Lainey stood and walked to the pantry door, where the clipboards showed inventory records, cleaning checklists, and . . . guest dietary reminders. While Mr. Hornsby's tree-nut allergy was printed in big red font with a list of which nuts that covered and potential sources of allergens that wouldn't be obvious, there was no mention of Harlow except to emphasize her desire for low-carb, low-sugar options.

"So she hadn't been terrorizing the hotel staff," Lainey muttered.

"What?"

"Poisonings aside, is this normally how these TV shoots run or is it different because it's a special?" Lainey asked, turning to Findlay.

"Nothing about this has been normal, Lainey," Findlay told her. "This is not how TV productions are run. Outside funding? Sure, that happens, but having 'sponsors' on-site making production decisions? No. And I mean, some dramatization or reenacting is normal, but this . . . this filming things that have already happened and reframing them as Harlow's big discoveries? That's just not how we do things. I don't know if it's because of funding-slash-interference from the DBags or what, but this whole vibe is off. Don't you care that she's taking credit for what you're finding?"

Lainey chewed on a squishy peach. "Eh, this is something I'm doing for quick cash while I'm trying to stabilize everything else in my life. Besides, I don't think Harlow's production style is going to be a problem for you for long after this, particularly if the network blames her for Shelley."

"Do you honestly think Shelley or even the Sausage Slayer thing is going to hold Harlow back if she actually solves a glamorous cold case involving a beautiful woman, secret passageways, missing jewels, and secret codes?" Findlay scoffed. "Shelley will be a three-second in memoriam card at the end of the episode, and Harlow will get assigned a new producer. I guess Cameron is now technically our producer until the network can send someone out. Our bosses made it clear: We are obligated to produce the promised content. And they don't want the added cost of a delay. I have a feeling we're going to finish up no matter what."

Lainey scrubbed a hand over her face. It was too late, and she was too tired for this.

"I miss Shelley, and this feels like an awful thing to say when we're less than a hundred yards from her body, but this is not great for me. My rent is going up again, and I was sort of counting on the paycheck," Findlay said.

"Same." Lainey sighed, chewing on another peach. She hadn't even thought about what would happen if the network didn't pay her. Was it denial or self-preservation to focus on the potential murderer in her immediate vicinity? Probably a little of both.

Findlay glanced at the counter, noticing Lainey's decoding efforts for the first time. "Are you making a Ouija board?"

"I'm decoding some of the diaries we found in the speakeasy," she said, showing Findlay her progress so far.

"Interesting," Findlay said, forking another peach into her mouth. "If I agree to put away the potentially staining canned foods, would you like some help handling the very delicate historical documents?"

Lainey blinked at her, confused. No one had ever offered to be her assistant. Weird.

"Sure," Lainey said. They conscientiously washed and dried their hands before opening the diaries. They worked quietly together, each taking one page of the open book before moving on to the next. Findlay's handwriting was quite a bit neater than Lainey's, even if Lainey transcribed faster. She was so caught up in the chore of translating one letter at a time that she knew she wasn't absorbing information in the passages.

At the same time, it took her mind off the wind howling outside and the body down the hall. They were so immersed in their task that they almost didn't hear the footsteps in the dining room. Lainey reached over and turned off the light switch. Findlay stared at her, seeming unsure of whether to follow Lainey, who had already rolled off the counter, clutching her pepper spray and her knife.

"Are we sure— OK." Findlay huffed quietly, grabbed her own blade, and followed suit.

They hid behind the metal prep counter, clutching their knives. The kitchen door swung open and two basketball-shorts-clad legs stepped into view. Poor Milo looked very confused as he hit the light switch closest to the door.

"Hello?"

Findlay looked to Lainey as if to ask, *Do we trust him not to murder us?*

While Lainey tried to formulate a response, Milo called, "I can see the giant can of peaches you left on the counter."

Lainey rolled her eyes and stood. "I'm not going to take any crap from a guy who walked into a dark room in a murder hotel and called out 'Hello?' That's how they get you."

"Why are you holding a knife?" Milo cried, before he stopped himself. "OK, that's a dumb question. What are you doing in here?"

Findlay stood, waving her own knife. "Peach and Knife Club? It's a social media thing."

"OK, I expect this from Lainey," Milo told Findlay. "But you seem like such a reasonable person."

Lainey was only slightly offended.

Findlay told Lainey, "That's literally the only time a person has said that to me."

"Want some peaches?" Lainey asked.

"Will you put the knives away?" Milo huffed.

"Probably not," Lainey replied as she and Findlay resumed their positions. "Can't sleep, either, huh?"

"Actually, I was worried about you," he said. He leaned on the counter across from them. Lainey held out the peaches and he used her fork to take one. "I checked your room and your door was standing open."

"It wasn't when I left. I locked it and checked it twice," she said, frowning. Had someone snuck into her room? Had her paranoia about closing herself in the room actually paid off? Mr. Wesley would have a master key to all the rooms in the hotel . . . but then again, someone had busted into Mr. Wesley's office. Maybe the burglar had gained access to all the hotel rooms in one fell swoop. Was it possible that *nowhere* in the Crossings was safe? Lainey was thankful that she'd brought her purse and the diaries with her to the kitchen—even her phone, not that it was particularly useful at the moment. She just didn't want a murderous burglar asshole taking her ancient, but paid off, technology.

"So, you two are just sitting here, eating ill-gotten stone fruit, translating the manager's diaries?" he said.

"Gee, mister, you're so sexy and observant," Lainey cooed in a fake coquette voice. Milo blushed almost as red as his Bulls T-shirt.

"Also, they're non*poisoned* ill-gotten stone fruit," Findlay noted, pointing to the can label.

"What do you have so far?" Milo asked.

"We really haven't had time to read over it," Lainey said. "We were kind of in the zone."

"Lay it on me," Milo said, hitching his butt onto the countertop. He winced, then reached into his shorts pocket. He pulled out several latex resistance bands and set them on the metal surface.

"I am not prepared for that sort of party," Findlay said, staring at the out-of-context exercise equipment.

Lainey's eyes went wide. "I know I'm going to regret asking this, but why do you have those? And why did you have them when you were checking my room?"

"Have you not been paying attention?" Milo asked, gesturing toward the dining room. "Poison, murder, mayhem? Your whole personal mission statement."

"First of all, that's hurtful. And a little judgy. Secondly, why do you just happen to have person-sized rubber bands packed in your pocket?" Lainey asked. "Unless they came with your room, to which I say—unfair, all I got was a tiny mouthwash."

Findlay pouted. "You got a mouthwash?"

"There have been several . . . let's say 'playful incidents' involving the guys and work-based sleep deprivation and certain choices they made under the influence of energy drinks that aren't legal in the US, Canada, or Norway. I can usually keep them from hurting themselves if I can keep them contained. And I've gotten pretty good at looping these things around the guys' ankles. I've found it's better to be prepared."

"What is your life?" Lainey asked, shaking her head.

"On to less unnerving subjects." Findlay held up the pages she'd ripped from Lainey's notebook. "*May Twentieth, The Sharp Gentleman, Mr. D's behavior is an issue. It's not surprising. He's never been the most cooperative of guests, but he has insisted on bringing his 'home brew' with him, as he just took up chemistry at home. The beverage staff report that it smells terrible, but that Mr. D insists that he and his companion will* only *drink his libations.*"

"Mr. Crowder is trying so hard not to say things like 'cocktail,'" Lainey said. "I'm assuming a sharp gentleman named Mr. D is Timmy Dandridge, unreliable razor heir."

Findlay read on. "*Mr. D became quite annoyed with the staff when he realized they were serving him very weak mixtures. He has been camped at the card table since he arrived. He has already exhausted his cash reserves and all available credit. His guest, a young woman he calls 'Lady M,' has been amusing herself at the lakeside. Her manner is rough, but she has been polite to the staff, which is all I can ask for. This is not the first time Mr. D has brought a woman without means into our midst, pretending she is a viscountess or some such foolishness. I believe that's part of the thrill for him—daring the other guests to say something about Miss M's obviously fake accent. She's no more from London than I am from Seville.*

"That's so shitty," Findlay huffed, breaking from the narration. "Using Marguerite that way . . . And there are uncomfortable parallels with how you and Harlow are being treated by the DBags."

"Yep," Lainey said, sucking her teeth and hating the sound. "The similarities have occurred to me."

"What's your page say?" Findlay asked.

"*I don't believe Miss M is nearly as enamored of Mr. D as he'd like to believe,*" Lainey read aloud. "*In particular, she seems very annoyed that when not addressing her as 'Your Ladyship,' he uses a nickname, 'Pegs.' He says it's because of her long legs, which are remarkably lithe, but she seems to find it demeaning.*

"Ew," Lainey huffed. "The next few entries are just stuff about menu changes and bitching about the price of pineapple."

"Is 'pineapple' a euphemism?" Milo asked.

Findlay shook her head. "I don't think so. Pineapples would have been pretty expensive to grow or import back then. It's not like they had a big-box store."

"*May Twenty-Third—Mr. D's behavior continues to be an issue. He has taken to breaking apart certain celestial assets to cover his debts at the gaming tables. They have been secured in the lower vaults . . .*" Lainey trailed off. "And that's where we stopped because you came ambling in here like a hapless horror movie NPC just waiting to get stabbed."

"Celestial assets?" Findlay gasped. "Like the Star of Sikkim? He broke up that gorgeous necklace into scrap to pay off his gambling debts? What an *asshole.*"

"Findlay, let me explain something that I've learned over the years," Milo said. "The rich are different. And . . . terrible."

Findlay snorted, but Lainey told her, "Don't listen to him. He has stock options."

"I'm not rich. I'm comfortable," Milo shot back.

"Which is something that rich people say," Lainey told him. "Well, Timmy Dandridge wantonly destroying a family heirloom to pay off debt definitely explains the scrap metal and loose stone we found in the speakeasy."

"Still nothing about what happened to the big ol' diamond the size of a tangerine," Findlay muttered.

"We're guessing the size of an egg," Milo told her, waving his hand between himself and Lainey.

Findlay's brows rose. "Oh, pardon me, I didn't realize I was dealing with a 'we.'"

"I think *we're* all just hungry," Lainey said.

"OK, gimme some notebook paper," Milo told them. "I'm tagging in."

Lainey and Findlay chuckled as they gathered, heads bent, over the diary. Findlay and Milo each took a page and transcribed, while Lainey studied the translated passages. This was nice, she realized, having people to share the homework, to collaborate on the puzzle.

"Uh-oh," Lainey said. "The manager says that the doctor was called to treat Lady M. *She had been quite ill, suffering stomach distress and headache, and complained of blurred vision. Management encouraged Mr. D to throw out the 'homemade brew' he had been mixing into his rickeys all week, as it might be dangerous. Beverage service offered by the hotel was at least bottled in safe environs.*"

"Could have been something in the booze Mr. D was brewing," Milo suggested. "If you don't know what you're doing, distilling can be dangerous. You can make a chemical mistake you don't even know is possible. And Dandridge wasn't exactly the brightest bulb."

Lainey cringed as she read aloud. "*Mr. D insisted that couldn't possibly be true, because he'd brewed the gin himself, using only the best wood alcohols. And then proceeded to drink most of a bottle in front of management.*"

The three of them froze as they heard the Beatrice Room door creak open. Something clattered and squeaked, as if someone had bumped one of the dining chairs. A gruff voice hissed, "I don't like this. They catch us doing this, they're gonna call the cops. We won't have another chance to get her. Maybe we can take the boat when that maintenance guy is taking a piss?"

This was answered with a sharp *shush.*

Lainey locked eyes with her decoding compatriots and reached for the light switch, plunging the kitchen into darkness.

14

Lainey pressed a finger to her lips and pointed to the knives. Findlay looked as if she had her doubts, but Milo helped them quietly gather the diaries and shove them into Lainey's bag. They each grabbed sizable knives and crept backward, behind the now-familiar prep table.

Lainey flipped the cap on her pepper spray, truly prepared to use it for the first time that night. How many people were creeping toward the kitchen? Which "her" were they trying to get? Lainey prayed it wasn't her or Findlay.

The door swung open slowly and the people on the other side seemed to be listening for a reaction. The door moved farther, allowing Mr. Spiros and Mrs. Maynard to creep through. They were both holding flashlights, giving Lainey enough ambient light to see a little of them. Gone were Mrs. Maynard's elegant dresses and pearls, replaced by joggers and an ancient Cubs sweatshirt. Her short blond hair was drawn back into a stubby ponytail.

Milo pulled his phone out of his pocket and began filming

them. Lainey didn't know if the footage would be any good, but it couldn't hurt.

Mr. Spiros looked tired, the brackets around his mouth carved even deeper than usual. He was carrying a small white plastic cannister marked **Mega-Ultra-Bleach Powder**. Mrs. Maynard searched the counter until she found the Crystalline Greens cannister. Smirking, she screwed open the cap and began measuring scoops of the bleach powder into Harlow's juice mix. Both powders were white, and unless Harlow sniffed the blender first, she might not even notice the smell. Lainey wasn't sure what effects the bleach would have when mixed into Harlow's supplement . . . but it certainly wasn't going to help with her skin-care routine.

"How much of this stuff do you think she'll need to drink before it gets her?" Mr. Spiros whispered. "Maybe we can be out of here before that Drake bitch croaks? I didn't like watching that poor woman dying in front of us."

Lainey looked to Milo, who nodded. Findlay pointed toward the light switch and mimed flipping it. Lainey nodded, tucking her pepper spray into her back pocket. It seemed smart to keep an advantage hidden . . . while holding a big old knife. Milo's resistance bands were still on the counter.

Findlay flipped the switch. The pair of powder poisoners froze, overpowered by the glare of industrial fluorescent lighting.

Mrs. Maynard laughed and in her Southern belle accent huffed, "Well, Lord-a-mercy, Lainey, you scared me half to death. Why are you in here hiding in the dark with your friends? Are y'all sneaking a midnight snack?"

"You don't need that many knives for a midnight snack," Mr. Spiros muttered.

"You don't know our lives," Findlay retorted. While Lainey

appreciated Findlay's casual approach to conversations with potential murderers, she noted that Milo was tense and quiet. He propped his phone against the can of peaches to keep his hands free as it filmed.

"You don't have to keep pretending for me, Mrs. Maynard," Lainey told her.

"Well, honey, what do you mean?" Mrs. Maynard tittered, but the smile didn't reach her eyes. Her face turned a shade pastier with every word. Mr. Spiros was inching toward them in a way that was putting Lainey's teeth on edge.

"Lucinda Maynard could be your real name, but you're not from Mobile, Alabama."

"Yeah," Findlay said. Her head whipped toward Lainey. "What?"

"You said you're a longtime visitor of the Crossings, but Mr. Wesley didn't seem to know anything about you. You didn't know about the Gentlemen's Lounge. And your accent is wrong. You sound like you're from Virginia, or at best, Georgia. Frankly, I think you're doing an impersonation of Blanche from *The Golden Girls*. And our first night at dinner, you said 'bottle of pop.' My mom is from Kentucky. She's lived outside Chicago for almost thirty years and she *still* calls every kind of soft drink a 'Coke.' Most Southerners do. If she asks if you want a Coke, and you say yes, she'll clarify if you want a Diet Coke or a Sprite or a Mello Yello. At *best*, she'll say 'soda.' And if Lucinda Maynard was from Mobile, Alabama, she wouldn't say 'pop.'"

"Really?" Mrs. Maynard rolled her eyes. "That's how you caught me?"

"It got my attention. And then, when Shelley was lying on the floor, *dying*, the voice that came out of you was pure Midwest,"

Lainey added pointedly. "It's really hard to keep up a pretense like a fake accent under duress."

"We didn't have anything to do with that TV woman getting sick," Mr. Spiros insisted.

"Shut up," Mrs. Maynard hissed. "He's recording. And they don't know anything."

"Um, I know we have footage of you putting bleach in Harlow's drink powder," Lainey replied. "You honestly expect us to believe that you didn't kill a woman by poisoning her drink when we actively caught you trying to poison another drink? Meant for the same woman?"

"You don't know what you're talking about!" Mr. Spiros cried.

"Great, then tell me what I'm talking about," Lainey said. "You're not getting out of here. You can't get off the island. You're caught."

"Pete, do something," Mrs. Maynard muttered.

"You wouldn't stab a couple of older people. You don't have it in you," Mr. Spiros said, coming around the counter. Lainey was standing between him and Milo. She wasn't sure what Mr. Spiros's plan was—he was a burly man with those big fisherman's hands—but Milo was about three decades younger and had years of wrangling DBags on his side. Did Mr. Spiros really think he could take three much younger *armed* people, possessing only the confidence of a late-stage baby boomer?

"You're probably right about that," Lainey conceded. Mr. Spiros was only about ten feet away and gaining ground.

"Not about me," Findlay snorted. "I work in cable TV. I've seen shit. I *will* cut you."

Mr. Spiros was almost cornering them now, herding them against the wall. He casually grabbed one of the knives from the magnetic rack as he passed it. It was probably a mistake on their part, not taking *all* the knives. Behind her back, Lainey motioned toward her pocket, hoping to catch Findlay's attention.

"I think if I rushed you, you would drop those knives and run," Mr. Spiros said. He stamped his foot, as if he was going to do just that. Lainey tilted her head, frowning at him. Was foot-stamping a fighting technique that she'd never seen before?

Mr. Spiros lunged and swiped the knife at them. Lainey pulled the pepper spray cannister from her back pocket. Findlay pulled a resistant Milo away from the "blast zone" as Lainey released a jet of jellified capsaicin into Mr. Spiros's face.

It took all of two seconds for him to shriek as if all the demons of hell had just peed into his eye sockets. Mrs. Maynard made a break for the door.

Dropping his knife, Milo dashed around the other side of the table, probably to avoid the cloud of residual pepper spray. He snagged a resistance band as he passed, catching Mrs. Maynard's arm before she could run out. He pulled her back and looped the latex band around her wrists multiple times, securing her hands behind her back. Mrs. Maynard struggled against the stretchy bonds, but wriggling around just seemed to leave her red-faced and frustrated. Lainey had suffered a similar fate when she'd gotten overconfident with a triceps workout. Her neighbor, Sophie, had had to cut her out of the upper-body trap of her own making.

Milo dragged Mrs. Maynard back across the room and lifted her onto the counter. Then he bound her feet together while she called him a stream of highly inappropriate names. "Stay there."

"This is not the behavior of a responsible corporate officer!" Lainey shouted as Mr. Spiros thrashed on the floor, screaming.

Milo yelled back, "I'll worry about corporate consequences when I'm not dodging a great big knife."

Findlay rolled her eyes at them and fetched a three-gallon jug of two percent milk from the fridge. She and Lainey helped Mr. Spiros stand and hover over the sink. They endured a symphony of heretofore unknown insults as they poured the milk onto his face. Milo took this opportunity to loop a band around his wrists. He was surprisingly cooperative, which Lainey supposed was normal, given the burning of his face.

"Are you drowning him?" Mrs. Maynard demanded.

"No, we're washing the pepper spray out of his eyes," Findlay shot back. "Because we're not a couple of psychos."

"We can flush out his eyes with saline solution later," Lainey said. Findlay opened her mouth and Lainey added, "Don't ask me how I know. Just trust that I do."

"What in blazes is going on down here?" Mr. Wesley demanded, running into the kitchen wearing a Crossings-branded bathrobe over starched blue-and-white-striped pajamas. "I heard screaming . . ."

He trailed off as he took in the scene—a bound Mrs. Maynard on the counter, seething, while Lainey and Findlay were dousing Mr. Spiros in dairy products.

Milo cleared his throat. "I know this looks bad, but we can explain."

Mr. Wesley insisted on the restraints being removed from *his guests*, but—after Milo showed him the video of the drink-powder tampering—he agreed to place them in the brig until Vern could summon the police the next morning. Lainey locked the poisoned Crystalline Greens cannister in the bar cabinet. It felt inevitable in this comedy of errors that Harlow or Cameron would wake up before Lainey and prepare a bleach-infused juice—even if they left a note on it or something.

Lainey had thought Vern was kidding about the brig, but Mr. Wesley led them down the service corridor to the very rear of the building. The brig was a double jail cell, divided down the middle by bars. But instead of feather tick mattresses and metal toilets, the cell boasted a queen bed, fully made up with the same comforter and pillows as the hotel. A privacy screen walled off a small toilet cubicle with a sink and a proper porcelain throne. If the "guests" craned their necks, they would have a bit of a lake view from their cells. Frankly, Lainey was surprised not to see a minibar.

"When one is the steward of the Crossings, one must be prepared for every possibility," Mr. Wesley intoned. Mr. Spiros and Mrs. Maynard were released from the resistance bands. Mr. Spiros immediately ran for the sink to wash off more of the pepper spray.

"So why two cells?" Lainey asked.

"In case of a serious fight, we separate the warring factions," Mr. Wesley said.

"You can't keep us in here," Mrs. Maynard insisted. "This whole thing is a misunderstanding."

"How?" Milo asked.

"We haven't actually done anything wrong," Mr. Spiros insisted between splashes on his face.

"You were putting bleach powder in someone's drink mix," Lainey reminded him. "You do realize that we saw you, right?"

"But she didn't drink it," Mr. Spiros shot back.

"I'll explain. I won't confess to a crime, but I'll explain. You're not going to film me, though." Mrs. Maynard sighed, sinking onto her bed.

Lainey cast a sidelong glance at Findlay, who shrugged. "Filming is Harlow's problem. She can figure it out later."

"My name is Lucy Maynard *Restretto*," she said. "I wanted to add the 'Restretto' legally when I turned eighteen, but my mother wouldn't let me. She said it would upset my father too much. He didn't want people to know about us. Even now, she would probably disown me if I did it . . . so I didn't tell her I came here to make things right for him."

"Oh, shit." Lainey gaped at her. "Restretto? From the Sausage Slayer thing?"

"Don't call him that," Mrs. Maynard snapped as both Findlay and Milo cringed.

"I wasn't calling him anything," Lainey clarified. "I was just trying to give them some context."

She turned to Mr. Spiros, giving him a speculative look, trying to determine where there was a family resemblance between the two of them. It was sort of difficult to see one, but the red eyes and nose could be interfering there. Then again, unless Sam Restretto started fathering children as a preteen, she wasn't sure how Pete Spiros played into that picture. He saw Lainey studying him and raised his hands. "Oh, no, I'm not one of Sam's sons—I'm just a family friend. I stepped in and helped Lucy's mom out sometimes when Sam was busy with his boys. That shop was his whole life. The boys should have inherited it, been part of their father's legacy, but thanks to that Drake girl, all they've inherited is a mess. And heartache."

"I don't even get a part of the legacy," Mrs. Maynard said, crossing her arms. "I was his only daughter. My mother and I lived on that block my whole life, but no one acknowledged us, like we weren't part of one of the best things in the neighborhood. The only time my brothers have voluntarily spoken to me was to ask me to leave his funeral because it *looked bad.*

"It was just so stupid and pointless. Everybody in the neighborhood knew who my father was, including the boys *and* their mother. They just pretended we didn't exist. It was like we were ghosts, never a part of things, never seen. And my mother never left, because she was convinced that we couldn't make it without my dad's help."

"Your dad had a whole-ass second family?" Findlay marveled. "Within walking distance of the first family?"

Mr. Spiros cleared his throat. "Things were different back then. It was just understood that a man's needs were different."

"Way back in the 1970s?" Lainey retorted.

Pete Spiros ignored her. "When Harlow Drake accused my friend of being a murderer, using the worst sort of stereotypes about Italian Americans, something he took so seriously and personally, it just broke something inside of him. He was convinced people in the neighborhood were watching him, judging him, thinking the worst. He was a *cornerstone* in our neighborhood, someone people knew they could come to if they needed help, needed food for their families, needed a job, and he was afraid to walk down his own street."

"He would come to my house after work and just weep. And there was nothing I could do to make him feel better. He died thinking everybody saw him as a murderer. Harlow Drake doesn't just get to walk away from that, have her dreams, be on TV, after she did that to my dad. There has to be justice. Harlow loves justice, right?" Mrs. Maynard sniffed. "Pete was the only one who understood how angry I was. My mother is in a nursing home. She doesn't understand what's going on. Pete helped me come up with a plan."

"And the plan involved you pretending to be an aging Southern belle?" Lainey asked. "For accent misdirection?"

Suddenly, Mrs. Maynard's near-obsessive comments about her daddy and his preferences at the Crossings made so much more sense. This was clearly some sort of higher-level complex grief gone wrong.

"I didn't want anyone to see me as a threat," Mrs. Maynard groused. "I wanted the chance to get at Harlow when the time was right. I figured the best way to get people to avoid me was to talk a lot and talk really fast and really loud."

"Well, it certainly explains why Mr. Wesley looked at me all confused when I mentioned your daddy's favorite breakfast and your longtime patronage," Lainey said.

"I've never seen that woman before this week," Mr. Wesley told her.

"And you didn't get your own fictional persona?" Milo asked Mr. Spiros.

"Never been much of actor," Mr. Spiros muttered. "I always end up sounding like myself, but lying. We figured the best route was to pretend we didn't know each other."

"We found out from the internet that Harlow would be shooting a special here and we made reservations as soon as we could," Mrs. Maynard said.

"From Facebook?" Findlay asked. "People your age love Facebook."

Mrs. Maynard glared at her. Mr. Spiros didn't clarify their preferred platform. He just added, "We held out when the game company tried to pay us off. We didn't give a shit about our stay. We wanted to get close to Harlow."

Lainey glanced at Milo, who was just staring at the pair in disbelief. "So was poisoning Harlow's cocktail your first attempt or—"

"We didn't poison Harlow's cocktail," Mrs. Maynard insisted.

"You'll pardon my skepticism," Milo said dryly.

Lainey asked, "OK, have you done anything else to try to get back at Harlow since you got here? For that matter, did you have something to do with Mr. Hornsby dying?"

"I wouldn't hurt an old man," Mr. Spiros cried, sounding genuinely offended.

"We don't have to tell you anything," Mrs. Maynard said.

"They have us with the bleach powder," Mr. Spiros told her. "Do you think they're gonna care about us messing with a few buttons?"

"What kind of buttons?" Findlay asked. "Motherfucker—are you the ones who wrecked the elevator? You assholes! Do you *know* how many extra steps I've had to climb this week?"

Mr. Wesley made an indignant squawking noise. "How dare you?"

Lainey couldn't tell if Mr. Wesley was offended by Findlay's language or the abuse of precious Crossings buttons. She recalled Harlow's complaints about the elevator on her first day . . . and the light socket that sparked when she charged her phone. "Did you mess with the light sockets in Harlow's room?"

"I'm in the electricity business." Mr. Spiros sighed. "I thought it would be easy. Cross a few wires, produce a shock. It should have been enough to stop her heart, but I guess God protects idiots from themselves."

"Or maybe there's a big difference between selling electrical supplies and knowing how to rewire an antique elevator," Milo deadpanned. Mr. Spiros shrugged. "So you progressed to murder by mixology."

"We didn't poison the cocktail," Mr. Spiros said. "We just figured that if that Shelley lady died of poisoning, then if bleach got slipped into Harlow's juice mix, it would be blamed on the same killer. We thought the police would eventually figure out who poisoned Shelley, and it would be too hard to prove that person didn't poison Harlow, too."

Lainey stared at him. "You see our conundrum in believing *you* didn't poison Shelley with a drink meant for Harlow."

"Look, we're willing to ignore the knife threats if you talk to us about the poisonings," Milo said as Mr. Wesley paled.

Lainey whispered out of the side of her mouth, "We are?"

"What have you been doing in my hotel?" Mr. Wesley asked.

"Nothing!" Lainey cried.

"We did pepper spray them," Milo noted.

"We pepper sprayed *one* of them," Findlay said, shrugging, as if that was no big deal.

"We're going to leave you in here for our own safety. And we'll let the police figure Shelley's poisoning out, once Vern gets them here," Milo said. "If you didn't do anything, you don't have anything to worry about."

"Historically, that is not an attitude that has worked out in true-crime cases," Lainey told him. She looked at Mr. Wesley. "Any problem with that?"

Mr. Wesley sneered. "They damaged hotel property. Let them rot."

"Bold words from the guy who kept a case full of poisons barely locked around guests," Lainey pointed out.

When he gave her a confused frown, she added, "The display full of dangerous household chemicals from the roaring twenties? The lock on the case was pretty much decorative. And when I was in the archive the other night, a can of what I *think* was cyanide was missing from the display."

"And you didn't say anything?" Findlay asked.

"I didn't know it was cyanide at the time," Lainey told her, fishing a copy of the guest guide to the archive out of her purse and handing it to Findlay. "I figured it out tonight, you know, after Shelley."

"*Whoa whoa whoa,*" Mr. Spiros said, waving his arms. "We didn't know anything about any cyanide. Doesn't that prove we didn't do it?"

"No," Milo told him, his voice flat.

"That is not how evidence works," Lainey added. "At all."

"I unearthed those historically significant containers from the hotel's bomb shel—storage facility myself. They were wonderfully intact. I thought they shed an educational light on what the staff used to use to keep the hotel fit for its guests back in its epoch," Mr. Wesley said.

"So you *left* them intact?" Milo gasped.

"Of course I did," Mr. Wesley cried. "I would no more throw away the contents of the hotel's history than I would dump bottles of your precious champagne into the lake. Besides, I didn't think that pesticides would even be effective after a hundred years."

"Well, I don't think ingesting them would be *good* for you, no matter how old they are," Lainey said, throwing up her hands. "Also, Shelley had asthma. Maybe that made her more susceptible to a chemical that denies your body oxygen."

"Well, we'll get that sorted when we can move Ms. McMillan's body from the archive entrance," Mr. Wesley sneered. "For now, I suggest we all return to our rooms."

"So you're just going to leave us in here when there's a killer on the loose?" Mr. Spiros protested.

"Someone will stay here, keeping watch," Milo told them. "You might be safer in here than out in the hotel."

"Oh, I feel so much better," Mrs. Maynard shot back sarcastically.

"Actually, I think this room might be nicer than mine," Mr. Spiros said, glancing around his cell. Mr. Wesley gasped, clearly irate at the comparison.

"I'm going to go back to my room." Lainey looked at Mrs. Maynard. "Care to tell me what you took from it so I can emotionally prepare myself?"

"What's she talking about?" Mr. Spiros asked Mrs. Maynard.

The faux belle rolled her eyes. "You're not going to trick me into a confession of any extra crimes."

"Mr. Wesley, you probably need to count how many master keys are missing from your office," Milo told him. Something in Mr. Wesley's eyes seemed to snap. His lip curled back into an expression Lainey had never seen on the face of the obsequious hotelier—injured, aggressive, *unhinged*. Was it the feeling that he'd failed the hotel somehow, leaving the Crossings unprotected from the machinations of Mr. Spiros and Mrs. Maynard? Milo took a step between Lainey and Mr. Wesley. It was probably unnecessary, but she appreciated the gesture.

"I'll take the first watch," Findlay said. "I'll never sleep again, so it will be easy."

Lainey could sense Milo's hesitation and instantly understood. Milo had difficulty trusting people *before* the bleach powder and revelations of deception. She could almost hear him asking himself, *What if Findlay is one of them?*

"Look, we're Peach and Knife Club sisters," Lainey told him. "Findlay's on our side."

"I'll be happy to stay and supervise," Mr. Wesley offered, staring daggers at the detainees.

"I don't think that's a good idea," Findlay said, shaking her head.

Lainey leveled a look at Mr. Wesley. "I'm hiding all of the knives on my way back through the kitchen."

It turned out that coming back to your burgled hotel room after locking a pair of seniors in a not-quite-jail didn't lead to a restful night's sleep. Lainey had returned to her room expecting to find it tossed, but somehow it had been more unnerving to find nothing moved. The doorknob wasn't even damaged. It was just . . . unlocked, which only lent credence to the "misplaced master key" theory. Lainey wasn't sure what they had been looking for in the first place. She carried most of her important stuff in her shoulder bag, so there wasn't much for Mrs. Maynard and Mr. Spiros to take.

She was standing in her room, frowning, while Milo made up the love seat with spare guest bedding. He wasn't comfortable leaving Lainey alone in a room that had obviously been breached.

Lainey was happy that she'd prevented Harlow from drinking a tampered juice, because seeing one person die in a horrible manner right in front of her was enough. But . . . something didn't feel right about the situation. Besides the person dying right in front of her.

There was something about the riddle of this that nagged at her. The stakes were so much higher now because these were real people who had suffered real loss, getting hurt right in front of her.

"You all right?" Milo asked. "Which I realize sounds like a really dumb question to ask, now that it's come out of my mouth."

"Something's missing," she said, crossing the room to hand him extra pillows from her bed. "A question is unanswered, but I can't figure out what."

"You're not happy we caught the people who killed Shelley?" he said. She waggled her hand back and forth. "You're not actually believing Maynard and Spiros and their protestation of innocence, right?"

"It's just a hunch, which is really just another word for something that sticks in my brain when a puzzle piece isn't quite fitting in with everything else," she said. "I'd really like to get into the archive to look at something, but it feels disrespectful to move Shelley's body aside so we can open the door."

"It would not be the kindest thing I've ever seen," Milo admitted. "But also not the worst."

She hummed, and Milo kissed her. And this time his hands did not stay in the PG areas. She figured murder investigations had moved them beyond human resources concerns.

"So this distress, it's not at all connected to any guilt you may feel because I will be sleeping folded in half tonight?" he asked, jerking his head toward the love seat.

"I would offer to let you sleep in the bed with me, but I am *not* going to have sex with you in the murder hotel," Lainey told him.

"Right, right, right." He sighed.

"When we are no longer at the murder hotel, I would like to explore whatever this is with you," she said. "And not just because you're one of the few guys I've met who doesn't get freaked out about how my brain works."

"We could share the bed and *not* have sex."

"Do I look like the kind of girl who would fall for that?" she asked.

"It was worth a shot."

HARLOW DRAKE INVESTIGATES . . .

Webisode 31, "Lainey Suffers a Setback"
Posted—November 12, 2009

TRANSCRIPT EXCERPT

HARLOW: I know you're upset, but I don't think it's appropriate to take your anger out on my peanut butter M&M's.

LAINEY [SHOVING A FISTFUL OF M&M'S IN HER MOUTH]: This is at least a year's supply of candy and I'm kind of in crisis, Harlow.

HARLOW: OK, I'm assuming that there's been a problem with your dad's case? Remind the viewers of what was happening the last time we talked about your dad's accident that wasn't an accident.

LAINEY: I really hate it when you put me through your Diane Sawyer paces.

HARLOW: Humor me.

LAINEY: Dad's case was closed and the sheriff told us there was nothing else to be done. We asked for a case review from the state police, hoping that they would be a little more professional. Turns out *that* was a mistake. The evidence from my dad's case went missing from their lockup—my dad's computer, thumb drives, parts of his *car*. It's all gone.

HARLOW: What? How?

LAINEY: I don't know. Maybe Sheriff Pleasant didn't appreciate me accusing him of not knowing what the hell he was doing? The state police told us evidence just goes missing sometimes. I think they thought that was going to make us feel better?

HARLOW: I could ask my dad to look into it.

LAINEY: What's he going to do? Make evidence materialize again? His connections only go so far. I mean, it's not like I can file Freedom of Information requests. They're telling me the evidence is no longer there to request.

HARLOW: I'm sorry, Lainey.

LAINEY: You know, for once, I believe you.

HARLOW: Thanks . . . ?

LAINEY: I just fooled myself into thinking there were eventually going to be answers, and I feel like an idiot. There are no neat and tidy happy endings in this world. There are sad, angry girls face-deep in bags of peanut butter M&M's.

HARLOW: Which you will happily share with the owner of said M&M's.

LAINEY: No.

HARLOW: Fine. I'm not going to risk losing a hand. So, I'm just going to ask you, what are you going to do now?

LAINEY: I don't know. I don't think I can give up, even though my mom keeps telling me that we need to move on, accept that Dad's gone, and knowing what happened isn't going to bring him back. But it's the not knowing that gets you. My dad didn't have an *accident*, so how the hell am I supposed to live with the idea that someone took my dad from me, and they just walked off to live their life? They get to have meals with their family. They get holidays and vacations. And maybe by now they don't even think about my dad anymore. It's just some memory they buried, like a terrible song lyric they wrote in high school. And I'm just this person who's missing a piece, but no one else can see it. And people expect me to act "normal." I don't know what that is.

HARLOW: I don't think anyone knows what that is.

LAINEY: I know you don't.

HARLOW: I know you have to buy me like five pounds of M&M's to replace my stash.

LAINEY: That is fair.

15

Somehow, Milo managed to sleep better folded in half on the love seat than she did on the bed.

Lainey tossed and turned, sleeping intermittently. When she wasn't dozing, she was mulling over Mrs. Maynard and her motivations, the woman's devotion to a father who had held her at a distance, the need to avenge him. That, Lainey understood on a level that made her uncomfortable.

What Lainey didn't get was how Mrs. Maynard had poisoned the drink. She was fairly certain she knew *where* the cyanide came from, but she couldn't figure out *how* Mrs. Maynard had gotten it into the cocktail. Mrs. Maynard had been skulking around the perimeter of the room with Mr. Spiros up until she came to sit at the table, by which time the drink was already made. Mrs. Maynard only handled the drink once, to steady the glass when Lainey kicked the table. Had she managed it through sleight of hand? Poisoning a cocktail ingredient wouldn't guarantee that only Harlow was poisoned . . . unless it was something specific to Harlow . . .

Wait.

Harlow had been the only guest drinking bee's knees since they arrived at the hotel, which was the only cocktail on the menu that included honey syrup. Could the poison have been in the honey syrup? Lainey had secured the glass, but the honey syrup was sitting out on the bar. She realized that people weren't in a drinking mood at the moment, but that didn't seem safe.

This was not a night meant for Lainey to get sleep.

She scribbled a note to Milo telling him that she was going to relieve Findlay for the brig watch. It wasn't like she was going to sleep. She changed out of her pajamas into jeans and running shoes because, dammit, she wanted to be ready for anything at this point.

While she didn't feel *safe* dashing through the hotel in the dark, knowing that the brig was occupied made her feel saf*er*. The big knife and the backup pepper spray in her beloved shoulder bag helped.

This was part of the reason she didn't fly a lot.

The Beatrice Room was still in the state of chaos they'd left it, chairs overturned and drink glasses abandoned. Lainey rounded the bar, searching among the bottles and mixers for the squeeze bottle of honey syrup.

It was gone. She searched the entire dining room twice and couldn't find it. It wasn't like they'd secured the Beatrice Room after the scene with Shelley. She pulled the bar cabinet key from her shoulder bag and made sure the poisoned glass and bleach-infused Crystalline Greens powder were still locked up with all the other evidence-type items. When she saw they were secure, she relocked the cabinet and stashed the key in her bag.

Was it possible that Mrs. Maynard or Mr. Spiros had come in

to retrieve the honey while everybody else was running around discovering the many means of communication that had been cut off? They certainly hadn't had it on them in the kitchen. If Mr. Spiros was willing to pull knives on Lainey and her friends, he would be willing to spray them in the face with cyanide syrup.

Lainey made a quick stop in the kitchen for cups and a sealed bottle of orange juice from the fridge. Walking down the service corridor to the brig, Lainey realized that was something else that bothered her. It was a heck of a jump from fiddling with elevator buttons to cyanide. What had made them make that leap?

Unfortunately, neither conspirator was available for questions when she arrived at the double cell. They were both fast asleep, with Mr. Spiros snoring softly. Findlay was wide-awake, though, propped against the wall and reading her romance novel. She beamed at Lainey. "You came back!"

"Mr. Wesley left you alone?" she whispered, sitting cross-legged on the floor next to Findlay.

"I made him leave," Findlay replied. "Mr. Spiros made a crack about how the mattress in his cell was way less worn out than the one in his room and I thought Mr. Wesley was going to unlock the door and physically fight him."

"Good call," Lainey said. "Are you OK walking through the hotel alone to your room?"

She scoffed. "As long as Mr. Wesley isn't lurking in the lobby," she said.

"Not that I saw," Lainey told her.

"Taking my knife anyway," Findlay replied, pushing to her feet.

"Understood," Lainey said. "I would say text me when you get home, but you know, no cell signal."

"Just when we need it the most." Findlay sighed.

As Findlay padded away, Lainey took out the manager's diary to decode. It was surprising how long the detainees managed to sleep while being, well, detained. Maybe it was knowing they didn't have to hide anything anymore? They were caught. Police investigations were inevitable. Maybe they were relieved.

But she had plenty of time to transcribe the manager's opinions of Timmy Dandridge during his final stay at the hotel. It was not flattering. She sank into the world of the Crossings, reliving Marguerite's stay through Mr. Crowder's eyes—the glamour, the intrigue, the inept razor heir who left everything he touched in chaos.

When the sun crept through the windows, she closed her notebook, pretty sure that she was the only living person who knew what had happened to poor Marguerite Devereaux—a girl who tried to make her way in the world by pinning her hopes to unworthy men.

"Holy shit." She sighed, scrubbing a hand over her face.

"Language," Mrs. Maynard grumped from her bed.

Without looking up, Lainey shot back, "Yeah, I don't think I'll take criticisms of character from you."

16

Dawn brought Mr. Wesley back to the brig. After securing a promise from him that he would not threaten or harm their guests, Lainey walked through the kitchen, where Cassie was sorting through the pantry. The entire contents of canned goods were on the central prep table. Cassie was examining each container up close while Mrs. Rowland seemed to be writing a checklist of everything that was still usable.

"Morning," Lainey called. She put her knife and her bag on the counter. "Checking them for tampering?"

Cassie sighed. "Every can and carton. Andy has taken to his bed like a frail old lady, except he took a bottle of whiskey with him. He's really freaked out by the idea that someone got sick from something in his kitchen."

Was it suspicious that Chef Andre was hiding? Or should they be worried about someone who had isolated himself with the bar supplies? What if he took a bottle that had been tampered with?

"Has anyone checked on him?" Lainey asked.

Cassie nodded. "About ten minutes ago. He was snoring so loud I heard it through his door. He seemed fine."

"And you get stuck with all his work?" Lainey replied.

"It's not a big surprise," Cassie said, shrugging. "Also, he's not going to be able to hide there forever. Mr. Taggert declined the honor of cooking his own food, after he 'paid so damn much for this place.'"

"Charming," Mrs. Rowland muttered. She gave Lainey a sidelong look. "How are you this morning? Did you have something to do with the pepper spray we had to clean off the counters?"

"I am so sorry!" Lainey's jaw dropped. "We were so— I didn't even think about cleanup. That is not like me."

"Leaving messes for other people to clean up?" Mrs. Rowland asked, giving her a small smile. "I had a feeling, so I'll let it slide this once. Fortunately for you, I recognized it and knew to put gloves on."

"How did you know how to spot pepper spray?" Lainey asked her.

"You spend thirty years as an ER nurse, you know dried pepper spray when you see it," Mrs. Rowland said.

"Ah." Lainey nodded. Mrs. Rowland didn't come across as someone who'd had to work for a living. She came across as more of an old-money matriarch. She was so polished and worldly . . . and classy. She used all the right forks at dinner.

"I understand we have guests in the brig? What happened last night?" When Lainey's mouth drew back at the corners, Cassie added, "What *else* happened last night?"

"I'll let Mr. Wesley explain," Lainey told her. "But hey, you'll get to finally use those little slots in the cell doors to slide their plates through."

"It's actually not my first time," Cassie told her. "This place, it has a way of making people lose it a little bit. Anyway, I believe Mr. Wade was hoping to see you? He was heading out to the dock last time I saw him."

"Thanks, Cassie," Lainey replied. "Are you doing OK? You know, with everything?"

"I'm not," Cassie told her. "And I won't be for a while. But we don't have time for that right now, so I'm going to sort through this pantry, and as soon as the police are here and I'm cleared as a non-murderer, I'm quitting this job and getting the hell off this island. I don't care if Mr. Wesley gives me a reference or not."

"You have no idea how much I empathize," Lainey told her. Cassie winked and returned to her pantry sorting.

Walking across the island in the morning quiet was a balm to Lainey's nerves. There was a real world outside of their problems and suspicions—a world with sunlight and cool breezes that would still be here after they were gone. Vern, Tommy, and Milo were talking on the dock, looking very serious, which Lainey supposed was appropriate.

"Did you actually sleep out here?" Lainey asked Vern as she approached.

"Not the first time," Tommy said.

"Life at this hotel is more complex than I thought," Lainey said. She turned to Milo. "Cassie said you were looking for me."

"Yes, because you disappeared from your bed while I was asleep, despite the fact that I made it very clear that I was invested in you being safe and nonpoisoned and nonstabbed," Milo told her.

"That sentence started out sort of romantic and then it went way out of bounds," Vern said.

"Well, he was a terrible guard," Lainey said. "I was awake for most of the night, with the light on. And I left the room without him even noticing."

"In my defense, the adrenaline crash hit me really hard," Milo said. "But I do appreciate you leaving the note."

"Old people are weird," Tommy said before jogging away.

"He just called us 'old,'" Milo said.

Lainey *tsk*ed. "Gen Z knows right where to hit you."

"Well, as much as I appreciate watching this very awkward yuppie courtship play out, I should get going," Vern told them. "Milo, can you toss me those lines?"

"Excuse me!" Mrs. Rowland called, jogging down the path to the dock, holding a metal Thermos. "Cassie sent coffee from the kitchen. She said don't worry, she brewed it extra strong—from one of the sealed cans."

"Thanks," Vern said, his weathered cheeks flushing pink. Lainey watched the way he rubbed at his neck as he accepted the Thermos. Lainey didn't care if they were caught in a life-or-death nightmare. She shipped this couple.

"You're welcome," she said. "Godspeed."

Lainey waggled her eyebrows at Vern and then felt really weird about it.

"Shut it," Vern grumbled at her.

They helped Vern push the boat off the dock, and he waved at them as he sped away.

"Well, this is not how I expected this birthday trip to turn out," Mrs. Rowland said as they turned to walk back to the hotel. "But I suppose that it has been one to call home about—when I'm able to use my phone, that is."

"It's not how any of us expected anything to turn out. I don't know if Harlow would have asked me to join if she knew how this was going to go—especially when I tell her what I found when I was"—Lainey paused to glance at Milo—"researching last night."

"Oh, I think she's better off with you than without you," Mrs. Rowland said. "Don't let her take credit for whatever it is you found. You had a tendency to step back and take over when you were kids, when it was obvious that you were the one who put in the work."

When Lainey paused and stared at her, Mrs. Rowland laughed. "I watched your webisodes on occasion with my daughter. She liked you better. You got all the funny lines."

Lainey blanched. "You never said anything."

Mrs. Rowland waved away her exclamation. "Oh, I didn't want to come across as some annoying fan. And Harlow has nothing to be embarrassed about. Everyone has an experimental nose ring phase."

Lainey snorted and told Milo, "Harlow tried to have a rebellious phase her sophomore year of college. Her dad squashed it right away."

"Well, I'll leave you two to your research revelations," Mrs. Rowland said. "I think Cassie needs help sorting breakfast."

As Mrs. Rowland walked away from them, Milo said, "Believe it or not, the guys are already up. The crew is having a pre-breakfast meeting in the speakeasy. Harlow said it was the only space where she felt safe."

"They're still planning to film?" Lainey marveled. "Shelley's death had no effect on them?"

"I wouldn't say that, but Harlow told Cameron, Gordy, and Kenny that the best way to take their minds off of things was to work. And Bryce and Deke pointed out that even with Shelley's death, the construction timeline isn't going to change. You still have to be out of here in two weeks."

"The show must go on," Lainey mused. "That is pretty depressing."

"Helping Harlow gets you that much closer to getting your paycheck," he said, in an apparent attempt to cheer her up.

"Did Harlow find out that I locked up her juice powder as evidence?" Lainey asked.

"Yes, she did, and she was really upset about it," he said, slipping her hand into his. "I explained the bleaching, but she was unmoved. Maybe she thought Cameron could sift the bleach out or something."

"I'm sure he would give it his best try," she said.

"So, this research revelation, does it require going into the archive like you wanted last night? Because I don't know if I can sanction moving the body," Milo said.

"No, but do you mind stopping by the bomb shelter on the way to the speakeasy?"

He grinned at her. "You solved it, didn't you?"

"I halfway solved it," she said. "Which isn't quite the same thing."

"Further than anyone else has gotten," he reminded her as they approached the hotel. "Harlow is going to be super pissed."

"She'll survive," Lainey said. "Unless someone manages to slip bleach into one of her other beverages."

"Yeah, I get the feeling she's not really taking the threat seriously."

"Such a weird moment to choose to hold my hand," she teased him.

He glanced down at their joined hands, but he didn't let go.

"Yeah, it felt weird. But I'm invested now, so I might as well go with it, as long as it's OK with you."

"I'll allow it," she said, making him grin.

It was interesting how nonthreatening the secret passageway seemed when one knew what was waiting at the end of it. The bomb shelter was a less dramatic way to enter the passageway, but they did spend a good ten minutes restacking debris to get to the mystery item she thought might soften the blow to Harlow when she explained to the crew what she'd learned.

They prepared to slide the bomb shelter's exit-hiding dresser out of the way when Findlay and Gordy came in behind them through the hatch door from the service corridor. Gordy looked a little flustered and rumpled, but Findlay seemed determined to chase off evidence of her all-nighter with a fully contoured face. Lainey admired her defiance of the circadian cycle.

"I'm glad we found you before you caught up to the rest of the crew," Gordy told her.

"Mostly because I still refuse to go into the secret passageway," Findlay said. "I feel comfortable with my choices. Harlow can do her own eyeliner."

"I see you and your quiet rebellion," Lainey told her.

"How did you even know we were in here?" Milo asked.

"Mrs. Rowland said she saw you coming this way," Gordy said. "There aren't a lot of other options, in terms of destination. Lainey, I don't know how to tell you this, but Findlay says you're one of us now, after the creation of the Peach and Knife Club—which I *will* be joining, by the way. Since you shielded my favorite person from knife-wielding senior citizens, I hereby pledge my loyalty to you. You have my sword. Anyway, I'm trying to put this gently, so—"

"Harlow isn't your friend!" Findlay blurted out. "She's not a nice person and she doesn't like you!"

Milo blinked at her. "That was gently?"

"He was taking too long," Findlay said.

"Just listen to this," Gordy said, holding up a digital recorder. "It's a clip from when we were recording intro shots in front of the hotel when we first got here. Harlow's phone rang and she took the call near the croquet lawn. She didn't take off her lapel mic. She definitely didn't realize it was still recording. I think she's talking to her agent?"

Harlow's voice filled the bomb shelter. *"Yeah, she gets here this afternoon. I don't know, accounting or something? She's broke, I know that. She should just be happy I invited her at all. I mean, it was hard enough to put up with her in high school. 'Boo-hoo, my daddy died and the world has to stop so I can whine and wallow in my trauma.' Cry me a fucking river. Everybody knew her dad was a thieving drunk who wrapped his car around a tree. Big fucking deal. My mom ran off on me and you didn't hear me complaining about it. Better no mom than backwoods hillbilly trash like her mom. She's just like the Restrettos, clutching pearls and playing victim, when everybody knows—"*

Gordy pressed "Pause." "And the rest of it is a rant against you, the network's executive board, the Restretto family, and the entire population of Chicago in a manner that is so offensive I'm surprised she hasn't already been canceled, like, by telepathy."

"We tried to warn Shelley, but she told us to keep it to ourselves. We were already under a microscope with this project and we all just needed to put our heads down, survive this shoot, and get back to New York," Findlay said. "Which turned out to be weirdly prophetic."

"We just don't want you to keep trying to stay friends with her. She doesn't deserve it."

Lainey blinked rapidly, determined not to let her eyes tear up. It had been a very long time since someone had gone out of their way to look out for her. She had friends, but this kind of effort and protection, especially in a situation as fraught as this one—Lainey knew how valuable it was. She blew out a long breath and wrapped her arms around Findlay's and Gordy's necks simultaneously.

"Oh!" Findlay exclaimed. "A hug! I didn't expect that."

"She's taking it really well," Gordy noted over Lainey's shoulder.

"You two are very sweet," Lainey assured them. "But I know."

Findlay frowned at her. "You know?"

"I didn't know about the rant against the population of Chicago, specifically, but I know Harlow has never been my friend," Lainey told them. "I mean, an acquaintance at best, but never a real friend. I found out years ago. It took a while to deal with it, but it is what it is."

"How did you find out?" Gordy demanded.

"I've kind of got some other stuff going on right now!" she exclaimed. "I'm happy to go over the past with you two later."

"Wait, so if you knew Harlow is the living worst, then why did you bother coming to Murder Island?" Findlay asked.

"Did I not make my dire financial circumstances clear?" Lainey asked.

"You're just using Harlow for . . . money?" Gordy gasped, clutching his invisible pearls.

"Sort of," she said. "There's some nostalgia at work here. Also the deep personal satisfaction of outsmarting her. But yes, money played a big part in most of my decisions."

"Good for you," Findlay said, holding up her hand for a fist bump.

"Thank you," Lainey said, touching her knuckles to Findlay's. "Can we go down the secret passageway so I can throw some potential evidence in Harlow's face now?"

"Everybody but me," Findlay said.

"Everybody but Findlay," Lainey agreed.

They found the crew in the speakeasy, looking more glum than usual as they set up the shot, which made sense, she supposed, given their coworker's gruesome death. Even Deke and Bryce were pretty subdued. They weren't even trying to juggle any of the antique bottles. Mr. Wesley was notably absent, which Lainey assumed was related to his shift as guard.

Harlow didn't seem thrilled to see Lainey as she walked down the speakeasy stairs with Milo and Gordy, gingerly carrying an old suitcase. Lainey hadn't trusted herself to hold it by the handle, even if it seemed to be carved from actual hardwood. It felt like dry rot could snap it at any moment.

"That Crystalline Greens powder is ninety dollars a cannister," Harlow announced as Lainey set the case on a nearby table.

"Well, talk to the people who mixed bleach into it," Lainey told her. Then she began carefully laying out her transcribed portions of the diary.

"What's that?" Harlow asked.

"The manager's diaries we found in the drop box," Lainey said. "Remember? My homework."

Harlow blinked. "Oh, right."

"I'm assuming you'll just film Harlow explaining this later?" Lainey asked Kenny, who gave her a thumbs-up.

Lainey went over the substitution cipher in the diaries, which seemed to excite Deke and Bryce. Kenny slipped his camera onto his shoulder.

"You got to spend all night decoding a book written in obscure code?" Deke said breathily as he and Bryce pored over her papers. "*Lucky*!"

"It varies every year. I think the manager changed it annually to maintain confusion . . ." She trailed off when Bryce's head popped up and he stepped close to her.

"Marry me. Our babies would be so smart," Bryce said. Milo's jaw dropped. Bryce gestured toward Lainey and Harlow. "Oh, come on, man, you knew that eventually I was going to propose to one of them!"

"I appreciate the offer," Lainey said, patting Bryce's arm. "But do you mind if I keep explaining stuff?"

"Oh, sure," Bryce said, nodding with a serious expression on his face. "But think about it."

Lainey noticed that the longer the "boys" were away from the real world, the more tolerable they were. They weren't *terrible* people, they were just . . . obtuse to the feelings of other people. Coddled. Protected from reality by their money. They took the easiest and most indulgent options because those were right there at their fingertips. Maybe it would be good for them to spend time on . . . this murder island. That was probably going to be a hard argument to make.

Harlow stared at Lainey, mouth set in an unhappy line as she summarized Timmy Dandridge's condescending behavior toward the staff, Marguerite, and basically everybody—how he was insistent on using his own private stash of home brew, which he believed was perfectly safe because he used the finest wood alcohols.

"Wood alcohol?" Deke said. "Hilarious joke opportunities aside, that doesn't sound good."

"It's a highly poisonous solvent that was pretty common during Prohibition. It was unsafe, but people wanted a drink so badly, they used it anyway," Lainey said.

"Were they OK?" Bryce asked.

"Decidedly not," Lainey replied, "and Dandridge used it to make his gin because he didn't know what he was doing. The staff was mixing his drinks pretty weak, which probably gave him a few days' grace, but still, poison. So, according to what I read last night, the staff liked Marguerite a bit more. That loyalty meant they mixed her cocktails a little stronger than Dandridge's, so she got sick first. The manager, Mr. Crowder, begged Dandridge to throw out his bathtub gin, but to prove that it couldn't possibly be his gin making Marguerite sick, he drank most of his last bottle right in front of Crowder. *Expiration was almost immediate.* And then a few days later, the manager writes, *Lady M has departed.* He's being so careful not to use the word 'died,' but I don't think he means 'checked out of the hotel as a breathing person.'"

"They never made it off the island." Harlow smiled, but it didn't reach her eyes, and that was when Lainey knew that she'd made a mistake.

Yes, Harlow liked to delegate, but Lainey should have pulled Harlow aside and let her read over the diary transcription for herself. And Lainey found herself . . . not really caring. Lainey had done the work. Oh well, Harlow could deal with it.

"But what happened to the bodies?" Bryce said.

"And what about the Star of Sikkim?" Deke demanded. When Milo gave him a stern look, Deke huffed, "I don't really need the money. But I'm emotionally involved!"

"Well, that's why I brought the suitcase," Lainey said. "Our first day here, Harlow told us that Marguerite borrowed some clothes from her roommate."

"And some travel essentials," Harlow interjected. "That's how she said it in the police report, but I thought she meant nylons and fancy pajamas or something."

"Well, I noticed this suitcase when we were in the bomb shelter. I think the managers just chucked stuff in there over the years, like a lost and found. They probably moved stuff around from place to place in the hotel and never realized what they had—like my mom and the Christmas decorations in the attic."

Lainey paused to show them the initials scratched on the suitcase, *GM*—Gladys McComber. "And remember, you said Gladys was Southern. Look at the stamp: 'FrogMouth, Alabama—the Mouth of the South.' Kind of fits, right?"

"You think this is her suitcase?" Harlow demanded, grabbing it and yanking it across the table.

Lainey shrugged. "Some of the suitcases in the bomb shelter have clearly been in there for decades. From what I read in the diary, Mr. Crowder told the housekeeping staff to 'clear the room' as quickly as possible. He made it look like Dandridge and Marguerite had checked out quietly and left the island as planned. It was bad business for a son of a wealthy, powerful family to die on the property, especially when it was already connected to illegal activities. Better to let Timmy's habits and well-known tendency to screw up do the work of explaining his disappearance. And he assigned one of his assistants, a Rupert Leopold, to take Dandridge's luggage to the mainland shortly after, to pawn it. I think he meant to throw the Pinkertons off the scent, but I would have to read ahead in the diaries. I don't think he was worried about Marguerite's stuff because no one was going to come looking for her. So maybe the housekeepers just threw it in the lost and found?"

"Kenny." Harlow snapped her fingers and pointed to the suitcase. "We'll film me finding the suitcase in the bomb shelter later."

Cameron didn't say a word as Lainey backed out of the shot. Kenny filmed diligently as Harlow opened the suitcase. There were no sparkly stage clothes inside. They'd probably been left hanging up in Dandridge's room and then thrown out by the housekeepers. They did, however, find plenty of pretty lacy underthings and corsetry that made Lainey thankful for sports bras.

Harlow shouted in triumph as she pulled out a curling black-and-white snapshot of a younger, calico-clad Marguerite standing between an elderly couple in front of an old farmhouse. "It's hers!"

Deke and Bryce whooped and began clapping, earning a light glare from Gordy.

Milo drifted to Lainey's side. He squeezed her arm gently as Harlow rifled through the suitcase. She pulled out a cloudy glass bottle with a homemade label. *Timothy's Latest and Greatest Invention! Dandridge's Finest Gin* was scrawled on it in purpling ink in a lazy hand.

It did not look like something that Lainey wanted to drink.

Harlow gasped over a tiny blue lady's handbag sewn with glass seed beads. She opened it and several gambling slips fluttered to the table. Each of them was marked in scary red pencil—some variation of "Dandridge Owes House—$50." That was the 1927 equivalent to about a thousand modern dollars. And there were so, so many slips.

"Is the Star in the suitcase?" Deke asked as Harlow brandished a small pair of pliers.

"No," she said, now taking out a small silky bag with **Hairpins** embroidered on it. She opened the bag, and several rusty-looking, sharply pointed hairpins fell out into her hand, along with . . .

"Holy shit!" Bryce yelped as diamonds sparkled in the light of the schoolhouse lamps. There were five of them—the largest was about the size of an English pea, while there were several smaller stones, equally shiny.

"Celestial assets," Lainey murmured. Harlow glared at her, but Lainey added, "Crowder said Dandridge had liquidated his celestial assets. It's what you thought. He broke up the necklace to pay off his gambling debts, but the casino staff were also pissed because Dandridge refused to hand over the Star as collateral—which, considering the way he was gambling, made sense. And Crowder complained that Dandridge wandered around the hotel at night in closed areas, causing messes for the staff to clean up. Marguerite must have snagged a few gems for herself when no one was looking. It probably would have set her up in that cozy little California-starlet starter apartment if she'd lived through Dandridge's version of mixology."

"That is so sad," Bryce muttered.

"OK, but where is the Star?" Deke demanded. "The tiny diamonds are nice and all, but I can't set a tiny diamond in a belt buckle to serve as a conversation starter with girls and draw their eyes to the Promised Land."

"It might give them more realistic expectations," Bryce told him.

Milo stepping between them was the only thing that kept Deke and Bryce from fist-fighting and destroying the nearest tables. Lainey was frowning, but it wasn't due to the DBags' antics.

"Why are you making that face?" Harlow asked.

"Do you want me to tell you, or do you want to read ahead and find out for yourself?" Lainey asked.

"You knew where the Star was all this time?" Deke gasped.

"Of course not, but this is the journey," Lainey told him. He frowned and crossed his arms over his chest.

"Well, of course I want to know what happened," Harlow snapped.

"I skipped ahead a few weeks in the diaries and found Mr. Crowder lamenting his assistant Mr. Leopold's sharp decline in performance. He wrote that he kept finding Mr. Leopold obsessively cleaning the light fixtures, all over the hotel, in the middle of the night," Lainey said. "Leopold was one of the people who tended to Dandridge while he was sick."

"The light fixtures in the guest hallways that have little crystals dripping off them," Deke asked. "You think Dandridge snuck off and hid the Star somewhere in the hotel."

"Before he got too sick to retrieve it," Lainey said. "I think Leopold knew Dandridge hid it somewhere, but didn't know specifics. There was a hole drilled in the top of the diamond because it was a dangling briolette shape. It could have been wired into one of the sconces."

"We still have the black light," Bryce reminded Deke.

Bryce and Deke looked at each other for a half second, then took off running for the rotating door. Kenny, Gordy, and Cameron followed quickly after them.

"Aren't you going to go get them?" Lainey asked Milo.

"My job is to protect them from destroying the company's reputation," Milo replied. "If they smack their heads while running through a secret passageway in the dark, that's on them."

"You knew where it was," Harlow said, shaking her head. "You could have gone to find it while we were sleeping."

"Well, a couple of problems with that," Lainey said. "One, *I* don't have a black light, so I wouldn't be able to tell diamond from cut glass. And I wasn't going to go to Bryce's room in the middle of the night to ask for it. Two, I'm not about to go wandering around the hotel in the dark when there's a murderer on the loose. Three, I don't have any way off of the island to make my escape with my ill-gotten loot, and on that note, what was I going to do? Find a fence to sell it in a way that won't be noticed? With my limitless dark web contacts?"

Harlow continued to stare at her.

"Shouldn't you be having your moment, finding the Star with Deke and Bryce and their black light?" Lainey asked.

Harlow huffed out an annoyed breath and hustled up the stairs, leaving them behind.

"So, you solved it," Milo said.

"I think I'm still at sort of halfway solved. We still don't know what happened to their bodies, and we don't know for sure what happened to the Star."

"Never happy, are you?"

"I'm standing in a basement with you, near a stranger's hundred-year-old underwear," Lainey told him. "You figure it out."

17

When they reached the lobby, Lainey could hear the cries of Deke and Bryce as they rampaged up the second-floor guest hall with their black light. Harlow and the crew were running along with them. Milo jogged up the staircase to catch up. Lainey would have followed if she hadn't spotted Cameron sitting on one of the lobby couches, shaking, looking sweaty and pale.

"Cameron?"

"I'm OK . . ." He panted. "I was OK just a few minutes ago."

He stretched back on the couch, as if he was trying to find a comfortable position to sit. "I'm fine, I just need an— I don't know what I need."

Lainey knew almost nothing about first aid, but she knew his pulse was way too fast when she touched his wrist. "I think you're having a heart attack. I'm going to go get Mrs. Rowland. Just stay here, all right?"

Without waiting for an answer, Lainey ran across the lobby and the dining room to the kitchen, the last place she'd seen Mrs. Rowland. She stuck her head in the swinging kitchen door to find the lady herself, reviewing Cassie's inventory list. Lainey didn't spot the desk clerk as she gasped out, "Lobby, Cameron, help."

"Chest pains?" Mrs. Rowland nodded sharply. "Grab the portable AED."

Within seconds, Lainey had grabbed the cardiac kit from the bar, and Mrs. Rowland was jogging across the lobby just behind her. Lainey knew she was supposed to be calling for help, but she couldn't seem to catch her breath. *Damn*, she needed to work out more.

As Mrs. Rowland knelt next to Cameron, facing Lainey, she wondered—how had Mrs. Rowland known that Cameron was having chest pains? Lainey hadn't said anything about symptoms. But Mrs. Rowland had just known that they'd need the portable defibrillator? How?

Meanwhile, Cameron had teetered off the couch onto his face. He groaned as Mrs. Rowland turned him onto his back. She patted his shirt, searching his pockets. Lainey knelt next to them, her hands shaking as she unzipped the first-aid kit. Her bag frequently slipped off her shoulder, but Lainey made the best of it.

"I don't think Cameron was taking any medication, if that's what you're looking for," Lainey huffed, still catching her breath as Mrs. Rowland searched his pockets. "Do you think it was the stress or something? Cameron is awfully young for a heart attack."

"Well, it is happening a little ahead of schedule, but these things can be tricky." Mrs. Rowland tugged a lip balm out of his shirt and moved it to her back pocket.

Lainey watched, confused by Mrs. Rowland's failure to check Cameron's vitals or administer any aid whatsoever. Mrs. Rowland was too busy searching his pockets. "Wait, what are you— Oh, hell."

Mrs. Rowland knew a lot of things. She knew about the chest pains. She seemed to know about Harlow's fake pistachio allergy. She'd known about Harlow's nose ring.

Harlow had never worn her nose ring on-camera. She'd never posted about it on social media. She thought the piercing went against her brand. Lainey only knew about it because Harlow had accidentally texted her a picture of it—obviously meant for another friend. Only someone close to Harlow during college would have known about the nose ring.

Mrs. Rowland didn't seem to like Harlow very much.

Shit.

Mrs. Rowland moved so fast, Lainey barely registered the knife the other woman pulled from the back of her jeans before the tip was pressed to Lainey's neck.

"What is it with your age group and knife play?" Lainey grumbled as Mrs. Rowland gripped the back of her head, keeping the knifepoint against the jugular. She had remarkable strength for such a relatively slim woman. She forced Lainey to stand.

"No screaming and no sudden moves," Mrs. Rowland told her. "You left your knife in the kitchen this morning. You used your pepper spray last night. You're all alone here, Lainey."

"Are we just going to let Cameron die?" Lainey asked as Mrs. Rowland forced her to sidestep away from Cameron's body. To her relief, Mrs. Rowland didn't force her to drop her shoulder bag. Lainey kept it tucked against her side like a baby.

"It's not my fault that he chose to use the lip balm so often," Mrs. Rowland hissed. She turned Lainey toward the door and marched her forward. "If he'd moisturized his lips in moderation, he probably would have been mildly ill. The rate of digoxin absorption through the skin can be difficult to predict."

"So, what, you melted the balm down, mixed in foxglove, and poured it back into the tube?" Lainey asked, naming one of the few poisons she knew affected the heart. Thank you, Mom's old murder mystery movies.

Oh, Lainey's mom was going to be so mad at her if she died on this creepy island.

"No, I melted the lip balm and mixed it with crushed heart medication like a normal person," Mrs. Rowland shot back. As they moved, Lainey angled her shoulder bag so it rested against her right side, away from Mrs. Rowland's eyes. "I am a nurse. I have access to these things. Though I suppose you deserve some credit for knowing digoxin comes from foxglove. Cameron wasn't even supposed to get a tube. I dropped one in your gift bag and Harlow's. Careless, really, for the staff to leave them just sitting out at the front desk where anyone could get to them. I suppose Cameron stole Harlow's balm without her even seeing it. She doesn't seem like the type to handle anything personally, not even a gift."

Lainey snaked her hand into the bag. She tried to be subtle about the rummaging. All she could close her hand around was an oblong device that wouldn't do much as a weapon but might prove useful. Lainey fumbled with it for a second and found the right button. She pushed it and breathed in, hoping for stealth as she continued to search the bag for her next-best resource. She worked to keep her expression neutral as her fingers found a more helpful cylindrical object.

With the knife at her throat, she didn't know whether it would do enough damage to Mrs. Rowland's eyes and get the blade away from her jugular. So instead, she flipped the cylinder's lid open and sprinkled a little bit at a time behind them. She could only pray Milo would see it and know what it meant.

"It was so *frustrating* every time I saw him use the stupid balm when neither you nor Harlow seemed to touch it," Mrs. Rowland grumbled as they walked out the front entrance. "Even if it was my backup plan."

"What was your original plan?" she asked, recalling Mrs. Rowland pulling the pistachios out of Harlow's reach. "Something to do with Harlow's fake pistachio allergy?"

Keep her talking, Lainey told herself. *Keep sprinkling the glitter.* The confessional strategy had worked for her before with Lunch Lady Sybil, Mr. Raine. People with heavy consciences *loved* talking about what they'd done. They craved the feeling of being unburdened.

"Fake? What do you mean *fake*!" Mrs. Rowland exclaimed. "Who the hell does that? If you had any idea what I've seen in the ER, the kids who come in because relatives decided to 'test' their allergies—"

"Cecelia—may I call you 'Cecelia'?" Lainey asked. "Is that even your real name?"

"It is," Cecelia growled, never lessening her knife pressure against Lainey's neck as they walked along the path from the hotel. Lainey could only hope that they didn't trip over loose stones or something.

Sprinkle, sprinkle, sprinkle.

"I don't know how long you've been dealing with Harlow, but the needs of other people don't exactly factor into her decisions," Lainey told her. "She wants to make sure people are doing what she tells them. So you're the person who coated all the door handles on the first floor in a sticky, faintly nutty-smelling substance?"

"Pistachio oil," Cecelia grumbled. "I snuck around my first night here, before the crew arrived. I peeled the label off and threw the container away in the woods. I thought Harlow would maybe have an EpiPen for one exposure, maybe two. But no one carries a *case* of EpiPens with them, and I left possibilities for so many exposures. It would take too long for her to get to a hospital from here. But it just wasn't working."

"Instead of Harlow, the only person you managed to hurt was Mr. Hornsby—who had a real nut allergy."

"Really?" Cecelia sighed. "I was really hoping that he'd just passed in his sleep, like Mr. Wesley said. *He's* a very effective liar, you know. I really didn't mean to hurt that poor man. The group was so small, I didn't think there would be another person here with a nut allergy. But he was old. He'd lived a good long life, and . . . we all have to make sacrifices."

They were past the croquet lawn now. Somehow, it seemed so much creepier when she was in danger. Lainey asked, "So why did you move the pistachios out of her reach at dinner the other night?"

"Because I didn't know the little bitch was lying," Cecelia shot back. "And I realized with each day that passed without Harlow going into anaphylaxis or heart failure, to my increasing frustration, that either one of those deaths was too good for her. I wanted her to die ugly. I wanted her to hurt. I wanted her to die scared."

"And you snuck the Rat-B-Gone out of the archive and into the honey syrup?" Lainey guessed. "How easy were those display-case locks to pick?"

"Only took a hairpin and a little bit of elbow grease," Cecelia said. "It was, honestly, sort of shocking how little effort that Wesley lunatic put into safeguarding a bunch of poisons."

"That's what I said!" Lainey tried to turn her head to look at her, but Cecelia pressed the knife against her neck. Lainey grunted as she felt the blade bite into her skin.

"Be careful," she warned Lainey. "Don't mistake my good manners for weakness. We are not gabbing girlfriends."

"Well, I don't know how you were raised, but my mom taught me that threatening to bisect someone's jugular is the height of rudeness. Right up there with slipping cyanide into mixology stock," Lainey retorted. "It must have been infuriating, after you poisoned the bee's knees, realizing that once again, Harlow had managed to dodge getting poisoned."

"Just proof that God protects idiots from themselves. What the hell was that Shelley woman doing, drinking other people's cocktails? Who does that? Didn't she realize how carefully I had to keep track of every single person's preferences? How tedious that was? How difficult it was to cut this island off from communication with the outside world? I would have disabled the boat, too, if I'd had time, but I'm only one person."

Sprinkle, sprinkle, sprinkle.

"Poor you." Lainey *tsk*ed. "Shelley was just so focused on her phone that she didn't realize it was Harlow's drink."

"Yes, and that's as rude as anything else—phones at the table," Cecelia huffed. "Maybe she deserved it."

Pivoting, Lainey observed, "So, God protects idiots from themselves. That's an interesting turn of phrase."

She took deep breaths through her nose, trying not to think about the trickle of warm blood she could feel seeping into the collar of her shirt. The treetops seemed to be bowing over them, closing them in. "So how long have you known Mrs. Maynard and Mr. Spiros? Did you all plan this together on Facebook or—"

"I don't know either of those morons," Cecelia insisted. "And I've never had a Facebook account. We're all members of a certain internet forum for people who don't want their chat history documented. It was originally a subgroup for people who found Harlow's media persona to be grating—which, I will admit, felt a little unsettling for me, personally. I mean, I find her deplorable as a person, but I felt uncomfortable with the number of people who criticized her for how she looked or for being 'unlikable' when, honestly, what she was guilty of was being a woman working on television. I could go on, but my thoughts on postmodern feminism and media aren't the reason we're here today. I almost quit the group. I didn't find any satisfaction in seeing people complain about her new haircut or how she pronounced 'Saskatchewan.' But then I saw a post titled 'Has anyone here been personally victimized by Harlow Drake?' I was prepared for another litany of complaints about her hair, her makeup, her eyebrows. And that was there, but then I saw chatter from people who *knew Harlow in real life.* Spiros and Maynard all but announced their plans to 'do something *big*' while Harlow was shooting at the Crossings. I figured, best-case scenario, they take care of the hard work for me and I just sit back and enjoy watching. And if they were charmingly inept blowhards—which it turned out, they were—I would have perfect patsies to take the fall for my plans."

"So what are you going to do when Vern comes back here with the police . . . Oh, fuck-a-duck, what did you do to Vern's coffee?" Lainey cried.

"Same heart meds I put in the lip balm," Mrs. Rowland told her proudly. "You know, they say poison is a woman's weapon. But sometimes it's the only one left to us. It seeps in over time, building, spreading to everything we touch. Harlow's poison was just a different type; it seeps through the skin, one word at a time, crawling into the brain, changing everything you see and hear, turning it into a wound. You know that little bitch came to my daughter's funeral, looked me in the eye, and shook my hand. '*Such a shame, but you know Bella always did drive a little fast.*'" Mrs. Rowland's ability to mimic Harlow's insincere pleasantries voice was unnerving. She added, "And all these years later, she didn't even recognize me?"

Lainey stopped, hissing when Cecelia jerked her grip on her hair, pressing the blade to her throat. "Bella Faris's mom?"

Cecelia's stranglehold on her hair relaxed ever so slightly. "You remembered her name. I don't think Harlow could remember it, even now. I liked being Mrs. Rowland—my married name from my second husband. He left years ago. Sweet man, just couldn't deal with my grief. It felt good this week, to live in someone else's skin, to be someone who didn't wake up every morning with an endless emptiness inside because her child was gone.

"Her father and I tried for such a long time with no luck, but when she was born—I can't even remember the pain, just this sweet little bundle in my arms, healthy and hearty. She was such an easy baby, slept through the night at three months. I would go into her room to check on her just to make sure she was breathing. And because I missed her. She was such a good-natured little thing. We breezed right through the toddler and teen years with no real trouble. Not even when her dad and I divorced and I remarried. But we were complacent. When she got to college, Bella began complaining about her roommate. We thought, this is normal. Bella was an only child. She had to adjust to sharing. We told her it couldn't be as bad as she said, that she was being dramatic. Nobody was out to get her."

Cecelia sniffed. "I wish we would have listened. Someone was out to get her. Harlow Drake. Bella had been so excited to be sharing a room with *the* Harlow Drake. Her roommate was a *celebrity.* We thought it was going to be good for her to room with someone also in the prelaw program. We thought Harlow would encourage her, be a good influence. Instead, Bella got death by a thousand cuts, just little inconveniences to pick her apart. Harlow screaming at her for bringing anything nut-related into the room because of her *allergy.* Harlow unplugging Bella's phone from the charger in the middle of the night so it wouldn't be ready for the next day. Locking Bella out of the room when she recorded interviews because Harlow didn't want to be interrupted, and then 'forgetting' to let Bella back in. Moving Bella's things so she couldn't find them when she needed them. Setting multiple alarms and leaving them on when she left for the day, waking Bella up over and over. Cooking full meals in the middle of the night, banging pots around in their kitchen so Bella couldn't sleep. So many little games to keep her from sleeping. We just thought it was normal roommate conflicts, that she needed to sort it out. We didn't see how desperate she was becoming, the sleep deprivation. The laptop was the final straw. Both girls were applying to some special study abroad program and had to put together a multimedia project—which should have been easy for Harlow, right? Well, it wasn't enough to be good, she wanted to make sure Bella couldn't even turn in her application by the deadline. Harlow 'tripped' and spilled a full glass of soda onto Bella's laptop. It died. There was no backup of the file. I think that's what broke her."

"I thought Bella died driving home for winter break," Lainey said. The glitter jar was empty now. They'd reached the cemetery on the other end of the island. Lainey searched her bag for some other weapon. Could she fight free and make it into the crypt?

Sneak back through the hotel's secret passageway and warn the others?

Cecelia lowered the knife and shoved Lainey forward. She didn't stumble headfirst into the Peggy headstone, but it was a near thing. She was just glad not to have the knife near her throat anymore.

"Bella didn't finish the semester. Didn't take her finals. She didn't even pack a bag," Cecelia spat. Her eyes were red-rimmed now, face flushed with recounting her child's slow torture. "She just grabbed her keys and her purse and drove five hours home in the middle of the night. She was so tired and her nerves were stretched wire-thin. She texted us, said all she wanted was to get home. And nothing we said to her could get her to turn around. And she just . . . fell asleep at the wheel. She was so smart, so responsible. She never would have done that if Harlow hadn't put her in that state. Her last weeks on earth were torture because of Harlow. And she died knowing that her mother didn't believe her. She pulled away from me because she felt betrayed. I missed out on the last few weeks of my child's life because of Harlow Drake. She took someone important from me, and now, I'm going to take someone important from her. Her oldest and dearest friend."

"So that explains the lip balm in my bag," Lainey said. "Mrs. Rowland, I know what a destructive force that woman can be. I've seen it firsthand. But if you want to punish her, killing me isn't going to do it. Harlow Drake does not care about me."

"That's a lie. I've seen the way that she folds herself inside out trying to make sure you're impressed with her. She doesn't do that with anybody else," Cecelia said.

"Because I know her secrets. I'm a vulnerable spot for her."

"Exactly," Cecelia seethed. "Imagine how it will break Harlow, searching the whole island for you, only to find your body out here all alone. And poor Mrs. Rowland won't know anything about that."

She changed to her soft, sophisticated ladylike voice. *"'I've been reading by the window in my room all day, dear.'"*

Cecelia moved toward Lainey, who held up her hand and backed away. "OK, OK, OK. Mrs. Rowland. I understand what it's like to lose someone, trust me, but this is not going to make it better."

Behind her, Lainey could hear the slide of stone inside the crypt. Someone was coming up from inside the secret passage. She began circling away from Cecelia, positioning the woman so her back was to the crypt. She slipped her hand into her shoulder bag as far behind her as she could manage, so Cecelia couldn't see her.

"Oh, you're just worldly at your age," Cecelia huffed. "You're just so familiar with my pain, my life."

"Frankly, yes," Lainey said, staring at her. Her hand closed around the final and most useful treasure in her purse. "I know what it's like to feel like no one is listening. I know what it's like when no one seems to care that you've lost something so huge that the idea of just walking away and living like a normal person seems impossible." Cecelia seemed to relax ever so slightly as Lainey spoke, lowering the knife. Behind the older woman's back, Lainey spotted Milo and Gordy creeping quietly out of the crypt. "But I know something else."

Cecelia raised the knife again. "What's that?"

"I always have backup pepper spray." Lainey whipped her hand out of her purse, finger already pressing the plunger. The gel stream hit Cecelia's nose before Lainey adjusted her aim and hit her eyes. Cecelia screamed, dropping the knife as she swiped at her face. Milo and Gordy rushed forward. Milo kicked the knife out of the way and Gordy shoved the woman to the ground, holding her to the grass. He slipped one of Milo's resistance bands around her wrists as she continued to yell about her eyes.

Milo swept toward Lainey, hugging her to him. He looked her over, grimacing when he saw the shallow cut at her throat. "Are you all right?"

"She's a sad woman who lost someone and went off the rails a little bit . . . with some poison. A lot of poison. Like several different kinds of poison. She is an advanced poisoner. Someone will probably write a book about her. I hope it's not Harlow." Lainey sighed. "Secret crypt passageway?"

Milo nodded. "The rest of the group is sneaking up behind you through the woods. They're armed."

"That does not make me feel better," Lainey said. "I've seen what the DBags attempt with a sword."

Milo helped Gordy lift Cecelia off the ground. There was some attempt to rinse her eyes with bottled water from Lainey's bag, but Cecelia hissed at them about their poor handling of her medical emergency. The three of them carefully marched Cecelia through the woods, following the patches of purple glitter on the ground.

"Did the glitter trail help?" Lainey asked Milo.

"Sort of," Milo said, rummaging through her shoulder bag for one of her first-aid kits. "Tommy spotted it as he was walking into the hotel and mentioned it to me when I came downstairs looking for you. We found Cameron. I remembered what you said about the glitter and organized a search effort. I figured if you were heading in this direction, the crypt would give me the element of surprise."

"How long did it take you to realize I was missing?" she asked him.

"A few minutes," he admitted. When she snorted, he added, "There was a search for a priceless diamond on! It was like watching the boys do an Easter egg hunt on meth! I was distracted!"

"It was really very hectic," Gordy admitted. "Harlow tripped Deke while he was running up the stairs to the fourth floor. His lip was busted, but he couldn't be more thrilled."

"Is Cameron OK?" she asked.

"Findlay's taking care of him as best she can," Gordy assured her. "She sent me to help you."

Her heart warmed. Lainey smiled at him. "Did you at least find the diamond?"

"Not yet," Milo said. "But people cared enough about you to stop searching and save you from a murderer."

Lainey shrugged, oddly touched. "Six of one, half a dozen of the other."

"They'll start looking again, once we get the brig cleared out," Milo assured her, making her laugh.

They left the woods and saw a very official-looking boat slicing through the water toward their dock. Milo glanced down at Cecelia's bound hands, the streams of tears dripping from her red, capsaicin-burned eyes. "This is going to look bad."

"I mean, she is a murderer," Lainey said. "We should probably let Mr. Spiros and Mrs. Maynard out of the brig, though. And apologize."

"Mr. Spiros pulled a knife on us," Milo reminded her.

"Right, and the bleach powder thing. So much has happened, I kind of skimmed over that, mentally."

Cecelia started laughing. "Good luck proving anything. I'm a sad grieving old woman. I can explain and re-explain until I make this whole thing Spiros's and Maynard's fault, and this little trip to the cemetery a terrible misunderstanding."

"Well, this might not hold up in court, but it's a good starting point." Lainey pulled the digital voice recorder from her bag and pressed "Stop." She rewound it for a second and pressed "Play" just in time to hear Cecelia say *"He was old. He'd lived a good long life, and . . . we all have to make sacrifices."*

Cecelia's eyes narrowed and her lip curled back in a sneer. Milo waved at the approaching state trooper and turned to their resident poisoner. "Never underestimate the contents of Lainey Piper's shoulder bag."

18

Hours of questions later, Lainey was exhausted but not under arrest, which she took as a positive sign of how her day was going.

The police searched Lainey's bag for additional pepper sprays. She supposed she couldn't blame them after she'd explained the events of the past few days. She also presented them with Shelley's phone, the recording of Cecelia's lengthy confession, and the bee's knees glass and tampered-with juice powder she'd stashed under the bar.

A whole team of detectives, who apparently had much better radio reception than the *Acheron* did, arrived tout de suite to search the hotel for the murder weapon—the honey syrup bottle, which they found in Mrs. Rowland's bathroom.

A host of officials—specifically, the Wisconsin State Patrol, the very confused Coast Guard, and multiple medical examiners—arrived on the island with lots of questions, most of them to do with Mrs. Rowland and poor Cameron, who had a whole team of paramedics working on him.

Milo wouldn't let Lainey talk to the police without legal counsel, and since he was the closest thing she had, Lainey let him sit in. Unsurprisingly, Mrs. Rowland was waiting for her lawyer before she talked. Even Milo told her that was a good idea.

It wasn't all good news. It turned out Vern *had* summoned help to the island, but not in the way they'd anticipated. The state patrol sent a team out to the Crossings after finding the *Acheron* circling in open water, with Vern writhing on the deck in agony, unable to stand long enough to steer. He was in full cardiac arrest, Inspector Dubrev told them. While he'd been taken to the hospital as soon as he was found, it was uncertain whether he would make it.

Lainey's day was spent leading investigators around the island, ending at the cemetery and explaining how Milo and Gordy managed to pop up through the crypt behind Cecelia. Kenny filmed everything while Harlow seethed. She interjected occasionally about her history with Mrs. Rowland's daughter. That didn't get the response she expected, which only made Harlow's temper worse. Deke and Bryce could not stop cheering at every new development, to Milo's great annoyance.

In the end, Lainey was left standing off to the side, near the scary beehive fireplace, trying to breathe her way through three true things (she was alive, Milo was safe, everything else could be worked out) when Harlow sidled up to her. There was a smile on her face—after all, there were authorities present—but her voice was an icy blade cutting across the wind as she said, "I hope you enjoyed your little moment, because you're out of here."

"I'm sorry?"

"Yeah, you're sorry. You're always sorry, Lainey. Poor sad Lainey with the dead dad and all the nice-girl-next-door trauma," Harlow growled. "I don't know what I was thinking, bringing you out to the island. I felt sorry for you. Just like I always feel sorry for you. I'm forever saving your ass, Lainey. It's my fatal flaw."

"Trust me, I have quite the list of your potential flaws—your body being composed of eighty percent asshole being one of them—but your spirit of compassion is definitely not one," Lainey shot back. "You had nothing to do with the decision to bring me out here. And you have never once *saved* me."

"If it wasn't for me, you never would have graduated high school," Harlow hissed quietly. "Sheriff Pleasant would have sent you to juvie for the weed cookies. It would have been the big victim moment you'd always dreamed of. Convicted of a crime you didn't commit."

Lainey closed her eyes. There was no reason to protect Harlow from herself anymore. There were plenty of witnesses here, including people with weapons. And it was time Harlow learned what Lainey knew.

"Well, if it wasn't for you, I probably never would have been accused of making the weed cookies in the first place," Lainey said.

"What are you talking about?" Harlow scoffed, rolling her eyes.

"I know about the Narc Box, Harlow."

"Yeah, someone put your name in the Narc Box, I know," Harlow said. Lainey noticed that Kenny, Findlay, and the crew members were slowly wandering closer to them, listening intently.

"You remember when I told you about people back home throwing drinks on me?" Lainey asked. "The thing you thought was no big deal, because after all, it never happened to you. Well, our freshman year of college, I was sitting in the Qwik-E-Fuel parking lot, bawling my eyes out because Jeremy Roman's sister had just thrown a Mega-Glug at me. Jeremy had lost his full ride to SIU. The funding for his scholarship mysteriously disappeared because he had a recommendation from Mr. Burnham. He actually *deserved* the recommendation. His parents hadn't paid for it, but that didn't matter because kids from our class were tainted by association. I was sitting there, trying to figure out how the hell I was going to go home and explain to my mom why I was soaked in frozen cherry cola. And sweet little Janey McInerney comes over to me to tell me that she was sorry that happened, that she didn't think I deserved more of the blame for GradeGate than you did because you were the one out there giving press interviews and thinking about a book deal."

Harlow sighed. "And as usual, you were worried about what a bunch of small-town nobodies thought of you."

"Well, Janey really wanted to warn me what the small-town nobodies thought of *you*," Lainey shot back. "Janey was two years older than us, remember? She was an office aide in school. She got to sit at the front desk and sort mail and make copies . . . and listen to the office ladies' gossip. She was at the desk so much they basically forgot she was there and what she could hear—like the morning they were standing around the coffeepot, talking about poor, silly Lainey Piper, following Harlow Drake around like a faithful puppy when Harlow was the one who almost got her expelled freshman year."

The color drained from Harlow's face. "I don't know what you're talking about."

"You dropped my name in the Narc Box. I'm guessing you didn't know that the office ladies made copies of the reports and put them in our school files if they led to disciplinary action. And your handwriting is very distinctive. You always made those little crisscross lines at the top of your O's, kind of like Walt Disney.

The office ladies remembered it. And they didn't like you. I guess at some point they were introduced to your particular brand of charm."

"Lainey, I was the one who found out that Junior Cappick drugged the cookies. I saved you," Harlow insisted.

"You dropped me into shark-infested waters just so you could pull me out," Lainey shot back. "You wanted me to *see you* save me. You're like one of those moms with Munchausen syndrome by proxy."

"I think they call it factitious disorder now," Bryce said helpfully.

"Thank you, Bryce," Lainey said without looking at him. "My only question is, did you know Junior drugged the cookies before you dropped my name in the Narc Box, or was finding the actual culprit just a fun side benefit for you?"

"Lainey—"

"What?" Lainey yelled.

"I had to!" Harlow cried. "You were going to leave the show. We were just starting to get a following! And yeah, I downplayed how much you did on the webisodes, but people didn't want to just watch my face spewing out info. They wanted us bouncing ideas off each other, joking around, your deadpan sense of humor, your trying—"

"Trying what?"

Harlow glanced at Kenny and his camera. Lainey could see the wheels turn in Harlow's head, struggling to find a way to spin this to her favor. "Trying to find out what happened to your dad. People cared about you in a way they didn't care about me. And I didn't want to admit that. I still don't. Maybe that's what I hoped this project could be—recapturing that old magic. I wasn't a good friend to you back then, but I can be a better one. Maybe you can teach me."

Lainey's mouth clicked shut. She didn't want to be arrested for some of the things that could come out of her mouth. "You know, when we were kids, if you asked me to do something scary or stupid, I did it, because I thought I owed you. I maybe wasn't the most affectionate of friends, but I was loyal. But you— You're only loyal to one person, and that's yourself. I suppose it's nice that you're predictable."

Lainey turned, snagging Milo by the arm and charging toward the stairs. She could walk away. She could leave this island, shedding a big part of herself here. Her doubt. Her shame. All of the things that were keeping her from risking her secure little life. And while it might have served her better to leave Harlow with a mystery unresolved, knowing that it would drive her former partner into madness, it was time to stop pretending.

So she stopped.

"By the way, I'm pretty sure Marguerite is buried in that plot over there under 'Peggy,'" Lainey told Deke and Bryce. "Dandridge's nickname for Marguerite was 'Pegs,' which she hated. And I'm pretty sure the marker next to her, 'Dandy—1927,' is where Timmy Dandridge is buried."

"They buried them in a pet cemetery?" Gordy marveled. "Did they learn nothing from the movie?"

"It would have been an easy way to bury two people on the island in the one place no one looked for dead bodies, because they're already there," Lainey said. "They probably brought them up through the crypt in the middle of the night."

"You don't know that," Harlow scoffed. "You don't have the answers to all of the questions."

"None of us *knows* anything, Harlow, that's the whole point of being here," Lainey told her. "Have Deke and Bryce exhume the remains. If they turn out to be beloved pets, I will apologize. If the remains are human, contact the Dandridge family and ask if they want to do a DNA test. There, I did most of the things I'm *good at*, which is, let's face it, the work. My part of our agreement is done. If you feel the urge to call me again to do more work for you, do us both a favor and fuck off into the sun!"

Harlow gasped in indignation.

"You get all that?" Lainey asked Gordy and Kenny. Gordy made a gesture to his collarbone, indicating that Harlow's lapel mic was live. He gave Lainey a thumbs-up. "Great."

"That was awesome!" Deke told her. "I mean, it kind of destroyed one of my most cherished fandoms, knowing that Harlow was the villain all along, but I think that's probably part of being an adult in today's world."

"Seriously, I never saw the twist coming," Bryce told her. "Whatever you want funding-wise for future projects, you've got it. Webisodes. Specials. Your own podcast. A line of energy drinks."

"Thanks, but I really haven't enjoyed my time in front of the camera," Lainey told them. "No offense, Kenny."

"None taken!" Kenny promised her.

"No matter what, we're going to pay you double for this job," Deke told her.

"And we want to pay you with one of those really big checks like they give to lottery winners," Bryce added.

Deke nodded. "Because this has been the best trip of our lives."

"People died, bud," Milo reminded him.

"Obviously I mean other than the dead people," Deke shot back, raising his hands. "I'm just saying, Lainey, you really lived up to your end of the bargain. And if you ever wanted to meet up—"

"No," she said. "Thank you, but no."

"My marriage proposal still stands," Bryce told her.

"Still a no, but you—" Lainey sighed. "You guys are not what I thought you were. If you would just spend two minutes out of your day thinking about how your actions affect the people around you, I could see myself socializing with you."

"Really?" Deke asked, grinning at her.

"Casually, in a public place, when you and Milo get together," Lainey added. "Every few months."

"And then we can revisit the marriage proposal? I've heard about this really great proposal planner out of Tennessee—" Bryce stopped when Lainey scrunched her nose, and he added, "I'll let you think about it. Wait, Milo, aren't you going to try to argue with me about offering all that and the marriage proposal and the big check?"

"No," Milo replied. "In fact, we need to start talking about my transition away from the company."

"What?" Deke exclaimed. "Oh, come on, man, I was just kidding about the best trip ever stuff. Running the company wouldn't be any fun without you."

Bryce didn't seem to be picking up on Milo's very casual resignation, continuing to tell Lainey, "If you and Milo are hanging out, you could come over and play some detective games with us. Maybe you could even help us design something! About a girl solving murders on a creepy island!"

"Bryce, if your next game is about a big-boobed girl named Draney, I swear to God," Lainey said, sighing and feeling very much like Milo.

Bryce cackled as Deke said, “We could really use someone like you in our finance department.”

“I don’t think that would work out the way you imagine it would,” Lainey replied. Milo put his arm around her. Bryce seemed to pick up on the hint very quickly and stepped back. Lainey turned to Milo and asked, “Are they trying to keep me from suing them or *encouraging me* to sue them?”

“Little of both,” Milo told her. “I don’t think they can tell the difference.”

“I don’t know what the next few months is going to bring,” she told him. “But I hope I see more of you . . . and less of everybody else here.”

Findlay scowled, clearly offended. “Hey!”

“Except for Findlay.”

Lainey considered her near future and whether Bryce would show up at her apartment with a giant check and scare Locard. And she realized, she didn’t care. She was open to it. She was ready for whatever weird adventure life had to offer, even if it meant leaving her secure little corner of the world. She stopped walking, letting Milo drag her arm a bit. When he turned to check on her, she kissed him, and he returned it—with intent.

She blurted out, “I know I spend a lot of time making you question my judgment, but I am not the risk-taker in my romantic life. Taking up with a dude you met on a murder island definitely qualifies as a risk.”

“Why does it matter where we met?” he asked.

“Because when I tell people the story of how I met my boyfriend, I don’t want the words ‘murder island’ to be involved!”

His whole face lit up at the word “boyfriend.” Lainey knew her mom would love him.

Dammit.

"Any chance you might want to visit a very small apartment occupied by a neurotic but adorable cat?" she asked.

"Alternate proposal, you move in with me, so I'm protected," he said.

"Have there been any murders in your apartment?" she asked.

He bit his lip. "Not that I'm aware of. I can't make any guarantees. How adorable of a cat are we talking?"

"Extremely adorable."

"You've got a deal," he replied. He grinned and kissed her.

When she broke away from the temptation of his mouth, she asked, "Mr. Wesley did let Mr. Spiros and Mrs. Maynard out of the brig, right? They should probably be questioned by people with badges."

Milo grimaced and glanced around at the gathered emergency personnel. "We should check with somebody."

Epilogue

One Year Later
Crossings Hotel

A champagne picnic in a cemetery might have seemed ghoulish, but the survivors of *Harlow Drake Investigates* . . . thought non-poisonous booze and laughter were the most appropriate way to dedicate Marguerite Devereaux's corrected headstone.

Lainey stood at the center of a group of her favorite people, popping a bottle of champagne—without the aid of a sword. Vern, Tommy, Cassie, Cameron, Kenny, Findlay, and Gordy helped catch the spilling bubbles in flutes.

The Dandridge family had, in fact, requested that Timmy Dandridge's remains be returned to them for burial in the family plot. They even offered Lainey and Harlow a reward for their involvement in finding him. Lainey was happy to accept her portion. She needed the financial cushion while adjusting to living in the new apartment in Chicago she shared with Milo—and Locard, who had quickly established himself as new ruling head of Milo's Rat Pack Pride. (Locard tolerated Milo, but barely.)

"I can't believe you stayed here," Helen Piper-Wintrout said, shuddering as she surveyed the cemetery. After Lainey survived her time here, her mom and Robin insisted on joining her on the return visit. They had also insisted that the whole family leave before nightfall—which seemed fair.

"Most of our time was spent outside of the cemetery," Lainey reminded her.

"Lainey spent most of her time finding secret passages and hanging out in the kitchen hoarding peaches and knives," Milo added cheerfully.

"I beg your pardon?" Helen gasped.

"That's my girl," Robin chuckled.

"We agreed you wouldn't provide my mom with details," Lainey hissed. "It was our own little NDA."

"It wasn't legally binding, and the fact that you and your mom make the same face when you're annoyed is hilarious," Milo replied.

"You're going to learn not to do that if you want to survive," Robin told him.

"Yeah, continue to annoy me and you're not going to be invited to the housewarming," Helen told him. Lainey squeezed her mom's hand and leaned her head against her shoulder.

Things were looking up for Lainey, business-wise. Her debts were settled. Her savings was back to a more than reasonable level. She'd had an honest conversation with her mom and Robin about her finances and how they should all budget to keep them on a more realistic track in the future. Putting the old Piper homestead on the market had been the first step toward Helen and Robin relying on Lainey less. Selling would give them enough for a cozy condo closer to their office and a nice little nest egg.

"I'm helping you move and you're not going to invite me to the housewarming?" Milo asked, laughing at Helen.

"When you've spent more time around us, you'll realize the capacity of a Piper woman to hold an irrational grudge," Helen said primly.

"Oh, I've seen it in action," Milo said, shaking his head. "She hasn't taken back a single old client since the publicity from *The Disappearance of the Blue Rose* brought attention to Piper and Associates."

"That's *my* girl," Helen said.

While Lainey did nurse a grudge, she honestly couldn't take on old clients with the new tech-bro business Deke and Bryce were funneling her way for financial checkups. And then they'd sent a messenger to the apartment with an official Illinois private investigator's license and papers for an investigative corporation that Deke had set up in Lainey's name.

"Don't I have to pass a test or, you know . . . sign stuff for this to be legal?" Lainey had asked Milo as he'd reviewed the papers for her.

"I stopped asking questions about the things they do when I left the company," Milo had replied. She hated bothering him when he was reviewing the contract for his brand-new job at a real law firm, with real clients, who knew his real name.

But she would always call him Milo. And he would never object.

Lainey still hadn't decided whether she wanted to use the license or not. While she still enjoyed forensic accounting, the puzzles offered by the clients seeking out a private investigator . . . they were tempting. Maybe she could focus on financial crimes, stick with what she knew.

For now, she had contented herself with having tracked down the Ploppe family through a genetic tracing website and asking for a sample for comparative DNA. The tests showed that the remains in the Peggy plot were, in fact, Margaret Ploppe, aka Marguerite Devereaux. And while the Ploppes were grateful that the network had managed to track down their long-lost relative, they weren't exactly moved to travel to Bantam Island for a memorial for someone they'd never met.

Deke and Bryce were not present at the cemetery, much as they'd had the good sense not to attend Cecelia Rowland's trial. In the end, they'd changed their plans to turn the Crossings into a corporate retreat. Renovations for the Crossings Center for Women, a therapeutic facility for women recovering from trauma, were well underway. The DBags hadn't set foot on the island since the groundbreaking ceremony, which everyone agreed was the best outcome. Bryce did get a photo opportunity to present the Center's administration with a giant check, which he found thrilling.

Lainey suspected that the funding for the project came from the sale of the Star of Sikkim. Deke and Bryce found the gem in a chandelier in the Beatrice Room after unleashing a full team of black-light-wielding gemologists into the hotel as soon as the police cleared the scene. As far as Lainey could tell, Dandridge had used baling wire to tie it into the dining room's showiest light fixture, probably when it was lowered for cleaning and no one was around. It was a valiant attempt to try to keep it from being sold to his debtors. How he planned to get back to it to claim it—well,

Milo was right. Timmy Dandridge had not been the brightest bulb. It was delightfully weird to think that millions of dollars in diamond had dangled over generations of Crossings guests while they ate perch omelets and had no clue.

Deke and Bryce didn't advertise their sale of the gem. It wasn't as if the Dandridges could get upset about it not being returned, seeing as they had accepted an insurance payout for it nearly a century before.

As for Harlow . . .

The former future face of True Crime 24/7 was "taking some time away from her public-facing duties while she focused on her recovery from exhaustion." While the response to the special had been generally positive, the Chicagoland Sausage Slayer issue became the least of Harlow's problems when *someone* posted the hot-mic moment to Reddit. In their weekly meeting of the Peach and Knife Club, Gordy refused to confirm or deny it was him. The recorded hot-mic rant spread even faster than Harlow's podcast interview, and plans for additional *Harlow Drake Investigates* . . . episodes were in indefinite development hell.

Lainey couldn't help Harlow with that, and she didn't feel moved to. It was not the first time she'd felt this lack of generosity toward Harlow. But it was the most comfortable she'd been with it.

She was distracted from these thoughts by Milo opening another bottle of champagne.

Vern and Cameron had both retired after their ordeals, thanks to generous "Sorry our adventure almost got you killed" packages arranged by Milo as his last official act with DBag Games. Tommy and Cassie found jobs at significantly less dangerous off-island hotels. Kenny, Gordy, and Findlay still worked for the network but asked for prior approval before being assigned remote duties. Given their ordeal at the Crossings, the network agreed.

Milo put an arm around Lainey. "Do you want to say a few words?"

"As few as possible," she said. She smiled at the tasteful stone, inscribed with Marguerite's chosen name and her birth and death dates. The inscription read A SHORTENED LIFE, LONG REMEMBERED. It was flanked by two smaller memorial stones for Timothy Dandridge and Shelley McMillan, who were buried elsewhere.

"Marguerite, we're sorry that you went unrecognized for so long, and we hope that this stone and this resting place bring you some peace. Timothy, I hope you're spending your time on the other side learning. Shelley, we're sorry to have lost you. Rest well, friends."

The group clinked the flutes together and took sips of their champagne. Cameron seemed to think better of it.

"There's no way to tamper with champagne, right?" he asked.

"Probably not," Lainey said. "Unless you took a syringe and injected something through the cork."

The others spit their champagne into their flutes.

"Why would you put that into our heads?" Findlay demanded.

"He *asked*!" Lainey cried.

"Never change, Lainey Piper," Milo laughed, kissing her temple.

"I don't make any promises," she told him.

"So, have you figured out where I've hidden your engagement ring in the apartment?"

"I figured that out weeks ago," she scoffed. "I mean, the cat toy drawer, come on."

"Aw, man, you solved it."

"I half solved it." She grinned at him. "I still don't know how and when you're going to do it."

After a long pause, he told her, "Not here and now."

She nodded, glancing at their cemetery surroundings. "Yeah, that's a good call."

ACKNOWLEDGMENTS

Thank you so much to my wonder of an agent, Natanya Wheeler, and my editor, Esi Sogah, for their constant support and patience as I worked out my Scooby-Doo sleuthing issues. Thank you to Jeanette Battista, Lish McBride, Tirzah Price, Kristen Simmons, Chelsea Mueller, and Jaye Wells for listening to my endless rapid-fire texts of doubt. And thank you to Caroline Johnson, who is always there through all the shenanigans. My gratitude to the true-crime community—the podcasters, the documentarians, the people who understand my need to overanalyze what scares me.

I am not a "method" writer, but I did try Chartreuse liqueur for the first time while writing Lainey's story, and I have to say . . . my impression is reflected in Lainey's opinion. In fact, I worked with several different cocktail recipes while trying to figure out the bar scenes in this book. So thank you to my family for their support while I used phrases like "murder hotel" and talked about poisoned cocktails . . . while mixing cocktails. I am not easy to live with—I recognize that. I love you all.

Author photo: Kimber Johansen / Kimber Photo Co.

Molly Harper is the author of more than forty paranormal romance, contemporary romance, women's fiction, and young adult titles. A lifelong romance reader, she graduated with a master of fine arts from Seton Hill University, focusing on writing popular fiction. She lived in Kentucky for most of her life before recently moving to Michigan with her family . . . and she's still figuring out how to choose outerwear and play complicated winter card games.

VISIT MOLLY HARPER ONLINE

MollyHarper.com
MollyHarperAuth
MollyHarperAuthor
MollyHarperAuth